# MISS OR MRS? · THE HAUNTED HOTEL
# THE GUILTY RIVER

WILKIE COLLINS was born in London in 1824, the elder son of a successful painter, William Collins. He left school at 17, and after an unhappy spell as a clerk in a tea broker's office, during which he wrote his first, unpublished novel, he entered Lincoln's Inn as a law student in 1846. He considered a career as a painter, but after the publication, in 1848, of his life of his father, and a novel, *Antonina*, in 1850, his future as a writer was assured. His meeting with Dickens in 1851 was perhaps the turning-point of his career. The two became collaborators and lifelong friends. Collins contributed to Dickens's magazines *Household Words* and *All the Year Round*, and his two best-known novels, *The Woman in White* and *The Moonstone*, were first published in *All the Year Round*. Collins's private life was as complex and turbulent as his novels. He never married, but lived with a widow, Mrs Caroline Graves, from 1858 until his death. He also had three children by a younger woman, Martha Rudd, whom he kept in a separate establishment. Collins suffered from 'rheumatic gout', a form of arthritis which made him an invalid in his later years, and he became addicted to the laudanum he took to ease the pain of the illness. He died in 1889.

NORMAN PAGE is Emeritus Professor of Modern English Literature, University of Nottingham. His publications include *Wilkie Collins: The Critical Heritage* (1974) and editions of Collins's *Mad Monkton and Other Stories* (1994) and *Man and Wife* (1995) in the Oxford World's Classics series. He is currently editing *The Oxford Reader's Companion to Thomas Hardy*.

TORU SASAKI is an Associate Professor of Kyoto University, Japan, where he teaches English literature. His publications include an edition of Hardy's *The Hand of Ethelberta* and articles in the *Dickensian*, *Language and Literature*, and the *Thomas Hardy Journal*. He is also a contributor to the forthcoming *Oxford Reader's Companion to Thomas Hardy*.

# OXFORD WORLD'S CLASSICS

*For almost 100 years Oxford World's Classics have brought
readers closer to the world's great literature. Now with over 700
titles—from the 4,000-year-old myths of Mesopotamia to the
twentieth century's greatest novels—the series makes available
lesser-known as well as celebrated writing.*

*The pocket-sized hardbacks of the early years contained
introductions by Virginia Woolf, T.S. Eliot, Graham Greene,
and other literary figures which enriched the experience of reading.
Today the series is recognized for its fine scholarship and
reliability in texts that span world literature, drama and poetry,
religion, philosophy and politics. Each edition includes perceptive
commentary and essential background information to meet the
changing needs of readers.*

OXFORD WORLD'S CLASSICS

WILKIE COLLINS

# Miss or Mrs?
# The Haunted Hotel
# The Guilty River

*Edited with an Introduction and Notes by*
NORMAN PAGE *and* TORU SASAKI

Oxford   New York
OXFORD UNIVERSITY PRESS
1999

Oxford University Press, Great Clarendon Street, Oxford OX2 6DP

Oxford New York

Athens Auckland Bangkok Bogotá Buenos Aires Calcutta
Cape Town Chennai Dar es Salaam Delhi Florence Hong Kong Istanbul
Karachi Kuala Lumpur Madrid Melbourne Mexico City Mumbai
Nairobi Paris São Paulo Singapore Taipei Tokyo Toronto Warsaw

and associated companies in Berlin Ibadan

Oxford is a registered trade mark of Oxford University Press

Introduction and Notes © Norman Page and Toru Sasaki 1999
Chronology © Catherine Peters 1993, revised by Norman Page 1999

First published as an Oxford World's Classics paperback 1999

British Library Cataloguing in Publication Data

Data available

Library of Congress Cataloging in Publication Data
Collins, Wilkie, 1824–1889.
[Selections. 1999]
Miss or Mrs? The haunted hotel; The guilty river / Wilkie Collins;
edited with an introduction and notes by Norman Page and Tōru Sasaki.
(Oxford world's classics)
Includes bibliographical references (p.   ).
1. Detective and mystery stories, English. I. Page, Norman. II. Sasaki, Tōru, 1956– .
III. Title. IV. Title: Haunted hotel. V. Title: Guilty river. VI. Series: Oxford world's classics
(Oxford University Press)
PR4492.P34   1999   823'.8-dc21   98–22118

ISBN 0-19-283307-3

1 3 5 7 9 10 8 6 4 2

Typeset by Pure Tech India Ltd, Pondicherry
Printed in Great Britain by
Cox & Wyman Ltd, Reading, Berkshire

# CONTENTS

# INTRODUCTION

*Since this Introduction includes references to plots, readers may prefer to turn to it after reading the stories themselves.*

Wilkie Collins's career as a novelist is longer than that of George Eliot or Hardy or even Dickens: from *Antonina* (1850) to the unfinished and posthumously-published *Blind Love* (1890) is a period of almost forty years, covering the remarkable span of history that extends from the Great Exhibition to the age of the Aesthetes and the Decadents— in terms of the history of the novel, from *David Copperfield* to *The Picture of Dorian Gray*. For nearly a hundred years after his death, however, Collins was thought of almost exclusively as a novelist of the 1860s. It is true that the series of novels from *The Woman in White* (1860) to *The Moonstone* (1868) represents by general consent his most consistently brilliant work, but the 'achievement and decline' theory that for so long held sway no longer looks as plausible as it once appeared, and in recent years many of his novels of the 1870s and 1880s have been revived, reconsidered, reprinted and widely enjoyed.

The full-length novel in the orthodox 'three-decker' format was not, however, the only fictional medium in which Collins worked. The insatiable appetite of publishers, editors and readers of magazines and annuals created a demand for shorter fiction that Collins, as a hard-working professional author, was happy to satisfy. The long list of his publications, therefore, includes not only more than twenty full-length novels but a large number of short stories and novellas. A selection of his short stories has already appeared in Oxford World's Classics as *Mad Monkton and Other Stories* (1994); the present volume brings together three of the best of his exercises in what might awkwardly be referred to as the long short story.

## The Novella

There is no satisfactory term in English for what the French call a *nouvelle* (Henry James's 'beautiful and blessed *nouvelle*'), the Italians a *novella* and the Germans a *Novelle*: *novelette*, though dating from as early as 1780 and defined as 'a short novel', has acquired associations of sentimentality and commercial ephemerality. It has, however, been a favourite form not only of Continental writers such as Flaubert and Mann but of many English-language novelists, as examples as diverse and distinguished as Stevenson's *Dr Jekyll and Mr Hyde*, Melville's *Billy Budd*, James's own *The Turn of the Screw*, Conrad's *Heart of Darkness* and Lawrence's *St Mawr* attest. The form has early Victorian prototypes of which Dickens's *A Christmas Carol* and his other 'Christmas Books' of the 1840s are widely familiar instances. (Several decades later, two of the stories in the present volume perpetuated the Dickensian tradition by appearing as tales specifically for Christmas consumption.)

The three Collins novellas reprinted here between them cover a period of fifteen years, from 1871 to 1886. The earliest of the three, *Miss or Mrs?*, appeared at the end of 1871. *The Haunted Hotel* followed nearly seven years later, in 1878, and *The Guilty River* eight years later still, at Christmas 1886, and less than three years before the author's death. They thus represent aspects of Collins's work from his late forties to his early sixties—almost the whole of the period, that is, which followed the successes of the 1860s—and they deserve to share in the revalidation and revaluation of his later work.

As publishing ventures, they illustrate the wide variety of forms in which fiction was presented to the late-Victorian reading public. The first appeared in the special Christmas number of an 'illustrated newspaper' and a couple of years later became the title-story of a volume containing three of Collins's stories, published by the famous London firm of Bentley, which had been one of Dickens's publishers. *The Haunted Hotel* was serialized over a six-month period in a well-established monthly magazine and, on the completion of the serial, promptly appeared in tandem with another novella in what seems to have been a needlessly inflated and expensive two-volume format obviously intended for the circulating libraries. *The Guilty River* was issued by a Bristol publisher as the Victorian equivalent of a paperback: in flimsy paper covers and modestly priced at one shilling, it was offered for sale as a 'Christmas annual'. The first two brought the author a double profit, but the last was never collected in his lifetime.

It is not difficult to trace connections between these novellas and Collins's other writings. *Miss or Mrs?* continues the exploration of the legal aspects of marriage that had been undertaken at much greater length in his novel *Man and Wife*, which had appeared in the previous year, while the dramatic form in which the same story is presented reflects his extensive involvement with the theatre (a stage version of *The Woman in White* had, for instance, been produced in the same year). *The Haunted Hotel* returns to the theme of fate that had formed a central element in *Armadale* (1866).

Again, there are interesting connections between these works of fiction and Collins's personal experience. *The Haunted Hotel* draws on his knowledge of Venice: he had been taken there in 1836 at the age of 12, had been back in 1853 with Dickens and their mutual friend the painter Augustus Egg, and was there again in November 1877, not long before composition of this novella began. The plot of *Miss or Mrs?* incorporates elements from a real-life adventure in which the young Collins had been involved and which he drew on repeatedly in his fiction. And, as a continuous background to the depiction in these stories of unconventional relationships, there were his own irregular liaisons: in 1871, for instance, he had resumed his cohabitation with Caroline Graves—at about the same time that Martha Rudd had borne him a second daughter. If, in *The Guilty River* and elsewhere, Collins seems to be preoccupied by the figure of the Outsider, his self-exclusion from respectable Victorian society must form part of the explanation.

As a fictional genre the novella does not afford its practitioners the elbow-room either to construct elaborate plots and subplots or to exhibit the gradual development of character and relationships. Full-length novels such as *Middlemarch* or *The Mayor of Casterbridge* (both contemporary with stories in this volume) show the working-out of human destinies over many years, but the novella must create its effects more succinctly. Collins himself recognized this by insisting on attaching to one collection of his novellas the label 'stories in outline': as he points out in the preface to that volume, they are 'restricted within limits which alike precluded elaborate development of character and subtle handling of events' (see the Appendix to the present volume). In his hands the novella tends to concentrate on a single line of action and to focus the reader's interest on discovering the solution to a single mystery or the outcome of a single intrigue. In *Miss or Mrs?* chronology, and especially the heroine's birthday, is of crucial significance, and the inescapable sense of an impending deadline gives pace and urgency to the tale. In *The Haunted Hotel* we read on to learn the truth about a murder mystery, and the solution has an ingenuity and a gruesomeness of which neither Agatha Christie nor Edgar Allan Poe, respectively, need have been ashamed. Only in *The Guilty River*, perhaps, does Collins, near the end of his life, seem to be losing his enthusiasm for plot-making: here the real interest is in a group of unusual characters, placed in a picturesque but sinister setting, and in their problematic relationship to society.

## *Miss or Mrs?*

English law in all its intricacy plays a crucial role in the plotting of many Victorian novels. In *Wuthering Heights* Heathcliff is obsessed not only by his love for Catherine, alive and dead, but by a desire for revenge that finds fulfilment by exploiting the laws of real and personal property and inheritance, of which Heathcliff appears to have a deep though unexplained understanding. The part played by a will in *Little Dorrit* is so complex that one editor has supplied an appendix to explain exactly what is going on. Trollope, George Eliot, and many others also make extensive use of the law and legal processes, and among them Collins, who had been a law student at Lincoln's Inn, is one of the most prominent. The plot of *Miss or Mrs?* involves an unsolved murder attempt in the past, another attempted murder in the present, a blackmail plot, a clandestine marriage and a commercial fraud, and thus several distinct areas of the law.

The villain, an apparently prosperous businessman named Richard Turlington, has a murky past that comes to light before the story is concluded. He is also in serious financial difficulties, borrows money in circumstances that involve deception, and urgently needs to raise capital in order to prevent the discovery of his fraud. The impending expiry of the loan period is one of the elements contributing to narrative momentum: as so often, Collins, whose own professional life placed him constantly at the mercy of publishers' deadlines, situates his characters in a world dominated by calendars, timetables and deadlines. Marriage to the daughter of a rich and weak-minded friend seems to offer a solution to Turlington's problems: by a neat arithmetical chance, the £40,000 he owes is exactly half Sir Joseph

Graybrooke's fortune, and half of his fortune is precisely what Graybrooke is contemplating offering to Turlington in the mandatory discussion of the marriage settlement that ensues. While Collins's villains—including the Countess in *The Haunted Hotel* and the Lodger in *The Guilty River*—often go some way towards redeeming themselves in the reader's eyes through their final confessions, Turlington is perfunctorily dispatched: a reflection, perhaps, of the limitations of space imposed by the novella form.

This middle-aged suitor has, however, a rival in the shape of a handsome doctor fifteen years his junior, and Launcelot Linzie's own plans for elopement themselves become tangled in the meshes of the law. (Launcelot's romantic name owes something to Tennyson, whose *Idylls of the King* were still in progress when Collins wrote this story, but whose *Lancelot and Elaine* had appeared in 1859.) Since Natalie, his intended, is only 15, he cannot marry her by special licence because (as he explains) ' "I can only get a Licence by taking my oath that I marry her with her father's consent" ' (p.39), and such a declaration would involve perjury. The publishing of banns and a church wedding, with all the attendant hazards of publicity, are therefore unavoidable. Furthermore, having married Natalie, he cannot carry her off and live with her:

'Natalie is not yet sixteen years old . . . She must go straight back to her father's house from the church, and I must wait to run away with her till her next birthday. When she's turned sixteen, she's ripe for elopement—not an hour before. There's the law of Abduction! Despotism in a free country— that's what I call it!' (p. 41)

Collins has not only devised an ingeniously dramatic situation but has exposed to critical scrutiny and questioning a seemingly paradoxical area of the existing marriage laws: the provision that a man may marry a young woman but is not allowed to take her from the parental home. Natalie's fast-approaching sixteenth birthday furnishes another deadline and further quickens the narrative pace.

It is evident that the plot requires Natalie to be a 15-year-old, but Collins goes boldly, even audaciously, beyond this requirement in making her a sexually mature and nubile young woman. Natalie is another Outsider figure: she has inherited 'a mixture of Negro blood and French blood' from her mother, whose family 'settled originally in Martinique' (p. 9), and this is deemed sufficient explanation of

her maturity of both body and personality. She possesses not only
'her mother's warm dusky colour, her mother's superb black hair, and
her mother's melting lazy lovely brown eyes' but a 'remarkable bodily
development', for she displays 'the development of the bosom and
limbs, which in England is rarely attained before twenty'. There is
surely nothing in the works of Dickens or Trollope or perhaps even
Hardy that goes as far as this in evoking a highly sensuous female
physicality: beside Natalie's firm fleshiness most Victorian heroines
seem like paper dolls. In the scenes that follow, Natalie's self-
confident and flirtatious behaviour goes a long way towards matching
her precocious physical development, and she is by any standards a
remarkable inhabitant of a mid-Victorian story. Collins's account of
the courtship of Natalie and Launcelot, initially conducted in the
claustrophobically intimate surroundings of a small private yacht,
similarly refuses to have anything to do with the timid conventions of
contemporary fiction. Collins, it seems, is prepared to call into question not only the time-honoured provisions of the English law but the
sexless innocence of the English middle-class maiden as depicted in
most contemporary fiction.

  As the above outline has suggested, the world of *Miss or Mrs?* is
very largely the world of Victorian capitalism in which human lives
are motivated and moulded as much by investments, inherited
wealth, marriage settlements and conspicuous consumption as by
falling in love or the other natural impulses of the heart. There is,
however, one episode that stands in stark and sordid contrast to this
well-upholstered world of bourgeois affluence. In the 'Tenth Scene'
Turlington makes a foray into an East End opium den in search of a
hired murderer with the excessively felicitous name of Thomas Wildfang—a scene that is surely indebted to Dickens's *The Mystery of
Edwin Drood*, published only a couple of years earlier. (The influence
of Dickens, who is flatteringly referred to in the preface to the
collection that contained *Miss or Mrs?*, may also be detected in the
comic bickering of Natalie's father and her maiden aunt Lavinia.) As
Margaret Cardwell has shown, there are a considerable number of
similarities of plotting between Dickens's last novel and Collins's
novella: among these are, for instance, 'the appearance of a disguised
stranger in the locality of the crime on Christmas Eve' and 'the plan
for the accomplice to rob the victim of jewellery to make that appear
the motive of the crime, and to burn his own clothes in a lime

cauldron before escaping'.[1] One striking resemblance not noted by Cardwell is the use of a heroine from a non-European background, for Dickens's Helena Landless has lived in Ceylon and is 'of almost the gipsy type'.

Mindful of the fact that he was writing a Christmas story—its first appearance was on 13 December 1871—Collins makes Natalie's sixteenth birthday coincide with that season and brings his plot to a highly sensational conclusion at the same time. The scene has by now shifted from London to a remote Somerset village, where Natalie and her family are virtually incarcerated in an isolated house belonging to Turlington: a variant on that favourite motif of sensation fiction, the isolated country house where horrors can be perpetrated behind the facade of civilized and well-ordered life. Within a few pages we are given a murderous attack, a nick-of-time arrival of the hero, bullets fired through the door of a room in which the women have been held prisoner, and a lucky accident that disposes of the villain. Collins's plans, never realized, to turn his story into a stage melodrama are evident in the abundance of action as well as the conduct of the narrative through a series of brief 'scenes'.

This division reminds us that, though his greatest successes were achieved in fiction, and especially in the full-length novel, Collins had a long love-affair with the theatre. In this respect he was following in the footsteps of his friend and mentor Charles Dickens, and the two of them had collaborated on a three-act drama, *A Message from the Sea* (1861), and one in five acts, *No Thoroughfare* (1867). During the decade preceding *Miss or Mrs?* Collins also produced independently stage versions of several of his own novels—*No Name* (1863), *Armadale* (1866), a second version of *No Name* (1870), and *The Woman in White* (1871)—as well as an original play, *The Frozen Deep* (1866), that was to prove momentous in Dickens's personal and artistic life.

All this makes it unsurprising that Collins, confronted with the imperious demands of the novella form for compression and pace, should attempt to reproduce the fictional equivalents of dramatic dialogue and stage-directions—and, more broadly, to conduct fictional narrative through a series of separate and mostly short scenes

[1] Charles Dickens, *The Mystery of Edwin Drood*, ed. Margaret Cardwell (Oxford, 1972), 250.

set in a variety of locations that are indicated in the chapter-headings. The twelfth and final 'scene', for instance, in which the action moves to its sensational climax, opens with a phrase recalling a play-script ('The scene in the drawing-room . . .'), proceeds to make extensive use of dialogue, and lavishly exploits the dramatic effect of 'noises off': 'they heard the back door opened and closed again'; 'There was a sound of footsteps on the gravel walk'; 'Then there was a heavy shock, as of something falling outside'. The reader can almost catch the whiff of gaslamps and greasepaint, and nothing could be further from the analysis, commentary and allusiveness of the much more leisurely narratives that, for example, George Eliot was writing at the same time.

As Catherine Peters has shown, Collins partly based his plot on a real-life drama in which he had been closely involved a generation earlier.[2] On 4 May 1848 his friend Edward Ward, aged 33, had married a girl of not quite 16 by licence at All Souls, Langham Place, London, and Collins had given the bride away as well as being one of the witnesses. After the ceremony the young bride had returned to the home of her parents, who knew nothing of what had taken place. Ward had known his wife since she was a child (he had been her teacher) and they had become engaged when she was 14. Her parents had initially agreed that the marriage might take place after her sixteenth birthday and had then withdrawn this permission. Collins had given his friend legal advice, and long afterwards—for she lived to publish her memoirs in 1924—the bride recalled that he had 'impressed great caution and secrecy, as he planned out the whole affair with zest and enjoyment'. Much of that zest and enjoyment must have been derived from the sense of playing a battle of wits with the law. He had no doubt drawn Ward's attention to the fact that if he lived with the young Henrietta before her sixteenth birthday he could be charged with the abduction of a minor. The experience of the real Henrietta is at many points close to that of the fictional Natalie, and in fact Collins's fascination with the impact of the law upon his friend's romance had led him to make creative use of this episode more than once before he turned to it again in *Miss or Mrs?*—almost twenty years earlier in *Basil* and more recently in *Armadale*.

[2] Catherine Peters, *The King of Inventors: A Life of Wilkie Collins* (London, 1991), 80–1.

## The Haunted Hotel

In September 1877, in the hope of improving his poor health, a chronic problem in his later years—among other afflictions he was suffering from 'gout' in both eyes—Collins made a three-month tour of the Tyrol and Northern Italy. This trip included (as noted earlier) a sojourn in Venice, which must have helped to inspire *The Haunted Hotel: A Mystery of Modern Venice*. He started writing this novella in February 1878, but the task soon severely strained his eyesight. Charles Kent, who was an associate of Dickens, records that at that time Collins's eyes 'were literally enormous bags of blood'.[3] Nevertheless, Collins had confidence in his new work and was baffled when Harper, the American publishers with whom he had so far maintained an excellent relationship, declined for commercial reasons to buy the advance sheets. Collins thereupon got in touch with G.M. Rose, a Canadian publisher, who had been attempting to undercut Harper's business in the United States. He wrote: 'There is certainly a chance of attacking the Harper monopoly this time, for the story is a very strong one and has (as I believe) the elements of popular interest in it' (1 May 1878).[4]

Collins was not boasting. The novella turned out to be popular enough to lead the author to say, in the Preface added to the 1879 edition (see Appendix): 'The public favour, at home and abroad, has shown such marked approval of "The Haunted Hotel," during its periodical appearance, that I may trust the work to speak for itself in the form under which it now appeals to other circles of readers'. And the story is, indeed, 'a very strong one'. Having quickly established the mysterious figure of the Countess Narona, the energetic narrative maintains its drive up to the very end. The novella begins with the Countess, presented as an enigma confronting Dr Wybrow. In fact, Wybrow, who quickly drops out of the story, is not a character: he is a narrative function, standing in for the reader. Collins deftly arouses the reader's interest, much as the Countess intrigues the doctor. The reader, then, with the socially ignorant Wybrow, discovers that the notorious Countess is going to marry Lord Montbarry, who has jilted Agnes Lockwood. Montbarry soon dies in a Venetian palace, and the Countess receives a huge sum of insurance money. The palace in

[3] Quoted in Nuel Pharr Davis, *The Life of Wilkie Collins* (Urbana, 1956), 287–8.
[4] Ibid. 288.

which he died is converted into a fashionable hotel, and when the relations of the deceased Lord stay there, they go through uncanny experiences which culminate in Agnes's encounter with the ghost and the Countess's derangement.

The force of 'modern' in the subtitle of this novella is easily over-looked. From the Renaissance drama to the poetry of Byron and Browning, Venice had enjoyed a long literary tradition as a romantic setting, but in Collins's story the ancient *palazzo* has been transformed into a distinctively Victorian phenomenon—a well-run luxury hotel catering for the affluent foreign tourist and, potentially, a money-spinner for its investors. This seems firmly in line with the view of Collinsian 'sensation fiction' as domesticated Gothic, in which the horrors are situated not in a bygone and barbarous age but in a familiar contemporary setting. The hotel is, however, simultaneously modern and antique, its thickly carpeted corridors leading to rooms in which mysteries still lurk, and Collins contrives to accommodate within its venerable though renovated walls the nameless horrors of the past as well as the commonplace appurtenances of modern life.

Thus, whereas *Miss or Mrs?* in the present collection is a typical example of the 'sensation' genre, in which every mystery has a rational explanation, *The Haunted Hotel* reminds us that its author was also a master of the ghost story and the supernatural tale. As G. K. Chesterton observed,

Wilkie Collins was the one man of unmistakable genius who has a certain affinity with Dickens; an affinity in this respect, that they both combine in a curious way a modern and cockney and even commonplace opinion about things with a huge elemental sympathy with strange oracles and spirits and old night. There were no two men in Mid-Victorian England, with their top-hats and umbrellas, more typical of its rationality and dull reform; and there were no two men who could touch them at a ghost story. No two men would have more contempt for superstitions; and no two men could so create the superstitious thrill.[5]

With its combination of 'the superstitious' in a 'modern' setting, *The Haunted Hotel* goes far towards validating this observation.

Dickens and Collins were the subject of another early appreciation, equally perceptive and suggestive, by T. S. Eliot, which appeared in the *Times Literary Supplement* in 1927. Eliot's main interest in this essay was 'to illuminate the question of the difference between the dramatic and melodramatic in fiction', and he here employs the dialectic of Fate and Chance, the former being associated with Drama, and the latter with Melodrama. There is in his view, however, no clear-cut distinction between the two forms: 'great drama has something melodramatic in it, and the best melodrama partakes of the greatness of drama'. Eliot finds an instance of the latter phenomenon in *The Haunted Hotel*. Although this novella, he finds, is 'far from' Collins's best,

what makes it better than a mere readable second-rate ghost story is the fact that fatality in this story is no longer merely a wire jerking the figures. The principal character, the fatal woman, is herself obsessed by the idea of fatality; her motives are melodramatic; she therefore compels the coincidences to occur, feeling that she is compelled to compel them. In this story, as the chief character is internally melodramatic, the story itself ceases to be merely melodramatic, and partakes of true drama.[6]

What Eliot is saying here is that by internalizing the Countess's Melodrama, Collins achieves something of Drama. At the beginning of the novella, the Countess says to Dr Wybrow that Agnes is 'the evil genius' (p. 95) who will bring retribution to her, and she is obsessed with this idea. This is not merely 'superstitious', to borrow Chesterton's term. In presenting the Countess, another example of the Outsider-figure that recurs in so much of Collins's fiction, he offers a psychological study of self-destruction. Aware that there is a doom waiting for her, she still cannot escape from it—or rather, she is even attracted to it, with her 'fascination of terror' (p. 143). 'Some will that is stronger than mine drives me on to my destruction,' she says (p. 190), and she defines this 'will' as 'Destiny' or 'what fools call Chance' (p. 181). It is her belief in this 'Destiny' that propels the events, and this is where Eliot finds Drama in the novella. The climactic encounter of the Countess and Agnes is no coincidence; *The Haunted Hotel* differs from *Miss or Mrs?*, in which, as Collins cheerfully admits, 'The discovery of the marriage depends entirely on a chance meeting between the lord's daughters and the rector's wife' (p. 45).

---

[6] T. S. Eliot, 'Wilkie Collins and Dickens', *Selected Essays* (London, 1934), 469, 467.

Collins constructs a playful Chinese box when Francis Westwick, the theatre manager, hits upon the idea of a play called *The Haunted Hotel*. As the Countess, having lost all her money, buttonholes him about the possibility of her writing a play, he suggests: ' "What do you say, Countess, to entering the lists with Shakespeare, and trying a drama with a ghost in it?" ' (p. 185) He further advises that she should use the occurrences in the hotel as raw material. ' "Sad stuff, if you look at it reasonably," ' he says: ' "But there is something dramatic in the notion of the ghostly influence making itself felt by the relations in succession, as they one after another enter the fatal room—until the one chosen relative comes who will see the Unearthly Creature, and know the terrible truth. Material for a play, Countess—first-rate material for a play!" ' (pp. 185–6). This is good-natured satire at the expense of the genre of stage melodrama, not without a touch of self-mockery at his own practice, but the Countess's compulsive confession in the form of a play, which is inspired by Francis's words, is seriously meant, and it succeeds admirably. Given Francis's reference to Shakespeare, Collins may have had in mind *Macbeth* in particular, with Lady Macbeth's compulsive washing of her hands. The Countess's confession has a ring of truth, but one cannot take everything in it at face value. For example, she paints herself as a noble character who sacrifices herself to her brother. But is Baron Rivar really her brother, as she claims? One very much doubts it, but Collins leaves the question mysterious to the end.

Recently an allegorical interpretation of this ending has been proposed. Seizing upon the fact that the Countess, after her death, continues to breathe in a way the doctor describes as 'purely mechanical' (p. 230), Tamar Heller argues: 'Many readers would claim that this image of the animated corpse is all too symbolic of Collins's career after *The Moonstone*'.[7] According to this interpretation, in his later works Collins obsessively returns to the stories about femininity cast in the mode of what Heller identifies as 'the female Gothic' (the tradition of Gothic writing by women, which maps a plot of domestic victimization), first seriously adopted by Collins in *The Dead Secret* (1857). Writing in this mode, as she points out, Collins often uses the motif of buried writing, such as the housemaid Sarah Leeson's document in that novel in which she writes down her mistress's

---

[7] Tamar Heller, *Dead Secrets: Wilkie Collins and the Female Gothic* (New Haven, 1992), 164.

deathbed confession, and the Countess's manuscript in the novella now under discussion. According to Heller, Collins needed to return to the issue—the tension between female marginality and male exclusion and control of women—that animated his earlier fiction. The later works are structured, she adds, by the desire at once to identify with rebellious women and to contain their rebellion.

Thus, in *The Haunted Hotel*, Countess Narona is subjected in the novel's first scene to the gaze of a male physician; after her death the male readers of her play—figures for critics—consign it to the flames. Since Collins, by killing off his anti-heroine, participates in taming her energy, he allies himself with these figures for the male diagnostician of female deviance; as in *The Woman in White*, however, his writing is also identified with that of his marginalized character. Since the Countess claims that she is writing her play because of a desperate need for money, like Leah Kerby in *After Dark*, she represents the popular author, and the fate of her Gothic melodrama is a grim commentary on the critical reception of the Victorian sensation writer.[8]

This is a stimulating view, but while there is no denying that Collins's creativity declined later in his career, he was still able to produce works like this novella. Swinburne was surely misguided when he regarded it as 'hideous fiction' and 'a bad parody' of an earlier story, 'The Yellow Mask'.[9] The latter, though admittedly an effective one, is a rather simple story of jealousy that has hardly any compelling interest. We may well agree with Nuel Pharr Davis that *The Haunted Hotel* is 'one of the best ghost stories of the century'.[10]

## The Guilty River

*The Guilty River* is a novella that fully deserves to be brought out of oblivion. In his last years, Collins suffered from angina, neuralgia, rheumatic gout and bronchitis and increasingly came to rely upon opium to ease the pain. But despite all this he was constantly working hard to meet the steady demand for his work. He started writing *The Guilty River* in September 1886 and finished it in early November. Although he was exhausted by the rush, Collins was able to say to his

[8] Ibid. 167.
[9] Norman Page (ed.), *Wilkie Collins: The Critical Heritage* (London, 1974), 263.
[10] Davis, 288.

friend, Frank Archer, 'considering that I was twelve hours a day at work for the last week of my labours, I have no reason to complain of my constitution.'[11] The publishers, Arrowsmith, liked the story and, eager to promote it, mounted various advertising campaigns, including (as Collins reported with gratification) 'a hundred "sandwich men" promenading London with *Guilty River* all over them'[12]—a remarkable publicity effort on behalf of a little book priced at just one shilling. It sold 20,000 copies in the first week after publication, but sales thereafter must have fallen off dramatically, since Arrowsmith was to complain after Collins's death that he still had 25,000 copies left on his hands.[13]

Into this novella Collins has combined various elements from his previous works. Roylake, an Englishman who behaves like a foreigner, looks back to Franklin Blake in *The Moonstone*. In his earlier works Collins had also featured a number of characters with physical handicaps like the deaf Lodger here, notably the deaf-mute Mary Grice in *Hide and Seek* (1854) and the blind Lucilla in *Poor Miss Finch* (1872). The latter novel, in fact, has twin brothers (one good, the other evil) competing for the same girl, and if we regard the Lodger as Roylake's double, the dark side of himself, we see the motif repeated here again. In this respect it is interesting that the Lodger and Ozias Midwinter in *Armadale*, another novel using the *Doppelgänger* motif, are both grandchildren of slaves.

Collins, however, manages to make *The Guilty River* wholly distinctive by investing it with a peculiarly haunting atmosphere that promptly declares itself in the early pages. The story begins with Roylake, the narrator, coming back home after many years of exile in Europe, where he was dispatched by his hated father, now dead. He catches moths in the woods familiar to him from his childhood, and then falls asleep from fatigue, or by 'the controlling influences of the dark and silent night':

I was awakened by a light falling on my face. The moon had risen. In the outward part of the wood, beyond which I had not advanced, the pure and welcome light penetrated easily through the scattered trees. I got up and looked about me. A path into the wood now showed itself, broader and

---

[11] Quoted in Kenneth Robinson, *Wilkie Collins: A Biography* (London, 1951), 282.
[12] Ibid. 283.
[13] Peters, 419.

better kept than any path that I could remember in the days of my boyhood. The moon showed it to me plainly, and my curiosity was aroused. (p. 248)

Following the track he chances upon a spring, which reminds him of the river nearby and the water-mill on its bank: 'The image of the great turning wheel, which half-frightened half-fascinated me when I was a child, now presented itself to my memory for the first time after an interval of many years.' He asks himself if he should revisit this scene from the past. This trifling question, however, gives him 'fantastic difficulties so absurd that they might have been difficulties encountered in a dream'. Of course he follows the path, and re-encounters Cristel, known from childhood, the meeting setting in train the remarkable events that follow. The dream-like atmosphere thus established permeates the whole novella, and Peters suggests that it is as though Collins, in reverie, is 'summing up much about himself':[14] the dark beauty, Cristel, with her courage and forthrightness, is perhaps modelled upon his mistress Martha Rudd, while the Lodger, with his auburn hair, his deep blue eyes and his artistic talent combined with depression and monomania, recalls the author's younger brother Charlie, who died in 1873 (they were, however, not rivals, for there was a strong mutual attachment).

R. V. Andrew claims of this novella that 'the construction is careless in the extreme'.[15] Though this is surely going too far, there are a few details which remain unexplained and seemingly unexplored. Roylake says that whilst he was in Germany he was enigmatically informed of his father's second marriage by 'some friend (or enemy)—I never discovered the person' (p. 247). This parallels a curious letter addressed to the Lodger's mother, telling her about the unsavoury past of her husband's family. The Lodger, too, reports, 'I cannot even guess who my mother's devoted friend may have been' (p. 263). One might expect Collins to have provided explanations about these mysterious informers: in, for example, 'A Plot in Private Life' (1858), an estranged wife receives an anonymous letter informing her that her husband has committed bigamy, and the identity of the author is later revealed. But they remain mysterious to the end and are perhaps simply loose ends Collins has forgotten to tie up.

---

[14] Ibid.
[15] R. V. Andrew, *Wilkie Collins: A Critical Survey of His Prose Fiction with a Bibliography* (New York, 1979), 305.

It remains interesting that curious incidents of this nature should be involved in the lives of the Lodger and Roylake alike. It is less surprising, however, when one remembers that in significant ways they resemble each other. Crucially, they are both Outsiders. Roylake, after years of Continental residence, finds many aspects of the way of life of the English upper classes incomprehensible or unappealing, and his ironical comments in Chapter 7 on 'the best society' obviously have the author's endorsement. He is a 'stranger among my own country people' (p. 248). To Mrs Roylake, he ' "looked more like a foreigner than an Englishman" ' (p. 247). Correspondingly, part of the heroine's attraction for him may be her foreignness: she has a German name, Cristel, derived from a German mother. In a different way, the deaf Lodger is a man, in Roylake's words, 'whose pitiable infirmity seemed to place him beyond the pale of social intercourse' (p. 255).

Also importantly, the mother is the key figure in the lives of both: ' "Our mothers have the most sacred of all claims on our gratitude and our love" ' (p. 246), declares Roylake, while the Lodger, in a moving scene at the end, confesses that his mother's ' "spirit has been with me ever since my hearing was restored" ' (p. 351), and it is through listening to her voice that he decides, in atonement, to give the woman he loves to the man he has wronged. It is natural, then, that when reading the Lodger's memoirs, Roylake should think: 'At one time, his tone in writing of his early life, and his allusions to his mother, won my sympathy and respect' (p. 273).

Indeed, Roylake's own early life is inseparably connected with the memory of his mother, with the strong presence of the river behind it, as is observed in a telling scene (p. 314), again dream-like, when he goes to see Cristel just before having tea with the Lodger: 'I walked hand in hand with my mother, among the scenes that were round me . . . and we found a companion of tender years, hiding from us. She showed herself, blushing, hesitating, offering a nosegay of wild flowers.' At this point Cristel appears, and dream and reality merge. This scene brings to mind the Lodger's confession that all his dreams 'without exception connect Cristel with the river':

Look at the stealthy current that makes no sound. In my last night's sleep, it made itself heard; it was flowing in my ears with a water-music of its own. No longer my deaf ears; I heard, in my dream, as well as you can hear. Yes;

the same water-music, singing over and over again the same horrid song: 'Fool, fool, no Cristel for you; bid her good-bye, bid her good-bye' (p. 294).

This, as we have seen, is precisely what his mother urges when his hearing is restored. Thus Roylake and the Lodger are alike attracted to Cristel, the attraction being closely related to both the river and the mother. One is tempted to speculate that Collins is here recalling his own mother, who died in 1868 and for whom he had a deep affection; he repeatedly called her death the greatest sorrow of his life.[16]

As for Collins's use of the river, this may show the influence of Dickens's last completed novel, *Our Mutual Friend* (1865), which also has a heroine who lives with a widowed father by the river and handles a rowing-boat with skill. Both heroines, too, are loved by men who are greatly their social superiors. More broadly, both works are pervaded by an atmosphere of half-light and gloom associated with river scenery that is almost painterly. As Collins has the Lodger observe at one point, the 'growing shadows and fading lights' constitute a fit subject for the brush of 'Rembrandt and Turner' (p. 317).

The Lodger has something curiously feminine about him. When Roylake sees him for the first time, he is surprised by the beautiful face, 'and it was the face of a man!' (p. 254). Clearly he thinks at first that he has seen a woman, but the Lodger has 'the expression of power which made it impossible to mistake [him] for a woman, although his hair grew long and he was without either moustache or beard' (p. 254). Later Roylake adds that the other man's deeply dark blue eyes 'were so entirely beautiful that they had no right to be in a man's face' (p. 277). Perhaps Collins is here offering a covert version of his 'female Gothic', as Heller defines it. Interestingly, the motif of the buried writing is also present here. The Lodger has the manuscript of a story, based upon an episode in a volume of French Trials, in which a young girl is cleverly abducted. He intends to use the plan himself, but it is cunningly stolen by Cristel's father.

In the Lodger Collins portrays a tragic figure who suffers from 'the family taint, developed by a deaf man's isolation among his fellow-creatures' (p. 351). Originally a good man, he gradually falls, or is made by circumstances to fall, and one stage of this downward journey towards moral corruption is powerfully captured in the

---

[16] Peters, 292.

episode where he sees a brutal carter beating an over-loaded horse, then turns that scene into a drawing (p. 269). In the drawing, however, he depicts the carter receiving at his own hands the thrashing he deserves but did not in actuality receive. Recalling this act of self-therapy, he observes: ' "Strange to say, this representation of what I ought to have done, relieved my mind as if I had actually done it" ' (p. 270). Eventually he does not scruple to make an attempt at murder, but his confession at the end, unlike that of the Countess in *The Haunted Hotel*, or that of Count Fosco in *The Woman in White*, carries a haunting sadness. Roylake notes, 'I say there was good in that suffering man; and I thank God I was not quite wrong about him after all' (p. 351), and we are likely to concur with this judgment when we have reached the end of the story.

Thomas Hardy, who early in his own career as a novelist fell under the influence of Collins, insisted that every writer of fiction was an Ancient Mariner and every story should be worth the telling. Perhaps Collins's supreme gift is his bulldog grip on the reader's attention and curiosity: his plot-devices can occasionally be implausible or even absurd, but once we have started reading it is difficult to stop until the last page has been turned. Varied in setting and atmosphere though they are, the three novellas that follow suggest that this is as true of his shorter fiction as of his more widely familiar full-length novels.

# NOTE ON THE TEXT

The texts of the novellas printed in this edition are based on the first editions to appear in volume form.

*Miss or Mrs?* first appeared in the Christmas Number of *The Graphic*, a London weekly newspaper, on 25 December 1871, with the subtitle 'A Christmas Story, in Twelve Scenes'. It was accompanied by ten full-page illustrations, of which six have a direct bearing upon the story, the rest depicting seasonal events such as 'The Snow Battle'. The story appeared in a volume entitled *Miss or Mrs? And Other Stories in Outline*, with 'Blow up with the Brig!' and 'The Fatal Cradle', in 1873, published by Richard Bentley and Son. A few typographical errors were corrected in a New Edition of 1875 which, in addition, contained 'A Mad Marriage'.

*The Haunted Hotel* first appeared in *Belgravia* in 1878. In each monthly issue there was one full-page illustration (by Arthur Hopkins). The serialization ran as follows: June Chapters 1–5; July 6–10; August 11–15; September 16–20; October 21–25; November 26–Postscript. The novella came out in two volumes with 'My Lady's Money' in 1879, published by Chatto & Windus and with the original illustrations.

*The Guilty River* was never serialized but first appeared in paper covers as Arrowsmith's Christmas Annual for 1886 (Arrowsmith Bristol Library, vol. 19).

When putting the first two of these novellas into volume form, Collins made a number of corrections. In the case of *Miss or Mrs?*, he revised the punctuation in more than twenty places and altered phrasing in almost thirty places. For instance, Natalie's 'languid brown' eyes (p. 38) were originally 'superb black' eyes; 'in his [Launce's] affairs' (p. 42) was 'in his love affairs'. For *The Haunted Hotel* Collins made more than fifty emendations. To give a few examples, Agnes's 'undignified conduct' (p. 112) was originally 'superstitious fears'; 'a supernatural movement' (p. 203) was 'a momentary movement'; 'He drew her nearer to him' (p. 218) was 'He drew her to his bosom'. As these examples suggest, the alterations are not drastic, but where changes are substantial, or deemed interesting, notes have been added.

A few obvious misprints have been silently corrected, and spelling has been modernized in a few cases (for example, 'ensconced' for 'ensconsed'; 'secrecy' for 'secresy'; 'decrepit' for 'decripid') where the original forms might distract readers. In addition, the text has been made to conform to Oxford World's Classics house style. Thus, for instance, full stops after common abbreviations (Mr, Mrs, etc.) have been deleted, and single quotation marks, instead of double, are used in introducing dialogue. In other respects Collins's punctuation, rhetorical and dramatic rather than strictly logical, and somewhat heavier than modern practice, has been retained.

The editors wish to thank The Harry Ransom Humanities Research Center, University of Texas at Austin, for making available the texts of original periodical publications.

# SELECT BIBLIOGRAPHY

The place of publication is London unless otherwise stated.

## Biography

By far the most thoroughly researched biography is Catherine Peters's admirable *The King of Inventors: A Life of Wilkie Collins* (1991). There are earlier biographies by Kenneth Robinson (*Wilkie Collins* (1951)), Nuel Pharr Davis (*The Life of Wilkie Collins* (Urbana, 1956)) and William Clarke (*The Secret Life of Wilkie Collins* (1988)).

## Bibliographies

Andrew, R. V., 'A Wilkie Collins Check-list', *English Studies in Africa*, 3 (1960), 79–98.

Ashley, Robert, 'Wilkie Collins', in George H. Ford (ed.), *Victorian Fiction: A Second Guide to Research* (New York, 1978).

Beetz, Kirk H., *Wilkie Collins: An Annotated Bibliography, 1889–1976* (1976).

Lohrli, Anne (ed.), *Household Words* (Toronto, 1973).

Wolff, Robert L., 'Wilkie Collins', in *Nineteenth Century Fiction: A Bibliographical Catalogue* (New York, 1981–6), i. 254–72.

## Criticism

Andrew, R. V., *Wilkie Collins: A Critical Survey of His Prose Fiction with a Bibliography* (New York, 1979).

Ashley, Robert, *Wilkie Collins* (1952).

Heller, Tamar, *Dead Secrets: Wilkie Collins and the Female Gothic* (New Haven, 1992).

Lonoff, Sue, *Wilkie Collins and His Victorian Readers* (New York, 1982).

Marshall, William H., *Wilkie Collins* (New York, 1970).

Page, Norman (ed.), *Wilkie Collins: The Critical Heritage* (1974).

Rance, Nicholas, *Wilkie Collins and Other Sensation Novelists* (1991).

## General Background

Collins, Philip, *Dickens and Crime* (1964)

Gilmour, Robin, *The Victorian Period: The Intellectual and Cultural Context of Literature 1830–90* (1993)

Hughes, Winnifred, *The Maniac in the Cellar: The Sensation Novel of the 1860s* (Princeton, 1980)

Punter, David, *The Literature of Terror* (2nd edn., 1996)

Pykett, Lyn, *The Sensation Novel* (1994)
Wheeler, Michael, *English Fiction of the Victorian Period 1830–90* (2nd edn., 1994)

### Further Reading in Oxford World's Classics

Braddon, Mary Elizabeth, *Lady Audley's Secret*, ed. David Skilton
—— *Aurora Floyd*, ed. P. D. Edwards
—— *The Doctor's Wife*, ed. Lyn Pykett
Collins, Wilkie, *Armadale*, ed. Catherine Peters
—— *Basil*, ed. Dorothy Goldman
—— *The Law and the Lady*, ed. Jenny Bourne Taylor
—— *Mad Monkton and Other Stories*, ed. Norman Page
—— *Man and Wife*, ed. Norman Page
—— *The Moonstone*, ed. Anthea Trodd
—— *No Name*, ed. Virginia Blain
—— *The Woman in White*, ed. John Sutherland
Dickens, Charles, *The Mystery of Edwin Drood*, ed. Margaret Cardwell

# A CHRONOLOGY OF WILKIE COLLINS

| *Life* | *Historical and cultural background* |
|---|---|
| 1824 (8 Jan.) Born at 11 New Cavendish Street, St Marylebone, London, elder son of William Collins, RA (1788–1847), artist, and Harriet Collins, née Geddes (1790–1868). | Death of Byron. Scott, *Redgauntlet* |
| 1825 | Stockton–Darlington railway opened. |
| 1826 (Spring) Family moves to Pond Street, Hampstead. | Hazlitt, *Spirit of the Age* |
| 1827 | Death of Blake; University College London founded. |
| 1828 (25 Jan.) Brother, Charles Allston Collins, born. | Birth of Meredith, D. G. Rossetti; Catholic Emancipation Act. |
| 1829 (Autumn) Family moves to Hampstead Square. | Balzac's *La Comédie humaine* begins publication |
| 1830 Family moves to Porchester Terrace, Bayswater. | Death of George IV and accession of William IV; July Revolution in France. Hugo, *Hernani* Tennyson, *Poems Chiefly Lyrical* |
| 1831 | British Association for the Advancement of Science founded; Britain annexes Mysore. |
| 1832 | Deaths of Bentham, Crabbe, Goethe, Scott; First Reform Bill passed. |
| 1833 | Slavery abolished throughout British Empire. Carlyle, *Sartor Resartus* |
| 1834 | Deaths of Coleridge, Lamb; new Poor Law comes into effect; Tolpuddle Martyrs. |
| 1835 (13 Jan.) Starts school, the Maida Hill Academy. | Dickens, *Sketches by Boz* (1st series) |
| 1836 (19 Sept.–15 Aug. 1838) Family visits France and Italy. | |
| 1837 | Death of William IV and accession of Victoria. |

Carlyle, *The French Revolution*
Dickens, *Pickwick Papers*

1838 (Aug.) Family moves to 20       Anti-Corn Law League founded;
Avenue Road, Regent's Park.          Chartist petitions published; London–
Attends Mr Cole's boarding           Birmingham railway opened; Anglo-
school, Highbury Place, until        Afghan War.
Dec. 1840.                           Dickens, *Oliver Twist*

1840 (Summer) Family moves to 85     Birth of Hardy; Marriage of Victoria and
Oxford Terrace, Bayswater.           Albert; penny postage introduced.
                                     Browning, *Sordello*
                                     Darwin, *Voyage of H.M.S. Beagle*
                                     Dickens, *The Old Curiosity Shop*

1841 (Jan.) Apprenticed to Antrobus &   Carlyle, *Heroes and Hero-Worship*
Co., tea merchants, Strand.

1842 (June–July) Trip to Highlands of   Child and female underground labour
Scotland, and Shetland, with         becomes illegal; Chartist riots; Act for
William Collins.                     inspection of asylums.
                                     Browning, *Dramatic Lyrics*
                                     Comte, *Cours de philosophie positive*
                                     Macaulay, *Lays of Ancient Rome*
                                     Tennyson, *Poems*

1843 (Aug.) First signed publication    Birth of Henry James; Thames Tunnel
'The Last Stage Coachman' in the     opened.
*Illuminated Magazine*.              Carlyle, *Past and Present*
                                     Dickens, *A Christmas Carol*
                                     Ruskin, *Modern Painters* begins
                                     publication

1844 Writes his first (unpublished)     Factory Act.
novel, 'Iolani; or Tahiti as it was; a   Chambers, *Vestiges of the Natural
Romance'.                            History of Creation*
                                     Elizabeth Barrett, *Poems*

1845 (Jan.) 'Iolani' submitted to       Boom in railway speculation; Newman
Chapman & Hall, rejected (8          joins Church of Rome.
Mar.).                               Disraeli, *Sybil*
                                     Engels, *Condition of the Working Class in
                                     England in 1844*
                                     Poe, *Tales of Mystery and Imagination*

1846 (17 May) Admitted student of       Repeal of Corn Laws; Irish potato
Lincoln's Inn.                       famine.
                                     Lear, *Book of Nonsense*

1847 (17 Feb.) Death of William         Ten-hour Factory Act; California gold
Collins.                             rush.
                                     Emily Brontë, *Wuthering Heights*
                                     Charlotte Brontë, *Jane Eyre*
                                     Tennyson, *The Princess*

1848 (Summer) Family move to 38 Blandford Square.
(Nov.) First book, *Memoirs of the Life of William Collins, Esq., R. A.* published.

Death of Emily Brontë; Pre-Raphaelite Brotherhood founded; Chartist Petition; cholera epidemic; Public Health Act; revolutions in Europe.
Dickens, *Dombey and Son*
Gaskell, *Mary Barton*
Marx and Engels, *Communist Manifesto*
Thackeray, *Vanity Fair*

1849 Exhibits a painting at the Royal Academy summer exhibition.

Thackeray, *Pendennis*
Ruskin, *Seven Lamps of Architecture*

1850 (27 Feb.) First published novel, *Antonina*; (Summer) Family move to 17 Hanover Terrace.

Deaths of Balzac, Wordsworth; Tennyson becomes Poet Laureate; Public Libraries Act.
Dickens, *David Copperfield*
Charles Kingsley, *Alton Locke*
Tennyson, *In Memoriam*
Wordsworth, *The Prelude*
Dickens starts *Household Words*

1851 (Jan.) Travel book on Cornwall, *Rambles Beyond Railways*, published.
(Mar.) Meets Dickens for the first time.
(May) Acts with Dickens in Bulwer-Lytton's *Not So Bad as We Seem.*

Death of Turner; Great Exhibition in Hyde Park; Australian gold rush.
Ruskin, *The Stones of Venice*

1852 (Jan.) *Mr Wray's Cash Box* published, with frontispiece by Millais.
(24 Apr.) 'A Terribly Strange Bed', first contribution to *Household Words.*
(May) Goes on tour with Dickens's company of amateur actors.
(16 Nov.) *Basil* published.

Death of Wellington; Louis Napoleon becomes Emperor of France.
Stowe, *Uncle Tom's Cabin*
Thackeray, *Henry Esmond*

1853 (Oct.–Dec.) Tours Switzerland and Italy with Dickens and Augustus Egg.

Arnold, *Poems*
Charlotte Brontë, *Villette*
Dickens, *Bleak House*
Gaskell, *Cranford*

1854 (5 June) *Hide and Seek* published.

Birth of Wilde; outbreak of Crimean War; Working Men's College founded.
Dickens, *Hard Times*

1855 (Feb.) Spends a holiday in Paris with Dickens.

Browning, *Men and Women*

(16 June) First play, *The Lighthouse*, performed by Dickens's theatrical company at Tavistock House.
(Nov.–Dec.) *Mad Monkton* serialized.

Gaskell, *North and South*
Trollope, *The Warden*
Death of Charlotte Brontë.

1856 (Feb.) *After Dark*, a collection of short stories, published.
(Feb.–Apr.) Spends six weeks in Paris with Dickens.
(Mar.) *A Rogue's Life* serialized in *Household Words*.
(Oct.) Joins staff of *Household Words* and begins collaboration with Dickens in *The Wreck of the Golden Mary* (Dec.).

Birth of Freud, Shaw; Crimean War ends.
E. B. Browning, *Aurora Leigh*

1857 (Jan.–June) *The Dead Secret* serialized in *Household Words*, published in volume form (June).
(6 Jan.) *The Frozen Deep* performed by Dickens's theatrical company at Tavistock House.
(Aug.) *The Lighthouse* performed at the Olympic Theatre.
(Sept.) Spends a working holiday in the Lake District with Dickens, their account appearing as *The Lazy Tour of Two Idle Apprentices*, serialized in *Household Words* (Oct.).
Collaborates with Dickens on *The Perils of Certain English Prisoners*.

Birth of Conrad; Matrimonial Causes Act establishes divorce courts; Indian Mutiny.
Dickens, *Little Dorrit*
Flaubert, *Madame Bovary*
Trollope, *Barchester Towers*

1858 (May) Dickens separates from his wife.
(Oct.) *The Red Vial* produced at the Olympic Theatre; a failure.

Victoria proclaimed Empress of India.
Eliot, *Scenes of Clerical Life*

1859 From this year no longer living with his mother; lives for the rest of his life (with one interlude) with Mrs Caroline Graves. (Jan.–Feb.) Living at 124 Albany Street; (May–Dec.) Living at 2a Cavendish Street.
(Apr.) *All the Year Round* begins publication.

War of Italian Liberation.
Darwin, *Origin of Species*
Eliot, *Adam Bede*
Meredith, *The Ordeal of Richard Feverel*
Mill, *On Liberty*
Samuel Smiles, *Self-Help*
Tennyson, *Idylls of the King*
Dickens starts *All the Year Round*

(Oct.) *The Queen of Hearts*, a
collection of short stories,
published.
(26 Nov.–25 Aug. 1860) *The
Woman in White* serialized in *All
the Year Round*.
(Dec.) Moves to 12 Harley Street.

1860 (Aug.) *The Woman in White*
published in volume form: a best-
seller in Britain and the United
States, and rapidly translated into
most European languages.

British Association meeting at Oxford
(Huxley–Wilberforce debate).
Eliot, *The Mill on the Floss*

1861 (Jan.) Resigns from *All the Year
Round*.

Death of Albert, Prince Consort;
Offences Against the Person Act
(includes provisions on bigamy);
outbreak of American Civil War.
Dickens, *Great Expectations*
Eliot, *Silas Marner*
Palgrave, *Golden Treasury*
Reade, *The Cloister and the Hearth*

1862 (15 Mar.–17 Jan. 1863) *No Name*
serialized in *All the Year Round*,
published in volume form (31
Dec.).

Clough, *Poems*

1863 *My Miscellanies*, a collection of
journalism from *Household Words*
and *All the Year Round*,
published.

Eliot, *Romola*
Huxley, *Man's Place in Nature*
Lyell, *Antiquity of Man*
Mill, *Utilitarianism*
Death of Thackeray.

1864 (Nov.–June 1866) *Armadale*
serialized in *The Cornhill*.
(Dec.) Moves to 9 Melcombe
Place, Dorset Square.

Albert Memorial constructed.
Newman, *Apologia pro Vita Sua*

1865

Birth of Kipling, Yeats; death of
Gaskell.
Arnold, *Essays in Criticism* (1st series)
Carroll, *Alice's Adventures in Wonderland*
Dickens, *Our Mutual Friend*
Tolstoy, *War and Peace*
Wagner, *Tristan und Isolde*

1866 (May) *Armadale* published in two
volumes.
(Oct.) *The Frozen Deep* produced
at the Olympic Theatre.

Birth of Wells.
Dostoyevsky, *Crime and Punishment*
Swinburne, *Poems and Ballads*

1867  (Sept.) Moves to 90 Gloucester Place, Portman Square. Collaborates with Dickens on *No Thoroughfare*, published as Christmas Number of *All the Year Round*; dramatic version performed at the Adelphi Theatre (Christmas Eve).

Second Reform Bill passed; Paris Exhibition.
Bagehot, *English Constitution*
Marx, *Das Kapital*

1868  (4 Jan.–8 Aug.) *The Moonstone* serialized in *All the Year Round*; published in three volumes (July).
(19 Mar.) Mother, Harriet Collins, dies.
Collins forms liaison with Martha Rudd ('Mrs Dawson').
(4 Oct.) Caroline Graves marries Joseph Charles Clow.

Report of Royal Commission on the Laws of Marriage.
Browning, *The Ring and the Book*

1869  (Mar.) *Black and White*, written in collaboration with Charles Fechter, produced at the Adelphi Theatre.
(4 July) Daughter, Marian Dawson, born to Collins and Martha Rudd, at 33 Bolsover Street, Portland Place.

Suez Canal opened.
Arnold, *Culture and Anarchy*
Mill, *On the Subjection of Women*

1870  (June) *Man and Wife* published in volume form.
(9 June) Dickens dies.
(Aug.) Dramatic version of *The Woman in White* tried out in Leicester.

Education Act; Married Woman's Property Act; Franco-Prussian War; fall of Napoleon III.
D. G. Rossetti, *Poems*
Spencer, *Principles of Psychology*

1871  (14 May) Second daughter, Harriet Constance Dawson, born at 33 Bolsover Street.
(May) Caroline Graves again living with Collins.
(Oct.) *The Woman in White* produced at the Olympic Theatre.
(Oct.–Mar. 1872) *Poor Miss Finch* serialized in *Cassell's Magazine*.
(25 Dec.) *Miss or Mrs?* published.

Trades unions become legal; first Impressionist Exhibition held in Paris; religious tests abolished at Oxford, Cambridge, Durham.
Darwin, *Descent of Man*
Eliot, *Middlemarch*

1872  (Feb.) *Poor Miss Finch* published in volume form.

Butler, *Erewhon*

| | |
|---|---|
| 1873 (Feb.) Dramatic version of *Man and Wife* performed at the Prince of Wales Theatre.<br>(9 Apr.) Brother, Charles Allston Collins, dies.<br>(May) *The New Magdalen* published in volume form; dramatic version performed at the Olympic Theatre.<br>*Miss or Mrs? And Other Stories in Outline* published.<br>(Sept.–Mar. 1874) Tours United States and Canada, giving readings from his work. | Mill, *Autobiography*<br>Pater, *Studies in the Renaissance* |
| 1874 (Nov.) *The Frozen Deep and Other Stories*.<br>(25 Dec.) Son, William Charles Dawson, born, 10 Taunton Place, Regent's Park. | Factory Act; Public Worship Act.<br>Hardy, *Far from the Madding Crowd* |
| 1875 Copyrights in Collins's work transferred to Chatto & Windus, who become his main publisher.<br>*The Law and the Lady* serialized in *The London Graphic*; published in volume form. | Artisans' Dwellings Act; Public Health Act. |
| 1876 (Apr.) *Miss Gwilt* (dramatic version of *Armadale*) performed at the Globe Theatre.<br>*The Two Destinies* published in volume form. | Invention of telephone and phonograph.<br>Eliot, *Daniel Deronda*<br>James, *Roderick Hudson*<br>Lombroso, *The Criminal* |
| 1877 (Sept.) Dramatic version of *The Moonstone* performed at the Olympic Theatre.<br>*My Lady's Money* and *Percy and the Prophet*, short stories, published. | Annexation of Transvaal.<br>Ibsen, *The Pillars of Society*<br>Tolstoy, *Anna Karenina* |
| 1878 (June–Nov.) *The Haunted Hotel* serialized. | Whistler–Ruskin controversy; Congress of Berlin; Edison invents the incandescent electric lamp.<br>Hardy, *The Return of the Native* |
| 1879 *The Haunted Hotel* published in volume form.<br>*The Fallen Leaves—First Series* published in volume form. | Birth of E. M. Forster.<br>Ibsen, *A Doll's House* |

| | |
|---|---|
| | *A Rogue's Life* published in volume form. | |
| 1880 | *Jezebel's Daughter* published in volume form. | Deaths of George Eliot, Flaubert; Bradlaugh, an atheist, becomes an MP. Gissing, *Workers in the Dawn* Zola, *Nana* |
| 1881 | *The Black Robe* published in volume form. A. P. Watt becomes Collins's literary agent. | Death of Carlyle; Democratic Federation founded. Ibsen, *Ghosts* James, *Portrait of a Lady* |
| 1882 | | Birth of Joyce, Woolf; death of Darwin, D. G. Rossetti, Trollope; Married Woman's Property Act; Daimler invents the petrol engine. |
| 1883 | *Heart and Science* published in volume form. *Rank and Riches* produced at the Adelphi Theatre: a theatrical disaster. | Deaths of Marx, Wagner. Trollope, *An Autobiography* |
| 1884 | '*I Say No*' published in volume form. | Fabian Society founded; Third Reform Bill. |
| 1885 | | Birth of Lawrence; Criminal Law Amendment Act (raising age of consent to 16). Maupassant, *Bel-Ami* Pater, *Marius the Epicurean* Zola, *Germinal* |
| 1886 | *The Evil Genius* published in volume form. *The Guilty River* published in *Arrowsmith's Christmas Annual*. | Irish Home Rule Act; Contagious Diseases Acts repealed. Hardy, *The Mayor of Casterbridge* |
| 1887 | *Little Novels*, a collection of short stories, published. | Victoria's Golden Jubilee; Independent Labour Party founded. Hardy, *The Woodlanders* Strindberg, *The Father* |
| 1888 | *The Legacy of Cain* published in volume form. (Feb.) Moves to 82 Wimpole Street. | Death of Arnold; birth of T. S. Eliot. Kipling, *Plain Tales from the Hills* |
| 1889 | (23 Sept.) Dies at 82 Wimpole Street. | Deaths of Browning, Hopkins; dock strike in London. Booth, *Life and Labour of the People in London* Shaw, *Fabian Essays in Socialism* Ibsen's *A Doll's House* staged in London |

1890   *Blind Love* (completed by Walter Besant) published in volume form.

Death of Newman; Parnell case; first underground railway in London.
Booth, *In Darkest England*
Frazer, *The Golden Bough*
William James, *Principles of Psychology*

1895   (June) Caroline Graves dies and is buried in Wilkie Collins's grave.

Morris, *News from Nowhere*

1919   Martha Rudd (Dawson) dies.

# MISS OR MRS?

TO

BARON VON TAUCHNITZ

IN CORDIAL REMEMBRANCE

OF MY RELATIONS WITH HIM AS

PUBLISHER AND FRIEND*

# CONTENTS

# PERSONS OF THE STORY

Sir Joseph Graybrooke                    (*Knight*)
Richard Turlington              (*Of the Levant Trade*)
Launcelot Linzie          (*Of the College of Surgeons*)
James Dicas               (*Of the Roll of Attorneys*)
Thomas Wildfang           (*Superannuated Seaman*)
Miss Graybrooke                 (*Sir Joseph's Sister*)
Natalie Graybrooke            (*Sir Joseph's Daughter*)
Lady Winwood                     (*Sir Joseph's Niece*)
Amelia ⎫
Sophia  ⎬        (*Lady Winwood's Stepdaughters*)
Dorothea ⎭

*Period*: The present time. *Place*: England.

# FIRST SCENE

## AT SEA

The night had come to an end. The new-born day waited for its quickening light in the silence that is never known on land—the silence before sunrise, in a calm at sea.

Not a breath came from the dead air. Not a ripple stirred on the motionless water. Nothing changed, but the softly-growing light; nothing moved but the lazy mist, curling up to meet the sun, its master, on the eastward sea. By fine gradations, the airy veil of morning thinned in substance as it rose—thinned, till there dawned through it in the first rays of sunlight the tall white sails of a Schooner Yacht.

From stem to stern silence possessed the vessel—as silence possessed the sea.

But one-living creature was on deck—the man at the helm, dozing peaceably with his arm over the useless tiller. Minute by minute the light grew, and the heat grew with it; and still the helmsman slumbered, the heavy sails hung noiseless, the quiet water lay sleeping against the vessel's sides. The whole orb of the sun was visible above the water-line, when the first sound pierced its way through the morning silence. From far off over the shining white ocean, the cry of a sea-bird reached the yacht on a sudden out of the last airy circles of the waning mist.

The sleeper at the helm woke; looked up at the idle sails, and yawned in sympathy with them; looked out at the sea on either side of him, and shook his head obstinately at the superior obstinacy of the calm.

'Blow, my little breeze!' said the man, whistling the sailor's invocation to the wind softly between his teeth. 'Blow, my little breeze!'

'How's her head?' cried a bold and brassy voice, hailing the deck from the cabin staircase.

'Anywhere you like, master; all round the compass.'

The voice was followed by the man. The owner of the yacht appeared on deck.

Behold Richard Turlington, Esq., of the great Levant* firm of Pizzituti, Turlington, and Branca! Aged eight-and-thirty; standing stiffly and sturdily at a height of not more than five feet six— Mr Turlington presented to the view of his fellow-creatures a face of the perpendicular* order of human architecture. His forehead was a straight line, his upper lip was another, his chin was the straightest and the longest line of all. As he turned his swarthy countenance eastward, and shaded his light grey eyes from the sun, his knotty hand plainly revealed that it had got him his living by its own labour at one time or another in his life. Taken on the whole, this was a man whom it might be easy to respect, but whom it would be hard to love. Better company at the official desk than at the social table. Morally and physically—if the expression may be permitted—a man without a bend in him.

'A calm yesterday,' grumbled Richard Turlington, looking with stubborn deliberation all round him. 'And a calm to-day. Ha! next season I'll have the vessel fitted with engines. I hate this!'

'Think of the filthy coals, and the infernal vibration, and leave your beautiful schooner as she is. We are out for a holiday. Let the wind and the sea take a holiday too.'

Pronouncing those words of remonstrance, a slim, nimble, curly-headed young gentleman joined Richard Turlington on deck, with his clothes under his arm, his towels in his hand, and nothing on him but the nightgown in which he had stepped out of his bed.

'Launcelot Linzie, you have been received on board my vessel in the capacity of medical attendant on Miss Natalie Graybrooke, at her father's request. Keep your place, if you please. When I want your advice, I'll ask you for it.' Answering in those terms, the elder man fixed his colourless grey eyes on the younger with an expression which added plainly: 'There won't be room enough in this schooner much longer for me and for you.'

Launcelot Linzie had his reasons (apparently) for declining to let his host offend him, on any terms whatever.

'Thank you!' he rejoined, in a tone of satirical good-humour. 'It isn't easy to keep my place on board your vessel. I can't help presuming to enjoy myself as if I was the owner. The life is such a new one—to *me*! It's so delightfully easy, for instance, to wash yourself here. On shore it's a complicated question of jugs and basins and tubs; one is always in danger of breaking something or spoiling something. Here you have only to jump out of bed, to run up on deck, and to do this!'

He turned, and scampered to the bows of the vessel. In one instant he was out of his nightgown, in another he was on the bulwark, in a third he was gambolling luxuriously in sixty fathoms of salt water.

Turlington's eyes followed him with a reluctant uneasy attention as he swam round the vessel, the only moving object in view. Turlington's mind, steady and slow in all its operations, set him a problem to be solved, on given conditions, as follows:—

'Launcelot Linzie is fifteen years younger than I am. Add to that, Launcelot Linzie is Natalie Graybrooke's cousin. Given those two advantages—Query: Has he taken Natalie's fancy?'

Turning that question slowly over and over in his mind, Richard Turlington seated himself in a corner at the stern of the vessel. He was still at work on the problem, when the young surgeon returned to his cabin to put the finishing touches to his toilet. He had not reached the solution when the steward appeared an hour later and said, 'Breakfast is ready, sir!'

They were a party of five round the cabin table.

First, Sir Joseph Graybrooke. Inheritor of a handsome fortune made by his father and his grandfather in trade. Mayor, twice elected, of a thriving provincial town. Officially privileged, while holding that dignity, to hand a silver trowel to a royal personage condescending to lay a first stone of a charitable edifice. Knighted accordingly, in honour of the occasion. Worthy of the honour and worthy of the occasion. A type of his eminently respectable class. Possessed of an amiable rosy face, and soft silky white hair. Sound in his principles; tidy in his dress; blest with moderate politics and a good digestion—a harmless, healthy, spruce, speckless, weak-minded old man.

Secondly, Miss Lavinia Graybrooke, Sir Joseph's maiden sister. Personally, Sir Joseph in petticoats. If you knew one you knew the other.

Thirdly, Miss Natalie Graybrooke—Sir Joseph's only child.

She had inherited the personal appearance and the temperament of her mother—dead many years since. There had been a mixture of Negro blood and French blood in the late Lady Graybrooke's family, settled originally in Martinique. Natalie had her mother's warm dusky colour, her mother's superb black hair, and her mother's melting lazy lovely brown eyes. At fifteen years of age (dating from her last birthday) she possessed the development of the bosom and limbs, which in England is rarely attained before twenty. Everything about the girl—except her little rosy ears—was on a grand Amazonian scale. Her shapely hand was long and large; her supple waist was the waist of a woman. The indolent grace of all her movements had its motive power in an almost masculine firmness of action, and profusion of physical resource. This remarkable bodily development was far from being accompanied by any corresponding development of character. Natalie's manner was the gentle, innocent manner of a young girl. She had her father's sweet temper engrafted on her mother's variable Southern nature. She moved like a goddess, and she laughed like a child. Signs of maturing too rapidly—of outgrowing her strength, as the phrase went—had made their appearance in Sir Joseph's daughter during the spring. The family doctor had suggested a sea-voyage, as a wise manner of employing the fine summer months. Richard Turlington's yacht was placed at her disposal—with Richard Turlington himself included as one of the fixtures of the vessel. With her father and her aunt to keep up round her the atmosphere of home—with cousin Launcelot (more commonly known as 'Launce') to carry out, if necessary, the medical treatment prescribed by superior authority on shore—the lovely invalid embarked on her summer cruise, and sprang up into a new existence in the life-giving breezes of the sea. After two happy months of lazy coasting round the shores of England, all that remained of Natalie's illness was represented by a delicious langour in her eyes, and an utter inability to devote herself to anything which took the shape of a serious occupation. As she sat at the cabin breakfast-table that morning, in her quaintly-made sailing dress of old-fashioned nankeen*—her inbred childishness of manner contrasting delightfully with the blooming maturity of her form—the man must have been trebly armed indeed in the modern philosophy who could have denied that the first of a woman's rights is the right of being beautiful; and the foremost of a woman's merits, the merit of being young!

The other two persons present at the table, were the two gentlemen who have already appeared on the deck of the yacht.

'Not a breath of wind stirring!' said Richard Turlington. 'The weather has got a grudge against us. We have drifted about four or five miles in the last eight-and-forty hours. You will never take another cruise with me—you must be longing to get on shore.'

He addressed himself to Natalie: plainly eager to make himself agreeable to the young lady—and plainly unsuccessful in producing any impression on her. She made a civil answer; and looked at her tea-cup, instead of looking at Richard Turlington.

'You might fancy yourself on shore at this moment,' said Launce. 'The vessel is as steady as a house, and the swing-table we are eating our breakfast on is as even as your dining-room table at home.'

He too addressed himself to Natalie—but without betraying the anxiety to please her which had been shown by the other. For all that, *he* diverted the girl's attention from her tea-cup; and *his* idea instantly awakened a responsive idea in Natalie's mind.

'It will be so strange on shore,' she said, 'to find myself in a room that never turns on one side, and to sit at a table that never tilts down to my knees at one time, or rises up to my chin at another. How I shall miss the wash of the water at my ear, and the ring of the bell on deck, when I am awake at night on land! No interest there in how the wind blows, or how the sails are set. No asking your way of the sun, when you are lost, with a little brass instrument and a morsel of pencil and paper. No delightful wandering wherever the wind takes you, without the worry of planning beforehand where you are to go. Oh, how I shall miss the dear changeable inconstant sea! And how sorry I am I'm not a man and a sailor!'

This to the guest, admitted on board on sufferance—and not one word of it addressed, even by chance, to the owner of the yacht!

Richard Turlington's heavy eyebrows contracted with an unmistakable expression of pain.

'If this calm weather holds,' he went on, addressing himself to Sir Joseph, 'I am afraid, Graybrooke, I shall not be able to bring you back to the port we sailed from, by the end of the week.'

'Whenever you like, Richard,' answered the old gentleman, resignedly. 'Any time will do for me.'

'Any time within reasonable limits, Joseph,' said Miss Lavinia—evidently feeling that her brother was conceding too much. She spoke with Sir Joseph's amiable smile and Sir Joseph's softly-pitched voice. Two twin babies could hardly have been more like one another.

While these few words were being exchanged among the elders, a private communication was in course of progress between the two young people, under the cabin table. Natalie's smartly-slippered foot felt its way cautiously inch by inch over the carpet till it touched

Launce's boot. Launce, devouring his breakfast, instantly looked up from his plate—and then, at a second touch from Natalie, looked down again in a violent hurry. After pausing to make sure that she was not noticed, Natalie took up her knife. Under a perfectly-acted pretence of toying with it absently, in the character of a young lady absorbed in thought, she began dividing a morsel of ham left on the edge of her plate, into six tiny pieces. Launce's eye looked in sidelong expectation at the divided and subdivided ham. He was evidently waiting to see the collection of morsels put to some telegraphic use, previously determined on between his neighbour and himself.

In the mean while the talk proceeded among the other persons at the breakfast-table. Miss Lavinia addressed herself to Launce.

'Do you know, you careless boy, you gave me a fright this morning? I was sleeping with my cabin-window open, and I was awoke by an awful splash in the water. I called for the stewardess. I declare I thought somebody had fallen overboard!'

Sir Joseph looked up briskly; his sister had accidentally touched on an old association.

'Talking of falling overboard,' he began, 'reminds me of an extraordinary adventure——'

There Launce broke in, making his apologies.

'It shan't occur again, Miss Lavinia,' he said. 'To-morrow morning I'll oil myself all over, and slip into the water as silently as a seal.'

'Of an extraordinary adventure,' persisted Sir Joseph, 'which happened to me many years ago, when I was a young man. Lavinia?'

He stopped, and looked interrogatively at his sister. Miss Graybrooke nodded her head responsively, and settled herself in her chair, as if summoning her attention in anticipation of a coming demand on it. To persons well acquainted with the brother and sister these proceedings were ominous of an impending narrative, protracted to a formidable length. The two always told a story in couples, and always differed with each other about the facts, the sister politely contradicting the brother when it was Sir Joseph's story, and the brother politely contradicting the sister when it was Miss Lavinia's story. Separated one from the other, and thus relieved of their own habitual interchange of contradiction, neither of them had ever been known to attempt the relation of the simplest series of events, without breaking down.

'It was five years before I knew you, Richard,' proceeded Sir Joseph.

'Six years,' said Miss Graybrooke.

'Excuse me, Lavinia.'

'No, Joseph, I have it down in my diary.'

'Let us waive the point.' (Sir Joseph invariably used this formula as a means of at once conciliating his sister, and getting a fresh start for his story.) 'I was cruising off the Mersey in a Liverpool pilot-boat.* I had hired the boat in company with a friend of mine, formerly notorious in London society, under the nickname (derived from the peculiar brown colour of his whiskers) of "Mahogany Dobbs." '

'The colour of his liveries, Joseph, not the colour of his whiskers.'

'My dear Lavinia, you are thinking of "Seagreen Shaw," so called from the extraordinary liveries he adopted for his servants in the year when he was sheriff.'

'I think not, Joseph.'

'I beg your pardon, Lavinia.'

Richard Turlington's knotty fingers drummed impatiently on the table. He looked towards Natalie. She was idly arranging her little morsels of ham in a pattern on her plate. Launcelot Linzie, still more idly, was looking at the pattern. Seeing what he saw now, Richard solved the problem which had puzzled him on deck. It was simply impossible that Natalie's fancy could be really taken by such an empty-headed fool as that!

Sir Joseph went on with his story—

'We were some ten or a dozen miles off the mouth of the Mersey—'

'Nautical miles,* Joseph.'

'It doesn't matter, Lavinia.'

'Excuse me, brother, the late great and good Doctor Johnson* said accuracy ought always to be studied even in the most trifling things.'

'They were common miles, Lavinia.'

'They were nautical miles, Joseph.'

'Let us waive the point. Mahogany Dobbs and I happened to be below in the cabin, occupied—'

Here Sir Joseph paused (with his amiable smile) to consult his memory. Miss Lavinia waited (with *her* amiable smile) for the coming opportunity of setting her brother right. At the same moment Natalie laid down her knife and softly touched Launce under the table. When she thus claimed his attention the six pieces of ham were arranged as follows in her plate:—Two pieces were placed opposite each other, and four pieces were ranged perpendicularly under them. Launce looked, and twice touched Natalie under the table. Interpreted by the Code agreed on between the two, the signal in the plate meant, 'I must see you in private.' And Launce's double touch answered, 'After breakfast.'

Sir Joseph proceeded with his story. Natalie took up her knife again. Another signal coming!

'We were both down in the cabin, occupied in finishing our dinner—'

'Just sitting down to lunch, Joseph.'

'My dear! I ought to know.'

'I only repeat what I heard, brother. The last time you told the story, you and your friend were sitting down to lunch.'

'We won't particularise, Lavinia. Suppose we say occupied over a meal?'

'If it is of no more importance than that, Joseph, it would be surely better to leave it out altogether?'

'Let us waive the point. Well, we were suddenly alarmed by a shout on deck, "Man overboard!" We both rushed up the cabin stairs, naturally under the impression that one of our crew had fallen into the sea: an impression shared, I ought to add, by the man at the helm, who had given the alarm.'

Sir Joseph paused again. He was approaching one of the great dramatic points in his story, and was naturally anxious to present it as impressively as possible. He considered with himself, with his head a little on one side. Miss Lavinia considered with *herself*, with *her* head a little on one side. Natalie laid down her knife again, and again touched Launce under the table. This time there were five pieces of ham ranged longitudinally on the plate, with one piece immediately under them at the centre of the line. Interpreted by the Code, this signal indicated two ominous words, 'Bad news.' Launce looked significantly at the owner of the yacht (meaning of the look, 'Is he at the bottom of it?'). Natalie frowned in reply (meaning of the frown, 'Yes, he is'). Launce looked down again into the plate. Natalie instantly pushed all the pieces of ham together in a little heap (meaning of the heap, 'No more to say').

'Well?' said Richard Turlington, turning sharply on Sir Joseph. 'Get on with your story. What next?'

Thus far he had not troubled himself to show even a decent pretence of interest in his old friend's perpetually-interrupted narrative. It was only when Sir Joseph had reached his last sentence—intimating that the man overboard might turn out in course of time not to be a man of the pilot-boat's crew—it was only then that Turlington sat up in his chair, and showed signs of suddenly feeling a strong interest in the progress of the story.

Sir Joseph went on—

'As soon as we got on deck, we saw the man in the water, astern. Our vessel was hove up in the wind, and the boat was lowered. The master and one of the men took the oars. All told, our crew were seven in number. Two away in the boat, a third at the helm, and, to my amazement, when I looked round, the other four behind me, making our number complete. At the same moment Mahogany Dobbs, who was looking through a telescope, called out, "Who the devil can he be? The man is floating on a hen-coop, and we have got nothing of the sort on board this pilot-boat."'

The one person present who happened to notice Richard Turlington's face when those words were pronounced was Launcelot Linzie. He—and he alone—saw the Levant trader's swarthy complexion fade slowly to a livid ashen grey; his eyes the while fixing themselves on Sir Joseph Graybrooke with a furtive glare in them like the glare in the eyes of a wild beast. Apparently conscious that Launce was looking at him—though he never turned his head Launce's way—he laid his elbow on the table, lifted his arm, and so rested his face on his hand, while the story went on, as to screen it effectually from the young surgeon's view.

'The man was brought on board,' proceeded Sir Joseph, 'sure enough with a hen-coop—on which he had been found floating. The poor wretch was blue with terror and exposure in the water; he fainted when we lifted him on deck. When he came to himself he told us a horrible story. He was a sick and destitute foreign seaman, and he had hidden himself in the hold of an English vessel (bound to a port in his native country) which had sailed from Liverpool that morning. He had been discovered, and brought before the captain. The captain, a monster in human form, if ever there was one yet—'

Before the next word of the sentence could pass Sir Joseph's lips, Turlington startled the little party in the cabin by springing suddenly to his feet.

'The breeze!' he cried; 'the breeze at last!'

As he spoke, he wheeled round to the cabin door so as to turn his back on his guests, and hailed the deck.

'Which way is the wind?'

'There is not a breath of wind, sir.'

Not the slightest movement in the vessel had been perceptible in the cabin; not a sound had been audible indicating the rising of the breeze. The owner of the yacht—accustomed to the sea; capable, if necessary, of sailing his own vessel—had surely committed a strange mistake! He turned again to his friends, and made his apologies with an excess of polite regret, far from characteristic of him at other times, and under other circumstances.

'Go on,' he said to Sir Joseph, when he had got to the end of his excuses; 'I never heard such an interesting story in my life. Pray go on!'

The request was not an easy one to comply with. Sir Joseph's ideas had been thrown into confusion. Miss Lavinia's contradictions (held in reserve) had been scattered beyond recall. Both brother and sister were, moreover, additionally hindered in recovering the control of their own resources by the look and manner of their host. He alarmed, instead of encouraging the two harmless old people, by fronting them almost fiercely, with his elbows squared on the table, and his face expressive of a dogged resolution to sit there and listen, if need be, for the rest of his life. Launce was the person who set Sir Joseph going again. After first looking attentively at Richard, he took his uncle straight back to the story by means of a question thus:—

'You don't mean to say that the captain of the ship threw the man overboard?'

'That is just what he did, Launce. The poor wretch was too ill to work his passage. The captain declared he would have no idle foreign vagabond in his ship to eat up the provisions of Englishmen who worked. With his own hands he cast the hen-coop into the water, and (assisted by one of his sailors) he threw the man after it, and told him to float back to Liverpool with the evening tide.'

'A lie!' cried Turlington, addressing himself, not to Sir Joseph, but to Launce.

'Are you acquainted with the circumstances?' asked Launce, quietly.

'I know nothing about the circumstances. I say, from my own experience, that foreign sailors are even greater blackguards than English sailors. The man had met with an accident, no doubt. The rest of his story was a lie—and the object of it was to open Sir Joseph's purse.'

Sir Joseph mildly shook his head.

'No lie, Richard. Witnesses proved that the man had spoken the truth.'

'Witnesses? Pooh! More liars, you mean.'

'I went to the owners of the vessel,' pursued Sir Joseph. 'I got from them the names of the officers and the crew; and I waited, leaving the case in the hands of the Liverpool police. The ship was wrecked at the mouth of the Amazon. But the crew and the cargo were saved. The men belonging to Liverpool came back. They were a bad set, I grant you. But they were examined separately about the treatment of the foreign sailor, and they all told the same story. They could give no account of their captain, nor of the sailor who had been his accomplice in the crime, except that they had not embarked in the ship which brought the rest of the crew to England. Whatever may have become of the captain since, he certainly never returned to Liverpool.'

'Did you find out his name?'

The question was asked by Turlington. Even Sir Joseph, the least observant of men, noticed that it was put with a perfectly unaccountable irritability of manner.

'Don't be angry, Richard,' said the old gentleman. 'What is there to be angry about?'

'I don't know what you mean. I'm not angry—I'm only curious. *Did* you find out who he was?'

'I did. His name was Goward. He was well-known at Liverpool as a very clever and a very dangerous man. Quite young at the time I am speaking of, and a first-rate sailor: famous for taking command of unseaworthy ships and vagabond crews. Report described him to me as having made considerable sums of money in that way, for a man in his position; serving firms, you know, with a bad name, and running all sorts of desperate risks. A sad ruffian, Richard! More than once in trouble, on both sides of the Atlantic, for acts of violence and cruelty. Dead, I daresay, long since.'

'Or possibly,' said Launce, 'alive, under another name, and thriving in a new way of life, with more desperate risks in it, of some other sort.'

'Are *you* acquainted with the circumstances?' asked Turlington, retorting Launce's question on him, with a harsh ring of defiance in his brassy voice.

'What became of the poor foreign sailor, papa?' said Natalie; purposely interrupting Launce before he could meet the question angrily asked of him, by an angry reply.

'We made a subscription, and spoke to his consul, my dear. He went back to his country, poor fellow, comfortably enough.'

'And there is an end of Sir Joseph's story,' said Turlington, rising noisily from his chair. 'It's a pity we haven't got a literary man on board—he would make a novel of it.' He looked up at the skylight as he got on his feet. 'Here is the breeze, this time,' he exclaimed, 'and no mistake!'

It was true. At last the breeze had come. The sails flapped, the main boom swung over with a thump, and the stagnant water, stirred at last, bubbled merrily past the vessel's sides.

'Come on deck, Natalie, and get some fresh air,' said Miss Lavinia, leading the way to the cabin-door.

Natalie held up the skirt of her nankeen dress, and exhibited the purple trimming torn away over an extent of some yards.

'Give me half an hour first, aunt, in my cabin,' she said, 'to mend this.'

Miss Lavinia elevated her venerable eyebrows in amazement.

'You have done nothing but tear your dresses, my dear, since you have been in Mr Turlington's yacht. Most extraordinary! I have torn none of mine during the whole cruise.'

Natalie's dark colour deepened a shade. She laughed a little uneasily. 'I am so awkward on board ship,' she replied, and turned away, and shut herself up in her cabin.

Richard Turlington produced his case of cigars.

'Now is the time,' he said to Sir Joseph, 'for the best cigar of the day—the cigar after breakfast. Come on deck.'

'You will join us, Launce?' said Sir Joseph.

'Give me half an hour first, over my books,' Launce replied. 'I mustn't let my medical knowledge get musty at sea, and I might not feel inclined to study later in the day.'

'Quite right, my dear boy, quite right.'

Sir Joseph patted his nephew approvingly on the shoulder. Launce turned away on *his* side, and shut himself up in his cabin.

The other three ascended together to the deck.

## SECOND SCENE
### THE STORE-ROOM

Persons possessed of sluggish livers and tender hearts find two serious drawbacks to the enjoyment of a cruise at sea. It is exceedingly difficult to get enough walking exercise; and it is next to impossible (where secrecy is an object) to make love without being found out. Reverting for the moment to the latter difficulty only, life within the narrow and populous limits of a vessel may be defined as essentially life in public. From morning to night you are in your neighbour's way, or your neighbour is in your way. As a necessary result of these conditions, the rarest of existing men may be defined as the man who is capable of stealing a kiss at sea without discovery. An inbred capacity for stratagem of the finest sort; inexhaustible inventive resources; patience which can flourish under superhuman trials; presence of mind which can keep its balance victoriously under every possible stress of emergency—these are some of the qualifications which must accompany Love on a cruise, when Love embarks in the character of a contraband commodity not duly entered on the papers of the ship.

Having established a Code of Signals which enabled them to communicate privately, while the eyes and ears of others were wide open on every side of them, Natalie and Launce were next confronted by the more serious difficulty of finding a means of meeting together at stolen interviews on board the yacht. Possessing none of those precious moral qualifications already enumerated as the qualifications of an accomplished lover at sea, Launce had proved unequal to grapple with the obstacles in his way. Left to her own inventive resources, Natalie had first suggested the young surgeon's medical studies as Launce's unanswerable excuse for shutting himself up at intervals in the lower regions—and had then hit on the happy idea of tearing her trimmings, and condemning herself to repair her own carelessness, as the all-sufficient reason for similar acts of self-seclusion on her side. In this way the lovers contrived, while the innocent ruling authorities were on deck, to meet privately below them, on the neutral ground of the main cabin—and there, by previous arrangement at the breakfast-table, they were about to meet privately now.

Natalie's door was, as usual on these occasions, the first that opened; for this sound reason, that Natalie's quickness was the quickness to be depended on in case of accident.

She looked up at the skylight. There were the legs of the two gentlemen and the skirts of her aunt visible (and stationary) on the lee side of the deck. She advanced a few steps and listened. There was a pause in the murmur of the voices above. She looked up again. One pair of legs (not her father's) had disappeared. Without an instant's hesitation, Natalie darted back to her own door, just in time to escape Richard Turlington descending the cabin stairs. All he did was to go to one of the drawers under the main-cabin book-case, and to take out a map, ascending again immediately to the deck. Natalie's guilty conscience rushed instantly, nevertheless, to the conclusion that Richard suspected her. When she showed herself for the second time, instead of venturing into the cabin, she called across it in a whisper,

'Launce!'

Launce appeared at his door. He was peremptorily checked before he could cross the threshold.

'Don't stir a step! Richard has been down in the cabin! Richard suspects us!'

'Nonsense! Come out.'

'Nothing will induce me, unless you can find some other place than the cabin.'

Some other place? How easy to find it on land! How apparently impossible at sea! There was the forecastle (full of men) at one end of the vessel. There was the sail-room (full of sails) at the other. There was the ladies' cabin (used as the ladies' dressing-room; inaccessible, in that capacity, to every male human being on board). Was there any disposable enclosed space to be found amidships? On one side there were the sleeping-berths of the sailing master and his mate (impossible to borrow *them*). On the other side was the steward's store-room. Launce considered for a moment. The steward's store-room was just the thing!

'Where are you going?' asked Natalie, as her lover made straight for a closed door at the lower extremity of the main-cabin.

'To speak to the steward, darling. Wait one moment, and you will see me again.'

Launce opened the store-room door, and discovered, not the steward, but his wife, who occupied the situation of stewardess on board the vessel. The accident was, in this case, a lucky one. Having stolen several kisses at sea, and having been discovered (in every case) either by the steward or his wife, Launce felt no difficulty in prefacing his request to be allowed the use of the room by the plainest allusion to his relations with Natalie. He could count on the silence of the sympathising authorities in this region of the vessel, having wisely secured them as accomplices by the usual persuasion of the pecuniary sort. Of the two, however, the stewardess, as a woman, was the more likely to lend a ready ear to Launce's entreaties in his present emergency. After a faint show of resistance, she consented, not only to leave the room, but to keep her husband out of it, on the understanding that it was not to be occupied for more than ten minutes. Launce made the signal to Natalie at one door, while the stewardess went out by the other. In a moment more the lovers were united in a private room. Is it necessary to say in what language the proceedings were opened? Surely not! There is an inarticulate language of the lips in use on these occasions in which we are all proficient, though we sometimes forget it in later life. Natalie seated herself on a locker. The tea, sugar, and spices were at her back, a side of bacon swung over her head, and a net full of lemons dangled before her face. It might not be roomy, but it was snug and comfortable.

'Suppose they call for the steward?' she suggested. ('Don't, Launce!')

'Never mind. We shall be safe enough if they do. The steward has only to show himself on deck, and they will suspect nothing.'

'Do be quiet, Launce! I have got dreadful news to tell you. And, besides, my aunt will expect to see me with my braid sewn on again.'

She had brought her needle and thread with her. Whipping up the skirt of her dress on her knee, she bent forward over it, and set herself industriously to the repair of the torn trimming. In this position her lithe figure showed charmingly its firm yet easy line. The needle, in her dexterous brown fingers, flew through its work. The locker was a broad one; Launce was able to seat himself partially behind her. In this position who could have resisted the temptation to lift up her great knot of broadly-plaited black hair, and to let the warm, dusky nape of her neck disclose itself to view? Who, looking at it, could fail to revile the senseless modern fashion of dressing the hair, which hides the double beauty of form and colour that nestles at the back of a woman's neck? From time to time, as the interview proceeded, Launce's lips emphasised the more important words occurring in his share of the conversation on the soft fragrant skin which the lifted hair let him see at intervals. In Launce's place, sir, you would have done it too.

'Now, Natalie, what is the news?'

'He has spoken to papa, Launce.'

'Richard Turlington?'

'Yes.'

'Damn him!'

Natalie started. A curse addressed to the back of your neck, instantly followed by a blessing in the shape of a kiss, *is* a little trying when you are not prepared for it.

'Don't do that again, Launce! It was while you were on deck, smoking, and when I was supposed to be fast asleep. I opened the ventilator in my cabin door, dear, and I heard every word they said. He waited till my aunt was out of the way, and he had got papa all to himself, and then he began it in that horrible, downright voice of his—"Graybrooke! how much longer am I to wait?"'

'Did he say that?'

'No more swearing, Launce! Those were the words. Papa didn't understand them. He only said (poor dear!)—"Bless my soul, Richard, what do you want?" Richard soon explained himself. "Who could he be waiting for—but Me?" Papa said something about my being so young. Richard stopped his mouth directly. "Girls were like fruit; some ripened soon, and some ripened late. Some were women at twenty, and some were women at sixteen. It was impossible to look at me, and not see that I was like a new being after my two months at sea," and so on and so on. Papa behaved like an angel. He still tried to put it off. "Plenty of time, Richard, plenty of time." "Plenty of time for *her*" (was the wretch's answer to that); "but not for *me*. Think of all I have to offer her" (as if I cared for his money!); "think how long I have looked upon her as growing up to be my wife" (growing up for *him*—monstrous!), "and don't keep me in a state of uncertainty, which it gets harder and harder for a man in my position to endure!" He was really quite eloquent. His voice trembled. There is no doubt, dear, that he is very, very fond of me.'

'And you feel flattered by it, of course?'

'Don't talk nonsense. I feel a little frightened at it, I can tell you.'

'Frightened? Did *you* notice him this morning?'

'I? When?'

'When your father was telling that story about the man overboard.'

'No. What did he do? Tell me, Launce.'

'I'll tell you directly. How did it all end last night? Did your father make any sort of promise?'

'You know Richard's way; Richard left him no other choice. Papa had to promise before he was allowed to go to bed.'

'To let Turlington marry you?'

'Yes; the week after my next birthday.'

'The week after next Christmas Day?'

'Yes. Papa is to speak to me as soon as we are at home again, and my married life is to begin with the New Year.'

'Are you in earnest, Natalie? Do you really mean to say it has gone as far as that?'

'They have settled everything. The splendid establishment we are to set up, the great income we are to have. I heard papa tell Richard that half his fortune should go to me on my wedding-day. It was sickening to hear how much they made of Money, and how little they thought of Love. What am I to do, Launce?'

'That's easily answered, my darling. In the first place, you are to make up your mind not to marry Richard Turlington—'

'Do talk reasonably. You know I have done all I could. I have told papa that I can think of Richard as a friend, but not as a husband. He only laughs at me, and says, "Wait a little, and you will alter your opinion, my dear." You see Richard is everything to him; Richard has always managed his affairs, and has saved him from losing by bad speculations; Richard has known me from the time when I was a child; Richard has a splendid business, and quantities of money. Papa can't even imagine that I can resist Richard. I have tried my aunt; I have told her he is too old for me. All she says is, "Look at your father; he was much older than your mother, and what a happy marriage theirs was." Even if I said in so many words, "I won't marry Richard," what good would it do to *us*? Papa is the best and dearest old man in the world; but oh, he is so fond of money! He believes in nothing else. He would be furious—yes, kind as he is, he would be furious—if I even hinted that I was fond of *you*. Any man who proposed to marry me—if he couldn't match the fortune that I should bring him by a fortune of his own—would be a lunatic in papa's eyes. He wouldn't think it necessary to answer him; he would ring the bell, and have him shown out of the house. I am exaggerating nothing, Launce; you know I am speaking the truth. There is no hope in the future—that I can see—for either of us.'

'Have you done, Natalie? I have something to say on my side if you have.'

'What is it?'

'If things go on as they are going on now, shall I tell you how it will end? It will end in your being Turlington's wife.'

'Never!'

'So you say now; but you don't know what may happen between this and Christmas Day. Natalie, there is only one way of making sure that you will never marry Richard. Marry *me*.'

'Without papa's consent?'

'Without saying a word to anybody till it's done.'

'Oh, Launce! Launce!'

'My darling, every word you have said proves there is no other way. Think of it, Natalie, think of it.'

There was a pause. Natalie dropped her needle and thread, and hid her face in her hands. 'If my poor mother was only alive,' she said; 'if I only had an elder sister to advise me, and to take my part.'

She was evidently hesitating. Launce took a man's advantage of her indecision. He pressed her without mercy.

'Do you love me?' he whispered, with his lips close to her ear.

'You know I do, dearly.'

'Put it out of Richard's power to part us, Natalie.'

'Part us? We are cousins: we have known each other since we were both children. Even if he proposed parting us, papa wouldn't allow it.'

'Mark my words, he *will* propose it. As for your father, Richard has only to lift his finger and your father obeys him. My love, the happiness of both our lives is at stake.' He wound his arm round her, and gently drew her head back on his bosom. 'Other girls have done it, darling,' he pleaded, 'why shouldn't you?'

The effort to answer him was too much for her. She gave it up. A low sigh fluttered through her lips. She nestled closer to him, and faintly closed her eyes. The next instant she started up, trembling from head to foot, and looked at the skylight. Richard Turlington's voice was suddenly audible on deck exactly above them.

'Graybrooke, I want to say a word to you about Launcelot Linzie.'

Natalie's first impulse was to fly to the door. Hearing Launce's name on Richard's lips, she checked herself. Something in Richard's tone roused in her the curiosity which suspends fear. She waited, with her hand in Launce's hand.

'If you remember,' the brassy voice went on, 'I doubted the wisdom of taking him with us on this cruise. You didn't agree with me, and, at your express request, I gave way. I did wrong. Launcelot Linzie is a very presuming young man.'

Sir Joseph's answer was accompanied by Sir Joseph's mellow laugh.

'My dear Richard! Surely you are a little hard on Launce?'

'You are not an observant man, Graybrooke. I am. I see signs of his presuming with all of us, and especially with Natalie. I don't like the manner in which he speaks to her, and looks at her. He is unduly familiar; he is insolently confidential. There must be a stop put to it. In my position, my feelings ought to be regarded. I request you to check the intimacy when we get on shore.'

Sir Joseph's next words were spoken more seriously. He expressed his surprise.

'My dear Richard, they are cousins, they have been playmates from childhood. How *can* you think of attaching the slightest importance to anything that is said or done by poor Launce?'

There was a good-humoured contempt in Sir Joseph's reference to 'poor Launce' which jarred on his daughter. He might almost have been alluding to some harmless domestic animal. Natalie's colour deepened. Her hand pressed Launce's hand gently.

Turlington still persisted.

'I must once more request—seriously request—that you will check this growing intimacy. I don't object to your asking him to the house when you ask other friends. I only wish you (and expect you) to stop his "dropping in," as it is called, at any hour of the day or evening when he may have nothing to do. Is that understood between us?'

'If you make a point of it, Richard, of course it's understood between us.'

Launce looked at Natalie, as weak Sir Joseph consented in those words.

'What did I tell you?' he whispered.

Natalie hung her head in silence. There was a pause in the conversation on deck. The two gentlemen walked away slowly towards the forward part of the vessel.

Launce pursued his advantage.

'Your father leaves us no alternative,' he said. 'The door will be closed against me as soon as we get on shore. If I lose you, Natalie, I don't care what becomes of me. My profession may go to the devil. I have nothing left worth living for.'

'Hush! hush! don't talk in that way!'

Launce tried the soothing influence of persuasion once more.

'Hundreds and hundreds of people in our situation have married privately—and have been forgiven afterwards,' he went on. 'I won't ask you to do anything in a hurry. I will be guided entirely by your wishes. All I want to quiet my mind is to know that you are mine. Do, do, do make me feel sure that Richard Turlington can't take you away from me.'

'Don't press me, Launce.' She dropped on the locker. 'See!' she said. 'It makes me tremble only to think of it!'

'Who are you afraid of, darling? Not your father, surely?'

'Poor papa! I wonder whether he would be hard on me for the first time in his life?' She stopped; her moistening eyes looked up imploringly in Launce's face. 'Don't press me!' she repeated faintly. 'You know it's wrong. We should have to confess it—and then what would happen?' She paused again. Her eyes wandered nervously to the deck. Her voice dropped to its lowest tones. 'Think of Richard!' she said, and shuddered at the terrors which that name conjured up. Before it was possible to say a quieting word to her, she was again on her feet. Richard's name had suddenly recalled to her memory Launce's mysterious allusion, at the outset of the interview, to the owner of the yacht. 'What was that you said about Richard just now?' she asked. 'You saw something (or heard something) strange while papa was telling his story. What was it?'

'I noticed Richard's face, Natalie, when your father told us that the man overboard was not one of the pilot-boat's crew. He turned ghastly pale. He looked guilty—'

'Guilty? Of what?'

'He was present—I am certain of it—when the sailor was thrown into the sea. For all I know, he may have been the man who did it.'

Natalie started back in horror.

'Oh, Launce! Launce! that is too bad. You may not like Richard—you may treat Richard as your enemy. But to say such a horrible thing of him as that—! It's not generous. It's not like *you*.'

'If you had seen him you would have said it too. I mean to make inquiries—in your father's interests as well as in ours. My brother knows one of the Commissioners of Police; and my brother can get it done for me. Turlington has not always been in the Levant trade—I know that already.'

'For shame, Launce! for shame!'

The footsteps on deck were audible, coming back. Natalie sprang to the door leading into the cabin. Launce stopped her, as she laid her hand on the lock. The footsteps went straight on towards the stern of the vessel. Launce clasped both arms round her. Natalie gave way.

'Don't drive me to despair!' he said. 'This is my last opportunity. I don't ask you to say at once that you will marry me—I only ask you to think of it. My darling! my angel! will you think of it?'

As he put the question, they might have heard (if they had not been too completely engrossed in each other to listen) the footsteps returning—one pair of footsteps only, this time. Natalie's prolonged absence had begun to surprise her aunt, and had roused a certain vague distrust in Richard's mind. He walked back again along the deck by himself. He looked absently into the main-cabin as he passed it. The store-room skylight came next. In his present frame of mind would he look absently into the store-room too?

'Let me go!' said Natalie.

Launce only answered, 'Say yes,' and held her as if he would never let her go again.

At the same moment Miss Lavinia's voice rose shrill from the deck, calling for Natalie. There was but one way of getting free from him. She said, 'I'll think of it.' Upon that, he kissed her and let her go.

The door had barely closed on her when the lowering face of Richard Turlington appeared on a level with the side of the sky-light—looking down into the store-room at Launce.

'Hullo!' he called out roughly. 'What are you doing in the steward's room?'

Launce took up a box of matches on the dresser. 'I'm getting a light,' he answered readily.

'I allow nobody below, forward of the main-cabin, without my leave. The steward has permitted a breach of discipline on board my vessel. The steward will leave my service.'

'The steward is not to blame.'

'I am the judge of that. Not you.'

Launce opened his lips to reply. An outbreak between the two men appeared to be inevitable—when the sailing-master of the yacht joined his employer on deck, and directed Turlington's attention to a question which is never to be trifled with at sea, the question of wind and tide.

The yacht was then in the Bristol Channel, at the entrance to Bideford Bay. The breeze, fast freshening, was also fast changing the direction from which it blew. The favourable tide had barely three hours more to run.

'The wind's shifting, sir,' said the sailing-master. 'I'm afraid we shan't get round the point this tide, unless we lay her off on the other tack.'

Turlington shook his head.

'There are letters waiting for me at Bideford,' he said. 'We have lost two days in the calm. I must send ashore to the Post-office, whether we lose the tide or not.'

The vessel held on her course. Off the port of Bideford, the boat was sent ashore to the Post-office; the yacht standing off and on, waiting the appearance of the letters. In the shortest time in which it was possible to bring them on board, the letters were in Turlington's hands.

The men were hauling the boat up to the davits,* the yacht was already heading off from the land, when Turlington startled everybody by one peremptory word—'Stop!'

He had thrust all his letters but one into the pocket of his sailing jacket, without reading them. The one letter which he had opened, he held in his closed hand. Rage was in his staring eyes; consternation was on his pale lips.

'Lower the boat!' he shouted; 'I must get to London to-night.' He stopped Sir Joseph, approaching him with open mouth. 'There's no time for questions and answers. I must get back.' He swung himself over the side of the yacht, and addressed the sailing-master from the boat. 'Save the tide if you can; if you can't, put them ashore to-morrow, at Minehead, or Watchet—wherever they like.' He beckoned to Sir Joseph to lean over the bulwark, and hear something he had to say in private. 'Remember what I told you about Launcelot Linzie!' he whispered fiercely. His parting look was for Natalie. He spoke to her with a strong constraint on himself, as gently as he could. 'Don't be alarmed; I shall see you in London.' He seated himself in the boat, and took the tiller. The last words they heard him say were words urging the men at the oars to lose no time. He was invariably brutal with the men. 'Pull, you lazy beggars!' he exclaimed, with an oath. 'Pull for your lives!'

## THIRD SCENE

### THE MONEY MARKET

Let us be serious.—Business!

The new scene plunges us head-foremost into the affairs of the Levant trading-house of Pizzituti, Turlington, and Branca. What on earth do we know about the Levant Trade? Courage! If we have ever known what it is to want money, we are perfectly familiar with the subject at starting. The Levant Trade does occasionally get into difficulties.—Turlington wanted money.

The letter which had been handed to him on board the yacht was from his third partner, Mr Branca, and was thus expressed:—

'A crisis in the trade. All right, so far—except our business with the small foreign firms. Bills to meet from those quarters (say), forty thousand pounds—and, I fear, no remittances to cover them. Particulars stated in another letter addressed to you at Post-office, Ilfracombe. I am quite broken down with anxiety, and confined to my bed. Pizzituti is still detained at Smyrna.* Come back at once.'

The same evening Turlington was at his office in Austin Friars, investigating the state of affairs, with his head clerk to help him.

Stated briefly, the business of the firm was of the widely miscellaneous sort. They plied a brisk trade, in a vast variety of commodities. Nothing came amiss to them, from Manchester cotton manufactures to Smyrna figs. They had branch houses at Alexandria and Odessa; and correspondents, here, there, and everywhere, along the shores of the Mediterranean, and in the ports of the East. These correspondents were the persons alluded to in Mr Branca's letter, as 'small foreign firms'; and they had produced the serious financial crisis in the affairs of the great house in Austin Friars, which had hurried Turlington up to London.

Every one of these minor firms claimed, and received, the privilege of drawing bills on Pizzituti, Turlington, and Branca, for amounts varying from four to six thousand pounds—on no better security than a verbal understanding that the money to pay the bills should be forwarded before they fell due. Competition, it is needless to say, was at the bottom of this insanely reckless system of trading. The native firms laid it down as a rule, that they would decline to transact business with any house in the trade which refused to grant them their privilege. In the case of Turlington's house, the foreign merchants had drawn their bills on him for sums, large in the aggregate, if not large in themselves; had, long since, turned those bills into cash in their own markets, for their own necessities; and had now left the money which their paper represented, to be paid by their London correspondents as it fell due. In some instances, they had sent nothing but promises and excuses. In others, they had forwarded drafts on firms which had failed already, or which were about to fail, in the crisis. After first exhausting his resources in ready money, Mr Branca had provided for the more pressing necessities, by pledging the credit of the house, so far as he *could* pledge it without exciting suspicion of the truth. This done, there were actually left, between that time and Christmas, liabilities to be met to the extent of forty thousand pounds, without a farthing in hand to pay that formidable debt.

After working through the night, this was the conclusion at which Richard Turlington arrived, when the rising sun looked in at him through the windows of his private room.

The whole force of the blow had fallen on *him*. The share of his partners in the business was of the most trifling nature. The capital was his; the risk was his. Personally and privately, *he* had to find the money, or to confront the one other alternative—ruin.

How was the money to be found?

With his position in the City, he had only to go to the famous money-lending and discounting house of Bulpit Brothers—reported to 'turn over' millions in their business every year—and to supply himself at once with the necessary funds. Forty thousand pounds was a trifling transaction to Bulpit Brothers.

Having got the money, how, in the present state of his trade, was the loan to be paid back?

His thoughts reverted to his marriage with Natalie.

'Curious!' he said to himself, recalling his conversation with Sir Joseph on board the yacht. 'Graybrooke told me he would give his daughter half his fortune on her marriage. Half Graybrooke's fortune happens to be just forty thousand pounds!' He took a turn in the room. No! It was impossible to apply to Sir Joseph. Once shake Sir Joseph's conviction of his commercial solidity, and the marriage would be certainly deferred—if not absolutely broken off. Sir Joseph's fortune could be made available, in the present emergency, in but one way—he might use it to repay his debt. He had only to make the date at which the loan expired coincide with the date of his marriage, and there was his father-in-law's money at his disposal, or at his wife's disposal—which meant the same thing. 'It's well I pressed Graybrooke about the marriage when I did!' he thought. 'I can borrow the money at a short date. In three months from this Natalie will be my wife.'

He drove to his club, to get breakfast, with his mind cleared, for the time being, of all its anxieties but one.

Knowing where he could procure the loan, he was by no means equally sure of being able to find the security on which he could borrow the money. Living up to his income; having no expectations from any living creature; possessing in landed property only some thirty or forty acres in Somersetshire, with a quaint little dwelling, half-farmhouse, half-cottage, attached—he was incapable of providing the needful security from his own personal resources. To appeal to wealthy friends in the City would be to let those friends into the secret of his embarrassments, and to put his credit in peril. He finished his breakfast, and went back to Austin Friars—failing entirely, so far, to see how he was to remove the last obstacle now left in his way.

The doors were open to the public; business had begun. He had not been ten minutes in his room before the shipping-clerk knocked at the door and interrupted him, still absorbed in his own anxious thoughts.

'What is it?' he asked, irritably.

'Duplicate Bills of Lading, sir,' answered the clerk, placing the documents on his master's table.

Found! There was the security on his writing-desk, staring him in the face! He dismissed the clerk and examined the papers.

They contained an account of goods shipped to the London house, on board vessels sailing from Smyrna and Odessa, and they were signed by the masters of the ships, who thereby acknowledged the receipt of the goods, and undertook to deliver them safely to the persons owning them, as directed. First copies of these papers had already been placed in the possession of the London house. The duplicates had now followed, in case of accident. Richard Turlington instantly determined to make the duplicates serve as his security, keeping the first copies privately under lock and key, to be used in obtaining possession of the goods at the customary time. The fraud was a fraud in appearance only. The security was a pure formality. His marriage would supply him with the funds needed for repaying the money, and the profits of his business would provide, in course of time, for restoring the dowry of his wife. It was simply a question of preserving his credit by means which were legitimately at his disposal. Within the lax limits of mercantile morality, Richard Turlington had a conscience. He put on his hat and took his false security to the money-lenders, without feeling at all lowered in his own estimation as an honest man.

Bulpit Brothers, long desirous of having such a name as his on their books, received him with open arms. The security (covering the amount borrowed) was accepted as a matter of course. The money was lent, for three months, with a stroke of the pen. Turlington stepped out again into the street, and confronted the City of London in the character of the noblest work of mercantile creation—a solvent man.[1]

The Fallen Angel,* walking invisibly behind, in Richard's shadow, flapped his crippled wings in triumph. From that moment the Fallen Angel had got him.

---

[1] It may not be amiss to remind the incredulous reader that a famous firm in the City accepted precisely the same security as that here accepted by Bulpit Brothers, with the same sublime indifference to troubling themselves by making any inquiry about it.

# FOURTH SCENE
## MUSWELL HILL

The next day Turlington drove to the suburbs, on the chance of finding the Graybrookes at home again. Sir Joseph disliked London, and could not prevail on himself to live any nearer to the metropolis than Muswell Hill. When Natalie wanted a change, and languished for balls, theatres, flower-shows, and the like, she had a room especially reserved for her in the house of Sir Joseph's married sister, Mrs Sancroft, living in that central deep of the fashionable whirlpool, known among mortals as Berkeley Square.

On his way through the streets, Turlington encountered a plain proof that the Graybrookes must have returned. He was passed by Launce, driving, in company with a gentleman, in a cab. The gentleman was Launce's brother, and the two were on their way to the Commissioner of Police to make the necessary arrangements for instituting an inquiry into Turlington's early life.

Arrived at the gate of the villa, the information received only partially fulfilled the visitor's expectations. The family had returned on the previous evening. Sir Joseph and his sister were at home, but Natalie was away again already. She had driven into town to lunch with her aunt.

Turlington went into the house.

'Have you lost any money?' Those were the first words uttered by Sir Joseph when he and Richard met again, after the parting on board the yacht.

'Not a farthing. I might have lost seriously, if I had not got back in time to set things straight. Stupidity on the part of my people left in charge—nothing more. It's all right now.'

Sir Joseph lifted his eyes, with heartfelt devotion, to the ceiling. 'Thank God, Richard!' he said, in tones of the deepest feeling. He rang the bell. 'Tell Miss Graybrooke Mr Turlington is here.' He turned again to Richard. 'Lavinia is like me—Lavinia has been so anxious about you. We have both of us passed a sleepless night.' Miss Lavinia came in. Sir Joseph hurried to meet her, and took her affectionately by both hands. 'My dear! the best of all good news, Richard has not lost a farthing.' Miss Lavinia lifted *her* eyes to the ceiling with heartfelt devotion, and said, 'Thank God, Richard!'—

like the echo of her brother's voice; a little late, perhaps, for its reputation as an echo, but accurate to half a note in its perfect repetition of sound.

Turlington asked the question which it had been his one object to put in paying his visit to Muswell Hill.

'Have you spoken to Natalie?'

'This morning,' replied Sir Joseph. 'An opportunity offered itself after breakfast. I took advantage of it, Richard—you shall hear how.'

He settled himself in his chair for one of his interminable stories; he began his opening sentence—and stopped, struck dumb at the first word. There was an unexpected obstacle in the way—his sister was not attending to him; his sister had silenced him at starting. The story touching, this time, on the question of marriage, Miss Lavinia had her woman's interest in seeing full justice done to the subject. She seized on her brother's narrative as on property in her own right.

'Joseph should have told you,' she began, addressing herself to Turlington, 'that our dear girl was unusually depressed in spirits this morning. Quite in the right frame of mind for a little serious talk about her future life. She ate nothing at breakfast, poor child, but a morsel of dry toast.'

'And marmalade,' said Sir Joseph, striking in at the first opportunity. The story, on this occasion, being Miss Lavinia's story, the polite contradictions necessary to its successful progress were naturally transferred from the sister to the brother, and became contradictions on Sir Joseph's side.

'No,' said Miss Lavinia, gently, 'if you *will* have it, Joseph—jam.'

'I beg your pardon,' persisted Sir Joseph, 'marmalade.'

'What *does* it matter, brother?'

'Sister! the late great and good Doctor Johnson said accuracy ought always to be studied even in the most trifling things.'

'You *will* have your way, Joseph'—(this was the formula—answering to Sir Joseph's 'Let us waive the point'—which Miss Lavinia used, as a means of conciliating her brother, and getting a fresh start for her story). 'Well, we took dear Natalie out between us, after breakfast, for a little walk in the grounds. My brother opened the subject with infinite delicacy and tact. "Circumstances," he said, "into which it was not then necessary to enter, made it very desirable, young as she was, to begin to think of her establishment in life." And then he referred, Richard (so nicely), to your faithful and devoted attachment—'

'Excuse me, Lavinia, I began with Richard's attachment, and then I got on to her establishment in life.'

'Excuse *me*, Joseph. You managed it much more delicately than you suppose. You didn't drag Richard in by the head and shoulders in that way.'

'Lavinia! I began with Richard.'

'Joseph! Your memory deceives you.'

Turlington's impatience broke through all restraint.

'How did it end?' he asked. 'Did you propose to her that we should be married in the first week of the New Year?'

'Yes!' said Miss Lavinia.

'No!' said Sir Joseph.

The sister looked at the brother, with an expression of affectionate surprise. The brother looked at the sister with a fund of amiable contradiction, expressed in a low bow.

'Do you really mean to deny, Joseph, that you told Natalie we had decided on the first week in the New Year?'

'I deny the New Year, Lavinia. I said early in January.'

'You *will* have your way, Joseph! We were walking in the shrubbery at the time. I had our dear girl's arm in mine, and I felt it tremble. She suddenly stopped. "Oh," she said, "not so soon!" I said, "My dear, consider Richard!" She turned to her father. She said, "Don't, pray don't press it so soon, papa! I respect Richard; I like Richard as your true and faithful friend; but I don't love him as I ought to love him if I am to be his wife." Imagine her talking in that way! What could she possibly know about it? Of course we both laughed —'

'*You* laughed, Lavinia.'

'*You* laughed, Joseph.'

'Get on, for God's sake!' cried Turlington, striking his hand passionately on the table by which he was sitting. 'Don't madden me by contradicting each other! Did she give way or not?'

Miss Lavinia turned to her brother. 'Contradicting each other, Joseph!' she exclaimed, lifting her hands in blank amazement.

'Contradicting each other!' repeated Sir Joseph, equally astonished on his side. 'My dear Richard, what can you be thinking of? I contradict my sister! We never disagreed in our lives.'

'I contradict my brother! We have never had a cross word between us from the time when we were children.'

Turlington internally cursed his own irritable temper.

'I beg your pardon—both of you,' he said. 'I didn't know what I was saying. Make some allowance for me. All my hopes in life are centred in Natalie; and you have just told me (in her own words, Miss Lavinia) that she doesn't love me. You don't mean any harm, I dare say; but you cut me to the heart.'

This confession, and the look that accompanied it, touched the ready sympathies of the two old people in the right place. The remainder of the story dropped between them by common consent. They vied with each other in saying the comforting words which would allay their dear Richard's anxiety. How little he knew of young girls. How could he be so foolish, poor fellow! as to attach any serious importance to what Natalie had said? As if a young creature in her teens knew the state of her own heart! Protestations and entreaties were matters of course, in such cases. Tears even might be confidently expected from a right-minded girl. It had all ended exactly as Richard would have wished it to end. Sir Joseph had said, 'My child! this is a matter of experience; love will come when you are married.' And Miss Lavinia had added, 'Dear Natalie, if you remembered your poor mother as I remember her, you would know that your father's experience is to be relied on.' In that way they had put it to her; and she had hung her head and had given—all that maiden modesty could be expected to give—a silent consent. 'The wedding-day was fixed for the first week in the New Year. (No, Joseph; not January—the New Year.) And God bless you, Richard! and may your married life be a long and happy one.'

So the average ignorance of human nature, and the average belief in conventional sentiment, complacently contemplated the sacrifice of one more victim on the all-devouring altar of Marriage! So Sir Joseph and his sister provided Launcelot Linzie with the one argument which he wanted to convince Natalie: 'Choose between making the misery of your life by marrying *him*, and making the happiness of your life by marrying *me*.'

'When shall I see her?' asked Turlington, with Miss Lavinia (in tears which did *her* credit) in possession of one of his hands, and Sir Joseph (in tears which did *him* credit) in possession of the other.

'She will be back to dinner, dear Richard. Stay and dine.'

'Thank you. I must go into the City first. I will come back and dine.'

With that arrangement in prospect, he left them.

An hour later a telegram arrived from Natalie. She had consented to dine, as well as lunch, in Berkeley Square—sleeping there that night, and returning the next morning. Her father instantly telegraphed back by the messenger, insisting on Natalie's return to Muswell Hill that evening, in time to meet Richard Turlington at dinner.

'Quite right, Joseph,' said Miss Lavinia, looking over her brother's shoulder, while he wrote the telegram.

'She is showing a disposition to coquette with Richard,' rejoined Sir Joseph, with the air of a man who knew female human nature in its remotest corners. 'My telegram, Lavinia, will have its effect.'

Sir Joseph was quite right. His telegram *had* its effect. It not only brought his daughter back to dinner—it produced another result which his prophetic faculty had altogether failed to foresee.

The message reached Berkeley Square at five o'clock in the afternoon. Let us follow the message.

# FIFTH SCENE
## THE SQUARE

Between four and five in the afternoon—when the women of the western regions are in their carriages, and the men are at their clubs—London presents few places more conveniently adapted for purposes of private talk than the solitary garden enclosure of a Square.

On the day when Richard Turlington paid his visit to Muswell Hill, two ladies (with a secret between them) unlocked the gate of the railed garden in Berkeley Square. They shut the gate, after entering the enclosure, but carefully forbore to lock it as well, and carefully restricted their walk to the westward side of the garden. One of them was Natalie Graybrooke. The other was Mrs Sancroft's eldest daughter. A certain temporary interest attached, in the estimation of society, to this young lady. She had sold well in the marriage market. In other words, she had recently been raised to the position of Lord

Winwood's second wife; his lordship conferring on the bride not only the honours of the peerage, but the additional distinction of being step-mother to his three single daughters, all older than herself. In person, Lady Winwood was little and fair. In character, she was dashing and resolute—a complete contrast to Natalie, and (on that very account) Natalie's bosom friend.

'My dear, one ambitious marriage in the family is quite enough! I have made up my mind that *you* shall marry the man you love. Don't tell me your courage is failing you—the excuse is contemptible; I decline to receive it. Natalie! the men have a phrase which exactly describes your character. You want back-bone!'

The bonnet of the lady who expressed herself in these peremptory terms barely reached the height of Natalie's shoulder. Natalie might have blown the little airy, light-haired, unsubstantial creature over the railings of the garden if she had taken a good long breath and stooped low enough. But who ever met with a tall woman who had a will of her own? Natalie's languid brown eyes looked softly down in submissive attention from an elevation of five feet seven. Lady Winwood's brisk blue eyes looked brightly up in despotic command from an elevation of four feet eleven (in her shoes).

'You are trifling with Mr Linzie, my dear. Mr Linzie is a nice fellow. I like him. I won't have that.'

'Louisa!'

'Mr Turlington has nothing to recommend him. He is not a well-bred old gentleman of exalted rank. He is only an odious brute who happens to have made money. You shall *not* marry Mr Turlington. And you *shall* marry Launcelot Linzie.'

'Will you let me speak, Louisa?'

'I will let you answer—nothing more. Didn't you come crying to me this morning? Didn't you say, "Louisa, they have pronounced sentence on me! I am to be married in the first week of the New Year. Help me out of it, for Heaven's sake!" You said all that, and more. And what did I do when I had heard your story?'

'Oh, you were so kind—'

'Kind doesn't half express it. I have committed crimes on your account. I have deceived my husband and my mother. For your sake I got mamma to ask Mr Linzie to lunch (as *my* friend!). For your sake I have banished my unoffending husband, not an hour since, to his club.

You wretched girl, who arranged a private conference in the library? Who sent Mr Linzie off to consult his friend in the Temple on the law of clandestine marriage? Who suggested your telegraphing home, and stopping here for the night? Who made an appointment to meet your young man privately in this detestable place in ten minutes' time? I did! I did! I did! All in your interests. All to prevent you from doing what I have done—marrying to please your family instead of to please yourself. (I don't complain, mind, of Lord Winwood, or of his daughters. *He* is charming; his daughters I shall tame in course of time. You are different. And Mr Turlington, as I observed before, is a brute.) Very well. Now what do you owe me on your side? You owe it to me at least to know your own mind. You don't know it. You coolly inform me that you daren't run the risk after all, and that you can't face the consequences on second thoughts. I'll tell you what! You don't deserve that nice fellow who worships the very ground you tread on. You are a bread-and-butter miss. I don't believe you are fond of him!'

'Not fond of him!' Natalie stopped, and clasped her hands in despair of finding language strong enough for the occasion. At the same moment the sound of a closing gate caught her ear. She looked round. Launce had kept his appointment before his time. Launce was in the garden, rapidly approaching them.

'Now for the Law of Clandestine Marriage!' said Lady Winwood. 'Mr Linzie, we will take it sitting.' She led the way to one of the benches in the garden, and placed Launce between Natalie and herself. 'Well, Chief Conspirator, have you got the License? No? Does it cost too much? Can I lend you the money?'

'It costs perjury, Lady Winwood, in my case,' said Launce. 'Natalie is not of age. I can only get a License by taking my oath that I marry her with her father's consent.' He turned piteously to Natalie. 'I couldn't very well do that,' he said, in the tone of a man who feels bound to make an apology, 'could I?' Natalie shuddered; Lady Winwood shrugged her shoulders.

'In your place a woman wouldn't have hesitated,' her ladyship remarked. 'But men are so selfish. Well? I suppose there is some other way?'

'Yes, there is another way,' said Launce. 'But there is a horrid condition attached to it—'

'Something worse than perjury, Mr Linzie? Murder?'

'I'll tell you directly, Lady Winwood. The marriage comes first. The condition follows. There is only one chance for us. We must be married by Banns.'*

'Banns!' cried Natalie. 'Why, banns are publicly proclaimed in church!'

'They needn't be proclaimed in *your* church, you goose,' said Lady Winwood. 'And, even if they were, nobody would be the wiser. You may trust implicitly, my dear, in the elocution of an English clergyman!'

'That's just what my friend said,' cried Launce. ' "Take a lodging near a large parish church, in a remote part of London,"—(this is my friend's advice)—"go to the clerk, tell him you want to be married by Banns, and say you belong to that parish. As for the lady, in your place I should simplify it. I should say she belonged to the parish too. Give an address, and have some one there to answer questions. How is the clerk to know? He isn't likely to be over-anxious about it—his fee is eighteen-pence. The clerk makes his profit out of you, after you are married. The same rule applies to the parson. He will have your names supplied to him on a strip of paper, with dozens of other names; and he will read them out all together in one inarticulate jumble in church. You will stand at the altar when your time comes, with Brown and Jones, Nokes and Styles, Jack and Gill. All that you will have to do is, to take care that your young lady doesn't fall to Jack, and you to Gill, by mistake—and there you are, married by Banns." My friend's opinion, stated in his own words.'

Natalie sighed, and wrung her hands in her lap. 'We shall never get through it,' she said, despondingly.

Lady Winwood took a more cheerful view.

'I see nothing very formidable, as yet, my dear. But we have still to hear the end of it. You mentioned a condition just now, Mr Linzie.'

'I am coming to the condition, Lady Winwood. You naturally suppose, as I did, that I put Natalie into a cab, and run away with her from the church-door?'

'Certainly. And I throw an old shoe after you for luck, and go home again.'

Launce shook his head ominously.

'Natalie must go home again as well as you!'

Lady Winwood started. 'Is that the condition you mentioned just now?' she asked.

'That is the condition. I may marry her without anything serious coming of it. But, if I run away with her afterwards, and if you are there, aiding and abetting me, we are guilty of Abduction, and we may stand, side by side, at the bar of the Old Bailey* to answer for it!'

Natalie sprang to her feet in horror. Lady Winwood held up one finger warningly, signing to her to let Launce go on.

'Natalie is not yet sixteen years old,' Launce proceeded. 'She must go straight back to her father's house from the church, and I must wait to run away with her till her next birthday. When she's turned sixteen, she's ripe for elopement—not an hour before. There is the law of Abduction! Despotism in a free country—that's what I call it!'

Natalie sat down again with an air of relief.

'It's a very comforting law, *I* think,' she said. 'It doesn't force one to take the dreadful step of running away from home all at once. It gives one time to consider, and plan, and make up one's mind. I can tell you this, Launce, if I *am* to be persuaded into marrying you, the law of Abduction is the only thing that will induce me to do it. You ought to thank the law, instead of abusing it.'

Launce listened—without conviction.

'It's a pleasant prospect,' he said, 'to part at the church-door, and to treat my own wife on the footing of a young lady who is engaged to marry another gentleman.'

'Is it any pleasanter for *me*,' retorted Natalie, 'to have Richard Turlington courting me, when I am all the time your wife? I shall never be able to do it. I wish I was dead!'

'Come! come!' interposed Lady Winwood. 'It's time to be serious. Natalie's birthday, Mr Linzie, is next Christmas Day. She will be sixteen—'

'At seven in the morning,' said Launce; 'I got that out of Sir Joseph. At one minute past seven, Greenwich mean-time, we may be off together. I got *that* out of the lawyer.'

'And it isn't an eternity to wait from now till Christmas Day. You get that, by way of completing the list of your acquisitions, out of *me*. In the mean time, can you, or can you not, manage to meet the difficulties in the way of the marriage?'

'I have settled everything,' Launce answered confidently. 'There is not a single difficulty left.'

He turned to Natalie, listening to him in amazement; and explained himself. It had struck him that he might appeal—with his purse in his hand, of course—to the interest felt in his affairs by the late stewardess of the yacht. That excellent woman had volunteered to do all that she could to help him. Her husband had obtained situations for his wife and himself on board another yacht—and they were both eager to assist in any conspiracy in which their late merciless master was destined to play the part of victim. When on shore, they lived in a populous London parish, far away from the fashionable district of Berkeley Square, and farther yet from the respectable suburb of Muswell Hill. A room in the house could be nominally engaged for Natalie, in the assumed character of the stewardess's niece—the stewardess undertaking to answer any purely formal questions which might be put by the Church authorities, and to be present at the marriage ceremony. As for Launce, he would actually, as well as nominally, live in the district close by; and the steward, if needful, would answer for *him*. Natalie might call at her parochial residence occasionally, under the wing of Lady Winwood; gaining leave of absence from Muswell Hill, on the plea of paying one of her customary visits at her aunt's house. The conspiracy, in brief, was arranged in all its details. Nothing was now wanting but the consent of the young lady; obtaining which, Launce would go to the parish church and give the necessary notice of a marriage by Banns on the next day. There was the plot. What did the ladies think of it?

Lady Winwood thought it perfect.

Natalie was not so easily satisfied.

'My father has always been so kind to me!' she said. 'The one thing I can't get over, Launce, is distressing papa. If he had been hard on me—as some fathers are—I shouldn't mind.' She suddenly brightened, as if she saw her position in a new light. 'Why should you hurry me?' she asked. 'I am going to dine at my aunt's to-day, and you are coming in the evening. Give me time! Wait till to-night.'

Launce instantly entered his protest against wasting a moment longer. Lady Winwood opened her lips to support him. They were both silenced at the same moment by the appearance of one of Mrs Sancroft's servants, opening the gate of the square.

Lady Winwood went forward to meet the man. A suspicion crossed her mind that he might be bringing bad news.

'What do you want?' she asked.

'I beg your pardon, my lady—the house-keeper said you were walking here with Miss Graybrooke. A telegram for Miss Graybrooke.'

Lady Winwood took the telegram from the man's hand; dismissed him, and went back with it to Natalie. Natalie opened it nervously. She read the message—and instantly changed. Her cheeks flushed deep; her eyes flashed with indignation. 'Even papa can be hard on me, it seems, when Richard asks him!' she exclaimed. She handed the telegram to Launce. Her eyes suddenly filled with tears. '*You* love me,' she said gently—and stopped. 'Marry me!' she added, with a sudden burst of resolution. 'I'll risk it!'

As she spoke those words, Lady Winwood read the telegram. It ran thus:—

'Sir Joseph Graybrooke, Muswell Hill. To Miss Natalie Graybrooke, Berkeley Square. Come back immediately. You are engaged to dine here with Richard Turlington.'

Lady Winwood folded up the telegram with a malicious smile. 'Well done, Sir Joseph!' thought her ladyship. 'We might never have persuaded Natalie—but for You!'*

# SIXTH SCENE
## THE CHURCH

The time is morning; the date is early in the month of November. The place is a church, in a poor and populous parish in the undiscovered regions of London, eastward of the Tower, and hard by the riverside.

A marriage procession of five approaches the altar. The bridegroom is pale, and the bride is frightened. The bride's friend (a resolute-looking little lady) encourages her in whispers. The two respectable persons, apparently man and wife, who complete the procession, seem to be not quite clear as to the position which they occupy at the ceremony. The beadle,* as he marshals them before the altar, sees something under the surface in this wedding-party. Marriages in the lower ranks of life are the only marriages celebrated here. Is this a runaway match? The beadle anticipates something out of the common, in the shape of a fee.

The clergyman (the junior curate) appears from the vestry in his robes. The clerk takes his place. The clergyman's eye rests with a sudden interest and curiosity on the bride and bridegroom, and on the bride's friend; notices the absence of elderly relatives; remarks, in the two ladies especially, evidences of refinement and breeding, entirely unparalleled in his professional experience of brides and brides' friends standing before the altar of that church; questions, silently and quickly, the eye of the clerk, occupied also in observing the strangers with interest. 'Jenkinson' (the clergyman's look asks), 'is this all right?' 'Sir' (the clerk's look answers), 'a marriage by banns; all the formalities have been observed.' The clergyman opens his book. The formalities have been observed; his duty lies plainly before him. Attention, Launcelot! Courage, Natalie! The service begins.

Launce casts a last furtive look round the church. Will Sir Joseph Graybrooke start up and stop it from one of the empty pews? Is Richard Turlington lurking in the organ loft, and only waiting till the words of the service appeal to him to prohibit the marriage, or 'else hereafter for ever to hold his peace?'* No. The clergyman proceeds steadily, and nothing happens. Natalie's charming face grows paler and paler, Natalie's heart throbs faster and faster, as the time comes nearer for reading the words which unite them for life. Lady Winwood herself feels an unaccustomed fluttering in the region of the bosom. Her ladyship's thoughts revert, not altogether pleasantly, to her own marriage: 'Ah, me! what was *I* thinking of when I was in this position? Of the bride's beautiful dress, and of Lady Winwood's coming presentation at Court!'

The service advances to the words in which they plight their troth. Launce has put the Ring on her finger. Launce has repeated the words after the clergyman. Launce has married her! Done! Come what may of it, done!

The service ends. Bridegroom, bride, and witnesses go into the vestry to sign the book. The signing, like the service, is serious. No trifling with the truth is possible here. When it comes to Lady Winwood's turn, Lady Winwood must write her name. She does it, but without her usual grace and decision. She drops her handkerchief. The clerk picks it up for her, and notices that a coronet is embroidered in one corner.

The fees are paid. They leave the vestry. Other couples, when it is over, are talkative and happy. These two are more silent and more embarrassed than ever. Stranger still, while other couples go off with relatives and friends, all socially united in honour of the occasion, these two and their friends part at the church door. The respectable man and his wife go their way on foot. The little lady with the coronet on her handkerchief puts the bride into a cab, gets in herself, and directs the driver to close the door, while the bridegroom is standing on the church steps! The bridegroom's face is clouded, as well it may be. He puts his head in at the window of the cab; he possesses himself of the bride's hand; he speaks in a whisper; he is apparently not to be shaken off. The little lady exerts her authority, separates the clasped hands, pushes the bridegroom away, and cries peremptorily to the driver to go on. The cab starts; the deserted husband drifts desolately anyhow down the street. The clerk, who has seen it all, goes back to the vestry, and reports what has happened.

The rector (with his wife on his arm) has just dropped into the vestry on business in passing. He and the curate are talking about the strange marriage. The rector, gravely bent on ascertaining that no blame rests with the Church, interrogates, and is satisfied. The rector's wife is not so easy to deal with. She has looked at the signatures in the book. One of the names is familiar to her. She cross-examines the clerk as soon as her husband has done with him. When she hears of the coronet on the handkerchief she points to the signature of 'Louisa Winwood,' and says to the rector, 'I know who it is! Lord Winwood's second wife. I went to school with his lordship's daughters by his first marriage. We occasionally meet at the Sacred Concerts (on the "Ladies' Committee"); I shall find an opportunity of speaking to them. One moment, Mr Jenkinson, I will write down the names before you put away the book. "Launcelot Linzie," "Natalie Graybrooke." Very pretty names; quite romantic. I do delight in a romance. Good-morning.'

She gives the curate a parting smile, and the clerk a parting nod, and sails out of the vestry. Natalie, silently returning in Lady Winwood's company to Muswell Hill; and Launce, cursing the law of Abduction as he roams the streets—little think that the ground is already mined under their feet. Richard Turlington may hear of it now, or may hear of it later. The discovery of the marriage depends entirely on a chance meeting between the lord's daughters and the rector's wife.

# SEVENTH SCENE
## THE EVENING PARTY

> MR TURLINGTON
> LADY WINWOOD *At Home.*
> *Wednesday, December 15th—Ten o'clock.*

'DEAREST NATALIE,—As the brute insists, the brute must have the invitation which I enclose. Never mind, my child. You and Launce are coming to dinner, and I will see that you have your little private opportunities of retirement afterwards. All I expect of you in return is, *not* to look (when you come back) as if your husband had been kissing you. You will certainly let out the secret of those stolen kisses, if you don't take care. At mamma's dinner yesterday, your colour (when you came out of the conservatory) was a sight to see. Even your shoulders were red! They are charming shoulders, I know, and men take the strangest fancies sometimes. But, my dear, suppose you wear a chemisette* next time, if you haven't authority enough over him to prevent his doing it again!—Your affectionate LOUISA.'

The private history of the days that had passed since the marriage was written in that letter. An additional chapter—of some importance in its bearing on the future—was contributed by the progress of events at Lady Winwood's party.

By previous arrangement with Natalie, the Graybrookes (invited to dinner) arrived early. Leaving her husband and her step-daughters to entertain Sir Joseph and Miss Lavinia, Lady Winwood took Natalie into her own boudoir, which communicated by a curtained opening with the drawing-room.

'My dear! you are looking positively haggard this evening. Has anything happened?'

'I am nearly worn out, Louisa. The life I am leading is so unendurable that, if Launce pressed me, I believe I should consent to run away with him when we leave your house to-night.'

'You will do nothing of the sort, if you please. Wait till you are sixteen. I delight in novelty, but the novelty of appearing at the Old Bailey is beyond my ambition. Is the brute coming to-night?'

'Of course. He insists on following me wherever I go. He lunched at Muswell Hill to-day. More complaints of my incomprehensible coldness to him. Another scolding from papa. A furious letter from Launce. If I let Richard kiss my hand again in his presence, Launce warns me he will knock him down. Oh, the meanness and the guiltiness of the life I am leading now! I am in the falsest of all false positions, Louisa, and you encouraged me to do it. I believe Richard Turlington suspects us. The last two times Launce and I tried to get a minute together at my aunt's, he contrived to put himself in our way. There he was, my dear, with his scowling face, looking as if he longed to kill Launce. Can you do anything for us to-night? Not on my account. But Launce is so impatient. If he can't say two words to me alone this evening, he declares he will come to Muswell Hill, and catch me in the garden tomorrow.'

'Compose yourself, my dear; he shall say his two words to-night.'

'How?'

Lady Winwood pointed through the curtained entrance of the boudoir to the door of the drawing-room. Beyond the door was the staircase landing. And beyond the landing was a second drawing-room, the smallest of the two.

'There are only three or four people coming to dinner,' her ladyship proceeded; 'and a few more in the evening. Being a small party, the small drawing-room will do for us. This drawing-room will not be lit, and there will be only my reading-lamp here in the boudoir. I shall give the signal for leaving the dining-room earlier than usual. Launce will join us before the evening-party begins. The moment he appears, send him in here—boldly before your aunt and all of us.'

'For what?'

'For your fan. Leave it there under the sofa-cushion before we go down to dinner. You will sit next to Launce, and you will give him private instructions not to find the fan. You will get impatient—you will go to find it yourself—and there you are. Take care of your shoulders, Mrs Linzie! I have nothing more to say.'

The guests asked to dinner began to arrive. Lady Winwood was recalled to her duties as mistress of the house.

It was a pleasant little dinner—with one drawback. It began too late. The ladies only reached the small drawing-room at ten minutes to ten. Launce was only able to join them as the clock struck.

'Too late!' whispered Natalie. 'He will be here directly.'

'Nobody comes punctually to an evening party,' said Launce. 'Don't let us lose a moment. Send me for your fan.'

Natalie opened her lips to say the necessary words. Before she could speak, the servant announced—'Mr Turlington.'

He came in, with his stiffly-upright shirt collar and his loosely-fitting glossy black clothes. He made his sullen and clumsy bow to Lady Winwood. And then he did, what he had done dozens of times already—he caught Natalie, with her eyes still bright and her face still animated (after talking to Launce)—a striking contrast to the cold and unimpulsive young lady whom he was accustomed to see while Natalie was talking to *him*.

Lord Winwood's daughters were persons of some celebrity in the world of amateur music. Noticing the look that Turlington cast at Launce, Lady Winwood whispered to Miss Lavinia—who instantly asked the young ladies to sing. Launce, in obedience to a sign from Natalie, volunteered to find the music-books. It is needless to add that he pitched on the wrong volume at starting. As he lifted it from the piano to take it back to the stand, there dropped out from between the leaves a printed letter, looking like a circular. One of the young ladies took it up, and ran her eye over it, with a start.

'The Sacred Concerts!' she exclaimed.

Her two sisters, standing by, looked at each other guiltily: 'What will the Committee say to us? We entirely forgot the meeting last month.'

'Is there a meeting this month?'

They all looked anxiously at the printed letter.

'Yes! The twenty-third of December. Put it down in your book, Amelia.' Amelia, then and there, put it down among the engagements for the latter end of the month. And Natalie's unacknowledged husband placidly looked on.

So did the merciless irony of circumstances make Launce the innocent means of exposing his own secret to discovery. Thanks to his success in laying his hand on the wrong music-book, there would now be a meeting—two good days before the elopement could take place—between the lord's daughters and the rector's wife!

The guests of the evening began to appear by twos and threes. The gentlemen below-stairs left the dinner-table, and joined them. The small drawing-room was pleasantly filled, and no more. Sir Joseph

Graybrooke, taking Turlington's hand, led him eagerly to their host. The talk in the dining-room had turned on finance. Lord Winwood was not quite satisfied with some of his foreign investments; and Sir Joseph's 'dear Richard' was the very man to give him a little sound advice. The three laid their heads together in a corner. Launce (watching them) slily pressed Natalie's hand. A renowned 'virtuoso' had arrived, and was thundering on the piano. The attention of the guests generally was absorbed in the performance. A fairer chance of sending Launce for the fan could not possibly have offered itself. While the financial discussion was still proceeding, the married lovers were ensconced together, alone in the boudoir.

Lady Winwood (privately observant of their absence) kept her eye on the corner, watching Richard Turlington.

He was talking earnestly—with his back towards the company. He neither moved nor looked round. It came to Lord Winwood's turn to speak. He preserved the same position, listening. Sir Joseph took up the conversation next. Then his attention wandered—he knew beforehand what Sir Joseph would say. His eyes turned anxiously towards the place in which he had left Natalie. Lord Winwood said a word. His head turned back again towards the corner. Sir Joseph put an objection. He glanced once more over his shoulder—this time, at the place in which Launce had been standing. The next moment his host recalled his attention, and made it impossible for him to continue his scrutiny of the room. At the same time, two among the evening-guests, bound for another party, approached to take leave of the lady of the house. Lady Winwood was obliged to rise, and attend to them. They had something to say to her before they left, and they said it at terrible length; standing so as to intercept her view of the proceedings of the enemy. When she had got rid of them at last, she looked—and behold Lord Winwood and Sir Joseph were the only occupants of the corner!

Delaying one moment, to set the 'virtuoso' thundering once more, Lady Winwood slipped out of the room, and crossed the landing. At the entrance to the empty drawing-room she heard Turlington's voice, low and threatening, in the boudoir. Jealousy has a Second Sight of its own. He had looked in the right place at starting—and, oh heavens! he had caught them.

Her ladyship's courage was beyond dispute; but she turned pale, as she approached the entrance to the boudoir.

There stood Natalie—at once angry and afraid—between the man to whom she was ostensibly engaged, and the man to whom she was actually married. Turlington's rugged face expressed a martyrdom of suppressed fury. Launce—in the act of offering Natalie her fan—smiled, with the cool superiority of a man who knew that he had won his advantage, and who triumphed in knowing it.

'I forbid you to take your fan from that man's hands,' said Turlington, speaking to Natalie, and pointing to Launce.

'Isn't it rather too soon to begin "forbidding"?' asked Lady Winwood, good-humouredly.

'Exactly what I say!' exclaimed Launce. 'It seems necessary to remind Mr Turlington that he is not married to Natalie yet!'

Those last words were spoken in a tone which made both the women tremble inwardly for results. Lady Winwood took the fan from Launce with one hand, and took Natalie's arm with the other.

'There is your fan, my dear,' she said in her easy off-hand manner. 'Why do you allow these two barbarous men to keep you here while the great Bootmann is playing the Nightmare Sonata in the next room? Launce! Mr Turlington! follow me, and learn to be musical directly! You have only to shut your eyes, and you will fancy you hear four modern German composers playing, instead of one, and not the ghost of a melody among all the four.' She led the way out with Natalie, and whispered, 'Did he catch you?' Natalie whispered back, 'I heard him in time. He only caught us looking for the fan.' The two men waited behind to have two words together, alone in the boudoir.

'This doesn't end here, Mr Linzie!'

Launce smiled satirically. 'For once, I agree with you,' he answered. 'It doesn't end here, as you say.'

Lady Winwood stopped, and looked back at them from the drawing-room door. They were keeping her waiting—they had no choice but to follow the mistress of the house.

Arrived in the next room, both Turlington and Launce resumed their places among the guests with the same object in view. As a necessary result of the scene in the boudoir, each had his own special remonstrance to address to Sir Joseph. Even here, Launce was beforehand with Turlington. He was the first to get possession of Sir Joseph's private ear. His complaint took the form of a protest against Turlington's jealousy, and an appeal for a reconsideration of the sentence which excluded him from Muswell Hill. Watching them from a distance, Turlington's suspicious eye detected the appearance of something unduly confidential in the colloquy between the two. Under cover of the company, he stole behind them and listened.

The great Bootmann had arrived at that part of the Nightmare Sonata in which musical sound, produced principally with the left hand, is made to describe, beyond all possibility of mistake, the rising of the moon in a country churchyard, and a dance of Vampires round a maiden's grave. Sir Joseph, having no chance against the Vampires in a whisper, was obliged to raise his voice to make himself audible in answering and comforting Launce. 'I sincerely sympathise with you,' Turlington heard him say; 'and Natalie feels about it as I do. But Richard is an obstacle in our way. We must look to the consequences, my dear boy, supposing Richard found us out.' He nodded kindly to his nephew; and, declining to pursue the subject, moved away to another part of the room.

Turlington's jealous distrust, wrought to the highest pitch of irritability for weeks past, instantly associated the words he had just heard with the words spoken by Launce in the boudoir, which had reminded him that he was not married to Natalie yet. Was there treachery at work under the surface? and was the object to persuade weak Sir Joseph to reconsider his daughter's contemplated marriage in a sense favourable to Launce? Turlington's blind suspicion overleapt at a bound all the manifest improbabilities which forbade such a conclusion as this. After an instant's consideration with himself, he decided on keeping his own counsel, and on putting Sir Joseph's good faith then and there to a test which he could rely on as certain to take Natalie's father by surprise.

'Graybrooke!'

Sir Joseph started at the sight of his future son-in-law's face.

'My dear Richard, you are looking very strangely! Is the heat of the room too much for you?'

'Never mind the heat! I have seen enough to-night to justify me in insisting that your daughter and Launcelot Linzie shall meet no more between this and the day of my marriage.' Sir Joseph attempted to speak. Turlington declined to give him the opportunity. 'Yes! yes! your opinion of Linzie isn't mine, I know. I saw you as thick as thieves together just now.' Sir Joseph once more attempted to make himself heard. Wearied by Turlington's perpetual complaints of his daughter and his nephew, he was sufficiently irritated by this time to have reported what Launce had actually said to him if he had been allowed the chance. But Turlington persisted in going on. 'I cannot prevent Linzie from being received in this house, and at your sister's,' he said; 'but I can keep him out of *my* house in the country, and to the country let us go. I propose a change in the arrangements. Have you any engagement for the Christmas holidays?'

He paused, and fixed his eyes attentively on Sir Joseph. Sir Joseph, looking a little surprised, replied briefly that he had no engagement.

'In that case,' resumed Turlington, 'I invite you all to Somersetshire, and I propose that the marriage shall take place from my house, and not from yours. Do you refuse?'

'It is contrary to the usual course of proceeding in such cases, Richard,' Sir Joseph began.

'Do you refuse?' reiterated Turlington. 'I tell you plainly, I shall place a construction of my own upon your motive if you do.'

'No, Richard,' said Sir Joseph quietly, 'I accept.'

Turlington drew back a step in silence. Sir Joseph had turned the tables on him, and had taken *him* by surprise.

'It will upset several plans, and be strongly objected to by the ladies,' proceeded the old gentleman. 'But if nothing less will satisfy you, I say, Yes! I shall have occasion when we meet tomorrow at Muswell Hill to appeal to your indulgence under circumstances which may greatly astonish you. The least I can do in the mean time is to set an example of friendly sympathy and forbearance on my side. No more now, Richard. Hush! the music!'

It was impossible to make him explain himself further that night. Turlington was left to interpret Sir Joseph's mysterious communication with such doubtful aid to success as his own unassisted ingenuity might afford.

The meeting of the next day at Muswell Hill had for its object—as Turlington had already been informed—the drawing of Natalie's marriage settlement. Was the question of money at the bottom of Sir Joseph's contemplated appeal to his indulgence? He thought of his commercial position. The depression in the Levant trade still continued. Never had his business at any previous time required such constant attention, and repaid that attention with so little profit. The Bills of Lading had been already used by the firm, in the ordinary course of trade, to obtain possession of the goods. The duplicates in the hands of Bulpit Brothers were literally waste paper. Repayment of the loan of forty thousand pounds (with interest) was due in less than a month's time. There was his commercial position! Was it possible that money-loving Sir Joseph had any modification to propose in the matter of his daughter's dowry? The bare dread that it might be so, struck him cold. He quitted the house—and forgot to wish Natalie good-night.

Meanwhile, Launce had left the evening party before him—and Launce also found matter for serious reflection presented to his mind before he slept that night. In other words, he found, on reaching his lodgings, a letter from his brother, marked 'private.' Had the inquiry into the secrets of Turlington's early life—now prolonged over some weeks—led to positive results at last? Launce eagerly opened the letter. It contained a Report and a Summary. He passed at once to the Summary, and read these words:

'If you only want moral evidence to satisfy your own mind, your end is gained. There is, morally, no doubt that Turlington and the sea captain who cast the foreign sailor overboard to drown, are one and the same man. Legally, the matter is beset by difficulties, Turlington having destroyed all provable connection between his present self and his past life. There is only one chance for us. A sailor on board the ship (who was in his master's secrets) is supposed to be still living (under his master's protection). All the black deeds of Turlington's early life are known to this man. He can prove the facts, if we can find him, and make it worth his while to speak. Under what *alias* he is hidden we do not know. His own name is Thomas Wildfang. If we are to make the attempt to find him, not a moment is to be lost. The expenses may be serious. Let me know whether we are to go on, or whether enough has been done to attain the end you have in view.'

Enough had been done—not only to satisfy Launce, but to produce the right effect on Sir Joseph's mind if Sir Joseph proved obdurate when the secret of the marriage was revealed. Launce wrote a line directing the stoppage of the proceedings at the point which they had now reached. 'Here is a reason for her not marrying Turlington,' he said to himself, as he placed the papers under lock and key. 'And if she doesn't marry Turlington,' he added, with a lover's logic, 'why shouldn't she marry Me?'

# EIGHTH SCENE
## THE LIBRARY

The next day Sir Joseph Graybrooke, Sir Joseph's lawyer, Mr Dicas (highly respectable and immensely rich), and Richard Turlington were assembled in the library at Muswell Hill, to discuss the question of Natalie's marriage settlement.

After the usual preliminary phrases had been exchanged, Sir Joseph showed some hesitation in openly approaching the question which the little party of three had met to debate. He avoided his lawyer's eye; and he looked at Turlington rather uneasily.

'Richard,' he began at last, 'when I spoke to you about your marriage, on board the yacht, I said I would give my daughter—' Either his courage or his breath failed him at that point. He was obliged to wait a moment before he could go on.

'I said I would give my daughter half my fortune on her marriage,' he resumed. 'Forgive me, Richard. I can't do it!'

Mr Dicas, waiting for his instructions, laid down his pen, and looked at Sir Joseph's son-in-law elect. What would Mr Turlington say?

He said nothing. Sitting opposite the window, he rose when Sir Joseph spoke, and placed himself at the other side of the table, with his back to the light.

'My eyes are weak this morning,' he said, in an unnaturally low tone of voice. 'The light hurts them.'

He could find no more plausible excuse than that for concealing his face in shadow from the scrutiny of the two men on either side of him. The continuous moral irritation of his unhappy courtship—a courtship which had never advanced beyond the frigid familiarity of kissing Natalie's hand in the presence of others—had physically deteriorated him. Even *his* hardy nerves began to feel the long strain of suspicion that had been laid unremittingly on them for weeks past. His power of self-control—he knew it himself—was not to be relied on. He could hide his face: he could no longer command it.

'Did you hear what I said, Richard?'

'I heard. Go on.'

Sir Joseph proceeded, gathering confidence as he advanced.

'Half my fortune!' he repeated. 'It's parting with half my life; it's saying good-bye for ever to my dearest friend! My money has been such a comfort to me, Richard; such a pleasant occupation for my mind. I know no reading so interesting and so instructive as the reading of one's Banker's Book. To watch the outgoings on one side,' said Sir Joseph, with a gentle and pathetic solemnity, 'and the incomings on the other—the sad lessening of the balance at one time, and the cheering and delightful growth of it at another—what absorbing reading! The best novel that ever was written isn't to be mentioned in a breath with it. I cannot, Richard, I really can *not*, see my nice round balance shrink up to half the figure that I have been used to for a life-time. It may be weak of me,' proceeded Sir Joseph, evidently feeling that it was not weak of him at all, 'but we all have our tender place, and my Banker's Book is mine. Besides, it isn't as if you wanted it. If you wanted it, of course—But you don't want it. You are a rich man; you are marrying my dear Natalie for love, not for money. You and she and my grandchildren will have it all at my death. It *can* make no difference to you to wait a few years till the old man's chair at the fireside is empty. Will you say the fourth part, Richard, instead of the half? Twenty thousand,' pleaded Sir Joseph, piteously. 'I can bear twenty thousand off. For God's sake don't ask me for more!'

The lips of the lawyer twisted themselves sourly into an ironical smile. He was quite as fond of his money as Sir Joseph. He ought to have felt for his client; but rich men have no sympathy with one another. Mr Dicas openly despised Sir Joseph.

There was a pause. The robin-redbreasts in the shrubbery outside must have had prodigious balances at their bankers; they hopped up on the window-sill so fearlessly; they looked in with so little respect at the two rich men.

'Don't keep me in suspense, Richard,' proceeded Sir Joseph. 'Speak out. Is it yes or no?'

Turlington struck his hand excitedly on the table, and burst out on a sudden with the answer which had been so strangely delayed.

'Twenty thousand with all my heart!' he said. 'On this condition, Graybrooke, that every farthing of it is settled on Natalie, and on her children after her. Not a halfpenny to me!' he cried magnanimously, in his brassiest tones. 'Not a halfpenny to me!'

Let no man say the rich are heartless. Sir Joseph seized his son-in-law's hand in silence, and burst into tears.

Mr Dicas, habitually a silent man, uttered the first two words that had escaped him since the business began. 'Highly creditable,' he said, and took a note of his instructions on the spot.

From that point the business of the settlement flowed smoothly on to its destined end. Sir Joseph explained his views at the fullest length, and the lawyer's pen kept pace with him. Turlington, remaining in his place at the table,* restricted himself to a purely passive part in the proceedings. He answered briefly when it was absolutely necessary to speak, and he agreed with the two elders in everything. A man has no attention to place at the disposal of other people when he stands at a crisis in his life. Turlington stood at that crisis, at the trying moment when Sir Joseph's unexpected proposal pressed instantly for a reply. Two merciless alternatives confronted him. Either he must repay the borrowed forty thousand pounds on the day when repayment was due, or he must ask Bulpit Brothers to grant him an extension of time, and so inevitably provoke an examination into the fraudulent security deposited with the firm, which could end in but one way. His last, literally his last chance, after Sir Joseph had diminished the promised dowry by one half, was to adopt the high-minded tone which became his position, and to conceal the truth until he could reveal it to his father-in-law in the privileged character of Natalie's husband. 'I owe forty thousand pounds, sir, in a fortnight's time, and I have not got a farthing of my own. Pay for me, or you will see your son-in-law's name in the Bankrupts' List.' For his daughter's sake—who could doubt it?—Sir Joseph would produce the money. The one thing needful was to be married in time. If either by accident or treachery Sir Joseph was led into deferring the appointed day, by so much as a fortnight only, the fatal 'call' would come, and the firm of Pizzituti, Turlington, and Branca would appear in the Gazette.*

So he reasoned, standing on the brink of the terrible discovery which was soon to reveal to him that Natalie was the wife of another man.

'Richard!'

'Mr Turlington!'

He started, and roused his attention to present things. Sir Joseph on one side, and the lawyer on the other, were both appealing to him, and both regarding him with looks of amazement.

'Have you done with the settlement?' he asked.

'My dear Richard, we have done with it long since,' replied Sir Joseph. 'Have you really not heard what I have been saying for the last quarter of an hour to good Mr Dicas here? What *can* you have been thinking of?'

Turlington did not attempt to answer the question. 'Am I interested,' he asked, 'in what you have been saying to Mr Dicas?'

'You shall judge for yourself,' answered Sir Joseph, mysteriously; 'I have been giving Mr Dicas his instructions for making my Will. I wish the Will and the Marriage Settlement to be executed at the same time. Read the instructions, Mr Dicas.'

Sir Joseph's contemplated Will proved to have two merits—it was simple and it was short. Excepting one or two trifling legacies to distant relatives, he had no one to think of (Miss Lavinia being already provided for) but his daughter and the children who might be born of her marriage. In its various provisions, made with these two main objects in view, the Will followed the precedents established in such cases. It differed in no important respect from the tens of thousands of other wills made under similar circumstances. Sir Joseph's motive in claiming special attention for it still remained unexplained, when Mr Dicas reached the clause devoted to the appointment of executors and trustees; and announced that this portion of the document was left in blank.

'Sir Joseph Graybrooke, are you prepared to name the persons whom you appoint?' asked the lawyer.

Sir Joseph rose, apparently for the purpose of giving special importance to the terms in which he answered his lawyer's question.

'I appoint,' he said, 'as sole executor and trustee—Richard Turlington.'

It was no easy matter to astonish Mr Dicas. Sir Joseph's reply absolutely confounded him. He looked across the table at his client and delivered himself on this special occasion of as many as three words.

'Are you mad?' he asked.

Sir Joseph's healthy complexion slightly reddened. 'I never was in more complete possession of myself, Mr Dicas, than at this moment.'

Mr Dicas was not to be silenced in that way.

'Are you aware of what you do,' persisted the lawyer, 'if you appoint Mr Turlington as sole executor and trustee? You put it in the power of your daughter's husband, sir, to make away with every farthing of your money after your death.'

Turlington had hitherto listened with an appearance of interest in the proceedings, which he assumed as an act of politeness. To his view, the future was limited to the date at which Bulpit Brothers had a right to claim the repayment of their loan. The Will was a matter of no earthly importance to him, by comparison with the infinitely superior interest of the Marriage. It was only when the lawyer's brutally plain language forced his attention to it, that the question of his pecuniary interest in his father-in-law's death assumed its fit position in his mind.

*His* colour rose; and *he* too showed that he was offended by what Mr Dicas had just said.

'Not a word, Richard! Let me speak for you as well as for myself,' said Sir Joseph. 'For seven years past,' he continued, turning to the lawyer, 'I have been accustomed to place the most unlimited trust in Richard Turlington. His disinterested advice has enabled me largely to increase my income, without placing a farthing of the principal in jeopardy. On more than one occasion, I have entreated him to make use of my money in his business. He has invariably refused to do so. Even his bitterest enemies, sir, have been obliged to acknowledge that my interests were safe when committed to his care. Am I to begin distrusting him, now that I am about to give him my daughter in marriage? Am I to leave it on record that I doubt him for the first time—when my Will is opened after my death? No! I can confide the management of the fortune which my child will inherit after me, to no more competent or more honourable hands than the hands of the man who is to marry her. I maintain my appointment, Mr Dicas! I persist in placing the whole responsibility under my Will in my son-in-law's care.'

Turlington attempted to speak. The lawyer attempted to speak. Sir Joseph—with a certain simple dignity which had its effect on both of them—declined to hear a word on either side. 'No, Richard! as long as I am alive this is my business, not yours. No, Mr Dicas! I understand that it is your business to protest professionally. You have protested. Fill in the blank space as I have told you. Or leave the instructions on the table, and I will send for the nearest solicitor to complete them in your place.'

Those words placed the lawyer's position plainly before him. He had no choice but to do as he was bid, or to lose a good client. He did as he was bid, and grimly left the room.

Sir Joseph, with old-fashioned politeness, followed him as far as the hall. Returning to the library to say a few friendly words before finally dismissing the subject of the Will, he found himself seized by the arm, and dragged without ceremony, in Turlington's powerful grasp, to the window.

'Richard!' he exclaimed, 'what does this mean?'

'Look!' cried the other, pointing through the window to a grassy walk in the grounds, bounded on either side by shrubberies, and situated at a little distance from the house. 'Who is that man?—quick! before we lose sight of him—the man crossing there from one shrubbery to the other?' Sir Joseph failed to recognise the figure before it disappeared. Turlington whispered fiercely, close to his ear—'Launcelot Linzie!'

In perfect good faith Sir Joseph declared that the man could not possibly have been Launce. Turlington's frenzy of jealous suspicion was not to be so easily calmed. He asked significantly for Natalie. She was reported to be walking in the grounds. 'I knew it!' he said, with an oath—and hurried out into the grounds to discover the truth for himself.

Some little time elapsed before he came back to the house. He had discovered Natalie—alone. Not a sign of Launce had rewarded his search. For the hundredth time he had offended Natalie. For the hundredth time he was compelled to appeal to the indulgence of her father and her aunt. 'It won't happen again,' he said, sullenly penitent. 'You will find me quite another man when I have got you all at my house in the country. Mind!' he burst out, with a furtive look, which expressed his inveterate distrust of Natalie and of every one about her. 'Mind! it's settled that you all come to me in Somersetshire, on Monday next.' Sir Joseph answered rather drily that it *was* settled. Turlington turned to leave the room—and suddenly came back. 'It's understood,' he went on, addressing Miss Lavinia, 'that the seventh of next month is the date fixed for the marriage. Not a day later!' Miss Lavinia replied rather drily, on her side, 'Of course, Richard; not a day later.' He muttered, 'All right'—and hurriedly left them.

Half an hour afterwards Natalie came in, looking a little confused.

'Has he gone?' she asked, whispering to her aunt.

Relieved on this point, she made straight for the library—a room which she rarely entered, at that, or any other period of the day. Miss

Lavinia followed her, curious to know what it meant. Natalie hurried to the window, and waved her handkerchief—evidently making a signal to some one outside. Miss Lavinia instantly joined her, and took her sharply by the hand.

'Is it possible, Natalie?' she asked. 'Has Launcelot Linzie really been here, unknown to your father or to me?'

'Where is the harm if he has?' answered Natalie, with a sudden outbreak of temper. 'Am I never to see my cousin again, because Mr Turlington happens to be jealous of him?'

She suddenly turned away her head. The rich colour flowed over her face and neck. Miss Lavinia, proceeding sternly with the administration of the necessary reproof, was silenced midway by a new change in her niece's variable temper. Natalie burst into tears. Satisfied with this appearance of sincere contrition, the old lady consented to overlook what had happened; and, for this occasion only, to keep her niece's secret. They would all be in Somersetshire, she remarked, before any more breaches of discipline could be committed. Richard had fortunately made no discoveries; and the matter might safely be trusted, all things considered, to rest where it was.

Miss Lavinia might possibly have taken a less hopeful view of the circumstances, if she had known that one of the men-servants at Muswell Hill was in Richard Turlington's pay—and that this servant had seen Launce leave the grounds by the back garden gate.

## NINTH SCENE

### THE DRAWING-ROOM

'Amelia!'

'Say something.'

'Ask him to sit down.'

Thus addressing one another in whispers, the three step-daughters of Lady Winwood stood bewildered in their own drawing-room, helplessly confronting an object which appeared before them on the threshold of the door.

The date was the 23rd of December. The time was between two and three in the afternoon. The occasion was the return of the three sisters from the Committee meeting of the Sacred Concerts' Society. And the object was Richard Turlington.

He stood hat in hand at the door, amazed by his reception. 'I have come up this morning from Somersetshire,' he said. 'Haven't you heard? A matter of business at the office has forced me to leave my guests at my house in the country. I return to them to-morrow. When I say my guests, I mean the Graybrookes. Don't you know they are staying with me? Sir Joseph and Miss Lavinia and Natalie—?' On the utterance of Natalie's name, the sisters roused themselves. They turned about and regarded each other with looks of dismay. Turlington's patience began to fail him. 'Will you be so good as to tell me what all this means?' he said, a little sharply. 'Miss Lavinia asked me to call here when she heard I was coming to town. I was to take charge of a pattern for a dress, which she said you would give me. You ought to have received a telegram explaining it all, hours since. Has the message not reached you?'

The leading spirit of the three sisters was Miss Amelia. She was the first who summoned presence of mind enough to give a plain answer to Turlington's plain question.

'We received the telegram this morning,' she said. 'Something has happened since which has shocked and surprised us. We beg your pardon.' She turned to one of her sisters. 'Sophia, the pattern is ready in the drawer of that table behind you. Give it to Mr Turlington.'

Sophia produced the packet. Before she handed it to the visitor, she looked at her sister. 'Ought we to let Mr Turlington go,' she asked, 'as if nothing had happened?'

Amelia considered silently with herself. Dorothea, the third sister (who had not spoken yet), came forward with a suggestion. She proposed, before proceeding further, to inquire whether Lady Winwood was in the house. The idea was instantly adopted. Sophia rang the bell. Amelia put the questions when the servant appeared.

Lady Winwood had left the house for a drive immediately after luncheon. Lord Winwood—inquired for next—had accompanied her ladyship. No message had been left indicating the hour of their return.

The sisters looked at Turlington, uncertain what to say or do next. Miss Amelia addressed him as soon as the servant had left the room.

'Is it possible for you to remain here until either my father or Lady Winwood return?' she asked.

'It is quite impossible. Minutes are of importance to me to-day.'

'Will you give us one of your minutes? We want to consider something which we may have to say to you before you go.'

Turlington, wondering, took a chair. Miss Amelia put the case before her sisters from the sternly conscientious point of view, at the opposite end of the room.

'We have not found out this abominable deception by any under-hand means,' she said. 'The discovery has been forced upon us, and we stand pledged to nobody to keep the secret. Knowing as we do how cruelly this gentleman has been used, it seems to me that we are bound in honour to open his eyes to the truth. If we remain silent we make ourselves Lady Winwood's accomplices. I, for one—I don't care what may come of it—refuse to do that.'

Her sisters agreed with her. The first chance their clever step-mother had given them of asserting their importance against hers was now in their hands. Their jealous hatred of Lady Winwood assumed the mask of Duty—duty towards an outraged and deceived fellow-creature. Could any earthly motive be purer than that? 'Tell him, Amelia!' cried the two young ladies, with the headlong recklessness of the sex which only stops to think when the time for reflection has gone by.

A vague sense of something wrong began to stir uneasily in Turlington's mind.

'Don't let me hurry you,' he said, 'but if you really have anything to tell me—'

Miss Amelia summoned her courage, and began.

'We have something very dreadful to tell you,' she said, interrupting him. 'You have been presented in this house, Mr Turlington, as a gentleman engaged to marry Lady Winwood's cousin, Miss Natalie Graybrooke.' She paused there—at the outset of the disclosure. A sudden change of expression passed over Turlington's face, which daunted her for the moment. 'We have hitherto understood,' she went on, 'that you were to be married to that young lady early in next month.'

'Well?'

He could say that one word. Looking at their pale faces, and their eager eyes, he could say no more.

'Take care!' whispered Dorothea, in her sister's ear. 'Look at him, Amelia! Not too soon.'

Amelia went on more carefully.

'We have just returned from a musical meeting,' she said. 'One of the ladies there was an acquaintance, a former school-fellow of ours. She is the wife of the rector of St Columb Major—a large church, far from this—at the East-end of London.'

'I know nothing about the woman or the church,' interposed Turlington, sternly.

'I must beg you to wait a little. I can't tell you what I want to tell you unless I refer to the rector's wife. She knows Lady Winwood by name. And she heard of Lady Winwood recently under very strange circumstances—circumstances connected with a signature in one of the books of the church.'

Turlington lost his self-control. 'You have got something against my Natalie,' he burst out; 'I know it by your whispering, I see it in your looks! Say it at once in plain words.'

There was no trifling with him now. In plain words Amelia said it.

\* \* \* \* \* \* \*

There was silence in the room. They could hear the sound of passing footsteps in the street. He stood perfectly still on the spot where they had struck him dumb by the disclosure, supporting himself with his right hand laid on the head of a sofa near him. The sisters drew back horror-struck into the farthest corner of the room. His face turned them cold. Through the mute misery which it had expressed at first, there appeared, slowly forcing its way to view, a look of deadly vengeance which froze them to the soul. They whispered feverishly one to the other, without knowing what they were talking of, without hearing their own voices. One of them said, 'Ring the bell!' Another said, 'Offer him something, he will faint.' The third shuddered, and repeated, over and over again, 'Why did we do it? Why did we do it?'

He silenced them on the instant by speaking on his side. He came on slowly, by a step at a time, with the big drops of agony falling slowly over his rugged face. He said, in a hoarse whisper, 'Write me down the name of the church—there.' He held out his open pocket-book to Amelia, while he spoke. She steadied herself, and wrote the address. She tried to say a word to soften him. The word died on her lips. There was a light in his eyes as they looked at her, which transfigured his face to something superhuman and devilish. She turned away from him, shuddering.

He put the book back in his pocket, and passed his handkerchief over his face. After a moment of indecision, he suddenly and swiftly stole out of the room, as if he was afraid of their calling somebody in, and stopping him. At the door he turned round for a moment, and said, 'You will hear how this ends. I wish you good morning.'

The door closed on him. Left by themselves, they began to realise it. They thought of the consequences when his back was turned and it was too late.

The Graybrookes! Now he knew it, what would become of the Graybrookes? What would he do when he got back? Even at ordinary times—when he was on his best behaviour—he was a rough man. What would happen? Oh, good God! what would happen when he and Natalie next stood face to face? It was a lonely house—Natalie had told them about it—no neighbours near; nobody by to interfere but the weak old father and the maiden aunt. Something ought to be done. Some steps ought to be taken to warn them. Advice—who could give advice? Who was the first person who ought to be told of what had happened? Lady Winwood? No! even at that crisis the sisters still shrank from their stepmother—still hated her with the old hatred! Not a word to *her*! They owed no duty to *her*! Who else could they appeal to? To their father? Yes! There was the person to advise them. In the meanwhile, silence towards their stepmother— silence towards everyone till their father came back!

They waited and waited. One after another the precious hours, pregnant with the issues of life and death, followed each other on the dial. Lady Winwood returned alone. She had left her husband at the House of Lords. Dinner-time came, and brought with it a note from his lordship. There was a Debate at the House. Lady Winwood and his daughters were not to wait dinner for him.

# TENTH SCENE

## GREEN ANCHOR LANE

An hour later than the time at which he had been expected, Richard Turlington appeared at his office in the City.

He met beforehand all the inquiries which the marked change in him must otherwise have provoked, by announcing that he was ill.

Before he proceeded to business, he asked if anybody was waiting to see him. One of the servants from Muswell Hill was waiting with another parcel for Miss Lavinia, ordered by telegram from the country that morning. Turlington (after ascertaining the servant's name) received the man in his private room. He there heard, for the first time, that Launcelot Linzie had been lurking in the grounds (exactly as he had supposed) on the day when the lawyer took his instructions for the Settlement and the Will.

In two hours more Turlington's work was completed. On leaving the office—as soon as he was out of sight of the door—he turned eastward, instead of taking the way that led to his own house in town. Pursuing his course, he entered the labyrinth of streets which led, in that quarter of East London, to the unsavoury neighbourhood of the river side.

By this time his mind was made up. The forecast shadow of meditated crime travelled before him already, as he threaded his way among his fellow-men.

He had been to the vestry of St Columb Major, and had satisfied himself that he was misled by no false report. There was the entry in the Marriage Register. The one unexplained mystery was the mystery of Launce's conduct in permitting his wife to return to her father's house. Utterly unable to account for this proceeding, Turlington could only accept facts as they were, and determine to make the most of his time, while the woman who had deceived him was still under his roof. A hideous expression crossed his face as he realised the idea that he had got her (unprotected by her husband) in his house. 'When Launcelot Linzie *does* come to claim her,' he said to himself, 'he shall find I have been even with him.' He looked at his watch. Was it possible to save the last train and get back that night? No—the last train had gone. Would she take advantage of his absence to escape? He had little fear of it. She would never have allowed her aunt to send him to Lord Winwood's house, if she had felt the slightest suspicion of his discovering the truth in that quarter. Returning by the first train the next morning, he might feel sure of getting back in time. Meanwhile, he had the hours of the night before him. He could give his mind to the serious question that must be settled before he left London—the question of repaying the forty thousand pounds. There was but one way of getting the money now. Sir Joseph had executed his Will; Sir Joseph's death would leave his sole executor and trustee (the lawyer had said it!) master of his fortune. Turlington determined to be master of it in four-and-twenty hours—striking the blow, without risk to himself, by means of another hand. In the face of the probabilities, in the face of the facts, he had now firmly persuaded himself that Sir Joseph was privy to the fraud that had been practised on him. The Marriage Settlement, the Will, the presence of the family at his country house—all these he believed to be so many stratagems invented to keep him deceived until the last moment. The truth was in those words which he had overheard between Sir Joseph and Launce—and in Launce's presence (privately encouraged, no doubt) at Muswell Hill. 'Her father shall pay me for it doubly: with his purse and with his life.' With that thought in his heart, Richard Turlington wound his way through the streets by the river side, and stopped at a blind alley called Green Anchor Lane, infamous to this day as the chosen resort of the most abandoned wretches whom London can produce.

The policeman at the corner cautioned him as he turned into the alley. 'They won't hurt *me!*' he answered, and walked on to a public house at the bottom of the lane.

The landlord at the door silently recognised him, and led the way in. They crossed a room filled with sailors of all nations drinking; ascended a staircase at the back of the house, and stopped at the door of a room on the second floor. There, the landlord spoke for the first time. 'He has outrun his allowance, sir, as usual. You will find him with hardly a rag on his back. I doubt if he will last much longer. He had another fit of the horrors* last night, and the doctor thinks badly of him.' With that introduction he opened the door, and Turlington entered the room.

On the miserable bed lay a grey-headed old man, of gigantic stature, with nothing on him but a ragged shirt and a pair of patched filthy trousers. At the side of the bed, with a bottle of gin on the ricketty table between them, sat two hideous, leering, painted monsters, wearing the dress of women. The smell of opium was in the room, as well as the smell of spirits. At Turlington's appearance, the old man rose on the bed and welcomed him with greedy eyes and outstretched hand.

'Money, master!' he called out hoarsely. 'A crown piece in advance, for the sake of old times!'

Turlington turned to the women without answering, purse in hand.

'His clothes are at the pawnbroker's, of course. How much?'

'Thirty shillings.'

'Bring them here, and be quick about it. You will find it worth your while when you come back.'

The women took the pawnbroker's tickets from the pockets of the man's trousers and hurried out.

Turlington closed the door, and seated himself by the bedside. He laid his hand familiarly on the giant's mighty shoulder; looked him full in the face, and said in a whisper:—

'Thomas Wildfang!'

The man started, and drew his huge hairy hand across his eyes, as if in doubt whether he was waking or sleeping. 'It's better than ten years, master, since you called me by my name. If I am Thomas Wildfang, what are You?'

'Your captain, once more.'

Thomas Wildfang sat up on the side of the bed, and spoke his next words cautiously in Turlington's ear.

'Another man in the way?'

'Yes.'

The giant shook his bald bestial head dolefully. 'Too late. I'm past the job. Look here.'

He held up his hand, and showed it trembling incessantly. 'I'm an old man,' he said, and let his hand drop heavily again on the bed beside him.

Turlington looked at the door, and whispered back—

'The man is as old as you are. And the money is worth having.'

'How much?'

'A hundred pounds.'

The eyes of Thomas Wildfang fastened greedily on Turlington's face. 'Let's hear,' he said. 'Softly, captain. Let's hear.'

\* \* \* \* \* \* \*

When the women came back with the clothes, Turlington had left the room. Their promised reward lay waiting for them on the table, and Thomas Wildfang was eager to dress himself and be gone. They could get but one answer from him to every question they put. He had business in hand, which was not to be delayed. They would see

him again in a day or two, with money in his purse. With that
assurance he took his cudgel from the corner of the room, and stalked
out swiftly by the back door of the house into the night.

## ELEVENTH SCENE

### OUTSIDE THE HOUSE

The evening was chilly, but not cold for the time of year. There was
no moon. The stars were out, and the wind was quiet. Upon the
whole, the inhabitants of the little Somersetshire village of Baxdale
agreed that it was as fine a Christmas Eve as they could remember for
some years past.

Towards eight in the evening the one small street of the village was
empty, except at that part of it which was occupied by the public-
house. For the most part, people gathered round their firesides, with
an eye to their suppers, and watched the process of cooking comfortably indoors. The old bare grey church, situated at some little
distance from the village, looked a lonelier object than usual in the
dim starlight. The vicarage, nestling close under the shadow of
the church tower, threw no illumination of firelight or candlelight
on the dreary scene. The clergyman's shutters fitted well, and the
clergyman's curtains were closely drawn. The one ray of light that
cheered the wintry darkness streamed from the unguarded window of
a lonely house, separated from the vicarage by the whole length of the
churchyard. A man stood at the window, holding back the shutter,
and looking out attentively over the dim void of the burial ground.
The man was Richard Turlington. The room in which he was
watching was a room in his own house.

A momentary spark of light flashed up, as from a kindled match,
in the burial ground. Turlington instantly left the empty room in
which he had been watching. Passing down the back garden of the
house, and crossing a narrow lane at the bottom of it, he opened a
gate in a low stone wall beyond, and entered the churchyard. The
shadowy figure of a man of great stature, lurking among the graves,
advanced to meet him. Midway in the dark and lonely place, the
two stopped and consulted together in whispers. Turlington spoke
first.

'Have you taken up your quarters at the public-house in the village?'

'Yes, master.'

'Did you find your way, while the daylight lasted, to the deserted malthouse behind my orchard wall?'

'Yes, master.'

'Now listen—we have no time to lose. Hide there, behind that monument. Before nine o'clock to-night you will see me cross the churchyard, as far as this place, with the man you are to wait for. He is going to spend an hour with the vicar, at the house yonder. I shall stop short here, and say to him, "You can't miss your way in the dark now—I will go back." When I am far enough away from him, I shall blow a call on my whistle. The moment you hear the call, follow the man, and drop him before he gets out of the churchyard. Have you got your cudgel?'

Thomas Wildfang held up his cudgel. Turlington took him by the arm, and felt it suspiciously.

'You have had an attack of the horrors, already,' he said. 'What does this trembling mean?'

He took a spirit-flask from his pocket as he spoke. Thomas Wildfang snatched it out of his hand, and emptied it at a draught. 'All right now, master,' he said. Turlington felt his arm once more. It was steadier already. Wildfang brandished his cudgel, and struck a heavy blow with it on one of the turf-mounds near them. 'Will that drop him, captain?' he asked. Turlington went on with his instructions.

'Rob him when you have dropped him. Take his money and his jewellery. I want to have the killing of him attributed to robbery as the motive. Make sure before you leave him that he is dead. Then go to the malthouse. There is no fear of your being seen; all the people will be indoors, keeping Christmas Eve. You will find a change of clothes hidden in the malthouse, and an old cauldron full of quicklime. Destroy the clothes you have got on, and dress yourself in the other clothes that you find. Follow the cross-road, and when it brings you into the high road, turn to the left; a four-mile walk will take you to the town of Harminster. Sleep there to-night, and travel to London by the train in the morning. The next day go to my office, see the head clerk, and say, "I have come to sign my receipt." Sign it in your own name, and you will receive your hundred pounds. There are your instructions. Do you understand them?'

Wildfang nodded his head in silent token that he understood, and disappeared again among the graves. Turlington went back to the house.

He had advanced midway across the garden, when he was startled by the sound of footsteps in the lane—at that part of it which skirted one of the corners of the house. Hastening forward, he placed himself behind a projection in the wall, so as to see the person pass across the stream of light from the uncovered window of the room that he had left. The stranger was walking rapidly. All Turlington could see, as he crossed the field of light, was that his hat was pulled over his eyes, and that he had a thick beard and moustachio. Describing the man to the servant on entering the house, he was informed that a stranger with a large beard had been seen about the neighbourhood for some days past. The account he had given of himself stated that he was a surveyor, engaged in taking measurements for a new map of that part of the country, shortly to be published.

The guilty mind of Turlington was far from feeling satisfied with the meagre description of the stranger thus rendered. He could not be engaged in surveying in the dark. What could he want in the desolate neighbourhood of the house and churchyard at that time of night?

The man wanted—what the man found a little lower down the lane, hidden in a dismantled part of the churchyard wall—a letter from a young lady. Read by the light of the pocket lantern which he carried with him, the letter first congratulated this person on the complete success of his disguise—and then promised that the writer would be ready at her bedroom window for flight the next morning, before the house was astir. The signature was 'Natalie,' and the person addressed was 'Dearest Launce.'

In the mean while, Turlington barred the window-shutters of the room, and looked at his watch. It wanted only a quarter to nine o'clock. He took his dog-whistle from the chimney-piece, and turned his steps at once in the direction of the drawing-room, in which his guests were passing the evening.

## TWELFTH SCENE

### INSIDE THE HOUSE

The scene in the drawing-room represented the ideal of domestic comfort. The fire of wood and coal mixed, burnt brightly; the lamps shed a soft glow of light; the solid shutters and the thick red curtains kept the cold night air on the outer side of two long windows, which opened on the back garden. Snug arm-chairs were placed in every part of the room. In one of them Sir Joseph reclined, fast asleep; in another, Miss Lavinia sat knitting; a third chair, apart from the rest, near a round table in one corner of the room, was occupied by Natalie. Her head was resting on her hand; an unread book lay open on her lap. She looked pale and harassed; anxiety and suspense had worn her down to the shadow of her former self. On entering the room, Turlington purposely closed the door with a bang. Natalie started. Miss Lavinia looked up reproachfully. The object was achieved—Sir Joseph was roused from his sleep.

'If you are going to the vicar's to-night, Graybrooke,' said Turlington, 'it's time you were off, isn't it?'

Sir Joseph rubbed his eyes, and looked at the clock on the mantelpiece. 'Yes, yes, Richard,' he answered drowsily, 'I suppose I must go. Where is my hat?'

His sister and his daughter both joined in trying to persuade him to send an excuse instead of groping his way to the vicarage in the dark. Sir Joseph hesitated as usual. He and the vicar had run up a sudden friendship, on the strength of their common enthusiasm for the old-fashioned game of backgammon. Victorious over his opponent on the previous evening at Turlington's house, Sir Joseph had promised to pass that evening at the vicarage, and give the vicar his revenge. Observing his indecision, Turlington cunningly irritated him by affecting to believe that he was really unwilling to venture out in the dark. 'I'll see you safe across the churchyard,' he said; 'and the vicar's servant will see you safe back.' The tone in which he spoke instantly roused Sir Joseph. 'I am not in my second childhood yet, Richard,' he replied, testily. 'I can find my way by myself.' He kissed his daughter on the forehead. 'No fear, Natalie. I shall be back in time for the mulled claret. No, Richard, I won't trouble you.' He kissed his hand to his sister and went out into the hall for his hat; Turlington following him with a rough apology, and asking as a favour to be permitted to accompany him part of the way only. The ladies, left behind in the drawing-room, heard the apology accepted by kind-hearted Sir Joseph. The two went out together.

'Have you noticed Richard since his return?' asked Miss Lavinia. 'I fancy he must have heard bad news in London. He looks as if he had something on his mind.'

'I haven't remarked it, aunt.'

For the time, no more was said. Miss Lavinia went monotonously on with her knitting. Natalie pursued her own anxious thoughts over the unread pages of the book in her lap. Suddenly the deep silence out of doors and in was broken by a shrill whistle, sounding from the direction of the churchyard. Natalie started with a faint cry of alarm. Miss Lavinia looked up from her knitting.

'My dear child! your nerves must be sadly out of order. What is there to be frightened at?'

'I'm not very well, aunt. It is so still here at night, the slightest noises startle me.'

There was another interval of silence. It was past nine o'clock when they heard the back door opened and closed again. Turlington came hurriedly into the drawing-room, as if he had some reason for wishing to rejoin the ladies as soon as possible. To the surprise of both of them, he sat down abruptly in a corner, with his face to the wall, and took up the newspaper, without casting a look at them or uttering a word.

'Is Joseph safe at the vicarage?' asked Miss Lavinia.

'All right.' He gave the answer in a short, surly tone, still without looking round.

Miss Lavinia tried him again. 'Did you hear a whistle while you were out? It quite startled Natalie in the stillness of this place.'

He turned half way round. 'My shepherd, I suppose,' he said, after a pause—'whistling for his dog.' He turned back again and immersed himself in his newspaper.

Miss Lavinia beckoned to her niece and pointed significantly to Turlington. After one reluctant look at him, Natalie laid her head wearily on her aunt's shoulder. 'Sleepy, my dear?' whispered the old lady. 'Uneasy, aunt—I don't know why,' Natalie whispered back. 'I would give the world to be in London, and to hear the carriages going by, and the people talking in the street.'

Turlington suddenly dropped his newspaper. 'What's the secret between you two?' he called out roughly. 'What are you whispering about?'

'We wish not to disturb you over your reading, that is all,' said Miss Lavinia, coldly. 'Has anything happened to vex you, Richard?'

'What the devil makes you think that?'

The old lady was offended, and showed it by saying nothing more. Natalie nestled closer to her aunt. One after another the clock ticked off the minutes with painful distinctness in the stillness of the room. Turlington suddenly threw aside the newspaper and left his corner. 'Let's be good friends!' he burst out, with a clumsy assumption of gaiety. 'This isn't keeping Christmas Eve. Let's talk and be sociable. Dearest Natalie!' He threw his arm roughly round Natalie, and drew her by main force away from her aunt. She turned deadly pale, and struggled to release herself. 'I am suffering—I am ill—let me go!' He was deaf to her entreaties. 'What! your husband that is to be, treated in this way? Mustn't I have a kiss?— I will!' He held her closer with one hand, and, seizing her head with the other, tried to turn her lips to him. She resisted with the inbred nervous strength which the weakest woman living has in reserve when she is outraged. Half indignant, half terrified, at Turlington's roughness, Miss Lavinia rose to interfere. In a moment more he would have had two women to overpower instead of one, when a noise outside the window suddenly suspended the ignoble struggle.

There was a sound of footsteps on the gravel walk which ran between the house-wall and the garden-lawn. It was followed by a tap—a single, faint tap, no more—on one of the panes of glass.

They all three stood still. For a moment more, nothing was audible. Then there was a heavy shock, as of something falling outside. Then a groan, then another interval of silence—a long silence, interrupted no more.

Turlington's arm dropped from Natalie. She drew back to her aunt. Looking at him instinctively, in the natural expectation that he would take the lead in penetrating the mystery of what had happened outside the window, the two women were thunderstruck to see that he was, to all appearance, even more startled and more helpless than they were. 'Richard,' said Miss Lavinia, pointing to the window, 'there is something wrong out there. See what it is.' He stood motionless, as if he had not heard her, his eyes fixed on the window, his face livid with terror.

The silence outside was broken once more; this time by a call for help.

A cry of horror burst from Natalie. The voice outside—rising wildly, then suddenly dying away again—was not entirely strange to *her* ears. She tore aside the curtain. With voice and hand she roused her aunt to help her. The two lifted the heavy bar from its socket; they opened the shutters and the window. The cheerful light of the room flowed out over the body of a prostrate man, lying on his face. They turned the man over. Natalie lifted his head.

Her father!

His face was bedabbled with blood. A wound, a frightful wound, was visible on the side of his bare head, high above the ear. He looked at her; his eyes recognised her, before he fainted again in her arms. His hands and his clothes were covered with earth stains. He must have traversed some distance: in that dreadful condition he must have faltered and fallen more than once before he reached the house. His sister wiped the blood from his face. His daughter called on him frantically to forgive her before he died—the harmless, gentle, kind-hearted father, who had never said a hard word to her! The father whom she had deceived!

The terrified servants hurried into the room. Their appearance roused their master from the extraordinary stupor that had seized him. He was at the window before the footman could get there. The two lifted Sir Joseph into the room, and laid him on the sofa. Natalie knelt by him, supporting his head. Miss Lavinia staunched the flowing blood with her handkerchief. The women-servants brought linen and cold water. The man hurried away for the doctor, who lived on the other side of the village. Left alone again with Turlington, Natalie noticed that his eyes were fixed in immovable scrutiny on her father's head. He never said a word. He looked, looked, looked at the wound.

The doctor arrived. Before either the daughter or the sister of the injured man could put the question, Turlington put it—'Will he live or die?'

The doctor's careful finger probed the wound.

'Make your minds easy. A little lower down, or in front, the blow might have been serious. As it is, there is no harm done. Keep him quiet and he will be all right again in two or three days.'

Hearing those welcome words, Natalie and her aunt sank on their knees in silent gratitude. After dressing the wound, the doctor looked round for the master of the house. Turlington, who had been so breathlessly eager but a few minutes since, seemed to have lost all interest in the case now. He stood apart, at the window, looking out towards the churchyard, thinking. The questions which it was the doctor's duty to ask, were answered by the ladies. The servants assisted in examining the injured man's clothes: they discovered that his watch and purse were both missing. When it became necessary to carry him upstairs, it was the footman who assisted the doctor. The footman's master, without a word of explanation, walked out bare-headed into the back garden, on the search, as the doctor and the servants supposed, for some trace of the robber who had attempted Sir Joseph's life.

His absence was hardly noticed at the time. The difficulty of conveying the wounded man to his room, absorbed the attention of all the persons present.

Sir Joseph partially recovered his senses while they were taking him up the steep and narrow stairs. Carefully as they carried the patient, the motion wrung a groan from him before they reached the top. The bedroom corridor, in the rambling irregularly built house, rose and fell on different levels. At the door of the first bed-chamber the doctor asked a little anxiously if that was the room. No; there were three more stairs to go down, and a corner to turn, before they could reach it. The first room was Natalie's. She instantly offered it for her father's use. The doctor (seeing that it was the airiest as well as the nearest room) accepted the proposal. Sir Joseph had been laid comfortably in his daughter's bed; the doctor had just left them, with renewed assurances that they need feel no anxiety—when they heard a heavy step below stairs. Turlington had re-entered the house.

(He had been looking, as they had supposed, for the ruffian who had attacked Sir Joseph; with a motive, however, for the search, at which it was impossible for other persons to guess. His own safety was now bound up in the safety of Thomas Wildfang. As soon as he was out of sight in the darkness, he made straight for the malthouse. The change of clothes was there untouched; not a trace of his accomplice was to be seen. Where else to look for him it was impossible to tell. Turlington had no alternative but to go back to the house, and ascertain if suspicion had been aroused in his absence.)

He had only to ascend the stairs, and to see, through the open door, that Sir Joseph had been placed in his daughter's room.

'What does this mean?' he asked roughly.

Before it was possible to answer him the footman appeared with a message. The doctor had come back to the door to say that he would take on himself the necessary duty of informing the constable of what had happened, on his return to the village. Turlington started and changed colour. If Wildfang was found by others, and questioned in his employer's absence, serious consequences might follow. 'The constable is my business,' said Turlington, hurriedly descending the stairs; 'I'll go with the doctor.' They heard him open the door below, then close it again (as if some sudden thought had struck him) and call to the footman. The house was badly provided with servants' bed-rooms. The women-servants only slept indoors. The footman occupied a room over the stables. Natalie and her aunt heard Turlington dismiss the man for the night, an hour earlier than usual at least. His next proceeding was stranger still. Looking cautiously over the stairs, Natalie saw him lock all the doors on the ground floor and take out the keys. When he went away she heard him lock the front door behind him. Incredible as it seemed, there could be no doubt of the fact—the inmates of the house were imprisoned till he came back. What did it mean?

(It meant that Turlington's vengeance still remained to be wreaked on the woman who had deceived him. It meant that Sir Joseph's life still stood between the man who had compassed his death and the money which the man was resolved to have. It meant that Richard Turlington was driven to bay, and that the horror and the peril of the night were not at an end yet.)

Natalie and her aunt looked at each other across the bed on which Sir Joseph lay. He had fallen into a kind of doze; no enlightenment could come to them from *him*. They could only ask each other, with beating hearts and baffled minds, what Richard's conduct meant—they could only feel instinctively that some dreadful discovery was hanging over them. The aunt was the calmer of the two—there was no secret weighing heavily on *her* conscience. *She* could feel the consolations of religion. 'Our dear one is spared to us, my love,' said the old lady gently. 'God has been good to us. We are in His hands. If we know that, we know enough.'

As she spoke there was a loud ring at the door bell. The women-servants crowded into the bedroom in alarm. Strong in numbers, and encouraged by Natalie—who roused herself and led the way—they confronted the risk of opening the window and of venturing out on the balcony which extended along that side of the house. A man was dimly visible below. He called to them in thick unsteady accents. The servants recognised him: he was the telegraphic messenger from the railway. They went down to speak to him—and returned with a telegram which had been pushed in under the door. The distance from the station was considerable; the messenger had been 'Keeping Christmas' in more than one beershop on his way to the house; and the delivery of the telegram had been delayed for some hours. It was addressed to Natalie. She opened it—looked at it—dropped it—and stood speechless; her lips parted in horror, her eyes staring vacantly straight before her.

Miss Lavinia took the telegram from the floor, and read these lines:—

'Lady Winwood, Hertford Street, London. To Natalie Gray-brooke, Church Meadows, Baxdale, Somersetshire. Dreadful news. R.T. has discovered your marriage to Launce. The truth has been kept from me till to-day (24th). Instant flight with your husband is your only chance. I would have communicated with Launce, but I do not know his address. You will receive this, I hope and believe, before R.T. can return to Somersetshire. Telegraph back, I entreat you, to say that you are safe. I shall follow my message if I do not hear from you in reasonable time.'

Miss Lavinia lifted her grey head, and looked at her niece. 'Is this true?' she said—and pointed to the venerable face laid back, white, on the white pillow of the bed. Natalie sank forward as her eyes met the eyes of her aunt. Miss Lavinia saved her from falling insensible on the floor.

*        *        *        *        *        *        *

The confession had been made. The words of penitence and the words of pardon had been spoken. The peaceful face of the father still lay hushed in rest. One by one, the minutes succeeded each other uneventfully in the deep tranquillity of the night. It was almost a relief when the silence was disturbed once more by another sound outside the house. A pebble was thrown up at the window, and a voice called out cautiously. 'Miss Lavinia!'

They recognised the voice of the man-servant, and at once opened the window.

He had something to say to the ladies in private. How could he say it? A domestic circumstance which had been marked by Launce, as favourable to the contemplated elopement, was now noticed by the servant as lending itself readily to effecting the necessary communication with the ladies. The lock of the gardener's tool-house (in the shrubbery close by) was under repair; and the gardener's ladder was accessible to any one who wanted it. At the short height of the balcony from the ground, the ladder was more than long enough for the purpose required. In a few minutes the servant had mounted to the balcony, and could speak to Natalie and her aunt at the window.

'I can't rest quiet,' said the man. 'I'm off on the sly to see what's going on down in the village. It's hard on ladies like you to be locked in here. Is there anything I can do for either of you?'

Natalie took up Lady Winwood's telegram. 'Launce ought to see this,' she said to her aunt. 'He will be here at daybreak,' she added, in a whisper, 'if I don't tell him what has happened.'

Miss Lavinia turned pale. 'If he and Richard meet—!' she began. 'Tell him!' she added hurriedly—'tell him before it is too late!'

Natalie wrote a few lines (addressed to Launce in his assumed name at his lodgings in the village) enclosing Lady Winwood's telegram, and entreating him to do nothing rash. When the servant had disappeared with the letter, there was one hope in her mind and in her aunt's mind, which each was ashamed to acknowledge to the other— the hope that Launce would face the very danger that they dreaded for him, and come to the house.

They had not been long alone again, when Sir Joseph drowsily opened his eyes and asked what they were doing in his room. They told him gently that he was ill. He put his hand up to his head, and said they were right; and so dropped off again into slumber. Worn out by the emotions through which they had passed, the two women silently waited for the march of events. The same stupor of resignation possessed them both. They had secured the door and the window. They had prayed together. They had kissed the quiet face on the pillow. They had said to each other, 'We will live with him or die with him as God pleases.' Miss Lavinia sat by the bedside. Natalie was on a stool at her feet—with her eyes closed, and her head on her aunt's knee.

Time went on. The clock in the hall had struck—ten or eleven, they were not sure which—when they heard the signal which warned them of the servant's return from the village. He brought news, and more than news, he brought a letter from Launce.

Natalie read these lines:—

'I shall be with you, dearest, almost as soon as you receive this. The bearer will tell you what has happened in the village—your note throws a new light on it all. I only remain behind to go to the vicar (who is also the magistrate here), and declare myself your husband. All disguise must be at an end now. My place is with you and yours. It is even worse than your worst fears. Turlington was at the bottom of the attack on your father. Judge if you have not need of your husband's protection after that! — L.'

Natalie handed the letter to her aunt, and pointed to the sentence which asserted Turlington's guilty knowledge of the attempt on Sir Joseph's life. In silent horror the two women looked at each other, recalling what had happened earlier in the evening, and understanding it now. The servant roused them to a sense of present things, by entering on the narrative of his discoveries in the village.

The place was all astir when he reached it. An old man—a stranger in Baxdale—had been found lying in the road, close to the church, in a fit; and the person who had discovered him had been no other than Launce himself. He had, literally, stumbled over the body of Thomas Wildfang in the dark, on his way back to his lodgings in the village.

'The gentleman gave the alarm, Miss,' said the servant, describing the event, as it had been related to him, 'and the man—a huge big old man—was carried to the inn. The landlord identified him; he had taken lodgings at the inn that day, and the constable found valuable property on him—a purse of money and a gold watch and chain. There was nothing to show who the money and the watch belonged to. It was only when my master and the doctor got to the inn that it was known whom he robbed and tried to murder. All he let out in his wanderings before they came, was that some person had set him on to do it. He called the person "Captain," and sometimes "Captain Goward." It was thought—if you could trust the ravings of a mad-man—that the fit took him while he was putting his hand on Sir Joseph's heart to feel if it had stopped beating. A sort of a vision (as I understand it) must have overpowered him at the moment. They tell me he raved about the sea bursting into the churchyard, and a drowning sailor floating by on a hen-coop; a sailor who dragged him down to hell by the hair of his head, and such like horrible nonsense, Miss. He was still screeching, at the worst of the fit, when my master and the doctor came into the room. At sight of one or other of them— it is thought of Mr Turlington, seeing that he came first—he held his peace on a sudden, and then fell back in convulsions in the arms of the men who were holding him. The doctor gave it a learned name, signifying drink-madness, and said the case was hopeless. However, he ordered the room to be cleared of the crowd to see what he could do. My master was reported to be still with the doctor, waiting to see whether the man lived or died, when I left the village, Miss, with the gentleman's answer to your note. I didn't dare stay to hear how it ended, for fear of Mr Turlington's finding me out.'

Having reached the end of his narrative, the man looked round restlessly towards the window. It was impossible to say when his master might not return, and it might be as much as his life was worth to be caught in the house after he had been locked out of it. He begged permission to open the window, and make his escape back to the stables while there was still time. As he unbarred the shutter they were startled by a voice hailing them from below. It was Launce's voice, calling to Natalie. The servant disappeared—and Natalie was in Launce's arms before she could breathe again.

For one delicious moment she let her head lie on his breast: then she suddenly pushed him away from her. 'Why do you come here? He will kill you if he finds you in the house. Where is he?'

Launce knew even less of Turlington's movements than the servant. 'Wherever he is, thank God, I am here before him!' That was all the answer he could give.

Natalie and her aunt heard him in silent dismay. Sir Joseph woke and recognised Launce before a word more could be said. 'Ah, my dear boy!' he murmured faintly. 'It's pleasant to see you again. How do you come here?' He was quite satisfied with the first excuse that suggested itself. 'We'll talk about it tomorrow,' he said, and composed himself to rest again.

Natalie made a second attempt to persuade Launce to leave the house.

'We don't know what may have happened,' she said. 'He may have followed you on your way here. He may have purposely let you enter his house. Leave us while you have the chance.'

Miss Lavinia added her persuasions. They were useless. Launce quietly closed the heavy window-shutters, lined with iron, and put up the bar. Natalie wrung her hands in despair.

'Have you been to the magistrate?' she asked. 'Tell us, at least, are you here by his advice? Is he coming to help us?'

Launce hesitated. If he had told the truth, he must have acknowledged that he was there in direct opposition to the magistrate's advice. He answered evasively, 'If the vicar doesn't come, the doctor will. I have told him Sir Joseph must be moved. Cheer up, Natalie! The doctor will be here as soon as Turlington.'

As the name passed his lips—without a sound outside to prepare them for what was coming—the voice of Turlington himself suddenly penetrated into the room, speaking close behind the window, on the outer side.

'You have broken into my house in the night,' said the voice. 'And you don't escape *this* way.'

Miss Lavinia sank on her knees. Natalie flew to her father. His eyes were wide open in terror; he moaned, feebly recognising the voice. The next sound that was heard was the sound made by the removal of the ladder from the balcony. Turlington, having descended by it, had taken it away. Natalie had but too accurately guessed what would happen. The death of the villain's accomplice had freed him from all apprehension in that quarter. He had deliberately dogged Launce's steps, and had deliberately allowed him to put himself in the wrong by effecting a secret entrance into the house.

There was an interval—a horrible interval—and then they heard the front door opened. Without stopping (judging by the absence of sound) to close it again, Turlington rapidly ascended the stairs and tried the locked door.

'Come out, and give yourself up!' he called through the door. 'I have got my revolver with me, and I have a right to fire on a man who has broken into my house. If the door isn't opened before I count three, your blood be on your own head. One!'

Launce was armed with nothing but his stick. He advanced, without an instant's hesitation, to give himself up. Natalie threw her arms round him and clasped him fast before he could reach the door.

'Two!' cried the voice outside, as Launce struggled to force her from him. At the same moment his eye turned towards the bed. It was exactly opposite the door—it was straight in the line of fire! Sir

Joseph's life (as Turlington had deliberately calculated) was actually in greater danger than Launce's life. He tore himself free, rushed to the bed, and took the old man in his arms to lift him out.

'Three!'

The crash of the report sounded. The bullet came through the door, grazed Launce's left arm, and buried itself in the pillow, at the very place on which Sir Joseph's head had rested the moment before. Launce had saved his father-in-law's life. Turlington had fired his first shot for the money, and had not got it yet.

They were safe in the corner of the room, on the same side as the door—Sir Joseph, helpless as a child, in Launce's arms; the women pale, but admirably calm. They were safe for the moment, when the second bullet (fired at an angle) tore its way through the wall on their right hand.

'I hear you,' cried the voice of the miscreant on the other side of the door. 'I'll have you yet—through the wall.'

There was a pause. They heard his hand sounding the wall, to find out where there was solid wood in the material of which it was built, and where there was plaster only. At that dreadful moment Launce's composure never left him. He laid Sir Joseph softly on the floor, and signed to Natalie and her aunt to lie down by him in silence. Their lives depended now on neither their voices nor their movements telling the murderer where to fire. He chose his place. The barrel of the revolver grated as he laid it against the wall. He touched the hair-trigger. A faint *click* was the only sound that followed. The third barrel had missed fire.

They heard him ask himself, with an oath, 'What's wrong with it now?'

There was a pause of silence.

Was he examining the weapon?

Before they could ask themselves the question, the report of the exploding charge burst on their ears. It was instantly followed by a heavy fall. They looked at the opposite wall of the room. No sign of a bullet there or anywhere.

Launce signed to them not to move yet. They waited, and listened. Nothing stirred on the landing outside.

Suddenly there was a disturbance of the silence in the lower regions—a clamour of many voices at the open house door. Had the firing of the revolver been heard at the vicarage? Yes! They recognised the vicar's voice among the others. A moment more, and they heard a general exclamation of horror on the stairs. Launce opened the door of the room. He instantly closed it again before Natalie could follow him.

The dead body of Turlington lay on the landing outside. The charge in the fourth barrel of the revolver had exploded while he was looking at it. The bullet had entered his mouth and killed him on the spot.

# DOCUMENTARY HINTS, IN CONCLUSION

### FIRST HINT

(*Derived from Lady Winwood's Card-Rack*.)

'Sir Joseph Graybrooke and Miss Graybrooke request the honour of Lord and Lady Winwood's company to dinner, on Wednesday, February 10, at half-past seven o'clock. To meet Mr and Mrs Launcelot Linzie on their return.'

### SECOND HINT

(*Derived from a recent money article in a morning newspaper*.)

'We are requested to give the fullest contradiction to unfavourable rumours lately in circulation respecting the firm of Pizzituti, Turlington, and Branca. Some temporary derangement in the machinery of the business was undoubtedly produced in consequence of the sudden death of the lamented managing partner, Mr Turlington, by the accidental discharge of a revolver which he was examining. Whatever temporary obstacles may have existed are now overcome. We are informed, on good authority, that the well-known house of Messrs Bulpit Brothers has an interest in the business, and will carry it on until further notice.'

# THE HAUNTED HOTEL

TO

MR & MRS SEBASTIAN SCHLESINGER*

IN REMEMBRANCE OF MUCH KINDNESS

AND OF MANY HAPPY DAYS

# THE FIRST PART

## CHAPTER I

In the year 1860, the reputation of Doctor Wybrow as a London physician reached its highest point. It was reported on good authority that he was in receipt of one of the largest incomes derived from the practice of medicine in modern times.

One afternoon, towards the close of the London season,* the Doctor had just taken his luncheon after a specially hard morning's work in his consulting-room, and with a formidable list of visits to patients at their own houses to fill up the rest of his day—when the servant announced that a lady wished to speak to him.

'Who is she?' the Doctor asked. 'A stranger?'

'Yes, sir.'

'I see no strangers out of consulting-hours. Tell her what the hours are, and send her away.'

'I have told her, sir.'

'Well?'

'And she won't go.'

'Won't go?' The Doctor smiled as he repeated the words. He was a humourist in his way; and there was an absurd side to the situation which rather amused him. 'Has this obstinate lady given you her name?' he inquired.

'No, sir. She refused to give any name—she said she wouldn't keep you five minutes, and the matter was too important to wait till to-morrow. There she is in the consulting-room; and how to get her out again is more than I know.'

Doctor Wybrow considered for a moment. His knowledge of women (professionally speaking) rested on the ripe experience of more than thirty years; he had met with them in all their varieties—especially the variety which knows nothing of the value of time, and never hesitates at sheltering itself behind the privileges of its sex. A glance at his watch informed him that he must soon begin his rounds among the patients who were waiting for him at their own houses. He decided forthwith on taking the only wise course that was open under the circumstances. In other words, he decided on taking to flight.

'Is the carriage at the door?' he asked.

'Yes, sir.'

'Very well. Open the house-door for me without making any noise, and leave the lady in undisturbed possession of the consulting-room. When she gets tired of waiting, you know what to tell her. If she asks when I am expected to return, say that I dine at my club, and spend the evening at the theatre. Now then, softly, Thomas! If your shoes creak, I am a lost man.'

He noiselessly led the way into the hall, followed by the servant on tip-toe.

Did the lady in the consulting-room suspect him? or did Thomas's shoes creak, and was her sense of hearing unusually keen? Whatever the explanation may be, the event that actually happened was beyond all doubt. Exactly as Doctor Wybrow passed his consulting-room, the door opened—the lady appeared on the threshold—and laid her hand on his arm.

'I entreat you, sir, not to go away without letting me speak to you first.'

The accent was foreign; the tone was low and firm. Her fingers closed gently, and yet resolutely, on the Doctor's arm.

Neither her language nor her action had the slightest effect in inclining him to grant her request. The influence that instantly stopped him, on the way to his carriage, was the silent influence of her face. The startling contrast between the corpse-like pallor of her complexion and the over-powering life and light, the glittering metallic brightness in her large black eyes, held him literally spell-bound. She was dressed in dark colours, with perfect taste; she was of middle height, and (apparently) of middle age—say a year or two over thirty. Her lower features—the nose, mouth, and chin—possessed the fineness and delicacy of form which is oftener seen among women of foreign races than among women of English birth. She was unquestionably a handsome person—with the one serious draw-back of her ghastly complexion, and with the less noticeable defect of a total want of tenderness in the expression of her eyes. Apart from his first emotion of surprise, the feeling she produced in the Doctor may be described as an overpowering feeling of professional curiosity. The case might prove to be something entirely new in his professional experience. 'It looks like it,' he thought; 'and it's worth waiting for.'

She perceived that she had produced a strong impression of some kind upon him, and dropped her hold on his arm.

'You have comforted many miserable women in your time,' she said. 'Comfort one more, to-day.'

Without waiting to be answered, she led the way back into the room.

The Doctor followed her, and closed the door. He placed her in the patients' chair, opposite the windows. Even in London the sun, on that summer afternoon, was dazzlingly bright. The radiant light flowed in on her. Her eyes met it unflinchingly, with the steely steadiness of the eyes of an eagle. The smooth pallor of her unwrinkled skin looked more fearfully white than ever. For the first time, for many a long year past, the Doctor felt his pulse quicken its beat in the presence of a patient.

Having possessed herself of his attention, she appeared, strangely enough, to have nothing to say to him. A curious apathy seemed to have taken possession of this resolute woman. Forced to speak first, the Doctor merely inquired, in the conventional phrase, what he could do for her.

The sound of his voice seemed to rouse her. Still looking straight at the light, she said abruptly: 'I have a painful question to ask.'

'What is it?'

Her eyes travelled slowly from the window to the Doctor's face. Without the slightest outward appearance of agitation, she put the 'painful question' in these extraordinary words:

'I want to know, if you please, whether I am in danger of going mad?'

Some men might have been amused, and some might have been alarmed. Doctor Wybrow was only conscious of a sense of disappointment. Was this the rare case that he had anticipated, judging rashly by appearances? Was the new patient only a hypochondriacal woman, whose malady was a disordered stomach and whose misfortune was a weak brain? 'Why do you come to *me*?' he asked sharply. 'Why don't you consult a doctor whose special employment is the treatment of the insane?'

She had her answer ready on the instant.

'I don't go to a doctor of that sort,' she said, 'for the very reason that he *is* a specialist: he has the fatal habit of judging everybody by lines and rules of his own laying down. I come to *you*, because my case is outside of all lines and rules, and because you are famous in your profession for the discovery of mysteries in disease. Are you satisfied?'

He was more than satisfied—his first idea had been the right idea, after all. Besides, she was correctly informed as to his professional position. The capacity which had raised him to fame and fortune was his capacity (unrivalled among his brethren) for the discovery of remote disease.

'I am at your disposal,' he answered. 'Let me try if I can find out what is the matter with you.'

He put his medical questions. They were promptly and plainly answered; and they led to no other conclusion than that the strange lady was, mentally and physically, in excellent health. Not satisfied with questions, he carefully examined the great organs of life. Neither his hand nor his stethoscope could discover anything that was amiss. With the admirable patience and devotion to his art which had distinguished him from the time when he was a student, he still subjected her to one test after another. The result was always the same. Not only was there no tendency to brain disease—there was not even a perceptible derangement of the nervous system. 'I can find nothing the matter with you,' he said. 'I can't even account for the extraordinary pallor of your complexion. You completely puzzle me.'

'The pallor of my complexion is nothing,' she answered a little impatiently. 'In my early life I had a narrow escape from death by poisoning. I have never had a complexion since—and my skin is so delicate, I cannot paint without producing a hideous rash. But that is of no importance. I wanted your opinion given positively. I believed in you, and you have disappointed me.' Her head dropped on her breast. 'And so it ends!' she said to herself bitterly.

The Doctor's sympathies were touched. Perhaps it might be more correct to say that his professional pride was a little hurt. 'It may end in the right way yet,' he remarked, 'if you choose to help me.'

She looked up again with flashing eyes. 'Speak plainly,' she said. 'How can I help you?'

'Plainly, madam, you come to me as an enigma, and you leave me to make the right guess by the unaided efforts of my art. My art will do much, but not all. For example, something must have occurred— something quite unconnected with the state of your bodily health—to frighten you about yourself, or you would never have come here to consult me. Is that true?'

She clasped her hands in her lap. 'That is true!' she said eagerly. 'I begin to believe in you again.'

'Very well. You can't expect me to find out the moral cause which has alarmed you. I can positively discover that there is no physical cause of alarm; and (unless you admit me to your confidence) I can do no more.'

She rose, and took a turn in the room. 'Suppose I tell you?' she said. 'But, mind, I shall mention no names!'

'There is no need to mention names. The facts are all I want.'

'The facts are nothing,' she rejoined. 'I have only my own impressions to confess—and you will very likely think me a fanciful fool when you hear what they are. No matter. I will do my best to content you—I will begin with the facts that you want. Take my word for it, *they* won't do much to help you.'

She sat down again. In the plainest possible words, she began the strangest and wildest confession that had ever reached the Doctor's ears.

## CHAPTER II

'It is one fact, sir, that I am a widow,' she said. 'It is another fact, that I am going to be married again.'

There she paused, and smiled at some thought that occurred to her. Doctor Wybrow was not favourably impressed by her smile—there was something at once sad and cruel in it. It came slowly, and it went away suddenly. He began to doubt whether he had been wise in acting on his first impression. His mind reverted to the commonplace patients and the discoverable maladies that were waiting for him, with a certain tender regret.

The lady went on.

'My approaching marriage,' she said, 'has one embarrassing circumstance connected with it. The gentleman whose wife I am to be, was engaged to another lady when he happened to meet with me, abroad: that lady, mind, being of his own blood and family, related to him as his cousin. I have innocently robbed her of her lover, and destroyed her prospects in life. Innocently, I say—because he told me nothing of his engagement until after I had accepted him. When we next met in England—and when there was danger, no doubt, of the affair coming to my knowledge—he told me the truth. I was naturally indignant. He had his excuse ready; he showed me a letter from the lady herself, releasing him from his engagement. A more noble, a more high-minded letter, I never read in my life. I cried over it—I who have no tears in me for sorrows of my own! If the letter had left him any hope of being forgiven, I would have positively refused to marry him. But the firmness of it—without anger, without a word of reproach, with heartfelt wishes even for his happiness—the firmness of it, I say, left him no hope. He appealed to my compassion; he appealed to his love for me. You know what women are. I too was soft-hearted—I said, Very well; yes! In a week more (I tremble as I think of it) we are to be married.'

She did really tremble—she was obliged to pause and compose herself, before she could go on. The Doctor, waiting for more facts, began to fear that he stood committed to a long story. 'Forgive me for reminding you that I have suffering persons waiting to see me,' he said. 'The sooner you can come to the point, the better for my patients and for me.'

The strange smile—at once so sad and so cruel—showed itself again on the lady's lips. 'Every word I have said is to the point,' she answered. 'You will see it yourself in a moment more.'

She resumed her narrative.

'Yesterday—you need fear no long story, sir; only yesterday—I was among the visitors at one of your English luncheon parties. A lady, a perfect stranger to me, came in late—after we had left the table, and had retired to the drawing-room. She happened to take a chair near me; and we were presented to each other. I knew her by name, as she knew me. It was the woman whom I had robbed of her lover, the woman who had written the noble letter. Now listen! You were impatient with me for not interesting you in what I said just now. I said it to satisfy your mind that I had no enmity of feeling towards the lady, on my side. I admired her, I felt for her—I had no cause to reproach myself. This is very important, as you will presently see. On her side, I have reason to be assured that the circumstances had been truly explained to her, and that she understood I was in no way to blame. Now, knowing all these necessary things as you do, explain to me, if you can, why, when I rose and met that woman's eyes looking at me, I turned cold from head to foot, and shuddered, and shivered, and knew what a deadly panic of fear was, for the first time in my life.'

The Doctor began to feel interested at last.

'Was there anything remarkable in the lady's personal appearance?' he asked.

'Nothing whatever!' was the vehement reply. 'Here is the true description of her:—The ordinary English lady; the clear cold blue eyes, the fine rosy complexion, the inanimately polite manner, the large good-humoured mouth, the too plump cheeks and chin: these, and nothing more.'

'Was there anything in her expression, when you first looked at her, that took you by surprise?'

'There was natural curiosity to see the woman who had been preferred to her; and perhaps some astonishment also, not to see a more engaging and more beautiful person; both those feelings restrained within the limits of good breeding, and both not lasting for more than a few moments—so far as I could see. I say, "so far," because the horrible agitation that she communicated to me disturbed my judgment. If I could have got to the door, I would have run out of the room, she frightened me so! I was not even able to stand up—I sank back in my chair; I stared horror-struck at the calm blue eyes that were only looking at me with a gentle surprise. To say they affected me like the eyes of a serpent is to say nothing. I felt her soul in them, looking into mine—looking, if such a thing can be, unconsciously to her own mortal self. I tell you my impression, in all its horror and in all its folly! That woman is destined (without knowing it herself) to be the evil genius* of my life. Her innocent eyes saw hidden capabilities of wickedness in me that I was not aware of myself, until I felt them stirring under her look. If I commit faults in my life to come—if I am even guilty of crimes—she will bring the retribution, without (as I firmly believe) any conscious exercise of her own will. In one indescribable moment I felt all this—and I suppose my face showed it. The good artless creature was inspired by a sort of gentle alarm for me. "I am afraid the heat of the room is too much for you; will you try my smelling bottle?" I heard her say those kind words; and I remember nothing else—I fainted. When I recovered my senses, the company had all gone; only the lady of the house was with me. For the moment I could say nothing to her; the dreadful impression that I have tried to describe to you came back to me with the coming back of my life. As soon as I could speak, I implored her to tell me the whole truth about the woman whom I had supplanted. You see, I had a faint hope that her good character might not really be deserved, that her noble letter was a skilful piece of hypocrisy—in short, that she secretly hated me, and was cunning enough to hide it. No! the lady had been her friend from her girlhood, was as familiar with her as if they had been sisters—knew her positively to be as good, as innocent, as incapable of hating anybody, as the greatest saint that ever lived. My one last hope, that I had only felt an ordinary forewarning of danger in the presence of an ordinary enemy, was a hope destroyed for ever. There was one more effort I could make, and I made it. I went next to the man whom I am to marry. I implored him to release me from my promise. He refused. I declared I would break my engagement. He showed me letters from his sisters, letters from his brothers, and his dear friends—all entreating him to think again before he made me his wife; all repeating reports of me in Paris, Vienna, and London, which are so many vile lies. "If you refuse to marry me," he said, "you admit that these reports are true—you admit that you are afraid to face society in the character of my wife." What could I answer? There was no contradicting him—he was plainly right: if I persisted in my refusal, the utter destruction of my reputation would be the result. I consented to let the wedding take place as we had arranged it—and left him. The night has passed. I am here, with my fixed conviction—that innocent woman is ordained to have a fatal influence over my life. I am here with my one question to put, to the one man who can answer it. For the last time, sir, what am I—a demon who has seen the avenging angel? or only a poor mad woman, misled by the delusion of a deranged mind?'

Doctor Wybrow rose from his chair, determined to close the interview.

He was strongly and painfully impressed by what he had heard. The longer he had listened to her, the more irresistibly the conviction of the woman's wickedness had forced itself on him. He tried vainly to think of her as a person to be pitied—a person with a morbidly sensitive imagination, conscious of the capacities for evil which lie dormant in us all, and striving earnestly to open her heart to the counter-influence of her own better nature; the effort was beyond him. A perverse instinct in him said, as if in words, Beware how you believe in her!

'I have already given you my opinion,' he said. 'There is no sign of your intellect being deranged, or being likely to be deranged, that medical science can discover—as *I* understand it. As for the impressions you have confided to me, I can only say that yours is a case (as I venture to think) for spiritual rather than for medical advice. Of one thing be assured: what you have said to me in this room shall not pass out of it. Your confession is safe in my keeping.'

She heard him, with a certain dogged resignation, to the end.

'Is that all?' she asked.

'That is all,' he answered.

She put a little paper packet of money on the table. 'Thank you, sir. There is your fee.'

With those words she rose. Her wild black eyes looked upward, with an expression of despair so defiant and so horrible in its silent agony that the Doctor turned away his head, unable to endure the sight of it. The bare idea of taking anything from her—not money only, but anything even that she had touched—suddenly revolted him. Still without looking at her, he said, 'Take it back; I don't want my fee.'

She neither heeded nor heard him. Still looking upward, she said slowly to herself, 'Let the end come. I have done with the struggle: I submit.'

She drew her veil over her face, bowed to the Doctor, and left the room.

He rang the bell, and followed her into the hall. As the servant closed the door on her, a sudden impulse of curiosity—utterly unworthy of him, and at the same time utterly irresistible—sprang up in the Doctor's mind. Blushing like a boy, he said to the servant, 'Follow her home, and find out her name.' For one moment the man looked at his master, doubting if his own ears had not deceived him. Doctor Wybrow looked back at him in silence. The submissive servant knew what that silence meant—he took his hat and hurried into the street.

The Doctor went back to the consulting-room. A sudden revulsion of feeling swept over his mind. Had the woman left an infection of wickedness in the house, and had he caught it? What devil had possessed him to degrade himself in the eyes of his own servant? He had behaved infamously—he had asked an honest man, a man who had served him faithfully for years, to turn spy! Stung by the bare thought of it, he ran out into the hall again, and opened the door. The servant had disappeared; it was too late to call him back. But one refuge from his contempt for himself was now open to him—the refuge of work. He got into his carriage and went his rounds among his patients.

If the famous physician could have shaken his own reputation, he would have done it that afternoon. Never before had he made himself so little welcome at the bedside. Never before had he put off until to-morrow the prescription which ought to have been written, the opinion which ought to have been given, to-day. He went home earlier than usual—unutterably dissatisfied with himself.

The servant had returned. Dr Wybrow was ashamed to question him. The man reported the result of his errand, without waiting to be asked.

'The lady's name is the Countess Narona. She lives at——'

Without waiting to hear where she lived, the Doctor acknowledged the all-important discovery of her name by a silent bend of the head, and entered his consulting-room. The fee that he had vainly refused still lay in its little white paper covering on the table. He sealed it up in an envelope; addressed it to the 'Poor-box' of the nearest police-court; and, calling the servant in, directed him to take it to the magistrate the next morning. Faithful to his duties, the servant waited to ask the customary question, 'Do you dine at home to-day, sir?'

After a moment's hesitation he said, 'No: I shall dine at the club.'

The most easily deteriorated of all the moral qualities is the quality called 'conscience.' In one state of a man's mind, his conscience is the severest judge that can pass sentence on him. In another state, he and his conscience are on the best possible terms with each other in the comfortable capacity of accomplices. When Doctor Wybrow left his house for the second time, he did not even attempt to conceal from himself that his sole object, in dining at the club, was to hear what the world said of the Countess Narona.

## CHAPTER III

There was a time when a man in search of the pleasures of gossip sought the society of ladies. The man knows better now. He goes to the smoking-room of his club.

Doctor Wybrow lit his cigar, and looked round him at his brethren in social conclave assembled. The room was well filled; but the flow of talk was still languid. The Doctor innocently applied the stimulant that was wanted. When he inquired if anybody knew the Countess Narona, he was answered by something like a shout of astonishment. Never (the conclave agreed) had such an absurd question been asked before! Every human creature, with the slightest claim to a place in society, knew the Countess Narona. An adventuress with a European reputation of the blackest possible colour—such was the general description of the woman with the deathlike complexion and the glittering eyes.

Descending to particulars, each member of the club contributed his own little stock of scandal to the memoirs of the Countess. It was doubtful whether she was really, what she called herself, a Dalmatian* lady. It was doubtful whether she had ever been married to the Count whose widow she assumed to be. It was doubtful whether the man who accompanied her in her travels (under the name of Baron Rivar, and in the character of her brother) was her brother at all. Report pointed to the Baron as a gambler at every 'table' on the Continent. Report whispered that his so-called sister had narrowly escaped being implicated in a famous trial for poisoning at Vienna—that she had been known at Milan as a spy in the interests of Austria—that her 'apartment' in Paris had been denounced to the police as nothing less than a private gambling-house—and that her present appearance in England was the natural result of the discovery. Only one member of the assembly in the smoking-room took the part of this much-abused woman, and declared that her character had been most cruelly and most unjustly assailed. But as the man was a lawyer, his interference went for nothing: it was naturally attributed to the spirit of contradiction inherent in his profession. He was asked derisively what he thought of the circumstances under which the Countess had become engaged to be married; and he made the characteristic answer, that he thought the circumstances highly creditable to both parties, and that he looked on the lady's future husband as a most enviable man.

Hearing this, the Doctor raised another shout of astonishment by inquiring the name of the gentleman whom the Countess was about to marry.

His friends in the smoking-room decided unanimously that the celebrated physician must be a second 'Rip-van-Winkle,'* and that he had just awakened from a supernatural sleep of twenty years. It was all very well to say that he was devoted to his profession, and that he had neither time nor inclination to pick up fragments of gossip at dinner-parties and balls. A man who did not know that the Countess Narona had borrowed money at Homburg* of no less a person than Lord Montbarry, and had then deluded him into making her a proposal of marriage, was a man who had probably never heard of Lord Montbarry himself. The younger members of the club, humouring the joke, sent a waiter for the 'Peerage',* and read aloud the memoir of the nobleman in question, for the Doctor's benefit— with illustrative morsels of information interpolated by themselves.

'Herbert John Westwick. First Baron Montbarry, of Montbarry, King's County, Ireland. Created a Peer for distinguished military services in India. Born, 1812. Forty-eight years old, Doctor, at the present time. Not married. Will be married next week, Doctor, to the delightful creature we have been talking about. Heir presumptive, his lordship's next brother, Stephen Robert, married to Ella, youngest daughter of the Reverend Silas Marden, Rector of Runnigate, and has issue, three daughters. Younger brothers of his lordship, Francis and Henry, unmarried. Sisters of his lordship, Lady Barville, married to Sir Theodore Barville, Bart.; and Anne, widow of the late Peter Norbury, Esq., of Norbury Cross. Bear his lordship's relations well in mind, Doctor. Three brothers Westwick, Stephen, Francis, and Henry; and two sisters, Lady Barville and Mrs Norbury. Not one of the five will be present at the marriage; and not one of the five will leave a stone unturned to stop it, if the Countess will only give them a chance. Add to these hostile members of the family another offended relative not mentioned in the "Peerage," a young lady———'

A sudden outburst of protest in more than one part of the room stopped the coming disclosure, and released the Doctor from further persecution.

'Don't mention the poor girl's name; it's too bad to make a joke of that part of the business; she has behaved nobly under shameful provocation; there is but one excuse for Montbarry—he is either a madman or a fool.' In these terms the protest expressed itself on all sides. Speaking confidentially to his next neighbour, the Doctor discovered that the lady referred to was already known to him (through the Countess's confession) as the lady deserted by Lord Montbarry. Her name was Agnes Lockwood. She was described as being the superior of the Countess in personal attraction, and as being also by some years the younger woman of the two. Making all allowance for the follies that men committed every day in their relations with women, Montbarry's delusion was still the most monstrous delusion on record. In this expression of opinion every man present agreed—the lawyer even included. Not one of them could call to mind the innumerable instances in which the sexual influence has proved irresistible in the persons of women without even the pretension to beauty. The very members of the club whom the Countess (in spite of her personal disadvantages) could have most easily fascinated, if she had thought it worth her while, were the members who wondered most loudly at Montbarry's choice of a wife.

While the topic of the Countess's marriage was still the one topic of conversation, a member of the club entered the smoking-room whose appearance instantly produced a dead silence. Doctor Wybrow's next neighbour whispered to him, 'Montbarry's brother—Henry Westwick!'

The new-comer looked round him slowly, with a bitter smile.

'You are all talking of my brother,' he said. 'Don't mind me. Not one of you can despise him more heartily than I do. Go on, gentlemen—go on!'

But one man present took the speaker at his word. That man was the lawyer who had already undertaken the defence of the Countess.

'I stand alone in my opinion,' he said, 'and I am not ashamed of repeating it in anybody's hearing. I consider the Countess Narona to be a cruelly-treated woman. Why shouldn't she be Lord Montbarry's wife? Who can say she has a mercenary motive in marrying him?'

Montbarry's brother turned sharply on the speaker. '*I* say it!' he answered.

The reply might have shaken some men. The lawyer stood on his ground as firmly as ever.

'I believe I am right,' he rejoined, 'in stating that his lordship's income is not more than sufficient to support his station in life; also that it is an income derived almost entirely from landed property in Ireland, every acre of which is entailed.'

Montbarry's brother made a sign, admitting that he had no objection to offer so far.

'If his lordship dies first,' the lawyer proceeded, 'I have been informed that the only provision he can make for his widow consists in a rent-charge* on the property of no more than four hundred a year. His retiring pension and allowances, it is well known, die with him. Four hundred a year is therefore all that he can leave to the Countess, if he leaves her a widow.'

'Four hundred a year is *not* all,' was the reply to this. 'My brother has insured his life for ten thousand pounds; and he has settled the whole of it on the Countess, in the event of his death.'

This announcement produced a strong sensation. Men looked at each other, and repeated the three startling words, 'Ten thousand pounds!' Driven fairly to the wall, the lawyer made a last effort to defend his position.

'May I ask who made that settlement a condition of the marriage?' he said. 'Surely it was not the Countess herself?'

Henry Westwick answered, 'It was the Countess's brother'; and added, 'which comes to the same thing.'

After that, there was no more to be said—so long, at least, as Montbarry's brother was present. The talk flowed into other channels; and the Doctor went home.

But his morbid curiosity about the Countess was not set at rest yet. In his leisure moments he found himself wondering whether Lord Montbarry's family would succeed in stopping the marriage after all. And more than this, he was conscious of a growing desire to see the infatuated man himself. Every day during the brief interval before the wedding, he looked in at the club, on the chance of hearing some news. Nothing had happened, so far as the club knew. The Countess's position was secure; Montbarry's resolution to be her husband was unshaken. They were both Roman Catholics, and they were to be married at the chapel in Spanish Place. So much the Doctor discovered about them—and no more.

On the day of the wedding, after a feeble struggle with himself, he actually sacrificed his patients and their guineas, and slipped away secretly to see the marriage. To the end of his life, he was angry with anybody who reminded him of what he had done on that day!

The wedding was strictly private. A close carriage stood at the church door; a few people, mostly of the lower class, and mostly old women, were scattered about the interior of the building. Here and there Doctor Wybrow detected the faces of some of his brethren of the club, attracted by curiosity, like himself. Four persons only stood before the altar—the bride and bridegroom and their two witnesses. One of these last was an elderly woman, who might have been the Countess's companion or maid; the other was undoubtedly her brother, Baron Rivar. The bridal party (the bride herself included) wore their ordinary morning costume. Lord Montbarry, personally viewed, was a middle-aged military man of the ordinary type: nothing in the least remarkable distinguished him either in face or figure. Baron Rivar, again, in his way was another conventional representative of another well-known type. One sees his finely-pointed moustache, his bold eyes, his crisply-curling hair, and his dashing carriage of the head, repeated hundreds of times over on the Boulevards of Paris. The only noteworthy point about him was of the negative sort—he was not in the least like his sister. Even the officiating priest was only a harmless, humble-looking old man, who went through his duties resignedly, and felt visible rheumatic difficulties every time he bent his knees. The one remarkable person, the Countess herself, only raised her veil at the beginning of the ceremony, and presented nothing in her plain dress that was worth a second look. Never, on the face of it, was there a less interesting and less romantic marriage than this. From time to time the Doctor glanced round at the door or up at the galleries, vaguely anticipating the appearance of some protesting stranger, in possession of some terrible secret, commissioned to forbid the progress of the service. Nothing in the shape of an event occurred—nothing extraordinary, nothing dramatic. Bound fast together as man and wife, the two disappeared, followed by their witnesses, to sign the registers; and still Doctor Wybrow waited, and still he cherished the obstinate hope that something worth seeing must certainly happen yet.

The interval passed, and the married couple, returning to the church, walked together down the nave to the door. Doctor Wybrow drew back as they approached. To his confusion and surprise, the Countess discovered him. He heard her say to her husband, 'One moment; I see a friend.' Lord Montbarry bowed and waited. She stepped up to the Doctor, took his hand, and wrung it hard. He felt her overpowering black eyes looking at him through her veil. 'One step more, you see, on the way to the end!' She whispered those strange words, and returned to her husband. Before the Doctor could recover himself and follow her, Lord and Lady Montbarry had stepped into their carriage, and had driven away.

Outside the church door stood the three or four members of the club who, like Doctor Wybrow, had watched the ceremony out of curiosity. Near them was the bride's brother, waiting alone. He was evidently bent on seeing the man whom his sister had spoken to, in broad daylight. His bold eyes rested on the Doctor's face, with a momentary flash of suspicion in them. The cloud suddenly cleared away; the Baron smiled with charming courtesy, lifted his hat to his sister's friend, and walked off.

The members constituted themselves into a club conclave on the church steps. They began with the Baron. 'Damned ill-looking rascal!' They went on with Montbarry. 'Is he going to take that horrid woman with him to Ireland?' 'Not he! he can't face the tenantry; they know about Agnes Lockwood.' 'Well, but where *is* he going?' 'To Scotland.' 'Does *she* like that?' 'It's only for a fortnight; they come back to London, and go abroad.' 'And they will never return to England, eh?' 'Who can tell? Did you see how she looked at Montbarry, when she had to lift her veil at the beginning of the service? In his place, I should have bolted. Did *you* see her, Doctor?' By this time, Doctor Wybrow had remembered his patients, and had heard enough of the club gossip. He followed the example of Baron Rivar, and walked off.

'One step more, you see, on the way to the end,' he repeated to himself, on his way home. 'What end?'

## CHAPTER IV

On the day of the marriage Agnes Lockwood sat alone in the little drawing-room of her London lodgings, burning the letters which had been written to her by Montbarry in the bygone time.

The Countess's maliciously smart description of her, addressed to Doctor Wybrow, had not even hinted at the charm that most distinguished Agnes—the artless expression of goodness and purity which instantly attracted everyone who approached her. She looked by many years younger than she really was. With her fair complexion and her shy manner, it seemed only natural to speak of her as 'a girl,' although she was now really advancing towards thirty years of age. She lived alone with an old nurse devoted to her, on a modest little income which was just enough to support the two. There were none of the ordinary signs of grief in her face, as she slowly tore the letters of her false lover in two, and threw the pieces into the small fire which had been lit to consume them. Unhappily for herself, she was one of those women who feel too deeply to find relief in tears. Pale and quiet, with cold trembling fingers, she destroyed the letters one by one without daring to read them again. She had torn the last of the series, and was still shrinking from throwing it after the rest into the swiftly destroying flame, when the old nurse came in, and asked if she would see 'Master Henry,'—meaning that youngest member of the Westwick family, who had publicly declared his contempt for his brother in the smoking-room of the club.

Agnes hesitated. A faint tinge of colour stole over her face.

There had been a long past time when Henry Westwick had owned that he loved her. She had made her confession to him, acknowledging that her heart was given to his eldest brother. He had submitted to his disappointment; and they had met thenceforth as cousins and friends. Never before had she associated the idea of him with embarrassing recollections. But now, on the very day when his brother's marriage to another woman had consummated his brother's treason towards her, there was something vaguely repellent in the prospect of seeing him. The old nurse (who remembered them both in their cradles) observed her hesitation; and sympathising of course with the man, put in a timely word for Henry. 'He says, he's going away, my dear; and he only wants to shake hands, and say good-bye.' This plain statement of the case had its effect. Agnes decided on receiving her cousin.

He entered the room so rapidly that he surprised her in the act of throwing the fragments of Montbarry's last letter into the fire. She hurriedly spoke first.

'You are leaving London very suddenly, Henry. Is it business? or pleasure?'

Instead of answering her, he pointed to the flaming letter, and to some black ashes of burnt paper lying lightly in the lower part of the fireplace.

'Are you burning letters?'

'Yes.'

'*His* letters?'

'Yes.'

He took her hand gently. 'I had no idea I was intruding on you, at a time when you must wish to be alone. Forgive me, Agnes—I shall see you when I return.'

She signed to him, with a faint smile, to take a chair.

'We have known one another since we were children,' she said. 'Why should I feel a foolish pride about myself in your presence? Why should I have any secrets from you? I sent back all your brother's gifts to me some time ago. I have been advised to do more, to keep nothing that can remind me of him—in short, to burn his letters. I have taken the advice; but I own I shrank a little from destroying the last of the letters. No—not because it was the last, but because it had this in it.' She opened her hand, and showed him a lock of Montbarry's hair, tied with a morsel of golden cord. 'Well! well! let it go with the rest.'

She dropped it into the flame. For a while, she stood with her back to Henry, leaning on the mantel-piece, and looking into the fire. He took the chair to which she had pointed, with a strange contradiction of expression in his face: the tears were in his eyes, while the brows above were knit close in an angry frown. He muttered to himself, 'Damn him!'

She rallied her courage, and looked at him again when she spoke. 'Well, Henry, and why are you going away?'

'I am out of spirits, Agnes, and I want a change.'

She paused before she spoke again. His face told her plainly that he was thinking of *her* when he made that reply. She was grateful to him, but her mind was not with him: her mind was still with the man who had deserted her. She turned round again to the fire.

'Is it true,' she asked, after a long silence, 'that they have been married to-day?'

He answered ungraciously in the one necessary word:—'Yes.'

'Did you go to the church?'

He resented the question with an expression of indignant surprise. 'Go to the church?' he repeated. 'I would as soon go to——' He checked himself there. 'How can you ask?' he added in lower tones. 'I have never spoken to Montbarry, I have not even seen him, since he treated you like the scoundrel and the fool that he is.'

She looked at him suddenly, without saying a word. He understood her, and begged her pardon. But he was still angry. 'The reckoning comes to some men,' he said, 'even in this world. He will live to rue the day when he married that woman!'

Agnes took a chair by his side, and looked at him with a gentle surprise.

'Is it quite reasonable to be so angry with her, because your brother preferred her to me?' she asked.

Henry turned on her sharply. 'Do *you* defend the Countess, of all the people in the world?'

'Why not?' Agnes answered. 'I know nothing against her. On the only occasion when we met, she appeared to be a singularly timid, nervous person, looking dreadfully ill; and *being* indeed so ill that she fainted under the heat of the room. Why should we not do her justice? We know that she was innocent of any intention to wrong me; we know that she was not aware of my engagement——'

Henry lifted his hand impatiently, and stopped her. 'There is such a thing as being *too* just and *too* forgiving!' he interposed. 'I can't bear to hear you talk in that patient way, after the scandalously cruel manner in which you have been treated. Try to forget them both, Agnes. I wish to God I could help you to do it!'

Agnes laid her hand on his arm. 'You are very good to me, Henry; but you don't quite understand me. I was thinking of myself and my trouble in quite a different way, when you came in. I was wondering whether anything which has so entirely filled my heart, and so absorbed all that is best and truest in me, as my feeling for your brother, can really pass away as if it had never existed. I have destroyed the last visible things that remind me of him. In this world I shall see him no more. But is the tie that once bound us, completely broken? Am I as entirely parted from the good and evil fortune of his life as if we had never met and never loved? What do *you* think, Henry? I can hardly believe it.'

'If you could bring the retribution on him that he has deserved,' Henry Westwick answered sternly, 'I might be inclined to agree with you.'

As that reply passed his lips, the old nurse appeared again at the door, announcing another visitor.

'I'm sorry to disturb you, my dear. But here is little Mrs Ferrari wanting to know when she may say a few words to you.'

Agnes turned to Henry, before she replied. 'You remember Emily Bidwell, my favourite pupil years ago at the village school, and afterwards my maid? She left me, to marry an Italian courier, named Ferrari—and I am afraid it has not turned out very well. Do you mind my having her in here for a minute or two?'

Henry rose to take his leave. 'I should be glad to see Emily again at any other time,' he said. 'But it is best that I should go now. My mind is disturbed, Agnes; I might say things to you, if I stayed here any longer, which—which are better not said now. I shall cross the Channel by the mail to-night, and see how a few weeks' change will help me.' He took her hand. 'Is there anything in the world that I can do for you?' he asked very earnestly. She thanked him, and tried to release her hand. He held it with a tremulous lingering grasp. 'God bless you, Agnes!' he said in faltering tones, with his eyes on the ground. Her face flushed again, and the next instant turned paler than ever; she knew his heart as well as he knew it himself—she was too distressed to speak. He lifted her hand to his lips, kissed it fervently, and, without looking at her again, left the room. The nurse hobbled after him to the head of the stairs: she had not forgotten the time when the younger brother had been the unsuccessful rival of the elder for the hand of Agnes. 'Don't be down-hearted, Master Henry,' whispered the old woman, with the unscrupulous common sense of persons in the lower rank of life. 'Try her again, when you come back!'

Left alone for a few moments, Agnes took a turn in the room, trying to compose herself. She paused before a little water-colour drawing on the wall, which had belonged to her mother: it was her own portrait when she was a child. 'How much happier we should be,' she thought to herself sadly, 'if we never grew up!'

The courier's wife was shown in—a little meek melancholy woman, with white eyelashes, and watery eyes, who curtseyed deferentially and was troubled with a small chronic cough. Agnes shook hands with her kindly. 'Well, Emily, what can I do for you?'

The courier's wife made rather a strange answer: 'I'm afraid to tell you, Miss.'

'Is it such a very difficult favour to grant? Sit down, and let me hear how you are going on. Perhaps the petition will slip out while we are talking. How does your husband behave to you?'

Emily's light grey eyes looked more watery than ever. She shook her head and sighed resignedly. 'I have no positive complaint to make against him, Miss. But I'm afraid he doesn't care about me; and he seems to take no interest in his home—I may almost say he's tired of his home. It might be better for both of us, Miss, if he went travelling for a while—not to mention the money, which is beginning to be wanted sadly.' She put her handkerchief to her eyes, and sighed again more resignedly than ever.

'I don't quite understand,' said Agnes. 'I thought your husband had an engagement to take some ladies to Switzerland and Italy?'

'That was his ill-luck, Miss. One of the ladies fell ill—and the others wouldn't go without her. They paid him a month's salary as compensation. But they had engaged him for the autumn and winter—and the loss is serious.'

'I am sorry to hear it, Emily. Let us hope he will soon have another chance.'

'It's not his turn, Miss, to be recommended when the next applications come to the couriers' office. You see, there are so many of them out of employment just now. If he could be privately recommended——' She stopped, and left the unfinished sentence to speak for itself.

Agnes understood her directly. 'You want my recommendation,' she rejoined. 'Why couldn't you say so at once?'

Emily blushed. 'It would be such a chance for my husband,' she answered confusedly. 'A letter, inquiring for a good courier (a six months' engagement, Miss!) came to the office this morning. It's another man's turn to be chosen—and the secretary will recommend him. If my husband could only send his testimonials by the same post—with just a word in your name, Miss—it might turn the scale, as they say. A private recommendation between gentlefolks goes so far.' She stopped again, and sighed again, and looked down at the carpet, as if she had some private reason for feeling a little ashamed of herself.

Agnes began to be rather weary of the persistent tone of mystery in which her visitor spoke. 'If you want my interest with any friend of mine,' she said, 'why can't you tell me the name?'

The courier's wife began to cry. 'I'm ashamed to tell you, Miss.'

For the first time, Agnes spoke sharply. 'Nonsense, Emily! Tell me the name directly—or drop the subject—whichever you like best.'

Emily made a last desperate effort. She wrung her handkerchief hard in her lap, and let off the name as if she had been letting off a loaded gun:— 'Lord Montbarry!'

Agnes rose and looked at her.

'You have disappointed me,' she said very quietly, but with a look which the courier's wife had never seen in her face before. 'Knowing what you know, you ought to be aware that it is impossible for me to communicate with Lord Montbarry. I always supposed you had some delicacy of feeling. I am sorry to find that I have been mistaken.'

Weak as she was, Emily had spirit enough to feel the reproof. She walked in her meek noiseless way to the door. 'I beg your pardon, Miss. I am not quite so bad as you think me. But I beg your pardon, all the same.'

She opened the door. Agnes called her back. There was something in the woman's apology that appealed irresistibly to her just and generous nature. 'Come,' she said; 'we must not part in this way. Let me not misunderstand you. What *is* it that you expected me to do?'

Emily was wise enough to answer this time without any reserve. 'My husband will send his testimonials, Miss, to Lord Montbarry in Scotland. I only wanted you to let him say in his letter that his wife has been known to you since she was a child, and that you feel some little interest in his welfare on that account. I don't ask it now, Miss. You have made me understand that I was wrong.'

Had she really been wrong? Past remembrances, as well as present troubles, pleaded powerfully with Agnes for the courier's wife. 'It seems only a small favour to ask,' she said, speaking under the impulse of kindness which was the strongest impulse in her nature. 'But I am not sure that I ought to allow my name to be mentioned in your husband's letter. Let me hear again exactly what he wishes to say.' Emily repeated the words—and then offered one of those suggestions, which have a special value of their own to persons unaccustomed to the use of their pens. 'Suppose you try, Miss, how it looks in writing?' Childish as the idea was, Agnes tried the experiment. 'If I let you mention me,' she said, 'we must at least decide what you are to say.' She wrote the words in the briefest and plainest form:—'I venture to state that my wife has been known from her childhood to Miss Agnes Lockwood, who feels some little interest in my welfare on that account.' Reduced to this one sentence, there was surely nothing in the reference to her name which implied that Agnes had permitted it, or that she was even aware of it. After a last struggle with herself, she handed the written paper to Emily. 'Your husband must copy it exactly, without altering anything,' she stipulated. 'On that condition, I grant your request.' Emily was not only thankful— she was really touched. Agnes hurried the little woman out of the room. 'Don't give me time to repent and take it back again,' she said. Emily vanished.

'Is the tie that once bound us completely broken? Am I as entirely parted from the good and evil fortune of his life as if we had never met and never loved?' Agnes looked at the clock on the mantel-piece. Not ten minutes since, those serious questions had been on her lips. It almost shocked her to think of the commonplace manner in which they had already met with their reply. The mail of that night would appeal once more to Montbarry's remembrance of her—in the choice of a servant.

Two days later, the post brought a few grateful lines from Emily. Her husband had got the place. Ferrari was engaged, for six months certain, as Lord Montbarry's courier.

# THE SECOND PART

## CHAPTER V

After only one week of travelling in Scotland, my lord and my lady returned unexpectedly to London. Introduced to the mountains and lakes of the Highlands, her ladyship positively declined to improve her acquaintance with them. When she was asked for her reason, she answered with a Roman brevity, 'I have seen Switzerland.'

For a week more, the newly-married couple remained in London, in the strictest retirement. On one day in that week the nurse returned in a state of most uncustomary excitement from an errand on which Agnes had sent her. Passing the door of a fashionable dentist, she had met Lord Montbarry himself just leaving the house. The good woman's report described him, with malicious pleasure, as looking wretchedly ill. 'His cheeks are getting hollow, my dear, and his beard is turning grey. I hope the dentist hurt him!'

Knowing how heartily her faithful old servant hated the man who had deserted her, Agnes made due allowance for a large infusion of exaggeration in the picture presented to her. The main impression produced on her mind was an impression of nervous uneasiness. If she trusted herself in the streets by daylight while Lord Montbarry remained in London, how could she be sure that his next chance-meeting might not be a meeting with herself? She waited at home, privately ashamed of her own undignified conduct, for the next two days. On the third day the fashionable intelligence of the newspapers announced the departure of Lord and Lady Montbarry for Paris, on their way to Italy.

Mrs Ferrari, calling the same evening, informed Agnes that her husband had left her with all reasonable expression of conjugal kindness; his temper being improved by the prospect of going abroad. But one other servant accompanied the travellers—Lady Montbarry's maid, rather a silent, unsociable woman, so far as Emily had heard. Her ladyship's brother, Baron Rivar, was already on the Continent. It had been arranged that he was to meet his sister and her husband at Rome.

One by one the dull weeks succeeded each other in the life of Agnes. She faced her position with admirable courage, seeing her friends, keeping herself occupied in her leisure hours with reading and drawing, leaving no means untried of diverting her mind from the melancholy remembrance of the past. But she had loved too faithfully, she had been wounded too deeply, to feel in any adequate degree the influence of the moral remedies which she employed. Persons who met with her in the ordinary relations of life, deceived by her outward serenity of manner, agreed that 'Miss Lockwood seemed to be getting over her disappointment.' But an old friend and school companion who happened to see her during a brief visit to London, was inexpressibly distressed by the change that she detected in Agnes. This lady was Mrs Westwick, the wife of that brother of Lord Montbarry who came next to him in age, and who was described in the 'Peerage' as presumptive heir to the title. He was then away, looking after his interests in some mining property which he possessed in America. Mrs Westwick insisted on taking Agnes back with her to her home in Ireland. 'Come and keep me company while my husband is away. My three little girls will make you their playfellow, and the only stranger you will meet is the governess, whom I answer for your liking beforehand. Pack up your things, and I will call for you to-morrow on my way to the train.' In those hearty terms the invitation was given. Agnes thankfully accepted it. For three happy months she lived under the roof of her friend. The girls hung round her in tears at her departure; the youngest of them wanted to go back with Agnes to London. Half in jest, half in earnest, she said to her old friend at parting, 'If your governess leaves you, keep the place open for me.' Mrs Westwick laughed. The wiser children took it seriously, and promised to let Agnes know.

On the very day when Miss Lockwood returned to London, she was recalled to those associations with the past which she was most anxious to forget. After the first kissings and greetings were over, the old nurse (who had been left in charge at the lodgings) had some startling information to communicate, derived from the courier's wife.

'Here has been little Mrs Ferrari, my dear, in a dreadful state of mind, inquiring when you would be back. Her husband has left Lord Montbarry, without a word of warning—and nobody knows what has become of him.'

Agnes looked at her in astonishment. 'Are you sure of what you are saying?' she asked.

The nurse was quite sure. 'Why, Lord bless you! the news comes from the couriers' office in Golden Square—from the secretary, Miss Agnes, the secretary himself!' Hearing this, Agnes began to feel alarmed as well as surprised. It was still early in the evening. She at once sent a message to Mrs Ferrari, to say that she had returned.

In an hour more the courier's wife appeared, in a state of agitation which it was not easy to control. Her narrative, when she was at last able to speak connectedly, entirely confirmed the nurse's report of it.

After hearing from her husband with tolerable regularity from Paris, Rome, and Venice, Emily had twice written to him after-wards—and had received no reply. Feeling uneasy, she had gone to the office in Golden Square, to inquire if he had been heard of there. The post of the morning had brought a letter to the secretary from a courier then at Venice. It contained startling news of Ferrari. His wife had been allowed to take a copy of it, which she now handed to Agnes to read.

The writer stated that he had recently arrived in Venice. He had previously heard that Ferrari was with Lord and Lady Montbarry, at one of the old Venetian palaces which they had hired for a term. Being a friend of Ferrari, he had gone to pay him a visit. Ringing at the door that opened on the canal, and failing to make anyone hear him, he had gone round to a side entrance opening on one of the narrow lanes of Venice. Here, standing at the door (as if she was waiting for him to try that way next), he found a pale woman with magnificent dark eyes, who proved to be no other than Lady Montbarry herself.

She asked, in Italian, what he wanted. He answered that he wanted to see the courier Ferrari, if it was quite convenient. She at once informed him that Ferrari had left the palace, without assigning any reason, and without even leaving an address at which his monthly salary (then due to him) could be paid. Amazed at this reply, the courier inquired if any person had offended Ferrari, or quarrelled with him. The lady answered, 'To my knowledge, certainly not. I am Lady Montbarry; and I can positively assure you that Ferrari was treated with the greatest kindness in this house. We are as much astonished as you are at his extraordinary disappearance. If you should hear of him, pray let us know, so that we may at least pay him the money which is due.'

After one or two more questions (quite readily answered) relating to the date and the time of day at which Ferrari had left the palace, the courier took his leave.

He at once entered on the necessary investigations—without the slightest result so far as Ferrari was concerned. Nobody had seen him. Nobody appeared to have been taken into his confidence. Nobody knew anything (that is to say, anything of the slightest importance) even about persons so distinguished as Lord and Lady Montbarry. It was reported that her ladyship's English maid had left her, before the disappearance of Ferrari, to return to her relatives in her own country, and that Lady Montbarry had taken no steps to supply her place. His lordship was described as being in delicate health. He lived in the strictest retirement—nobody was admitted to him, not even his own countrymen. A stupid old woman was discovered who did the housework at the palace, arriving in the morning and going away again at night. She had never seen the lost courier—she had never even seen Lord Montbarry, who was then confined to his room. Her ladyship, 'a most gracious and adorable mistress,' was in constant attendance on her noble husband. There was no other servant then in the house (so far as the old woman knew) but herself. The meals were sent in from a restaurant. My lord, it was said, disliked strangers. My lord's brother-in-law, the Baron, was generally shut up in a remote part of the palace, occupied (the gracious mistress said) with experiments in chemistry. The experiments sometimes made a nasty smell. A doctor had latterly been called in to his lordship—an Italian doctor, long resident in Venice. Inquiries being addressed to this gentleman (a physician of undoubted capacity and respectability), it turned out that he also had never seen Ferrari, having been summoned to the palace (as his memorandum book showed) at a date subsequent to the courier's disappearance. The doctor described Lord Montbarry's malady as bronchitis. So far, there was no reason to feel any anxiety, though the attack was a sharp one. If alarming symptoms should appear, he had arranged with her ladyship to call in another physician. For the rest, it was impossible to speak too highly of my lady; night and day, she was at her lord's bedside.

With these particulars began and ended the discoveries made by Ferrari's courier-friend. The police were on the look-out for the lost man—and that was the only hope which could be held forth for the present, to Ferrari's wife.

'What do you think of it, Miss?' the poor woman asked eagerly. 'What would you advise me to do?'

Agnes was at a loss how to answer her; it was an effort even to listen to what Emily was saying. The references in the courier's letter to Montbarry—the report of his illness, the melancholy picture of his secluded life—had reopened the old wound. She was not even thinking of the lost Ferrari; her mind was at Venice, by the sick man's bedside.

'I hardly know what to say,' she answered. 'I have had no experience in serious matters of this kind.'

'Do you think it would help you, Miss, if you read my husband's letters to me? There are only three of them—they won't take long to read.'

Agnes compassionately read the letters.

They were not written in a very tender tone. 'Dear Emily,' and 'Yours affectionately'—these conventional phrases, were the only phrases of endearment which they contained. In the first letter, Lord Montbarry was not very favourably spoken of:—'We leave Paris to-morrow. I don't much like my lord. He is proud and cold, and, between ourselves, stingy in money matters. I have had to dispute such trifles as a few centimes in the hotel bill; and twice already, some sharp remarks have passed between the newly-married couple, in consequence of her ladyship's freedom in purchasing pretty tempting things at the shops in Paris. "I can't afford it; you must keep to your allowance." She has had to hear those words already. For my part, I like her. She has the nice, easy foreign manners—*she* talks to me as if I was a human being like herself.'

The second letter was dated from Rome.

'My lord's caprices' (Ferrari wrote) 'have kept us perpetually on the move. He is becoming incurably restless. I suspect he is uneasy in his mind. Painful recollections, I should say—I find him constantly reading old letters, when her ladyship is not present. We were to have stopped at Genoa, but he hurried us on. The same thing at Florence. Here, at Rome, my lady insists on resting. Her brother has met us at this place. There has been a quarrel already (the lady's maid tells me) between my lord and the Baron. The latter wanted to borrow money of the former. His lordship refused in language which offended Baron Rivar. My lady pacified them, and made them shake hands.'

The third, and last letter, was from Venice.

'More of my lord's economy! Instead of staying at the hotel, we have hired a damp, mouldy, rambling old palace. My lady insists on having the best suites of rooms wherever we go—and the palace comes cheaper for a two months' term. My lord tried to get it for longer; he says the quiet of Venice is good for his nerves. But a foreign speculator has secured the palace, and is going to turn it into an hotel. The Baron is still with us, and there have been more disagreements about money matters. I don't like the Baron—and I don't find the attractions of my lady grow on me. She was much nicer before the Baron joined us. My lord is a punctual paymaster; it's a matter of honour with him; he hates parting with his money, but he does it because he has given his word. I receive my salary regularly at the end of each month—not a franc extra, though I have done many things which are not part of a courier's proper work. Fancy the Baron trying to borrow money of *me*! he is an inveterate gambler. I didn't believe it when my lady's maid first told me so—but I have seen enough since to satisfy me that she was right. I have seen other things besides, which—well! which don't increase my respect for my lady and the Baron. The maid says she means to give warning to leave. She is a respectable British female, and doesn't take things quite so easily as I do. It is a dull life here. No going into company—no company at home—not a creature sees my lord—not even the consul, or the banker. When he goes out, he goes alone, and generally towards nightfall. Indoors, he shuts himself up in his own room with his books, and sees as little of his wife and the Baron as possible. I fancy things are coming to a crisis here. If my lord's suspicions are once awakened, the consequences will be terrible. Under certain provocations, the noble Montbarry is a man who would stick at nothing. However, the pay is good—and I can't afford to talk of leaving the place, like my lady's maid.'

Agnes handed back the letters—so suggestive of the penalty paid already for his own infatuation by the man who had deserted her!—with feelings of shame and distress, which made her no fit counsellor for the helpless woman who depended on her advice.

'The one thing I can suggest,' she said, after first speaking some kind words of comfort and hope, 'is that we should consult a person of greater experience than ours. Suppose I write and ask my lawyer (who is also my friend and trustee) to come and advise us to-morrow after his business hours?'

Emily eagerly and gratefully accepted the suggestion. An hour was arranged for the meeting on the next day; the correspondence was left under the care of Agnes; and the courier's wife took her leave.

Weary and heartsick, Agnes lay down on the sofa, to rest and compose herself. The careful nurse brought in a reviving cup of tea. Her quaint gossip about herself and her occupations while Agnes had been away, acted as a relief to her mistress's overburdened mind. They were still talking quietly, when they were startled by a loud knock at the house door. Hurried footsteps ascended the stairs. The door of the sitting-room was thrown open violently; the courier's wife rushed in like a mad woman. 'He's dead! they've murdered him!' Those wild words were all she could say. She dropped on her knees at the foot of the sofa—held out her hand with something clasped in it—and fell back in a swoon.

The nurse, signing to Agnes to open the window, took the necessary measures to restore the fainting woman. 'What's this?' she exclaimed. 'Here's a letter in her hand. See what it is, Miss.'

The open envelope was addressed (evidently in a feigned handwriting) to 'Mrs Ferrari.' The post-mark was 'Venice.' The contents of the envelope were a sheet of foreign note-paper, and a folded enclosure.

On the note-paper, one line only was written. It was again in a feigned handwriting, and it contained these words:

'*To console you for the loss of your husband.*'

Agnes opened the enclosure next.

It was a Bank of England note for a thousand pounds.

## CHAPTER VI

The next day, the friend and legal adviser of Agnes Lockwood, Mr Troy, called on her by appointment in the evening.

Mrs Ferrari—still persisting in the conviction of her husband's death—had sufficiently recovered to be present at the consultation. Assisted by Agnes, she told the lawyer the little that was known relating to Ferrari's disappearance, and then produced the correspondence connected with that event. Mr Troy read (first) the three letters addressed by Ferrari to his wife; (secondly) the letter written by Ferrari's courier-friend, describing his visit to the palace and his interview with Lady Montbarry; and (thirdly) the one line of anonymous writing which had accompanied the extraordinary gift of a thousand pounds to Ferrari's wife.

Well known, at a later period, as the lawyer who acted for Lady Lydiard, in the case of theft, generally described as the case of 'My Lady's Money,'* Mr Troy was not only a man of learning and experience in his profession—he was also a man who had seen something of society at home and abroad. He possessed a keen eye for character, a quaint humour, and a kindly nature which had not been deteriorated even by a lawyer's professional experience of mankind. With all these personal advantages, it is a question, nevertheless, whether he was the fittest adviser whom Agnes could have chosen under the circumstances. Little Mrs Ferrari, with many domestic merits, was an essentially commonplace woman. Mr Troy was the last person living who was likely to attract her sympathies—he was the exact opposite of a commonplace man.

'She looks very ill, poor thing!' In these words the lawyer opened the business of the evening, referring to Mrs Ferrari as unceremoniously as if she had been out of the room.

'She has suffered a terrible shock,' Agnes answered.

Mr Troy turned to Mrs Ferrari, and looked at her again, with the interest due to the victim of a shock. He drummed absently with his fingers on the table. At last he spoke to her.

'My good lady, you don't really believe that your husband is dead?'

Mrs Ferrari put her handkerchief to her eyes. The word 'dead' was ineffectual to express her feelings. 'Murdered!' she said sternly, behind her handkerchief.

'Why? And by whom?' Mr Troy asked.

Mrs Ferrari seemed to have some difficulty in answering. 'You have read my husband's letters, sir,' she began. 'I believe he discovered——' She got as far as that, and there she stopped.

'What did he discover?'

There are limits to human patience—even the patience of a bereaved wife. This cool question irritated Mrs Ferrari into expressing herself plainly at last.

'He discovered Lady Montbarry and the Baron!' she answered, with a burst of hysterical vehemence. 'The Baron is no more that vile woman's brother than I am. The wickedness of those two wretches came to my poor dear husband's knowledge. The lady's maid left her place on account of it. If Ferrari had gone away too, he would have been alive at this moment. They have killed him. I say they have killed him, to prevent it from getting to Lord Montbarry's ears.' So, in short sharp sentences, and in louder and louder accents, Mrs Ferrari stated *her* opinion of the case.

Still keeping his own view in reserve, Mr Troy listened with an expression of satirical approval.

'Very strongly stated, Mrs Ferrari,' he said. 'You build up your sentences well; you clinch your conclusions in a workmanlike manner. If you had been a man, you would have made a good lawyer—you would have taken juries by the scruff of their necks. Complete the case, my good lady—complete the case. Tell us next who sent you this letter, enclosing the bank-note. The "two wretches" who murdered Mr Ferrari would hardly put their hands in their pockets and send you a thousand pounds. Who is it—eh? I see the post-mark on the letter is "Venice." Have you any friend in that interesting city, with a large heart, and a purse to correspond, who has been let into the secret and who wishes to console you anonymously?'

It was not easy to reply to this. Mrs Ferrari began to feel the first inward approaches of something like hatred towards Mr Troy. 'I don't understand you, sir,' she answered. 'I don't think this is a joking matter.'

Agnes interfered, for the first time. She drew her chair a little nearer to her legal counsellor and friend.

'What is the most probable explanation, in your opinion?' she asked.

'I shall offend Mrs Ferrari if I tell you,' Mr Troy answered.

'No, sir, you won't!' cried Mrs Ferrari, hating Mr Troy undisguisedly by this time.

The lawyer leaned back in his chair. 'Very well,' he said, in his most good-humoured manner. 'Let's have it out. Observe, madam, I don't dispute your view of the position of affairs at the palace in Venice. You have your husband's letters to justify you; and you have also the significant fact that Lady Montbarry's maid did really leave the house. We will say, then, that Lord Montbarry has presumably been made the victim of a foul wrong—that Mr Ferrari was the first to find it out—and that the guilty persons had reason to fear, not only that he would acquaint Lord Montbarry with his discovery, but that he would be a principal witness against them if the scandal was made public in a court of law. Now mark! Admitting all this, I draw a totally different conclusion from the conclusion at which you have arrived. Here is your husband left in this miserable household of three, under very awkward circumstances for *him*. What does he do? But for the bank-note and the written message sent to you with it, I should say that he had wisely withdrawn himself from association with a disgraceful discovery and exposure, by taking secretly to flight. The money modifies this view—unfavourably so far as Mr Ferrari is concerned. I still believe he is keeping out of the way. But I now say he is *paid* for keeping out of the way—and that bank-note there on the table is the price of his absence, sent by the guilty persons to his wife.'

Mrs Ferrari's watery grey eyes brightened suddenly; Mrs Ferrari's dull drab-coloured complexion became enlivened by a glow of brilliant red.

'It's false!' she cried. 'It's a burning shame to speak of my husband in that way!'

'I told you I should offend you!' said Mr Troy.

Agnes interposed once more—in the interests of peace. She took the offended wife's hand; she appealed to the lawyer to reconsider that side of his theory which reflected harshly on Ferrari. While she was still speaking, the servant interrupted her by entering the room with a visiting-card. It was the card of Henry Westwick; and there was an ominous request written on it in pencil. 'I bring bad news. Let me see you for a minute downstairs.' Agnes immediately left the room.

Alone with Mrs Ferrari, Mr Troy permitted his natural kindness of heart to show itself on the surface at last. He tried to make his peace with the courier's wife.

'You have every claim, my good soul, to resent a reflection cast upon your husband,' he began. 'I may even say that I respect you for speaking so warmly in his defence. At the same time, remember, that I am bound, in such a serious matter as this, to tell you what is really in my mind. I can have no intention of offending you, seeing that I am a total stranger to you and to Mr Ferrari. A thousand pounds is a large sum of money; and a poor man may excusably be tempted by it to do nothing worse than to keep out of the way for a while. My only interest, acting on your behalf, is to get at the truth. If you will give me time, I see no reason to despair of finding your husband yet.'

Ferrari's wife listened, without being convinced: her narrow little mind, filled to its extreme capacity by her unfavourable opinion of Mr Troy, had no room left for the process of correcting its first impression. 'I am much obliged to you, sir,' was all she said. Her eyes were more communicative—her eyes added, in *their* language, 'You may say what you please; I will never forgive you to my dying day.'

Mr Troy gave it up. He composedly wheeled his chair around, put his hands in his pockets, and looked out of window.

After an interval of silence, the drawing-room door was opened.

Mr Troy wheeled round again briskly to the table, expecting to see Agnes. To his surprise there appeared, in her place, a perfect stranger to him—a gentleman, in the prime of life, with a marked expression of pain and embarrassment on his handsome face. He looked at Mr Troy, and bowed gravely.

'I am so unfortunate as to have brought news to Miss Agnes Lockwood which has greatly distressed her,' he said. 'She has retired to her room. I am requested to make her excuses, and to speak to you in her place.'

Having introduced himself in those terms, he noticed Mrs Ferrari, and held out his hand to her kindly. 'It is some years since we last met, Emily,' he said. 'I am afraid you have almost forgotten the "Master Henry" of old times.' Emily, in some little confusion, made her acknowledgments, and begged to know if she could be of any use to Miss Lockwood. 'The old nurse is with her,' Henry answered; 'they will be better left together.' He turned once more to Mr Troy. 'I ought to tell you,' he said, 'that my name is Henry Westwick. I am the younger brother of the late Lord Montbarry.'

'The *late* Lord Montbarry!' Mr Troy exclaimed.

'My brother died at Venice yesterday evening. There is the telegram.' With that startling answer, he handed the paper to Mr Troy.

The message was in these words:

'Lady Montbarry, Venice. To Stephen Robert Westwick, Newbury's Hotel, London. It is useless to take the journey. Lord Montbarry died of bronchitis, at 8.40 this evening. All needful details by post.'

'Was this expected, sir?' the lawyer asked.

'I cannot say that it has taken us entirely by surprise,' Henry answered. 'My brother Stephen (who is now the head of the family) received a telegram three days since, informing him that alarming symptoms had declared themselves, and that a second physician had been called in. He telegraphed back to say that he had left Ireland for London, on his way to Venice, and to direct that any further message might be sent to his hotel. The reply came in a second telegram. It announced that Lord Montbarry was in a state of insensibility, and that, in his brief intervals of consciousness, he recognised nobody. My brother was advised to wait in London for later information. The third telegram is now in your hands. That is all I know, up to the present time.'

Happening to look at the courier's wife, Mr Troy was struck by the expression of blank fear which showed itself in the woman's face.

'Mrs Ferrari,' he said, 'have you heard what Mr Westwick has just told me?'

'Every word of it, sir.'

'Have you any questions to ask?'

'No, sir.'

'You seem to be alarmed,' the lawyer persisted. 'Is it still about your husband?'

'I shall never see my husband again, sir. I have thought so all along, as you know. I feel sure of it now.'

'Sure of it, after what you have just heard?'

'Yes, sir.'

'Can you tell me why?'

'No, sir. It's a feeling I have. I can't tell why.'

'Oh, a feeling?' Mr Troy repeated, in a tone of compassionate contempt. 'When it comes to feelings, my good soul——!' He left the sentence unfinished, and rose to take his leave of Mr Westwick. The truth is, he began to feel puzzled himself, and he did not choose to let Mrs Ferrari see it. 'Accept the expression of my sympathy, sir,' he said to Mr Westwick politely. 'I wish you good evening.'

Henry turned to Mrs Ferrari as the lawyer closed the door. 'I have heard of your trouble, Emily, from Miss Lockwood. Is there anything I can do to help you?'

'Nothing, sir, thank you. Perhaps, I had better go home after what has happened? I will call to-morrow, and see if I can be of any use to Miss Agnes. I am very sorry for her.' She stole away, with her formal curtsey, her noiseless step, and her obstinate resolution to take the gloomiest view of her husband's case.

Henry Westwick looked round him in the solitude of the little drawing-room. There was nothing to keep him in the house, and yet he lingered in it. It was something to be even near Agnes—to see the things belonging to her that were scattered about the room. There, in one corner, was her chair, with her embroidery on the work-table by its side. On the little easel near the window was her last drawing, not quite finished yet. The book she had been reading lay on the sofa, with her tiny pencil-case in it to mark the place at which she had left off. One after another, he looked at the objects that reminded him of the woman whom he loved—took them up tenderly—and laid them down again with a sigh. Ah, how far, how unattainably far from him, she was still! 'She will never forget Montbarry,' he thought to himself as he took up his hat to go. 'Not one of us feels his death as she feels it. Miserable, miserable wretch—how she loved him!'

In the street, as Henry closed the house-door, he was stopped by a passing acquaintance—a wearisome inquisitive man—doubly unwelcome to him, at that moment. 'Sad news, Westwick, this about your brother. Rather an unexpected death, wasn't it? We never heard at the club that Montbarry's lungs were weak. What will the insurance offices do?'

Henry started; he had never thought of his brother's life insurance. What could the offices do but pay? A death by bronchitis, certified by two physicians, was surely the least disputable of all deaths. 'I wish you hadn't put that question into my head!' he broke out irritably. 'Ah!' said his friend, 'you think the widow will get the money? So do I! so do I!'

## CHAPTER VII

Some days later, the insurance offices (two in number) received the formal announcement of Lord Montbarry's death, from her ladyship's London solicitors. The sum insured in each office was five thousand pounds—on which one year's premium only had been paid. In the face of such a pecuniary emergency as this, the Directors thought it desirable to consider their position. The medical advisers of the two offices, who had recommended the insurance of Lord Montbarry's life, were called into council over their own reports. The result excited some interest among persons connected with the business of life insurance. Without absolutely declining to pay the money, the two offices (acting in concert) decided on sending a commission of inquiry to Venice, 'for the purpose of obtaining further information.'

Mr Troy received the earliest intelligence of what was going on. He wrote at once to communicate his news to Agnes; adding, what he considered to be a valuable hint, in these words:

'You are intimately acquainted, I know, with Lady Barville, the late Lord Montbarry's eldest sister. The solicitors employed by her husband are also the solicitors to one of the two insurance offices. There may possibly be something in the report of the commission of inquiry touching on Ferrari's disappearance. Ordinary persons would not be permitted, of course, to see such a document. But a sister of the late lord is so near a relative as to be an exception to general rules. If Sir Theodore Barville puts it on that footing, the lawyers, even if they do not allow his wife to look at the report, will at least answer any discreet questions she may ask referring to it. Let me hear what you think of this suggestion, at your earliest convenience.'

The reply was received by return of post. Agnes declined to avail herself of Mr Troy's proposal.

'My interference, innocent as it was,' she wrote, 'has already been productive of such deplorable results, that I cannot and dare not stir any further in the case of Ferrari. If I had not consented to let that unfortunate man refer to me by name, the late Lord Montbarry would never have engaged him, and his wife would have been spared the misery and suspense from which she is suffering now. I would not even look at the report to which you allude if it was placed in my hands—I have heard more than enough already of that hideous life in the palace at Venice. If Mrs Ferrari chooses to address herself to Lady Barville (with your assistance), that is of course quite another thing. But, even in this case, I must make it a positive condition that my name shall not be mentioned. Forgive me, dear Mr Troy! I am very unhappy, and very unreasonable—but I am only a woman, and you must not expect too much from me.'

Foiled in this direction, the lawyer next advised making the attempt to discover the present address of Lady Montbarry's English maid. This excellent suggestion had one drawback: it could only be carried out by spending money—and there was no money to spend.

Mrs Ferrari shrank from the bare idea of making any use of the thousand-pound note. It had been deposited in the safe keeping of a bank. If it was even mentioned in her hearing, she shuddered and referred to it, with melodramatic fervour, as 'my husband's blood-money!'

So, under stress of circumstances, the attempt to solve the mystery of Ferrari's disappearance was suspended for a while.

It was the last month of the year 1860. The commission of inquiry was already at work; having begun its investigations on December 6. On the 10th, the term for which the late Lord Montbarry had hired the Venetian palace, expired. News by telegram reached the insurance offices that Lady Montbarry had been advised by her lawyers to leave for London with as little delay as possible. Baron Rivar, it was believed, would accompany her to England, but would not remain in that country, unless his services were absolutely required by her ladyship. The Baron, 'well known as an enthusiastic student of chemistry,' had heard of certain recent discoveries in connection with that science in the United States, and was anxious to investigate them personally.

These items of news, collected by Mr Troy, were duly communicated to Mrs Ferrari, whose anxiety about her husband made her a frequent, a too frequent, visitor at the lawyer's office. She attempted to relate what she had heard to her good friend and protectress. Agnes steadily refused to listen, and positively forbade any further conversation relating to Lord Montbarry's wife, now that Lord Montbarry was no more. 'You have Mr Troy to advise you,' she said; 'and you are welcome to what little money I can spare, if money is wanted. All I ask in return is that you will not distress me. I am trying to separate myself from remembrances—' her voice faltered; she paused to control herself—'from remembrances,' she resumed, 'which are sadder than ever since I have heard of Lord Montbarry's death. Help me by your silence to recover my spirits, if I can. Let me hear nothing more, until I can rejoice with you that your husband is found.'

Time advanced to the 13th of the month; and more information of the interesting sort reached Mr Troy. The labours of the insurance commission had come to an end—the report had been received from Venice on that day.

# CHAPTER VIII

On the 14th the Directors and their legal advisers met for the reading of the report, with closed doors. These were the terms in which the Commissioners related the results of their inquiry:

'*Private and confidential.*

'We have the honour to inform our Directors that we arrived in Venice on December 6, 1860. On the same day we proceeded to the palace inhabited by Lord Montbarry at the time of his last illness and death.

'We were received with all possible courtesy by Lady Montbarry's brother, Baron Rivar. "My sister was her husband's only attendant throughout his illness," the Baron informed us. "She is overwhelmed by grief and fatigue—or she would have been here to receive you personally. What are your wishes, gentlemen? and what can I do for you in her ladyship's place?"

'In accordance with our instructions, we answered that the death and burial of Lord Montbarry abroad made it desirable to obtain more complete information relating to his illness, and to the circumstances which had attended it, than could be conveyed in writing. We explained that the law provided for the lapse of a certain interval of time before the payment of the sum assured, and we expressed our wish to conduct the inquiry with the most respectful consideration for her ladyship's feelings, and for the convenience of any other members of the family inhabiting the house.

'To this the Baron replied, "I am the only member of the family living here, and I and the palace are entirely at your disposal." From first to last we found this gentleman perfectly straightforward, and most amiably willing to assist us.

'With the one exception of her ladyship's room, we went over the whole of the palace the same day. It is an immense place only partially furnished. The first floor and part of the second floor were the portions of it that had been inhabited by Lord Montbarry and the members of the household. We saw the bedchamber, at one extremity of the palace, in which his lordship died, and the small room communicating with it, which he used as a study. Next to this was a large apartment or hall, the doors of which he habitually kept locked, his object being (as we were informed) to pursue his studies uninterruptedly in perfect solitude. On the other side of the large hall were the bedchamber occupied by her ladyship, and the dressing-room in which the maid slept previous to her departure for England. Beyond these were the dining and reception rooms, opening into an antechamber, which gave access to the grand staircase of the palace.

'The only inhabited rooms on the second floor were the sitting-room and bedroom occupied by Baron Rivar, and another room at some distance from it, which had been the bedroom of the courier Ferrari.

'The rooms on the third floor and on the basement were completely unfurnished, and in a condition of great neglect. We inquired if there was anything to be seen below the basement—and we were at once informed that there were vaults beneath, which we were at perfect liberty to visit.

'We went down, so as to leave no part of the palace unexplored. The vaults were, it was believed, used as dungeons in the old times—say, some centuries since. Air and light were only partially admitted to these dismal places by two long shafts of winding construction, which communicated with the back yard of the palace, and the openings of which, high above the ground, were protected by iron gratings. The stone stairs leading down into the vaults could be closed at will by a heavy trap-door in the back hall, which we found open. The Baron himself led the way down the stairs. We remarked that it might be awkward if that trap-door fell down and closed the opening behind us. The Baron smiled at the idea. "Don't be alarmed, gentlemen," he said; "the door is safe. I had an interest in seeing to it myself, when we first inhabited the palace. My favourite study is the study of experimental chemistry—and my workshop, since we have been in Venice, is down here."

'These last words explained a curious smell in the vaults, which we noticed the moment we entered them. We can only describe the smell by saying that it was of a twofold sort—faintly aromatic, as it were, in its first effect, but with some after-odour very sickening in our nostrils. The Baron's furnaces and retorts, and other things, were all there to speak for themselves, together with some packages of chemicals, having the name and address of the person who had supplied them plainly visible on their labels. 'Not a pleasant place for study,' Baron Rivar observed, "but my sister is timid. She has a horror of chemical smells and explosions—and she has banished me to these lower regions, so that my experiments may neither be smelt nor heard." He held out his hands, on which we had noticed that he wore gloves in the house. "Accidents will happen sometimes," he said, "no matter how careful a man may be. I burnt my hands severely in trying a new combination the other day, and they are only recovering now."

'We mention these otherwise unimportant incidents, in order to show that our exploration of the palace was not impeded by any attempt at concealment. We were even admitted to her ladyship's own room—on a subsequent occasion, when she went out to take the air. Our instructions recommended us to examine his lordship's residence, because the extreme privacy of his life at Venice, and the remarkable departure of the only two servants in the house, might have some suspicious connection with the nature of his death. We found nothing to justify suspicion.

'As to his lordship's retired way of life, we have conversed on the subject with the consul and the banker—the only two strangers who held any communication with him. He called once at the bank to obtain money on his letter of credit, and excused himself from accepting an invitation to visit the banker at his private residence, on the ground of delicate health. His lordship wrote to the same effect on sending his card to the consul, to excuse himself from personally returning that gentleman's visit to the palace. We have seen the letter, and we beg to offer the following copy of it. "Many years passed in India have injured my constitution. I have ceased to go into society; the one occupation of my life now is the study of Oriental literature. The air of Italy is better for me than the air of England, or I should never have left home. Pray accept the apologies of a student and an invalid. The active part of my life is at an end." The self-seclusion of his lordship seems to us to be explained in these brief lines. We have not, however, on that account spared our inquiries in other directions. Nothing to excite a suspicion of anything wrong has come to our knowledge.

'As to the departure of the lady's maid, we have seen the woman's receipt for her wages, in which it is expressly stated that she left Lady Montbarry's service because she disliked the Continent, and wished to get back to her own country. This is not an uncommon result of taking English servants to foreign parts. Lady Montbarry has informed us that she abstained from engaging another maid in consequence of the extreme dislike which his lordship expressed to having strangers in the house, in the state of his health at that time.

'The disappearance of the courier Ferrari is, in itself, unquestionably a suspicious circumstance. Neither her ladyship nor the Baron can explain it; and no investigation that we could make has thrown the smallest light on this event, or has justified us in associating it, directly or indirectly, with the object of our inquiry. We have even gone the length of examining the portmanteau which Ferrari left behind him. It contains nothing but clothes and linen—no money, and not even a scrap of paper in the pockets of the clothes. The portmanteau remains in charge of the police.

'We have also found opportunities of speaking privately to the old woman who attends to the rooms occupied by her ladyship and the Baron. She was recommended to fill this situation by the keeper of the restaurant who has supplied the meals to the family throughout the period of their residence at the palace. Her character is most favourably spoken of. Unfortunately, her limited intelligence makes her of no value as a witness. We were patient and careful in questioning her, and we found her perfectly willing to answer us; but we could elicit nothing which is worth including in the present report.

'On the second day of our inquiries, we had the honour of an interview with Lady Montbarry. Her ladyship looked miserably worn and ill, and seemed to be quite at a loss to understand what we wanted with her. Baron Rivar, who introduced us, explained the nature of our errand in Venice, and took pains to assure her that it was a purely formal duty on which we were engaged. Having satisfied her ladyship on this point, he discreetly left the room.

'The questions which we addressed to Lady Montbarry related mainly, of course, to his lordship's illness. The answers, given with great nervousness of manner, but without the slightest appearance of reserve, informed us of the facts that follow:

'Lord Montbarry had been out of order for some time past—nervous and irritable. He first complained of having taken cold on November 13 last; he passed a wakeful and feverish night, and remained in bed the next day. Her ladyship proposed sending for medical advice. He refused to allow her to do this, saying that he could quite easily be his own doctor in such a trifling matter as a cold. Some hot lemonade was made at his request, with a view to producing perspiration. Lady Montbarry's maid having left her at that time, the courier Ferrari (then the only servant in the house) went out to buy the lemons. Her ladyship made the drink with her own hands. It was successful in producing perspiration—and Lord Montbarry had some hours of sleep afterwards. Later in the day, having need of Ferrari's services, Lady Montbarry rang for him. The bell was not answered. Baron Rivar searched for the man, in the palace and out of it, in vain. From that time forth not a trace of Ferrari could be discovered. This happened on November 14.

'On the night of the 14th, the feverish symptoms accompanying his lordship's cold returned. They were in part perhaps attributable to the annoyance and alarm caused by Ferrari's mysterious disappearance. It had been impossible to conceal the circumstance, as his lordship rang repeatedly for the courier; insisting that the man should relieve Lady Montbarry and the Baron by taking their places during the night at his bedside.

'On the 15th (the day on which the old woman first came to do the housework), his lordship complained of sore throat, and of a feeling of oppression on the chest. On this day, and again on the 16th, her ladyship and the Baron entreated him to see a doctor. He still refused. "I don't want strange faces about me; my cold will run its course, in spite of the doctor,"—that was his answer. On the 17th he was so much worse that it was decided to send for medical help whether he liked it or not. Baron

Rivar, after inquiry at the consul's, secured the services of Doctor Bruno, well known as an eminent physician in Venice; with the additional recommendation of having resided in England, and having made himself acquainted with English forms of medical practice.

'Thus far our account of his lordship's illness has been derived from statements made by Lady Montbarry. The narrative will now be most fitly continued in the language of the doctor's own report, herewith subjoined.

' "My medical diary informs me that I first saw the English Lord Montbarry, on November 17. He was suffering from a sharp attack of bronchitis. Some precious time had been lost, through his obstinate objection to the presence of a medical man at his bedside. Generally speaking, he appeared to be in a delicate state of health. His nervous system was out of order—he was at once timid and contradictory. When I spoke to him in English, he answered in Italian; and when I tried him in Italian, he went back to English. It mattered little—the malady had already made such progress that he could only speak a few words at a time, and those in a whisper.

' "I at once applied the necessary remedies. Copies of my prescriptions (with translation into English) accompany the present statement, and are left to speak for themselves.

' "For the next three days I was in constant attendance on my patient. He answered to the remedies employed—improving slowly, but decidedly. I could conscientiously assure Lady Montbarry that no danger was to be apprehended thus far. She was indeed a most devoted wife. I vainly endeavoured to induce her to accept the services of a competent nurse; she would allow nobody to attend on her husband but herself. Night and day this estimable woman was at his bedside. In her brief intervals of repose, her brother watched the sick man in her place. This brother was, I must say, very good company, in the intervals when we had time for a little talk. He dabbled in chemistry, down in the horrid under-water vaults of the palace; and he wanted to show me some of his experiments. I have enough of chemistry in writing prescriptions—and I declined. He took it quite good-humouredly.

' "I am straying away from my subject. Let me return to the sick lord.

' "Up to the 20th, then, things went well enough. I was quite unprepared for the disastrous change that showed itself, when I paid Lord Montbarry my morning visit on the 21st. He had relapsed, and seriously relapsed. Examining him to discover the cause, I found symptoms of pneumonia—that is to say, in unmedical language, inflammation of the substance of the lungs. He breathed with difficulty, and was only partially able to relieve himself by coughing. I made the strictest inquiries, and was assured that his medicine had been administered as carefully as usual, and that he had not been exposed to any changes of temperature. It was with great reluctance that I added to Lady Montbarry's distress; but I felt bound, when she suggested a consultation with another physician, to own that I too thought there was really need for it.

'"Her ladyship instructed me to spare no expense, and to get the best medical opinion in Italy. The best opinion was happily within our reach. The first and foremost of Italian physicians is Torello of Padua. I sent a special messenger for the great man. He arrived on the evening of the 21st, and confirmed my opinion that pneumonia had set in, and that our patient's life was in danger. I told him what my treatment of the case had been, and he approved of it in every particular. He made some valuable suggestions, and (at Lady Montbarry's express request) he consented to defer his return to Padua until the following morning.

'"We both saw the patient at intervals in the course of the night. The disease, steadily advancing, set our utmost resistance at defiance. In the morning Doctor Torello took his leave. 'I can be of no further use,' he said to me. 'The man is past all help—and he ought to know it.'

'"Later in the day I warned my lord, as gently as I could, that his time had come. I am informed that there are serious reasons for my stating what passed between us on this occasion, in detail, and without any reserve. I comply with the request.

'"Lord Montbarry received the intelligence of his approaching death with becoming composure, but with a certain doubt. He signed to me to put my ear to his mouth. He whispered faintly, 'Are you sure?' It was no time to deceive him; I said, 'Positively sure.' He waited a little, gasping for breath, and then he whispered again, 'Feel under my pillow.' I found under his pillow a letter, sealed and stamped, ready for the post. His next words were just audible and no more—'Post it yourself.' I answered, of course, that I would do so—and I did post the letter with my own hand. I looked at the address. It was directed to a lady in London. The street I cannot remember. The name I can perfectly recall: it was an Italian name—'Mrs Ferrari.'

'"That night my lord nearly died of asphyxia. I got him through it for the time; and his eyes showed that he understood me when I told him, the next morning, that I had posted the letter. This was his last effort of consciousness. When I saw him again he was sunk in apathy. He lingered in a state of insensibility, supported by stimulants, until the 25th, and died (unconscious to the last) on the evening of that day.

'"As to the cause of his death, it seems (if I may be excused for saying so) simply absurd to ask the question. Bronchitis, terminating in pneumonia—

there is no more doubt that this, and this only, was the malady of which he expired, than that two and two make four. Doctor Torello's own note of the case is added here to a duplicate of my certificate, in order (as I am informed) to satisfy some English offices in which his lordship's life was insured. The English offices must have been founded by that celebrated saint and doubter, mentioned in the New Testament, whose name was Thomas!"*

'Doctor Bruno's evidence ends here.

'Reverting for a moment to our inquiries addressed to Lady Montbarry, we have to report that she can give us no information on the subject of the letter which the doctor posted at Lord Montbarry's request. When his lordship wrote it? what it contained? why he kept it a secret from Lady Montbarry (and from the Baron also); and why he should write at all to the wife of his courier? these are questions to which we find it simply impossible to obtain any replies. It seems even useless to say that the matter is open to suspicion. Suspicion implies conjecture of some kind—and the letter under my lord's pillow baffles all conjecture. Application to Mrs Ferrari may perhaps clear up the mystery. Her residence in London will be easily discovered at the Italian Couriers' Office, Golden Square.

'Having arrived at the close of the present report, we have now to draw your attention to the conclusion which is justified by the results of our investigation.

'The plain question before our Directors and ourselves appears to be this: Has the inquiry revealed any extraordinary circumstances which render the death of Lord Montbarry open to suspicion? The inquiry has revealed extraordinary circumstances beyond all doubt—such as the disappearance of Ferrari, the remarkable absence of the customary establishment of servants in the house, and the mysterious letter which his lordship asked the doctor to post. But where is the proof that any one of these circumstances is associated—suspiciously and directly associated—with the only event which concerns us, the event of Lord Montbarry's death? In the absence of any such proof, and in the face of the evidence of two eminent physicians, it is impossible to dispute the statement on the certificate that his lordship died a natural death. We are bound, therefore, to report, that there are no valid grounds for refusing the payment of the sum for which the late Lord Montbarry's life was assured.

'We shall send these lines to you by the post of to-morrow, December 10; leaving time to receive your further instructions (if any), in reply to our telegram of this evening announcing the conclusion of the inquiry.'

## CHAPTER IX

'Now, my good creature, whatever you have to say to me, out with it at once! I don't want to hurry you needlessly; but these are business hours, and I have other people's affairs to attend to besides yours.'

Addressing Ferrari's wife, with his usual blunt good-humour, in these terms, Mr Troy registered the lapse of time by a glance at the watch on his desk, and then waited to hear what his client had to say to him.

'It's something more, sir, about the letter with the thousand-pound note,' Mrs Ferrari began. 'I have found out who sent it to me.'

Mr Troy started. 'This is news indeed!' he said. 'Who sent you the letter?'

'Lord Montbarry sent it, sir.'

It was not easy to take Mr Troy by surprise. But Mrs Ferrari threw him completely off his balance. For a while he could only look at her in silent surprise. 'Nonsense!' he said, as soon as he had recovered himself. 'There is some mistake—it can't be!'

'There is no mistake,' Mrs Ferrari rejoined, in her most positive manner. 'Two gentlemen from the insurance offices called on me this morning, to see the letter. They were completely puzzled—especially when they heard of the bank-note inside. But they know who sent the letter. His lordship's doctor in Venice posted it at his lordship's request. Go to the gentlemen yourself, sir, if you don't believe me. They were polite enough to ask if I could account for Lord Montbarry writing to me and sending me the money. I gave them my opinion directly—I said it was like his lordship's kindness.'

'Like his lordship's kindness?' Mr Troy repeated, in blank amazement.

'Yes, sir! Lord Montbarry knew me, like all the other members of his family, when I was at school on the estate in Ireland. If he could have done it, he would have protected my poor dear husband. But he was helpless himself in the hands of my lady and the Baron—and the only kind thing he could do was to provide for me in my widowhood, like the true nobleman he was!'

'A very pretty explanation!' said Mr Troy. 'What did your visitors from the insurance offices think of it?'

'They asked if I had any proof of my husband's death.'

'And what did you say?'

'I said, "I give you better than proof, gentlemen; I give you my positive opinion."'

'That satisfied them, of course?'

'They didn't say so in words, sir. They looked at each other—and wished me good-morning.'

'Well, Mrs Ferrari, unless you have some more extraordinary news for me, I think I shall wish you good-morning too. I can take a note of your information (very startling information, I own); and, in the absence of proof, I can do no more.'

'I can provide you with proof, sir—if that is all you want,' said Mrs Ferrari, with great dignity. 'I only wish to know, first, whether the law justifies me in doing it. You may have seen in the fashionable intelligence of the newspapers, that Lady Montbarry has arrived in London, at Newbury's Hotel. I propose to go and see her.'

'The deuce you do! May I ask for what purpose?'

Mrs Ferrari answered in a mysterious whisper. 'For the purpose of catching her in a trap! I shan't send in my name—I shall announce myself as a person on business, and the first words I say to her will be these: "I come, my lady, to acknowledge the receipt of the money sent to Ferrari's widow." Ah! you may well start, Mr Troy! It almost takes *you* off your guard, doesn't it? Make your mind easy, sir; I shall find the proof that everybody asks me for in her guilty face. Let her only change colour by the shadow of a shade—let her eyes only drop for half an instant—I shall discover her! The one thing I want to know is, does the law permit it?'

'The law permits it,' Mr Troy answered gravely; 'but whether her ladyship will permit it, is quite another question. Have you really courage enough, Mrs Ferrari, to carry out this notable scheme of yours? You have been described to me, by Miss Lockwood, as rather a nervous, timid sort of person—and, if I may trust my own observation, I should say you justify the description.'

'If you had lived in the country, sir, instead of living in London,' Mrs Ferrari replied, 'you would sometimes have seen even a sheep turn on a dog. I am far from saying that I am a bold woman—quite the reverse. But when I stand in that wretch's presence, and think of my murdered husband, the one of us two who is likely to be frightened is not *me*. I am going there now, sir. You shall hear how it ends. I wish you good-morning.'

With those brave words the courier's wife gathered her mantle about her, and walked out of the room.

Mr Troy smiled—not satirically, but compassionately. 'The little simpleton!' he thought to himself. 'If half of what they say of Lady Montbarry is true, Mrs Ferrari and her trap have but a poor prospect before them. I wonder how it will end?'

All Mr Troy's experience failed to forewarn him of how it *did* end.

## CHAPTER X

In the mean time, Mrs Ferrari held to her resolution. She went straight from Mr Troy's office to Newbury's Hotel.

Lady Montbarry was at home, and alone. But the authorities of the hotel hesitated to disturb her when they found that the visitor declined to mention her name. Her ladyship's new maid happened to cross the hall while the matter was still in debate. She was a Frenchwoman, and, on being appealed to, she settled the question in the swift, easy, rational French way. 'Madame's appearance was perfectly respectable. Madame might have reasons for not mentioning her name which Miladi might approve. In any case, there being no orders forbidding the introduction of a strange lady, the matter clearly rested between Madame and Miladi. Would Madame, therefore, be good enough to follow Miladi's maid up the stairs?'

In spite of her resolution, Mrs Ferrari's heart beat as if it would burst out of her bosom, when her conductress led her into an ante-room, and knocked at a door opening into a room beyond. But it is remarkable that persons of sensitively-nervous organisation are the very persons who are capable of forcing themselves (apparently by the exercise of a spasmodic effort of will) into the performance of acts of the most audacious courage. A low, grave voice from the inner room said, 'Come in.' The maid, opening the door, announced, 'A person to see you, Miladi, on business,' and immediately retired. In the one instant while these events passed, timid little Mrs Ferrari mastered her own throbbing heart; stepped over the threshold, conscious of her clammy hands, dry lips, and burning head; and stood in the presence of Lord Montbarry's widow, to all outward appearance as supremely self-possessed as her ladyship herself.

It was still early in the afternoon, but the light in the room was dim. The blinds were drawn down. Lady Montbarry sat with her back to the windows, as if even the subdued daylight were disagreeable to her. She had altered sadly for the worse in her personal appearance, since the memorable day when Doctor Wybrow had seen her in his consulting-room. Her beauty was gone—her face had fallen away to mere skin and bone; the contrast between her ghastly complexion and her steely glittering black eyes was more startling than ever. Robed in dismal black, relieved only by the brilliant whiteness of her widow's cap—reclining in a panther-like suppleness of attitude on a little green sofa—she looked at the stranger who had intruded on her, with a moment's languid curiosity, then dropped her eyes again to the hand-screen which she held between her face and the fire. 'I don't know you,' she said. 'What do you want with me?'

Mrs Ferrari tried to answer. Her first burst of courage had already worn itself out. The bold words that she had determined to speak were living words still in her mind, but they died on her lips.

There was a moment of silence. Lady Montbarry looked round again at the speechless stranger. 'Are you deaf?' she asked. There was another pause. Lady Montbarry quietly looked back again at the screen, and put another question. 'Do you want money?'

'Money!' That one word roused the sinking spirit of the courier's wife. She recovered her courage; she found her voice. 'Look at me, my lady, if you please,' she said, with a sudden outbreak of audacity.

Lady Montbarry looked round for the third time. The fatal words passed Mrs Ferrari's lips.

'I come, my lady, to acknowledge the receipt of the money sent to Ferrari's widow.'

Lady Montbarry's glittering black eyes rested with steady attention on the woman who had addressed her in those terms. Not the faintest expression of confusion or alarm, not even a momentary flutter of interest stirred the deadly stillness of her face. She reposed as quietly, she held the screen as composedly, as ever. The test had been tried, and had utterly failed.

There was another silence. Lady Montbarry considered with herself. The smile that came slowly and went away suddenly—the smile at once so sad and so cruel—showed itself on her thin lips. She lifted her screen, and pointed with it to a seat at the farther end of the room. 'Be so good as to take that chair,' she said.

Helpless under her first bewildering sense of failure—not knowing what to say or what to do next—Mrs Ferrari mechanically obeyed. Lady Montbarry, rising on the sofa for the first time, watched her with undisguised scrutiny as she crossed the room—then sank back into a reclining position once more. 'No,' she said to herself, 'the woman walks steadily; she is not intoxicated—the only other possibility is that she may be mad.'

She had spoken loud enough to be heard. Stung by the insult, Mrs Ferrari instantly answered her: 'I am no more drunk or mad than you are!'

'No?' said Lady Montbarry. 'Then you are only insolent? The ignorant English mind (I have observed) is apt to be insolent in the exercise of unrestrained English liberty. This is very noticeable to us foreigners among you people in the streets. Of course I can't be insolent to you, in return. I hardly know what to say to you. My maid was imprudent in admitting you so easily to my room. I suppose your respectable appearance misled her. I wonder who you are? You mentioned the name of a courier who left us very strangely. Was he married by any chance? Are you his wife? And do you know where he is?'

Mrs Ferrari's indignation burst its way through all restraints. She advanced to the sofa; she feared nothing, in the fervour and rage of her reply.

'I am his widow—and you know it, you wicked woman! Ah! it was an evil hour when Miss Lockwood recommended my husband to be his lordship's courier—!'

Before she could add another word, Lady Montbarry sprang from the sofa with the stealthy suddenness of a cat—seized her by both shoulders—and shook her with the strength and frenzy of a mad-woman. 'You lie! you lie! you lie!' She dropped her hold at the third repetition of the accusation, and threw up her hands wildly with a gesture of despair. 'Oh, Jesu Maria! is it possible?' she cried. '*Can* the courier have come to me through that woman?' She turned like lightning on Mrs Ferrari, and stopped her as she was escaping from the room. 'Stay here, you fool—stay here, and answer me! If you cry out, as sure as the heavens are above you, I'll strangle you with my own hands. Sit down again—and fear nothing. Wretch! It is I who am frightened—frightened out of my senses. Confess that you lied, when you used Miss Lockwood's name just now! No! I don't believe you on your oath; I will believe nobody but Miss Lockwood herself. Where does she live? Tell me that, you noxious stinging little insect—and you may go.' Terrified as she was, Mrs Ferrari hesitated. Lady Montbarry lifted her hands threateningly, with the long, lean, yellow-white fingers outspread and crooked at the tips. Mrs Ferrari shrank at the sight of them, and gave the address. Lady Montbarry pointed contemptuously to the door—then changed her mind. 'No! not yet! you will tell Miss Lockwood what has happened, and she may refuse to see me. I will go there at once, and you shall go with me. As far as the house—not inside of it. Sit down again. I am going to ring for my maid. Turn your back to the door—your cowardly face is not fit to be seen!'

She rang the bell. The maid appeared.

'My cloak and bonnet—instantly!'

The maid produced the cloak and bonnet from the bedroom.

'A cab at the door—before I can count ten!'

The maid vanished. Lady Montbarry surveyed herself in the glass, and wheeled round again, with her cat-like suddenness, to Mrs Ferrari.

'I look more than half dead already, don't I?' she said with a grim outburst of irony. 'Give me your arm.'

She took Mrs Ferrari's arm, and left the room. 'You have nothing to fear, so long as you obey,' she whispered, on the way downstairs. 'You leave me at Miss Lockwood's door, and never see me again.'

In the hall they were met by the landlady of the hotel. Lady Montbarry graciously presented her companion. 'My good friend Mrs Ferrari; I am so glad to have seen her.' The landlady accompanied them to the door. The cab was waiting. 'Get in first, good Mrs Ferrari,' said her ladyship; 'and tell the man where to go.'

They were driven away. Lady Montbarry's variable humour changed again. With a low groan of misery, she threw herself back in the cab. Lost in her own dark thoughts, as careless of the woman whom she had bent to her iron will as if no such person sat by her side, she preserved a sinister silence, until they reached the house where Miss Lockwood lodged. In an instant, she roused herself to action. She opened the door of the cab, and closed it again on Mrs Ferrari, before the driver could get off his box.

'Take that lady a mile farther on her way home!' she said, as she paid the man his fare. The next moment she had knocked at the house-door. 'Is Miss Lockwood at home?' 'Yes, ma'am.' She stepped over the threshold—the door closed on her.

'Which way, ma'am?' asked the driver of the cab.

Mrs Ferrari put her hand to her head, and tried to collect her thoughts. Could she leave her friend and benefactress helpless at Lady Montbarry's mercy? She was still vainly endeavouring to decide on the course that she ought to follow—when a gentleman, stopping at Miss Lockwood's door, happened to look towards the cab-window, and saw her.

'Are you going to call on Miss Agnes too?' he asked.

It was Henry Westwick. Mrs Ferrari clasped her hands in gratitude as she recognised him.

'Go in, sir!' she cried. 'Go in, directly. That dreadful woman is with Miss Agnes. Go and protect her!'

'What woman?' Henry asked.

The answer literally struck him speechless. With amazement and indignation in his face, he looked at Mrs Ferrari as she pronounced the hated name of 'Lady Montbarry.' 'I'll see to it,' was all he said. He knocked at the house-door; and he too, in his turn, was let in.

## CHAPTER XI

'Lady Montbarry, Miss.'

Agnes was writing a letter, when the servant astonished her by announcing the visitor's name. Her first impulse was to refuse to see the woman who had intruded on her. But Lady Montbarry had taken care to follow close on the servant's heels. Before Agnes could speak, she had entered the room.

'I beg to apologise for my intrusion, Miss Lockwood. I have a question to ask you, in which I am very much interested. No one can answer me but yourself.' In low hesitating tones, with her glittering black eyes bent modestly on the ground, Lady Montbarry opened the interview in those words.

Without answering, Agnes pointed to a chair. She could do this, and, for the time, she could do no more. All that she had read of the hidden and sinister life in the palace at Venice; all that she had heard of Montbarry's melancholy death and burial in a foreign land; all that she knew of the mystery of Ferrari's disappearance, rushed into her mind, when the black-robed figure confronted her, standing just inside the door. The strange conduct of Lady Montbarry added a new perplexity to the doubts and misgivings that troubled her. There stood the adventuress whose character had left its mark on society all over Europe—the Fury who had terrified Mrs Ferrari at the hotel—inconceivably transformed into a timid, shrinking woman! Lady Montbarry had not once ventured to look at Agnes, since she had made her way into the room. Advancing to take the chair that had been pointed out to her, she hesitated, put her hand on the rail to support herself, and still remained standing. 'Please give me a moment to compose myself,' she said faintly. Her head sank on her bosom: she stood before Agnes like a conscious culprit before a merciless judge.

The silence that followed was, literally, the silence of fear on both sides. In the midst of it, the door was opened once more—and Henry Westwick appeared.

He looked at Lady Montbarry with a moment's steady attention—bowed to her with formal politeness—and passed on in silence. At the sight of her husband's brother, the sinking spirit of the woman sprang to life again. Her drooping figure became erect. Her eyes met Westwick's look, brightly defiant. She returned his bow with an icy smile of contempt.

Henry crossed the room to Agnes.

'Is Lady Montbarry here by your invitation?' he asked quietly.

'No.'

'Do you wish to see her?'

'It is very painful to me to see her.'

He turned and looked at his sister-in-law. 'Do you hear that?' he asked coldly.

'I hear it,' she answered, more coldly still.

'Your visit is, to say the least of it, ill-timed.'

'Your interference is, to say the least of it, out of place.'

With that retort, Lady Montbarry approached Agnes. The presence of Henry Westwick seemed at once to relieve and embolden her. 'Permit me to ask my question, Miss Lockwood,' she said, with graceful courtesy. 'It is nothing to embarrass you. When the courier Ferrari applied to my late husband for employment, did you—' Her resolution failed her, before she could say more. She sank trembling into the nearest chair, and, after a moment's struggle, composed herself again. 'Did you permit Ferrari,' she resumed, 'to make sure of being chosen for our courier by using your name?'

Agnes did not reply with her customary directness. Trifling as it was, the reference to Montbarry, proceeding from *that* woman of all others, confused and agitated her.

'I have known Ferrari's wife for many years,' she began. 'And I take an interest——'

Lady Montbarry abruptly lifted her hands with a gesture of entreaty. 'Ah, Miss Lockwood, don't waste time by talking of his wife! Answer my plain question, plainly!'

'Let me answer her,' Henry whispered. 'I will undertake to speak plainly enough.'

Agnes refused by a gesture. Lady Montbarry's interruption had roused her sense of what was due to herself. She resumed her reply in plainer terms.

'When Ferrari wrote to the late Lord Montbarry,' she said, 'he did certainly mention my name.'

Even now, she had innocently failed to see the object which her visitor had in view. Lady Montbarry's impatience became ungovernable. She started to her feet, and advanced to Agnes.

'Was it with your knowledge and permission that Ferrari used your name?' she asked. 'The whole soul of my question is in *that*. For God's sake answer me—Yes, or No!'

'Yes.'

That one word struck Lady Montbarry as a blow might have struck her. The fierce life that had animated her face the instant before, faded out of it suddenly, and left her like a woman turned to stone. She stood, mechanically confronting Agnes, with a stillness so wrapt and perfect that not even the breath she drew was perceptible to the two persons who were looking at her.

Henry spoke to her roughly. 'Rouse yourself,' he said. 'You have received your answer.'

She looked round at him. 'I have received my Sentence,' she rejoined—and turned slowly to leave the room.

To Henry's astonishment, Agnes stopped her. 'Wait a moment, Lady Montbarry. I have something to ask on my side. You have spoken of Ferrari. I wish to speak of him too.'*

Lady Montbarry bent her head in silence. Her hand trembled as she took out her handkerchief, and passed it over her forehead. Agnes detected the trembling, and shrank back a step. 'Is the subject painful to you?' she asked timidly.

Still silent, Lady Montbarry invited her by a wave of the hand to go on. Henry approached, attentively watching his sister-in-law. Agnes went on.

'No trace of Ferrari has been discovered in England,' she said. 'Have you any news of him? And will you tell me (if you have heard anything), in mercy to his wife?'

Lady Montbarry's thin lips suddenly relaxed into their sad and cruel smile.

'Why do you ask *me* about the lost courier?' she said. 'You will know what has become of him, Miss Lockwood, when the time is ripe for it.'

Agnes started. 'I don't understand you,' she said. 'How shall I know? Will some one tell me?'

'Some one will tell you.'

Henry could keep silence no longer. 'Perhaps, your ladyship may be the person?' he interrupted with ironical politeness.

She answered him with contemptuous ease. 'You may be right, Mr Westwick. One day or another, I may be the person who tells Miss Lockwood what has become of Ferrari, if—' She stopped; with her eyes fixed on Agnes.

'If what?' Henry asked.

'If Miss Lockwood forces me to it.'

Agnes listened in astonishment. 'Force you to it?' she repeated. 'How can I do that? Do you mean to say my will is stronger than yours?'

'Do *you* mean to say that the candle doesn't burn the moth, when the moth flies into it?' Lady Montbarry rejoined. 'Have you ever heard of such a thing as the fascination of terror? I am drawn to you by a fascination of terror. I have no right to visit you, I have no wish to visit you: you are my enemy. For the first time in my life, against my own will, I submit to my enemy. See! I am waiting because you told me to wait—and the fear of you (I swear it!) creeps through me while I stand here. Oh, don't let me excite your curiosity or your pity! Follow the example of Mr Westwick. Be hard and brutal and unforgiving, like him. Grant me my release. Tell me to go.'

The frank and simple nature of Agnes could discover but one intelligible meaning in this strange outbreak.

'You are mistaken in thinking me your enemy,' she said. 'The wrong you did me when you gave your hand to Lord Montbarry was not intentionally done. I forgave you my sufferings in his lifetime. I forgive you even more freely now that he has gone.'

Henry heard her with mingled emotions of admiration and distress. 'Say no more!' he exclaimed. 'You are too good to her; she is not worthy of it.'

The interruption passed unheeded by Lady Montbarry. The simple words in which Agnes had replied seemed to have absorbed the whole attention of this strangely-changeable woman. As she listened, her face settled slowly into an expression of hard and tearless sorrow. There was a marked change in her voice when she spoke next. It expressed that last worst resignation which has done with hope.

'You good innocent creature,' she said, 'what does your amiable forgiveness matter? What are your poor little wrongs, in the reckoning for greater wrongs which is demanded of me? I am not trying to frighten you, I am only miserable about myself. Do you know what it is to have a firm presentiment of calamity that is coming to you—and yet to hope that your own positive conviction will not prove true? When I first met you, before my marriage, and first felt your influence over me, I had that hope. It was a starveling sort of hope that lived a lingering life in me until to-day. *You* struck it dead, when you answered my question about Ferrari.'

'How have I destroyed your hopes?' Agnes asked. 'What connection is there between my permitting Ferrari to use my name to Lord Montbarry, and the strange and dreadful things you are saying to me now?'

'The time is near, Miss Lockwood, when you will discover that for yourself. In the mean while, you shall know what my fear of you is, in the plainest words I can find. On the day when I took your hero from you and blighted your life—I am firmly persuaded of it!—you were made the instrument of the retribution that my sins of many years had deserved. Oh, such things have happened before to-day! One person has, before now, been the means of innocently ripening the growth of evil in another. You have done that already—and you have more to do yet. You have still to bring me to the day of discovery, and to the punishment that is my doom. We shall meet again—here in England, or there in Venice where my husband died—and meet for the last time.'

In spite of her better sense, in spite of her natural superiority to superstitions of all kinds, Agnes was impressed by the terrible earnestness with which those words were spoken. She turned pale as she looked at Henry. 'Do *you* understand her?' she asked.

'Nothing is easier than to understand her,' he replied contemptuously. 'She knows what has become of Ferrari; and she is confusing you in a cloud of nonsense, because she daren't own the truth. Let her go!'

If a dog had been under one of the chairs, and had barked, Lady Montbarry could not have proceeded more impenetrably with the last words she had to say to Agnes.

'Advise your interesting Mrs Ferrari to wait a little longer,' she said. '*You* will know what has become of her husband, and you will tell her. There will be nothing to alarm you. Some trifling event will bring us together the next time—as trifling, I dare say, as the engagement of Ferrari. Sad nonsense, Mr Westwick, is it not? But you make allowances for women; we all talk nonsense. Good morning, Miss Lockwood.'

She opened the door—suddenly, as if she was afraid of being called back for the second time—and left them.

## CHAPTER XII

'Do you think she is mad?' Agnes asked.

'I think she is simply wicked. False, superstitious, inveterately cruel—but not mad. I believe her main motive in coming here was to enjoy the luxury of frightening you.'

'She *has* frightened me. I am ashamed to own it—but so it is.'

Henry looked at her, hesitated for a moment, and seated himself on the sofa by her side.

'I am very anxious about you, Agnes,' he said. 'But for the fortunate chance which led me to call here to-day—who knows what that vile woman might not have said or done, if she had found you alone? My dear, you are leading a sadly unprotected solitary life. I don't like to think of it; I want to see it changed—especially after what has happened to-day. No! no! it is useless to tell me that you have your old nurse. She is too old; she is not in your rank of life—there is no sufficient protection in the companionship of such a person for a lady in your position. Don't mistake me, Agnes! what I say, I say in the sincerity of my devotion to you.' He paused, and took her hand. She made a feeble effort to withdraw it—and yielded. 'Will the day never come,' he pleaded, 'when the privilege of protecting you may be mine? when you will be the pride and joy of my life, as long as my life lasts?' He pressed her hand gently. She made no reply. The colour came and went on her face; her eyes were turned away from him. 'Have I been so unhappy as to offend you?' he asked.

She answered that—she said, almost in a whisper, 'No.'

'Have I distressed you?'

'You have made me think of the sad days that are gone.' She said no more; she only tried to withdraw her hand from his for the second time. He still held it; he lifted it to his lips.

'Can I never make you think of other days than those—of the happier days to come? Or, if you must think of the time that is passed, can you not look back to the time when I first loved you?'

She sighed as he put the question. 'Spare me, Henry,' she answered sadly. 'Say no more!'

The colour again rose in her cheeks; her hand trembled in his. She looked lovely, with her eyes cast down and her bosom heaving gently. At that moment he would have given everything he had in the world to take her in his arms and kiss her. Some mysterious sympathy, passing from his hand to hers, seemed to tell her what was in his mind. She snatched her hand away, and suddenly looked up at him. The tears were in her eyes. She said nothing; she let her eyes speak for her. They warned him—without anger, without unkindness—but still they warned him to press her no further that day.

'Only tell me that I am forgiven,' he said, as he rose from the sofa.

'Yes,' she answered quietly, 'you are forgiven.'

'I have not lowered myself in your estimation, Agnes?'

'Oh, no!'

'Do you wish me to leave you?'

She rose, in her turn, from the sofa, and walked to her writing-table before she replied. The unfinished letter which she had been writing when Lady Montbarry interrupted her, lay open on the blotting-book. As she looked at the letter, and then looked at Henry, the smile that charmed everybody showed itself in her face.

'You must not go just yet,' she said: 'I have something to tell you. I hardly know how to express it. The shortest way perhaps will be to let you find it out for yourself. You have been speaking of my lonely unprotected life here. It is not a very happy life, Henry—I own that.' She paused, observing the growing anxiety of his expression as he looked at her, with a shy satisfaction that perplexed him. 'Do you know that I have anticipated your idea?' she went on. 'I am going to make a great change in my life—if your brother Stephen and his wife will only consent to it.' She opened the desk of the writing-table while she spoke, took a letter out, and handed it to Henry.

He received it from her mechanically. Vague doubts, which he hardly understood himself, kept him silent. It was impossible that the 'change in her life' of which she had spoken could mean that she was about to be married—and yet he was conscious of a perfectly un-reasonable reluctance to open the letter. Their eyes met; she smiled again. 'Look at the address,' she said. 'You ought to know the hand-writing—but I dare say you don't.'

He looked at the address. It was in the large, irregular, uncertain writing of a child. He opened the letter instantly.

'Dear Aunt Agnes,—Our governess is going away. She has had money left to her, and a house of her own. We have had cake and wine to drink her health. You promised to be our governess if we wanted another. We want you. Mamma knows nothing about this. Please come before Mamma can get another governess. Your loving Lucy, who writes this. Clara and Blanche have tried to write too. But they are too young to do it. They blot the paper.'

'Your eldest niece,' Agnes explained, as Henry looked at her in amazement. 'The children used to call me aunt when I was staying with their mother in Ireland, in the autumn. The three girls were my inseparable companions—they are the most charming children I know. It is quite true that I offered to be their governess, if they ever wanted one, on the day when I left them to return to London. I was writing to propose it to their mother, just before you came.'

'Not seriously!' Henry exclaimed.

Agnes placed her unfinished letter in his hand. Enough of it had been written to show that she did seriously propose to enter the household of Mr and Mrs Stephen Westwick as governess to their children! Henry's bewilderment was not to be expressed in words.

'They won't believe you are in earnest,' he said.

'Why not?' Agnes asked quietly.

'You are my brother Stephen's cousin; you are his wife's old friend.'

'All the more reason, Henry, for trusting me with the charge of their children.'

'But you are their equal; you are not obliged to get your living by teaching. There is something absurd in your entering their service as a governess!'

'What is there absurd in it? The children love me; the mother loves me; the father has shown me innumerable instances of his true friendship and regard. I am the very woman for the place—and, as to my education, I must have completely forgotten it indeed, if I am not fit to teach three children the eldest of whom is only eleven years old. You say I am their equal. Are there no other women who serve as governesses, and who are the equals of the persons whom they serve? Besides, I don't know that I *am* their equal. Have I not heard that your brother Stephen was the next heir to the title? Will he not be the new lord? Never mind answering me! We won't dispute whether I am right or wrong in turning governess—we will wait the event. I am weary of my lonely useless existence here, and eager to make my life more happy and more useful, in the household of all others in which I should like most to have a place. If you will look again, you will see that I have these personal considerations still to urge before I finish my letter. You don't know your brother and his wife as well as I do, if you doubt their answer. I believe they have courage enough and heart enough to say Yes.'

Henry submitted without being convinced.

He was a man who disliked all eccentric departures from custom and routine; and he felt especially suspicious of the change proposed in the life of Agnes. With new interests to occupy her mind, she might be less favourably disposed to listen to him, on the next occasion when he urged his suit. The influence of the 'lonely useless existence' of which she complained, was distinctly an influence in his favour. While her heart was empty, her heart was accessible. But with his nieces in full possession of it, the clouds of doubt overshadowed his prospects. He knew the sex well enough to keep these purely selfish perplexities to himself. The waiting policy was especially the policy to pursue with a woman as sensitive as Agnes. If he once offended her delicacy he was lost. For the moment he wisely controlled himself and changed the subject.

'My little niece's letter has had an effect,' he said, 'which the child never contemplated in writing it. She has just reminded me of one of the objects that I had in calling on you to-day.'

Agnes looked at the child's letter. 'How does Lucy do that?' she asked.

'Lucy's governess is not the only lucky person who has had money left her,' Henry answered. 'Is your old nurse in the house?'

'You don't mean to say that nurse has got a legacy?'

'She has got a hundred pounds. Send for her, Agnes, while I show you the letter.'

He took a handful of letters from his pocket, and looked through them, while Agnes rang the bell. Returning to him, she noticed a printed letter among the rest, which lay open on the table. It was a 'prospectus,' and the title of it was 'Palace Hotel Company of Venice (Limited).' The two words, 'Palace' and 'Venice,' instantly recalled her mind to the unwelcome visit of Lady Montbarry. 'What is that?' she asked, pointing to the title.

Henry suspended his search, and glanced at the prospectus. 'A really promising speculation,' he said. 'Large hotels always pay well, if they are well managed. I know the man who is appointed to be manager of this hotel when it is opened to the public; and I have such entire confidence in him that I have become one of the shareholders of the Company.'

The reply did not appear to satisfy Agnes. 'Why is the hotel called the "Palace Hotel"?' she inquired.

Henry looked at her, and at once penetrated her motive for asking the question. 'Yes,' he said, 'it *is* the palace that Montbarry hired at Venice; and it has been purchased by the Company to be changed into an hotel.'

Agnes turned away in silence, and took a chair at the farther end of the room. Henry had disappointed her. His income as a younger son stood in need, as she well knew, of all the additions that he could make to it by successful speculation. But she was unreasonable enough, nevertheless, to disapprove of his attempting to make money already out of the house in which his brother had died. Incapable of under-standing this purely sentimental view of a plain matter of business, Henry returned to his papers, in some perplexity at the sudden change in the manner of Agnes towards him. Just as he found the letter of which he was in search, the nurse made her appearance. He glanced at Agnes, expecting that she would speak first. She never even looked up when the nurse came in. It was left to Henry to tell the old woman why the bell had summoned her to the drawing-room.

'Well, nurse,' he said, 'you have had a windfall of luck. You have had a legacy left you of a hundred pounds.'

The nurse showed no outward signs of exultation. She waited a little to get the announcement of the legacy well settled in her mind—and then she said quietly, 'Master Henry, who gives me that money, if you please?'

'My late brother, Lord Montbarry, gives it to you.' (Agnes instantly looked up, interested in the matter for the first time. Henry went on.) 'His will leaves legacies to the surviving old servants of the family. There is a letter from his lawyers, authorising you to apply to them for the money.'

In every class of society, gratitude is the rarest of all human virtues. In the nurse's class it is extremely rare. Her opinion of the man who had deceived and deserted her mistress remained the same opinion still, perfectly undisturbed by the passing circumstance of the legacy.

'I wonder who reminded my lord of the old servants?' she said. 'He would never have heart enough to remember them himself!'

Agnes suddenly interposed. Nature, always abhorring monotony, institutes reserves of temper as elements in the composition of the gentlest women living. Even Agnes could, on rare occasions, be angry. The nurse's view of Montbarry's character seemed to have provoked her beyond endurance.

'If you have any sense of shame in you,' she broke out, 'you ought to be ashamed of what you have just said! Your ingratitude disgusts me. I leave you to speak with her, Henry—*you* won't mind it!' With this significant intimation that he too had dropped out of his customary place in her good opinion, she left the room.

The nurse received the smart reproof administered to her with every appearance of feeling rather amused by it than not. When the door had closed, this female philosopher winked at Henry.

'There's a power of obstinacy in young women,' she remarked. 'Miss Agnes wouldn't give my lord up as a bad one, even when he jilted her. And now she's sweet on him after he's dead. Say a word against him, and she fires up as you see. All obstinacy! It will wear out with time. Stick to her, Master Henry—stick to her!'

'She doesn't seem to have offended you,' said Henry.

'*She?*' the nurse repeated in amazement—'she offend me? I like her in her tantrums; it reminds me of her when she was a baby. Lord bless you! when I go to bid her good-night, she'll give me a big kiss, poor dear—and say, Nurse, I didn't mean it! About this money, Master Henry? If I was younger I should spend it in dress and jewellery. But I'm too old for that. What shall I do with my legacy when I have got it?'

'Put it out at interest,' Henry suggested. 'Get so much a year for it, you know.'

'How much shall I get?' the nurse asked.

'If you put your hundred pounds into the Funds,* you will get between three and four pounds a year.'

The nurse shook her head. 'Three or four pounds a year? That won't do! I want more than that. Look here, Master Henry. I don't care about this bit of money—I never did like the man who has left it to me, though he *was* your brother. If I lost it all to-morrow, I shouldn't break my heart; I'm well enough off, as it is, for the rest of my days. They say you're a speculator. Put me in for a good thing, there's a dear! Neck-or-nothing—and *that* for the Funds!' She snapped her fingers to express her contempt for security of invest-ment at three per cent.

Henry produced the prospectus of the Venetian Hotel Company. 'You're a funny old woman,' he said. 'There, you dashing specu-lator—there is neck-or-nothing for you! You must keep it a secret from Miss Agnes, mind. I'm not at all sure that she would approve of my helping you to this investment.'

The nurse took out her spectacles. 'Six per cent. guaranteed,' she read; 'and the Directors have every reason to believe that ten per cent., or more, will be ultimately realised to the shareholders by the hotel.' 'Put me into that, Master Henry! And, wherever you go, for Heaven's sake recommend the hotel to your friends!'

So the nurse, following Henry's mercenary example, had *her* pecuniary interest, too, in the house in which Lord Montbarry had died.

Three days passed before Henry was able to visit Agnes again. In that time, the little cloud between them had entirely passed away. Agnes received him with even more than her customary kindness. She was in better spirits than usual. Her letter to Mrs Stephen Westwick had been answered by return of post; and her proposal had been joyfully accepted, with one modification. She was to visit the Westwicks for a month—and, if she really liked teaching the children, she was then to be governess, aunt, and cousin, all in one—and was only to go away in an event which her friends in Ireland persisted in contemplating, the event of her marriage.

'You see I was right,' she said to Henry.

He was still incredulous. 'Are you really going?' he asked.

'I am going next week.'

'When shall I see you again?'

'You know you are always welcome at your brother's house. You can see me when you like.' She held out her hand. 'Pardon me for leaving you—I am beginning to pack up already.'

Henry tried to kiss her at parting. She drew back directly.

'Why not? I am your cousin,' he said.

'I don't like it,' she answered.

Henry looked at her, and submitted. Her refusal to grant him his privilege as a cousin was a good sign—it was indirectly an act of encouragement to him in the character of her lover.

On the first day in the new week, Agnes left London on her way to Ireland. As the event proved, this was not destined to be the end of her journey. The way to Ireland was only the first stage on a round-about road—the road that led to the palace at Venice.

# THE THIRD PART

## CHAPTER XIII

In the spring of the year 1861, Agnes was established at the country-seat of her two friends—now promoted (on the death of the first lord, without offspring) to be the new Lord and Lady Montbarry. The old nurse was not separated from her mistress. A place, suited to her time of life, had been found for her in the pleasant Irish household. She was perfectly happy in her new sphere; and she spent her first half-year's dividend from the Venice Hotel Company, with characteristic prodigality, in presents for the children.

Early in the year, also, the Directors of the life insurance offices submitted to circumstances, and paid the ten thousand pounds. Immediately afterwards, the widow of the first Lord Montbarry (otherwise, the dowager Lady Montbarry) left England, with Baron Rivar, for the United States. The Baron's object was announced, in the scientific columns of the newspapers, to be investigation into the present state of experimental chemistry in the great American republic. His sister informed inquiring friends that she accompanied him, in the hope of finding consolation in change of scene after the bereavement that had fallen on her. Hearing this news from Henry Westwick (then paying a visit at his brother's house), Agnes was conscious of a certain sense of relief. 'With the Atlantic between us,' she said, 'surely I have done with that terrible woman now!'

Barely a week passed after those words had been spoken, before an event happened which reminded Agnes of the 'terrible woman' once more.

On that day, Henry's engagements had obliged him to return to London. He had ventured, on the morning of his departure, to press his suit once more on Agnes; and the children, as he had anticipated, proved to be innocent obstacles in the way of his success. On the other hand, he had privately secured a firm ally in his sister-in-law. 'Have a little patience,' the new Lady Montbarry had said, 'and leave me to turn the influence of the children in the right direction. If they can persuade her to listen to you—they shall!'

The two ladies had accompanied Henry, and some other guests who went away at the same time, to the railway station, and had just driven back to the house, when the servant announced that 'a person of the name of Rolland was waiting to see her ladyship.'

'Is it a woman?'

'Yes, my lady.'

Young Lady Montbarry turned to Agnes.

'This is the very person,' she said, 'whom your lawyer thought likely to help him, when he was trying to trace the lost courier.'

'You don't mean the English maid who was with Lady Montbarry at Venice?'

'My dear! don't speak of Montbarry's horrid widow by the name which is *my* name now. Stephen and I have arranged to call her by her foreign title, before she was married. I am "Lady Montbarry," and she is "the Countess." In that way there will be no confusion.—Yes, Mrs Rolland was in my service before she became the Countess's maid. She was a perfectly trustworthy person, with one defect that obliged me to send her away—a sullen temper which led to perpetual complaints of her in the servants' hall. Would you like to see her?'

Agnes accepted the proposal, in the faint hope of getting some information for the courier's wife. The complete defeat of every attempt to trace the lost man had been accepted as final by Mrs Ferrari. She had deliberately arrayed herself in widow's mourning; and was earning her livelihood in an employment which the unwearied kindness of Agnes had procured for her in London. The last chance of penetrating the mystery of Ferrari's disappearance seemed to rest now on what Ferrari's former fellow-servant might be able to tell. With highly-wrought expectations, Agnes followed her friend into the room in which Mrs Rolland was waiting.

A tall bony woman, in the autumn of life, with sunken eyes and iron-grey hair, rose stiffly from her chair, and saluted the ladies with stern submission as they opened the door. A person of unblemished character, evidently—but not without visible drawbacks. Big bushy eyebrows, an awfully deep and solemn voice, a harsh unbending manner, a complete absence in her figure of the undulating lines characteristic of the sex, presented Virtue in this excellent person under its least alluring aspect. Strangers, on a first introduction to her, were accustomed to wonder why she was not a man.

'Are you pretty well, Mrs Rolland?'

'I am as well as I can expect to be, my lady, at my time of life.'

'Is there anything I can do for you?'

'Your ladyship can do me a great favour, if you will please speak to my character while I was in your service. I am offered a place, to wait on an invalid lady who has lately come to live in this neighbourhood.'

'Ah, yes—I have heard of her. A Mrs Carbury, with a very pretty niece I am told. But, Mrs Rolland, you left my service some time ago. Mrs Carbury will surely expect you to refer to the last mistress by whom you were employed.'

A flash of virtuous indignation irradiated Mrs Rolland's sunken eyes. She coughed before she answered, as if her 'last mistress' stuck in her throat.

'I have explained to Mrs Carbury, my lady, that the person I last served—I really cannot give her her title in your ladyship's presence!—has left England for America. Mrs Carbury knows that I quitted the person of my own free will, and knows why, and approves of my conduct so far. A word from your ladyship will be amply sufficient to get me the situation.'

'Very well, Mrs Rolland, I have no objection to be your reference, under the circumstances. Mrs Carbury will find me at home tomorrow until two o'clock.'

'Mrs Carbury is not well enough to leave the house, my lady. Her niece, Miss Haldane, will call and make the inquiries, if your ladyship has no objection.'

'I have not the least objection. The pretty niece carries her own welcome with her. Wait a minute, Mrs Rolland. This lady is Miss Lockwood—my husband's cousin, and my friend. She is anxious to speak to you about the courier who was in the late Lord Montbarry's service at Venice.'

Mrs Rolland's bushy eyebrows frowned in stern disapproval of the new topic of conversation. 'I regret to hear it, my lady,' was all she said.

'Perhaps you have not been informed of what happened after you left Venice?' Agnes ventured to add. 'Ferrari left the palace secretly; and he has never been heard of since.'

Mrs Rolland mysteriously closed her eyes—as if to exclude some vision of the lost courier which was of a nature to disturb a respectable woman. 'Nothing that Mr Ferrari could do would surprise me,' she replied in her deepest bass tones.

'You speak rather harshly of him,' said Agnes.

Mrs Rolland suddenly opened her eyes again. 'I speak harshly of nobody without reason,' she said. 'Mr Ferrari behaved to me, Miss Lockwood, as no man living has ever behaved—before or since.'

'What did he do?'

Mrs Rolland answered, with a stony stare of horror:—

'He took liberties with me.'

Young Lady Montbarry suddenly turned aside, and put her handkerchief over her mouth in convulsions of suppressed laughter.

Mrs Rolland went on, with a grim enjoyment of the bewilderment which her reply had produced in Agnes: 'And when I insisted on an apology, Miss, he had the audacity to say that the life at the palace was dull, and he didn't know how else to amuse himself!'

'I am afraid I have hardly made myself understood,' said Agnes. 'I am not speaking to you out of any interest in Ferrari. Are you aware that he is married?'

'I pity his wife,' said Mrs Rolland.

'She is naturally in great grief about him,' Agnes proceeded.

'She ought to thank God she is rid of him,' Mrs Rolland interposed.

Agnes still persisted. 'I have known Mrs Ferrari from her childhood, and I am sincerely anxious to help her in this matter. Did you notice anything, while you were at Venice, that would account for her husband's extraordinary disappearance? On what sort of terms, for instance, did he live with his master and mistress?'

'On terms of familiarity with his mistress,' said Mrs Rolland, 'which were simply sickening to a respectable English servant. She used to encourage him to talk to her about all his affairs— how he got on with his wife, and how pressed he was for money, and such like—just as if they were equals. Contemptible—that's what I call it.'

'And his master?' Agnes continued. 'How did Ferrari get on with Lord Montbarry?'

'My lord used to live shut up with his studies and his sorrows,' Mrs Rolland answered, with a hard solemnity expressive of respect for his lordship's memory. 'Mr Ferrari got his money when it was due; and he cared for nothing else. "If I could afford it, I would leave the place too; but I can't afford it." Those were the last words he said to me, on the morning when I left the palace. I made no reply. After what had happened (on that other occasion) I was naturally not on speaking terms with Mr Ferrari.'

'Can you really tell me nothing which will throw any light on this matter?'

'Nothing,' said Mrs Rolland, with an undisguised relish of the disappointment that she was inflicting.

'There was another member of the family at Venice,' Agnes resumed, determined to sift the question to the bottom while she had the chance. 'There was Baron Rivar.'

Mrs Rolland lifted her large hands, covered with rusty black gloves, in mute protest against the introduction of Baron Rivar as a subject of inquiry. 'Are you aware, Miss,' she began, 'that I left my place in consequence of what I observed—?'

Agnes stopped her there. 'I only wanted to ask,' she explained, 'if anything was said or done by Baron Rivar which might account for Ferrari's strange conduct.'

'Nothing that I know of,' said Mrs Rolland. 'The Baron and Mr Ferrari (if I may use such an expression) were "birds of a feather," so far as I could see—I mean, one was as unprincipled as the other. I am a just woman; and I will give you an example. Only the day before I left, I heard the Baron say (through the open door of his room while I was passing along the corridor), "Ferrari, I want a thousand pounds. What would you do for a thousand pounds?" And I heard Mr Ferrari answer, "Anything, sir, as long as I was not found out." And then they both burst out laughing. I heard no more than that. Judge for yourself, Miss.'

Agnes reflected for a moment. A thousand pounds was the sum that had been sent to Mrs Ferrari in the anonymous letter. Was that enclosure in any way connected, as a result, with the conversation between the Baron and Ferrari? It was useless to press any more inquiries on Mrs Rolland. She could give no further information which was of the slightest importance to the object in view. There was no alternative but to grant her her dismissal. One more effort had been made to find a trace of the lost man, and once again the effort had failed.

They were a family party at the dinner-table that day. The only guest left in the house was a nephew of the new Lord Montbarry—the eldest son of his sister, Lady Barville. Lady Montbarry could not resist telling the story of the first (and last) attack made on the virtue of Mrs Rolland, with a comically-exact imitation of Mrs Rolland's deep and dismal voice. Being asked by her husband what was the object which had brought that formidable person to the house, she naturally mentioned the expected visit of Miss Haldane. Arthur Barville, unusually silent and pre-occupied so far, suddenly struck into the conversation with a burst of enthusiasm. 'Miss Haldane is the most charming girl in all Ireland!' he said. 'I caught sight of her yesterday, over the wall of her garden, as I was riding by. What time is she coming to-morrow? Before two? I'll look into the drawing-room by accident—I am dying to be introduced to her!'

Agnes was amused by his enthusiasm. 'Are you in love with Miss Haldane already?' she asked.

Arthur answered gravely, 'It's no joking matter. I have been all day at the garden wall, waiting to see her again! It depends on Miss Haldane to make me the happiest or the wretchedest man living.'

'You foolish boy! How can you talk such nonsense?'

He was talking nonsense undoubtedly. But, if Agnes had only known it, he was doing something more than that. He was innocently leading her another stage nearer on the way to Venice.

## CHAPTER XIV

As the summer months advanced, the transformation of the Venetian palace into the modern hotel proceeded rapidly towards completion.

The outside of the building, with its fine Palladian* front looking on the canal, was wisely left unaltered. Inside, as a matter of necessity, the rooms were almost rebuilt—so far at least as the size and the arrangement of them were concerned. The vast saloons were partitioned off into 'apartments' containing three or four rooms each. The broad corridors in the upper regions afforded spare space enough for rows of little bedchambers, devoted to servants and to travellers with limited means. Nothing was spared but the solid floors and the finely-carved ceilings. These last, in excellent preservation as to workmanship, merely required cleaning, and regilding here and there, to add greatly to the beauty and importance of the best rooms in the hotel. The only exception to the complete re-organisation of the interior was at one extremity of the edifice, on the first and second floors. Here there happened, in each case, to be rooms of such comparatively moderate size, and so attractively decorated, that the architect suggested leaving them as they were. It was afterwards discovered that these were no other than the apartments formerly occupied by Lord Montbarry (on the first floor), and by Baron Rivar (on the second). The room in which Montbarry had died was still fitted up as a bedroom, and was now distinguished as Number Fourteen. The room above it, in which the Baron had slept, took its place on the hotel-register as Number Thirty-Eight. With the ornaments on the walls and ceilings cleaned and brightened up, and with the heavy old-fashioned beds, chairs, and tables replaced by bright, pretty, and luxurious modern furniture, these two promised to be at once the most attractive and the most comfortable bedchambers in the hotel. As for the once-desolate and disused ground floor of the building, it was now transformed, by means of splendid dining-rooms, reception-rooms, billiard-rooms, and smoking-rooms, into a palace by itself. Even the dungeon-like vaults beneath, now lighted and ventilated on the most approved modern plan, had been turned as if by magic into kitchens, servants' offices, ice-rooms, and wine cellars, worthy of the splendour of the grandest hotel in Italy, in the now bygone period of seventeen years since.

Passing from the lapse of the summer months at Venice, to the lapse of the summer months in Ireland, it is next to be recorded that Mrs Rolland obtained the situation of attendant on the invalid Mrs Carbury; and that the fair Miss Haldane, like a female Caesar, came, saw, and conquered, on her first day's visit to the new Lord Montbarry's house.

The ladies were as loud in her praises as Arthur Barville himself. Lord Montbarry declared that she was the only perfectly pretty woman he had ever seen, who was really unconscious of her own attractions. The old nurse said she looked as if she had just stepped out of a picture, and wanted nothing but a gilt frame round her to make her complete. Miss Haldane, on her side, returned from her first visit to the Montbarrys charmed with her new acquaintances. Later on the same day, Arthur called with an offering of fruit and flowers for Mrs Carbury, and with instructions to ask if she was well enough to receive Lord and Lady Montbarry and Miss Lockwood on the morrow. In a week's time, the two households were on the friendliest terms. Mrs Carbury, confined to the sofa by a spinal malady, had been hitherto dependent on her niece for one of the few pleasures she could enjoy, the pleasure of having the best new novels read to her as they came out. Discovering this, Arthur volunteered to relieve Miss Haldane, at intervals, in the office of reader. He was clever at mechanical contrivances of all sorts, and he introduced improvements in Mrs Carbury's couch, and in the means of conveying her from the bed-chamber to the drawing-room, which alleviated the poor lady's sufferings and brightened her gloomy life. With these claims on the gratitude of the aunt, aided by the personal advantages which he unquestionably possessed, Arthur advanced rapidly in the favour of the charming niece. She was, it is needless to say, perfectly well aware that he was in love with her, while he was himself modestly reticent on the subject—so far as words went. But she was not equally quick in penetrating the nature of her own feelings towards Arthur. Watching the two young people with keen powers of observation, necessarily concentrated on them by the complete seclusion of her life, the invalid lady discovered signs of roused sensibility in Miss Haldane, when Arthur was present, which had never yet shown themselves in her social relations with other admirers eager to pay their addresses to her. Having drawn her own conclusions in private, Mrs Carbury took the first favourable opportunity (in Arthur's interests) of putting them to the test.

'I don't know what I shall do,' she said one day, 'when Arthur goes away.'

Miss Haldane looked up quickly from her work. 'Surely he is not going to leave us!' she exclaimed.

'My dear! he has already stayed at his uncle's house a month longer than he intended. His father and mother naturally expect to see him at home again.'

Miss Haldane met this difficulty with a suggestion, which could only have proceeded from a judgment already disturbed by the ravages of the tender passion. 'Why can't his father and mother go and see him at Lord Montbarry's?' she asked. 'Sir Theodore's place is only thirty miles away, and Lady Barville is Lord Montbarry's sister. They needn't stand on ceremony.'

'They may have other engagements,' Mrs Carbury remarked.

'My dear aunt, we don't know that! Suppose you ask Arthur?'

'Suppose *you* ask him?'

Miss Haldane bent her head again over her work. Suddenly as it was done, her aunt had seen her face—and her face betrayed her.

When Arthur came the next day, Mrs Carbury said a word to him in private, while her niece was in the garden. The last new novel lay neglected on the table. Arthur followed Miss Haldane into the garden. The next day he wrote home, enclosing in his letter a photograph of Miss Haldane. Before the end of the week, Sir Theodore and Lady Barville arrived at Lord Montbarry's, and formed their own judgment of the fidelity of the portrait. They had themselves married early in life—and, strange to say, they did not object on principle to the early marriages of other people. The question of age being thus disposed of, the course of true love had no other obstacles to encounter. Miss Haldane was an only child, and was possessed of an ample fortune. Arthur's career at the university had been creditable, but certainly not brilliant enough to present his withdrawal in the light of a disaster. As Sir Theodore's eldest son, his position was already made for him. He was two-and-twenty years of age; and the young lady was eighteen. There was really no producible reason for keeping the lovers waiting, and no excuse for deferring the wedding-day beyond the first week in September. In the interval, while the bride and bridegroom would be necessarily absent on the inevitable tour abroad, a sister of Mrs Carbury volunteered to stay with her during the temporary separation from her niece. On the conclusion of the honeymoon, the young couple were to return to Ireland, and were to establish themselves in Mrs Carbury's spacious and comfortable house.

These arrangements were decided upon early in the month of August. About the same date, the last alterations in the old palace at Venice were completed. The rooms were dried by steam; the cellars were stocked; the manager collected round him his army of skilled servants; and the new hotel was advertised all over Europe to open in October.

## CHAPTER XV

### (MISS AGNES LOCKWOOD TO MRS FERRARI)

'I promised to give you some account, dear Emily, of the marriage of Mr Arthur Barville and Miss Haldane. It took place ten days since. But I have had so many things to look after in the absence of the master and mistress of this house, that I am only able to write to you to-day.

'The invitations to the wedding were limited to members of the families on either side, in consideration of the ill health of Miss Haldane's aunt. On the side of the Montbarry family, there were present, besides Lord and Lady Montbarry, Sir Theodore and Lady Barville; Mrs Norbury (whom you may remember as his lordship's second sister); and Mr Francis Westwick, and Mr Henry Westwick. The three children and I attended the ceremony as bridesmaids. We were joined by two young ladies, cousins of the bride and very agreeable girls. Our dresses were white, trimmed with green in honour of Ireland; and we each had a handsome gold bracelet given to us as a present from the bridegroom. If you add to the persons whom I have already mentioned, the elder members of Mrs Carbury's family, and the old servants in both houses—privileged to drink the healths of the married pair at the lower end of the room—you will have the list of the company at the wedding-breakfast complete.

'The weather was perfect, and the ceremony (with music) was beautifully performed. As for the bride, no words can describe how lovely she looked, or how well she went through it all. We were very merry at the breakfast, and the speeches went off on the whole quite well enough. The last speech, before the party broke up, was made by Mr Henry Westwick, and was the best of all. He offered a happy suggestion, at the end, which has produced a very unexpected change in my life here.

'As well as I remember, he concluded in these words:—"On one point, we are all agreed—we are sorry that the parting hour is near, and we should be glad to meet again. Why should we not meet again? This is the autumn time of the year; we are most of us leaving home for the holidays. What do you say (if you have no engagements that will prevent it) to joining our young married friends before the close of their tour, and renewing the social success of this delightful breakfast by another festival in honour of the honeymoon? The bride and bridegroom are going to Germany and the Tyrol, on their way to Italy. I propose that we allow them a month to themselves, and that we arrange to meet them afterwards in the North of Italy—say at Venice."

'This proposal was received with great applause, which was changed into shouts of laughter by no less a person than my dear old nurse. The moment Mr Westwick pronounced the word "Venice," she started up among the servants at the lower end of the room, and called out at the top of her voice, "Go to our hotel, ladies and gentlemen! We get six per cent. on our money already; and if you will only crowd the place and call for the best of everything, it will be ten per cent. in our pockets in no time. Ask Master Henry!"

'Appealed to in this irresistible manner, Mr Westwick had no choice but to explain that he was concerned as a shareholder in a new Hotel Company at Venice, and that he had invested a small sum of money for the nurse (not very considerately, as I think) in the speculation. Hearing this, the company, by way of humouring the joke, drank a new toast:—Success to the nurse's hotel, and a speedy rise in the dividend!

'When the conversation returned in due time to the more serious question of the proposed meeting at Venice, difficulties began to present themselves, caused of course by invitations for the autumn which many of the guests had already accepted. Only two members of Mrs Carbury's family were at liberty to keep the proposed appointment. On our side we were more at leisure to do as we pleased. Mr Henry Westwick decided to go to Venice in advance of the rest, to test the accommodation of the new hotel on the opening day. Mrs Norbury and Mr Francis Westwick volunteered to follow him; and, after some persuasion, Lord and Lady Montbarry consented to a species of compromise. His lordship could not conveniently spare time enough for the journey to Venice, but he and Lady Montbarry arranged to accompany Mrs Norbury and Mr Francis Westwick as far on their way to Italy as Paris. Five days since, they took their departure to meet their travelling companions in London; leaving me here in charge of the three dear children. They begged hard, of course, to be taken with papa and mamma. But it was thought better not to interrupt the progress of their education, and not to expose them (especially the two younger girls) to the fatigues of travelling.

'I have had a charming letter from the bride, this morning, dated Cologne. You cannot think how artlessly and prettily she assures me of her happiness. Some people, as they say in Ireland, are born to good luck—and I think Arthur Barville is one of them.

'When you next write, I hope to hear that you are in better health and spirits, and that you continue to like your employment. Believe me, sincerely your friend,—A. L.'

Agnes had just closed and directed her letter, when the eldest of her three pupils entered the room with the startling announcement that Lord Montbarry's travelling-servant had arrived from Paris! Alarmed by the idea that some misfortune had happened, she ran out to meet the man in the hall. Her face told him how seriously he had frightened her, before she could speak. 'There's nothing wrong, Miss,' he hastened to say. 'My lord and my lady are enjoying themselves at Paris. They only want you and the young ladies to be with them.' Saying these amazing words, he handed to Agnes a letter from Lady Montbarry.

'Dearest Agnes,' (she read), 'I am so charmed with the delightful change in my life—it is six years, remember, since I last travelled on the Continent—that I have exerted all my fascinations to persuade Lord Montbarry to go on to Venice. And, what is more to the purpose, I have actually succeeded! He has just gone to his room to write the necessary letters of excuse in time for the post to England. May you have as good a husband, my dear, when your time comes! In the mean while, the one thing wanting now to make my happiness complete, is to have you and the darling children with us. Montbarry is just as miserable without them as I am—though he doesn't confess it so freely. You will have no difficulties to trouble you. Louis will deliver these hurried lines, and will take care of you on the journey to Paris. Kiss the children for me a thousand times—and never mind their education for the present! Pack up instantly, my dear, and I will be fonder of you than ever. Your affectionate friend, Adela Montbarry.'

Agnes folded up the letter; and, feeling the need of composing herself, took refuge for a few minutes in her own room.

Her first natural sensations of surprise and excitement at the prospect of going to Venice were succeeded by impressions of a less agreeable kind. With the recovery of her customary composure came the unwelcome remembrance of the parting words spoken to her by Montbarry's widow:—'We shall meet again—here in England, or there in Venice where my husband died—and meet for the last time.'

It was an odd coincidence, to say the least of it, that the march of events should be unexpectedly taking Agnes to Venice, after those words had been spoken! Was the woman of the mysterious warnings and the wild black eyes still thousands of miles away in America? Or was the march of events taking *her* unexpectedly, too, on the journey to Venice? Agnes started out of her chair, ashamed of even the momentary concession to superstition which was implied by the mere presence of such questions as these in her mind.

She rang the bell, and sent for her little pupils, and announced their approaching departure to the household. The noisy delight of the children, the inspiriting effort of packing up in a hurry, roused all her energies. She dismissed her own absurd misgivings from consideration, with the contempt that they deserved. She worked as only women *can* work, when their hearts are in what they do. The travellers reached Dublin that day, in time for the boat to England. Two days later, they were with Lord and Lady Montbarry at Paris.

# THE FOURTH PART

## CHAPTER XVI

It was only the twentieth of September, when Agnes and the children reached Paris. Mrs Norbury and her brother Francis had then already started on their journey to Italy—at least three weeks before the date at which the new hotel was to open for the reception of travellers.

The person answerable for this premature departure was Francis Westwick.

Like his younger brother Henry, he had increased his pecuniary resources by his own enterprise and ingenuity; with this difference, that his speculations were connected with the Arts. He had made money, in the first instance, by a weekly newspaper; and he had then invested his profits in a London theatre. This latter enterprise, admirably conducted, had been rewarded by the public with steady and liberal encouragement. Pondering over a new form of theatrical attraction for the coming winter season, Francis had determined to revive the languid public taste for the ballet by means of an entertainment of his own invention, combining dramatic interest with dancing. He was now, accordingly, in search of the best dancer (possessed of the indispensable personal attractions) who was to be found in the theatres of the Continent. Hearing from his foreign correspondents of two women who had made successful first appearances, one at Milan and one at Florence, he had arranged to visit those cities, and to judge of the merits of the dancers for himself, before he joined the bride and bridegroom. His widowed sister, having friends at Florence whom she was anxious to see, readily accompanied him. The Montbarrys remained at Paris, until it was time to present themselves at the family meeting in Venice. Henry found them still in the French capital, when he arrived from London on his way to the opening of the new hotel.

Against Lady Montbarry's advice, he took the opportunity of renewing his addresses to Agnes. He could hardly have chosen a more unpropitious time for pleading his cause with her. The gaieties of Paris (quite incomprehensibly to herself as well as to everyone about her) had a depressing effect on her spirits. She had no illness to complain of; she shared willingly in the ever-varying succession of amusements offered to strangers by the ingenuity of the liveliest people in the world—but nothing roused her: she remained persistently dull and weary through it all. In this frame of mind and body, she was in no humour to receive Henry's ill-timed addresses with favour, or even with patience: she plainly and positively refused to listen to him. 'Why do you remind me of what I have suffered?' she asked petulantly. 'Don't you see that it has left its mark on me for life?'

'I thought I knew something of women by this time,' Henry said, appealing privately to Lady Montbarry for consolation. 'But Agnes completely puzzles me. It is a year since Montbarry's death; and she remains as devoted to his memory as if he had died faithful to her—she still feels the loss of him, as none of *us* feel it!'

'She is the truest woman that ever breathed the breath of life,' Lady Montbarry answered. 'Remember that, and you will understand her. Can such a woman as Agnes give her love or refuse it, according to circumstances? Because the man was unworthy of her, was he less the man of her choice? The truest and best friend to him (little as he deserved it) in his lifetime, she naturally remains the truest and best friend to his memory now. If you really love her, wait; and trust to your two best friends—to time and to me. There is my advice; let your own experience decide whether it is not the best advice that I can offer. Resume your journey to Venice to-morrow; and when you take leave of Agnes, speak to her as cordially as if nothing had happened.'

Henry wisely followed this advice. Thoroughly understanding him, Agnes made the leave-taking friendly and pleasant on her side. When he stopped at the door for a last look at her, she hurriedly turned her head so that her face was hidden from him. Was that a good sign? Lady Montbarry, accompanying Henry down the stairs, said, 'Yes, decidedly! Write when you get to Venice. We shall wait here to receive letters from Arthur and his wife, and we shall time our departure for Italy accordingly.'

A week passed, and no letter came from Henry. Some days later, a telegram was received from him. It was despatched from Milan, instead of from Venice; and it brought this strange message:—'I have left the hotel. Will return on the arrival of Arthur and his wife. Address, meanwhile, Albergo Reale, Milan.'

Preferring Venice before all other cities of Europe, and having arranged to remain there until the family meeting took place, what unexpected event had led Henry to alter his plans? and why did he state the bare fact, without adding a word of explanation? Let the narrative follow him—and find the answer to those questions at Venice.

## CHAPTER XVII

The Palace Hotel, appealing for encouragement mainly to English and American travellers, celebrated the opening of its doors, as a matter of course, by the giving of a grand banquet, and the delivery of a long succession of speeches.

Delayed on his journey, Henry Westwick only reached Venice in time to join the guests over their coffee and cigars. Observing the splendour of the reception rooms, and taking note especially of the artful mixture of comfort and luxury in the bedchambers, he began to share the old nurse's view of the future, and to contemplate seriously the coming dividend of ten per cent. The hotel was beginning well, at all events. So much interest in the enterprise had been aroused, at home and abroad, by profuse advertising, that the whole accommodation of the building had been secured by travellers of all nations for the opening night. Henry only obtained one of the small rooms on the upper floor, by a lucky accident—the absence of the gentleman who had written to engage it. He was quite satisfied, and was on his way to bed, when another accident altered his prospects for the night, and moved him into another and a better room.

Ascending on his way to the higher regions as far as the first floor of the hotel, Henry's attention was attracted by an angry voice protesting, in a strong New England accent, against one of the greatest hardships that can be inflicted on a citizen of the United States—the hardship of sending him to bed without gas in his room.

The Americans* are not only the most hospitable people to be found on the face of the earth—they are (under certain conditions) the most patient and good-tempered people as well. But they are human; and the limit of American endurance is found in the obsolete institution of a bedroom candle. The American traveller, in the present case, declined to believe that his bedroom was in a completely finished state without a gas-burner. The manager pointed to the fine antique decorations (renewed and regilt) on the walls and the ceiling, and explained that the emanations of burning gas-light would certainly spoil them in the course of a few months. To this the traveller replied that it was possible, but that he did not understand decorations. A bedroom with gas in it was what he was used to, was what he wanted, and was what he was determined to have. The compliant manager volunteered to ask some other gentleman, housed on the inferior upper storey (which was lit throughout with gas), to change rooms. Hearing this, and being quite willing to exchange a small bedchamber for a large one, Henry volunteered to be the other gentleman. The excellent American shook hands with him on the spot. 'You are a cultured person, sir,' he said; 'and *you* will no doubt understand the decorations.'

Henry looked at the number of the room on the door as he opened it. The number was Fourteen.

Tired and sleepy, he naturally anticipated a good night's rest. In the thoroughly healthy state of his nervous system, he slept as well in a bed abroad as in a bed at home. Without the slightest assignable reason, however, his just expectations were disappointed. The luxurious bed, the well-ventilated room, the delicious tranquillity of Venice by night, all were in favour of his sleeping well. He never slept at all. An indescribable sense of depression and discomfort kept him waking through darkness and daylight alike. He went down to the coffee-room as soon as the hotel was astir, and ordered some breakfast. Another unaccountable change in himself appeared with the appearance of the meal. He was absolutely without appetite. An excellent omelette, and cutlets cooked to perfection, he sent away untasted— he, whose appetite never failed him, whose digestion was still equal to any demands on it!

The day was bright and fine. He sent for a gondola, and was rowed to the Lido.

Out on the airy Lagoon, he felt like a new man. He had not left the hotel ten minutes before he was fast asleep in the gondola. Waking, on reaching the landing-place, he crossed the Lido, and enjoyed a morning's swim in the Adriatic. There was only a poor restaurant on the island, in those days; but his appetite was now ready for anything; he ate whatever was offered to him, like a famished man.

He could hardly believe, when he reflected on it, that he had sent away untasted his excellent breakfast at the hotel.

Returning to Venice, he spent the rest of the day in the picture-galleries and the churches. Towards six o'clock his gondola took him back, with another fine appetite, to meet some travelling acquaintances with whom he had engaged to dine at the table d'hôte.*

The dinner was deservedly rewarded with the highest approval by every guest in the hotel but one. To Henry's astonishment, the appetite with which he had entered the house mysteriously and completely left him when he sat down to table. He could drink some wine, but he could literally eat nothing. 'What in the world is the matter with you?' his travelling acquaintances asked. He could honestly answer, 'I know no more than you do.'

When night came, he gave his comfortable and beautiful bedroom another trial. The result of the second experiment was a repetition of the result of the first. Again he felt the all-pervading sense of depression and discomfort. Again he passed a sleepless night. And once more, when he tried to eat his breakfast, his appetite completely failed him!

This personal experience of the new hotel was too extraordinary to be passed over in silence. Henry mentioned it to his friends in the public room, in the hearing of the manager. The manager, naturally zealous in defence of the hotel, was a little hurt at the implied reflection cast on Number Fourteen. He invited the travellers present to judge for themselves whether Mr Westwick's bedroom was to blame for Mr Westwick's sleepless nights; and he especially appealed to a grey-headed gentleman, a guest at the breakfast-table of an English traveller, to take the lead in the investigation. 'This is Doctor Bruno, our first physician in Venice,' he explained. 'I appeal to him to say if there are any unhealthy influences in Mr Westwick's room.'

Introduced to Number Fourteen, the doctor looked round him with a certain appearance of interest which was noticed by everyone present. 'The last time I was in this room,' he said, 'was on a melancholy occasion. It was before the palace was changed into an hotel. I was in professional attendance on an English nobleman who died here.' One of the persons present inquired the name of the nobleman. Doctor Bruno answered (without the slightest suspicion that he was speaking before a brother of the dead man), 'Lord Montbarry.'

Henry quietly left the room, without saying a word to anybody.

He was not, in any sense of the term, a superstitious man. But he felt, nevertheless, an insurmountable reluctance to remaining in the hotel. He decided on leaving Venice. To ask for another room would be, as he could plainly see, an offence in the eyes of the manager. To remove to another hotel, would be to openly abandon an establishment in the success of which he had a pecuniary interest. Leaving a note for Arthur Barville, on his arrival in Venice, in which he merely mentioned that he had gone to look at the Italian lakes, and that a line addressed to his hotel at Milan would bring him back again, he took the afternoon train to Padua—and dined with his usual appetite, and slept as well as ever that night.

The next day, a gentleman and his wife (perfect strangers to the Montbarry family), returning to England by way of Venice, arrived at the hotel and occupied Number Fourteen.

Still mindful of the slur that had been cast on one of his best bedchambers, the manager took occasion to ask the travellers the next morning how they liked their room. They left him to judge for himself how well they were satisfied, by remaining a day longer in Venice than they had originally planned to do, solely for the purpose of enjoying the excellent accommodation offered to them by the new hotel. 'We have met with nothing like it in Italy,' they said; 'you may rely on our recommending you to all our friends.'

On the day when Number Fourteen was again vacant, an English lady travelling alone with her maid arrived at the hotel, saw the room, and at once engaged it.

The lady was Mrs Norbury. She had left Francis Westwick at Milan, occupied in negotiating for the appearance at his theatre of the new dancer at the Scala. Not having heard to the contrary, Mrs Norbury supposed that Arthur Barville and his wife had already arrived at Venice. She was more interested in meeting the young married couple than in awaiting the result of the hard bargaining which delayed the engagement of the new dancer; and she volunteered to make her brother's apologies, if his theatrical business caused him to be late in keeping his appointment at the honeymoon festival.

Mrs Norbury's experience of Number Fourteen differed entirely from her brother Henry's experience of the room.

Falling asleep as readily as usual, her repose was disturbed by a succession of frightful dreams; the central figure in every one of them being the figure of her dead brother, the first Lord Montbarry. She saw him starving in a loathsome prison; she saw him pursued by assassins, and dying under their knives; she saw him drowning in immeasurable depths of dark water; she saw him in a bed on fire, burning to death in the flames; she saw him tempted by a shadowy creature to drink, and dying of the poisonous draught. The reiterated horror of these dreams had such an effect on her that she rose with the dawn of day, afraid to trust herself again in bed. In the old times, she had been noted in the family as the one member of it who lived on affectionate terms with Montbarry. His other sister and his brothers were constantly quarrelling with him. Even his mother owned that her eldest son was of all her children the child whom she least liked. Sensible and resolute woman as she was, Mrs Norbury shuddered with terror as she sat at the window of her room, watching the sunrise, and thinking of her dreams.

She made the first excuse that occurred to her, when her maid came in at the usual hour, and noticed how ill she looked. The woman was of so superstitious a temperament that it would have been in the last degree indiscreet to trust her with the truth. Mrs Norbury merely remarked that she had not found the bed quite to her liking, on account of the large size of it. She was accustomed at home, as her maid knew, to sleep in a small bed. Informed of this objection later in the day, the manager regretted that he could only offer to the lady the choice of one other bedchamber, numbered Thirty-eight, and situated immediately over the bedchamber which she desired to leave. Mrs Norbury accepted the proposed change of quarters. She was now about to pass her second night in the room occupied in the old days of the palace by Baron Rivar.

Once more, she fell asleep as usual. And, once more, the frightful dreams of the first night terrified her, following each other in the same succession. This time her nerves, already shaken, were not equal to the renewed torture of terror inflicted on them. She threw on her dressing-gown, and rushed out of her room in the middle of the night. The porter, alarmed by the banging of the door, met her hurrying headlong down the stairs, in search of the first human being she could find to keep her company. Considerably surprised at this last new manifestation of the famous 'English eccentricity,' the man looked at the hotel register, and led the lady upstairs again to the room occupied by her maid. The maid was not asleep, and, more wonderful still, was not even undressed. She received her mistress quietly. When they were alone, and when Mrs Norbury had, as a matter of necessity, taken her attendant into her confidence, the woman made a very strange reply.

'I have been asking about the hotel, at the servants' supper to-night,' she said. 'The valet of one of the gentlemen staying here has heard that the late Lord Montbarry was the last person who lived in the palace, before it was made into an hotel. The room he died in, ma'am, was the room you slept in last night. Your room tonight is the room just above it. I said nothing for fear of frightening you. For my own part, I have passed the night as you see, keeping my light in, and reading my Bible. In my opinion, no member of your family can hope to be happy or comfortable in this house.'

'What do you mean?'

'Please to let me explain myself, ma'am. When Mr Henry West-wick was here (I have this from the valet, too) he occupied the room his brother died in (without knowing it), like you. For two nights he never closed his eyes. Without any reason for it (the valet heard him tell the gentlemen in the coffee-room) he could *not* sleep; he felt so low and so wretched in himself. And what is more, when daytime came, he couldn't even eat while he was under this roof. You may laugh at me, ma'am—but even a servant may draw her own conclu-sions. It's my conclusion that something happened to my lord, which we none of us know about, when he died in this house. His ghost walks in torment until he can tell it—and the living persons related to him are the persons who feel he is near them. Those persons may yet see him in the time to come. Don't, pray don't stay any longer in this dreadful place! I wouldn't stay another night here myself—no, not for anything that could be offered me!'

Mrs Norbury at once set her servant's mind at ease on this last point.

'I don't think about it as you do,' she said gravely. 'But I should like to speak to my brother of what has happened. We will go back to Milan.'

Some hours necessarily elapsed before they could leave the hotel, by the first train in the forenoon.

In that interval, Mrs Norbury's maid found an opportunity of confidentially informing the valet of what had passed between her mistress and herself. The valet had other friends to whom he related the circumstances in his turn. In due course of time, the narrative, passing from mouth to mouth, reached the ears of the manager. He instantly saw that the credit of the hotel was in danger, unless something was done to retrieve the character of the room numbered Fourteen. English travellers, well acquainted with the peerage of their native country, informed him that Henry Westwick and Mrs Norbury were by no means the only members of the Montbarry family. Curiosity might bring more of them to the hotel, after hearing what had happened. The manager's ingenuity easily hit on the obvious means of misleading them, in this case. The numbers of all the rooms were enamelled in blue, on white china plates, screwed to the doors. He ordered a new plate to be prepared, bearing the number, '13 A'; and he kept the room empty, after its tenant for the time being had gone away, until the plate was ready. He then renumbered the room; placing the removed Number Fourteen on the door of his own room (on the second floor), which, not being to let, had not previously been numbered at all. By this device, Number Fourteen disappeared at once and for ever from the books of the hotel, as the number of a bedroom to let.

Having warned the servants to beware of gossiping with travellers, on the subject of the changed numbers, under penalty of being dismissed, the manager composed his mind with the reflection that he had done his duty to his employers. 'Now,' he thought to himself, with an excusable sense of triumph, 'let the whole family come here if they like! The hotel is a match for them.'

## CHAPTER XVIII

Before the end of the week, the manager found himself in relations with 'the family' once more. A telegram from Milan announced that Mr Francis Westwick would arrive in Venice on the next day; and would be obliged if Number Fourteen, on the first floor, could be reserved for him, in the event of its being vacant at the time.

The manager paused to consider, before he issued his directions.

The re-numbered room had been last let to a French gentleman. It would be occupied on the day of Mr Francis Westwick's arrival, but it would be empty again on the day after. Would it be well to reserve the room for the special occupation of Mr Francis? and when he had passed the night unsuspiciously and comfortably in 'No. 13 A,' to ask him in the presence of witnesses how he liked his bedchamber? In this case, if the reputation of the room happened to be called in question again, the answer would vindicate it, on the evidence of a member of the very family which had first given Number Fourteen a bad name. After a little reflection, the manager decided on trying the experiment, and directed that '13 A' should be reserved accordingly.

On the next day, Francis Westwick arrived in excellent spirits.

He had signed agreements with the most popular dancer in Italy; he had transferred the charge of Mrs Norbury to his brother Henry, who had joined him in Milan; and he was now at full liberty to amuse himself by testing in every possible way the extraordinary influence exercised over his relatives by the new hotel. When his brother and sister first told him what their experience had been, he instantly declared that he would go to Venice in the interest of his theatre. The circumstances related to him contained invaluable hints for a ghost-drama. The title occurred to him in the railway: 'The Haunted Hotel.' Post that in red letters six feet high, on a black ground, all over London—and trust the excitable public to crowd into the theatre!

Received with the politest attention by the manager, Francis met with a disappointment on entering the hotel. 'Some mistake, sir. No such room on the first floor as Number Fourteen. The room bearing that number is on the second floor, and has been occupied by me, from the day when the hotel opened. Perhaps you meant number 13 A, on the first floor? It will be at your service to-morrow—a charming room. In the mean time, we will do the best we can for you, to-night.'

A man who is the successful manager of a theatre is probably the last man in the civilised universe who is capable of being impressed with favourable opinions of his fellow-creatures. Francis privately set the manager down as a humbug, and the story about the numbering of the rooms as a lie.

On the day of his arrival, he dined by himself in the restaurant, before the hour of the table d'hôte, for the express purpose of questioning the waiter, without being overheard by anybody. The answer led him to the conclusion that '13 A' occupied the situation in the hotel which had been described by his brother and sister as the situation of '14.' He asked next for the Visitors' List; and found that the French gentleman who then occupied '13 A,' was the proprietor of a theatre in Paris, personally well known to him. Was the gentleman then in the hotel? He had gone out, but would certainly return for the table d'hôte. When the public dinner was over, Francis entered the room, and was welcomed by his Parisian colleague, literally, with open arms. 'Come and have a cigar in my room,' said the friendly Frenchman. 'I want to hear whether you have really engaged that woman at Milan or not.' In this easy way, Francis found his opportunity of comparing the interior of the room with the description which he had heard of it at Milan.

Arriving at the door, the Frenchman bethought himself of his travelling companion. 'My scene-painter is here with me,' he said, 'on the look-out for materials. An excellent fellow, who will take it as a kindness if we ask him to join us. I'll tell the porter to send him up when he comes in.' He handed the key of his room to Francis. 'I will be back in a minute. It's at the end of the corridor—13 A.'

Francis entered the room alone. There were the decorations on the walls and the ceiling, exactly as they had been described to him! He had just time to perceive this at a glance, before his attention was diverted to himself and his own sensations, by a grotesquely disagreeable occurrence which took him completely by surprise.

He became conscious of a mysteriously offensive odour in the room, entirely new in his experience of revolting smells. It was composed (if such a thing could be) of two mingling exhalations, which were separately-discoverable exhalations nevertheless. This strange blending of odours consisted of something faintly and unpleasantly aromatic, mixed with another underlying smell, so unutterably sickening that he threw open the window, and put his head out into the fresh air, unable to endure the horribly infected atmosphere for a moment longer.

The French proprietor joined his English friend, with his cigar already lit. He started back in dismay at a sight terrible to his country-men in general—the sight of an open window. 'You English people are perfectly mad on the subject of fresh air!' he exclaimed. 'We shall catch our deaths of cold.'

Francis turned, and looked at him in astonishment. 'Are you really not aware of the smell there is in the room?' he asked.

'Smell!' repeated his brother-manager. 'I smell my own good cigar. Try one yourself. And for Heaven's sake shut the window!'

Francis declined the cigar by a sign. 'Forgive me,' he said. 'I will leave you to close the window. I feel faint and giddy—I had better go out.' He put his handkerchief over his nose and mouth, and crossed the room to the door.

The Frenchman followed the movements of Francis, in such a state of bewilderment that he actually forgot to seize the opportunity of shutting out the fresh air. 'Is it so nasty as that?' he asked, with a broad stare of amazement.

'Horrible!' Francis muttered behind his handkerchief. 'I never smelt anything like it in my life!'

There was a knock at the door. The scene-painter appeared. His employer instantly asked him if he smelt anything.

'I smell your cigar. Delicious! Give me one directly!'

'Wait a minute. Besides my cigar, do you smell anything else—vile, abominable, overpowering, indescribable, never-never-never-smelt before?'

The scene-painter appeared to be puzzled by the vehement energy of the language addressed to him. 'The room is as fresh and sweet as a room can be,' he answered. As he spoke, he looked back with astonishment at Francis Westwick, standing outside in the corridor, and eyeing the interior of the bedchamber with an expression of undisguised disgust.

The Parisian director approached his English colleague, and looked at him with grave and anxious scrutiny.

'You see, my friend, here are two of us, with as good noses as yours, who smell nothing. If you want evidence from more noses, look there!' He pointed to two little English girls, at play in the corridor. 'The door of my room is wide open—and you know how fast a smell can travel. Now listen, while I appeal to these innocent noses, in the language of their own dismal island. My little loves, do you sniff a nasty smell here—ha?' The children burst out laughing, and answered emphatically, 'No.' 'My good Westwick,' the Frenchman resumed, in his own language, 'the conclusion is surely plain? There is something wrong, very wrong, with your own nose. I recommend you to see a medical man.'

Having given that advice, he returned to his room, and shut out the horrid fresh air with a loud exclamation of relief. Francis left the hotel, by the lanes that led to the Square of St Mark. The night-breeze soon revived him. He was able to light a cigar, and to think quietly over what had happened.

# CHAPTER XIX

Avoiding the crowd under the colonnades, Francis walked slowly up and down the noble open space of the square, bathed in the light of the rising moon.

Without being aware of it himself, he was a thorough materialist. The strange effect produced on him by the room—following on the other strange effects produced on the other relatives of his dead brother—exercised no perplexing influence over the mind of this sensible man. 'Perhaps,' he reflected, 'my temperament is more imaginative than I supposed it to be—and this is a trick played on me by my own fancy? Or, perhaps, my friend is right; something is physically amiss with me? I don't feel ill, certainly. But that is no safe criterion sometimes. I am not going to sleep in that abominable room to-night—I can well wait till to-morrow to decide whether I shall speak to a doctor or not. In the mean time, the hotel doesn't seem likely to supply me with the subject of a piece. A terrible smell from an invisible ghost is a perfectly new idea. But it has one draw-back. If I realise it on the stage, I shall drive the audience out of the theatre.'

As his strong common sense arrived at this facetious conclusion, he became aware of a lady, dressed entirely in black, who was observing him with marked attention. 'Am I right in supposing you to be Mr Francis Westwick?' the lady asked, at the moment when he looked at her.

'That is my name, madam. May I inquire to whom I have the honour of speaking?'

'We have only met once,' she answered a little evasively, 'when your late brother introduced me to the members of his family. I wonder if you have quite forgotten my big black eyes and my hideous complexion?' She lifted her veil as she spoke, and turned so that the moonlight rested on her face.

Francis recognised at a glance the woman of all others whom he most cordially disliked—the widow of his dead brother, the first Lord Montbarry. He frowned as he looked at her. His experience on the stage, gathered at innumerable rehearsals with actresses who had sorely tried his temper, had accustomed him to speak roughly to women who were distasteful to him. 'I remember you,' he said. 'I thought you were in America!'

She took no notice of his ungracious tone and manner; she simply stopped him when he lifted his hat, and turned to leave her.

'Let me walk with you for a few minutes,' she quietly replied. 'I have something to say to you.'

He showed her his cigar. 'I am smoking,' he said.

'I don't mind smoking.'

After that, there was nothing to be done (short of downright brutality) but to yield. He did it with the worst possible grace. 'Well?' he resumed. 'What do you want of me?'

'You shall hear directly, Mr Westwick. Let me first tell you what my position is. I am alone in the world. To the loss of my husband has now been added another bereavement, the loss of my companion in America, my brother—Baron Rivar.'

The reputation of the Baron, and the doubt which scandal had thrown on his assumed relationship to the Countess, were well known to Francis. 'Shot in a gambling-saloon?' he asked brutally.

'The question is a perfectly natural one on your part,' she said, with the impenetrably ironical manner which she could assume on certain occasions. 'As a native of horse-racing England, you belong to a nation of gamblers. My brother died no extraordinary death, Mr Westwick. He sank, with many other unfortunate people, under a fever prevalent in a Western city which we happened to visit. The calamity of his loss made the United States unendurable to me. I left by the first steamer that sailed from New York—a French vessel which brought me to Havre. I continued my lonely journey to the South of France. And then I went on to Venice.'

'What does all this matter to me?' Francis thought to himself. She paused, evidently expecting him to say something. 'So you have come to Venice?' he said carelessly. 'Why?'

'Because I couldn't help it,' she answered.

Francis looked at her with cynical curiosity. 'That sounds odd,' he remarked. 'Why couldn't you help it?'

'Women are accustomed to act on impulse,' she explained. 'Suppose we say that an impulse has directed my journey? And yet, this is the last place in the world that I wish to find myself in. Associations that I detest are connected with it in my mind. If I had a will of my own, I would never see it again. I hate Venice. As you see, however, I am here. When did you meet with such an unreasonable woman before? Never, I am sure!' She stopped, eyed him for a moment, and suddenly altered her tone. 'When is Miss Agnes Lockwood expected to be in Venice?' she asked.

It was not easy to throw Francis off his balance, but that extraordinary question did it. 'How the devil did you know that Miss Lockwood was coming to Venice?' he exclaimed.

She laughed—a bitter mocking laugh. 'Say, I guessed it!'

Something in her tone, or perhaps something in the audacious defiance of her eyes as they rested on him, roused the quick temper that was in Francis Westwick. 'Lady Montbarry—!' he began.

'Stop there!' she interposed. 'Your brother Stephen's wife calls herself Lady Montbarry now. I share my title with no woman. Call me by my name before I committed the fatal mistake of marrying your brother. Address me, if you please, as Countess Narona.'

'Countess Narona,' Francis resumed, 'if your object in claiming my acquaintance is to mystify me, you have come to the wrong man. Speak plainly, or permit me to wish you good evening.'

'If your object is to keep Miss Lockwood's arrival in Venice a secret,' she retorted, 'speak plainly, Mr Westwick, on *your* side, and say so.'

Her intention was evidently to irritate him; and she succeeded. 'Nonsense!' he broke out petulantly. 'My brother's travelling arrangements are secrets to nobody. He brings Miss Lockwood here, with Lady Montbarry and the children. As you seem so well informed, perhaps you know why she is coming to Venice?'

The Countess had suddenly become grave and thoughtful. She made no reply. The two strangely associated companions, having reached one extremity of the square, were now standing before the church of St Mark. The moonlight was bright enough to show the architecture of the grand cathedral in its wonderful variety of detail. Even the pigeons of St Mark were visible, in dark closely packed rows, roosting in the archways of the great entrance doors.

'I never saw the old church look so beautiful by moonlight,' the Countess said quietly; speaking, not to Francis, but to herself. 'Good-bye, St Mark's by moonlight! I shall not see you again.'

She turned away from the church, and saw Francis listening to her with wondering looks. 'No,' she resumed, placidly picking up the lost thread of the conversation, 'I don't know why Miss Lockwood is coming here, I only know that we are to meet in Venice.'

'By previous appointment?'

'By Destiny,' she answered, with her head on her breast, and her eyes on the ground. Francis burst out laughing. 'Or, if you like it better,' she instantly resumed, 'by what fools call Chance.' Francis answered easily, out of the depths of his strong common sense. 'Chance seems to be taking a queer way of bringing the meeting about,' he said. 'We have all arranged to meet at the Palace Hotel. How is it that your name is not on the Visitors' List? Destiny ought to have brought you to the Palace Hotel too.'

She abruptly pulled down her veil. 'Destiny may do that yet!' she said. 'The Palace Hotel?' she repeated, speaking once more to herself. 'The old hell, transformed into the new purgatory. The place itself! Jesu Maria! the place itself!' She paused and laid her hand on her companion's arm. 'Perhaps Miss Lockwood is not going there with the rest of you?' she burst out with sudden eagerness. 'Are you positively sure she will be at the hotel?'

'Positively! Haven't I told you that Miss Lockwood travels with Lord and Lady Montbarry? and don't you know that she is a member of the family? You will have to move, Countess, to our hotel.'

She was perfectly impenetrable to the bantering tone in which he spoke. 'Yes,' she said faintly, 'I shall have to move to your hotel.' Her hand was still on his arm—he could feel her shivering from head to foot while she spoke. Heartily as he disliked and distrusted her, the common instinct of humanity obliged him to ask if she felt cold.

'Yes,' she said. 'Cold and faint.'

'Cold and faint, Countess, on such a night as this?'

'The night has nothing to do with it, Mr Westwick. How do you suppose the criminal feels on the scaffold, while the hangman is putting the rope round his neck? Cold and faint, too, I should think. Excuse my grim fancy. You see, Destiny has got the rope round *my* neck—and *I* feel it.'

She looked about her. They were at that moment close to the famous café known as 'Florian's.' 'Take me in there,' she said; 'I must have something to revive me. You had better not hesitate. You are interested in reviving me. I have not said what I wanted to say to you yet. It's business, and it's connected with your theatre.'

Wondering inwardly what she could possibly want with his theatre, Francis reluctantly yielded to the necessities of the situation, and took her into the café. He found a quiet corner in which they could take their places without attracting notice. 'What will you have?' he inquired resignedly. She gave her own orders to the waiter, without troubling him to speak for her.

'Maraschino.* And a pot of tea.'

The waiter stared; Francis stared. The tea was a novelty (in connection with maraschino) to both of them. Careless whether she surprised them or not, she instructed the waiter, when her directions had been complied with, to pour a large wine-glass-full of the liqueur into a tumbler, and to fill it up from the teapot. 'I can't do it for myself,' she remarked, 'my hand trembles so.' She drank the strange mixture eagerly, hot as it was. 'Maraschino punch—will you taste some of it?' she said. 'I inherit the discovery of this drink. When your English Queen Caroline* was on the Continent, my mother was attached to her Court. That much injured Royal Person invented, in her happier hours, maraschino punch. Fondly attached to her gracious mistress, my mother shared her tastes. And I, in my turn, learnt from my mother. Now, Mr Westwick, suppose I tell you what my business is. You are manager of a theatre. Do you want a new play?'

'I always want a new play—provided it's a good one.'

'And you pay, if it's a good one?'

'I pay liberally—in my own interests.'

'If *I* write the play, will you read it?'

Francis hesitated. 'What has put writing a play into your head?' he asked.

'Mere accident,' she answered. 'I had once occasion to tell my late brother of a visit which I paid to Miss Lockwood, when I was last in England. He took no interest in what happened at the interview, but something struck him in my way of relating it. He said, "You describe what passed between you and the lady with the point and contrast of good stage dialogue. You have the dramatic instinct—try if you can write a play. You might make money." *That* put it into my head.'

Those last words seemed to startle Francis. 'Surely you don't want money!' he exclaimed.

'I always want money. My tastes are expensive. I have nothing but my poor little four hundred a year—and the wreck that is left of the other money: about two hundred pounds in circular notes—no more.'

Francis knew that she was referring to the ten thousand pounds paid by the insurance offices. 'All those thousands gone already!' he exclaimed.

She blew a little puff of air over her fingers. 'Gone like that!' she answered coolly.

'Baron Rivar?'

She looked at him with a flash of anger in her hard black eyes.

'My affairs are my own secret, Mr Westwick. I have made you a proposal—and you have not answered me yet. Don't say No, without thinking first. Remember what a life mine has been. I have seen more of the world than most people, playwrights included. I have had strange adventures; I have heard remarkable stories; I have observed; I have remembered. Are there no materials, here in my head, for writing a play—if the opportunity is granted to me?' She waited a moment, and suddenly repeated her strange question about Agnes.

'When is Miss Lockwood expected to be in Venice?'

'What has that to do with your new play, Countess?'

The Countess appeared to feel some difficulty in giving that question its fit reply. She mixed another tumbler full of the maraschino punch, and drank one good half of it before she spoke again.

'It has everything to do with my new play,' was all she said. 'Answer me.' Francis answered her.

'Miss Lockwood may be here in a week. Or, for all I know to the contrary, sooner than that.'

'Very well. If I am a living woman and a free woman in a week's time—or if I am in possession of my senses in a week's time (don't interrupt me; I know what I am talking about)—I shall have a sketch or outline of my play ready,* as a specimen of what I can do. Once again, will you read it?'

'I will certainly read it. But, Countess, I don't understand—'

She held up her hand for silence, and finished the second tumbler of maraschino punch.

'I am a living enigma—and you want to know the right reading of me,' she said. 'Here is the reading, as your English phrase goes, in a nutshell. There is a foolish idea in the minds of many persons that the natives of the warm climates are imaginative people. There never was a greater mistake. You will find no such unimaginative people anywhere as you find in Italy, Spain, Greece, and the other Southern countries. To anything fanciful, to anything spiritual, their minds are deaf and blind by nature. Now and then, in the course of centuries, a great genius springs up among them; and he is the exception which proves the rule. Now see! I, though I am no genius—I am, in my little way (as I suppose), an exception too. To my sorrow, I have some of that imagination which is so common among the English and the Germans—so rare among the Italians, the Spaniards, and the rest of them! And what is the result? I think it has become a disease in me. I am filled with presentiments which make this wicked life of mine one long terror to me. It doesn't matter, just now, what they are. Enough that they absolutely govern me—they drive me over land and sea at their own horrible will; they are in me, and torturing me, at this moment! Why don't I resist them? Ha! but I do resist them. I am trying (with the help of the good punch) to resist them now. At intervals I cultivate the difficult virtue of sound sense. Sometimes, sound sense makes a hopeful woman of me. At one time, I had the hope that what seemed reality to me was only mad delusion, after all—I even asked the question of an English doctor! At other times, other sensible doubts of myself beset me. Never mind dwelling on them now—it always ends in the old terrors and superstitions taking possession of me again. In a week's time, I shall know whether Destiny does indeed decide my future for me, or whether I decide it for myself. In the last case, my resolution is to absorb this self-tormenting fancy of mine in the occupation that I have told you of already. Do you understand me a little better now? And, our business being settled, dear Mr Westwick, shall we get out of this hot room into the nice cool air again?'

They rose to leave the café. Francis privately concluded that the maraschino punch offered the only discoverable explanation of what the Countess had said to him.

## CHAPTER XX

'Shall I see you again?' she asked, as she held out her hand to take leave. 'It is quite understood between us, I suppose, about the play?'

Francis recalled his extraordinary experience of that evening in the re-numbered room. 'My stay in Venice is uncertain,' he replied. 'If you have anything more to say about this dramatic venture of yours, it may be as well to say it now. Have you decided on a subject already? I know the public taste in England better than you do—I might save you some waste of time and trouble, if you have not chosen your subject wisely.'

'I don't care what subject I write about, so long as I write,' she answered carelessly. 'If *you* have got a subject in your head, give it to me. I answer for the characters and the dialogue.'

'You answer for the characters and the dialogue,' Francis repeated. 'That's a bold way of speaking for a beginner! I wonder if I should shake your sublime confidence in yourself, if I suggested the most ticklish subject to handle which is known to the stage? What do you say, Countess, to entering the lists with Shakespeare, and trying a drama with a ghost in it? A true story, mind! founded on events in this very city in which you and I are interested.'

She caught him by the arm, and drew him away from the crowded colonnade into the solitary middle space of the square. 'Now tell me!' she said eagerly. 'Here, where nobody is near us. How am I interested in it? How? how?'

Still holding his arm, she shook him in her impatience to hear the coming disclosure. For a moment he hesitated. Thus far, amused by her ignorant belief in herself, he had merely spoken in jest. Now, for the first time, impressed by her irresistible earnestness, he began to consider what he was about from a more serious point of view. With her knowledge of all that had passed in the old palace, before its transformation into an hotel, it was surely possible that she might suggest some explanation of what had happened to his brother, and sister, and himself. Or, failing to do this, she might accidentally reveal some event in her own experience which, acting as a hint to a competent dramatist, might prove to be the making of a play. The prosperity of his theatre was his one serious object in life. 'I may be on the trace of another "Corsican Brothers," '* he thought. 'A new piece of that sort would be ten thousand pounds in my pocket, at least.'

With these motives (worthy of the single-hearted devotion to dramatic business which made Francis a successful manager) he related, without further hesitation, what his own experience had been, and what the experience of his relatives had been, in the haunted hotel. He even described the outbreak of superstitious terror which had escaped Mrs Norbury's ignorant maid. 'Sad stuff, if you look at it reasonably,' he remarked. 'But there is something dramatic in the notion of the ghostly influence making itself felt by the relations in succession, as they one after another enter the fatal room—until the one chosen relative comes who will see the Unearthly Creature, and know the terrible truth. Material for a play, Countess—first-rate material for a play!'

There he paused. She neither moved nor spoke. He stooped and looked closer at her.

What impression had he produced? It was an impression which his utmost ingenuity had failed to anticipate. She stood by his side—just as she had stood before Agnes when her question about Ferrari was plainly answered at last—like a woman turned to stone. Her eyes were vacant and rigid; all the life in her face had faded out of it. Francis took her by the hand. Her hand was as cold as the pavement that they were standing on. He asked her if she was ill.

Not a muscle in her moved. He might as well have spoken to the dead.

'Surely,' he said, 'you are not foolish enough to take what I have been telling you seriously?'

Her lips moved slowly. As it seemed, she was making an effort to speak to him.

'Louder,' he said. 'I can't hear you.'

She struggled to recover possession of herself. A faint light began to soften the dull cold stare of her eyes. In a moment more she spoke so that he could hear her.

'I never thought of the other world,' she murmured, in low dull tones, like a woman talking in her sleep.

Her mind had gone back to the day of her last memorable interview with Agnes; she was slowly recalling the confession that had escaped her, the warning words which she had spoken at that past time. Necessarily incapable of understanding this, Francis looked at her in perplexity. She went on in the same dull vacant tone, steadily following out her own train of thought, with her heedless eyes on his face, and her wandering mind far away from him.

'I said some trifling event would bring us together the next time. I was wrong. No trifling event will bring us together. I said I might be the person who told her what had become of Ferrari, if she forced me to it. Shall I feel some other influence than hers? Will *he* force me to it? When *she* sees him, shall *I* see him too?'

Her head sank a little; her heavy eyelids dropped slowly; she heaved a long low weary sigh. Francis put her arm in his, and made an attempt to rouse her.

'Come, Countess, you are weary and over-wrought. We have had enough talking to-night. Let me see you safe back to your hotel. Is it far from here?'

She started when he moved, and obliged her to move with him, as if he had suddenly awakened her out of a deep sleep.

'Not far,' she said faintly. 'The old hotel on the quay. My mind's in a strange state; I have forgotten the name.'

'Danieli's?'

'Yes!'

He led her on slowly. She accompanied him in silence as far as the end of the Piazzetta. There, when the full view of the moonlit Lagoon revealed itself, she stopped him as he turned towards the Riva degli Schiavoni. 'I have something to ask you. I want to wait and think.'

She recovered her lost idea, after a long pause.

'Are you going to sleep in the room to-night?' she asked.

He told her that another traveller was in possession of the room that night. 'But the manager has reserved it for me to-morrow,' he added, 'if I wish to have it.'

'No,' she said. 'You must give it up.'

'To whom?'

'To me!'

He started. 'After what I have told you, do you really wish to sleep in that room to-morrow night?'

'I *must* sleep in it.'

'Are you not afraid?'

'I am horribly afraid.'

'So I should have thought, after what I have observed in you to-night. Why should you take the room? you are not obliged to occupy it, unless you like.'

'I was not obliged to go to Venice, when I left America,' she answered. 'And yet I came here. I must take the room, and keep the room, until—' She broke off at those words. 'Never mind the rest,' she said. 'It doesn't interest you.'

It was useless to dispute with her. Francis changed the subject. 'We can do nothing to-night,' he said. 'I will call on you to-morrow morning, and hear what you think of it then.'

They moved on again to the hotel. As they approached the door, Francis asked if she was staying in Venice under her own name.

She shook her head. 'As your brother's widow, I am known here. As Countess Narona, I am known here. I want to be unknown, this time, to strangers in Venice; I am travelling under a common English name.' She hesitated, and stood still. 'What has come to me?' she muttered to herself. 'Some things I remember; and some I forget. I forgot Danieli's—and now I forget my English name.' She drew him hurriedly into the hall of the hotel, on the wall of which hung a list of visitors' names. Running her finger slowly down the list, she pointed to the English name that she had assumed:—'Mrs James.'

'Remember that when you call to-morrow,' she said. 'My head is heavy. Good night.'

Francis went back to his own hotel, wondering what the events of the next day would bring forth. A new turn in his affairs had taken place in his absence. As he crossed the hall, he was requested by one of the servants to walk into the private office. The manager was waiting there with a gravely pre-occupied manner, as if he had something serious to say. He regretted to hear that Mr Francis Westwick had, like other members of the family, discovered mysterious sources of discomfort in the new hotel. He had been informed in strict confidence of Mr Westwick's extraordinary objection to the atmosphere of the bedroom upstairs. Without presuming to discuss the matter, he must beg to be excused from reserving the room for Mr Westwick after what had happened.

Francis answered sharply, a little ruffled by the tone in which the manager had spoken to him. 'I might, very possibly, have declined to sleep in the room, if you *had* reserved it,' he said. 'Do you wish me to leave the hotel?'

The manager saw the error that he had committed, and hastened to repair it. 'Certainly not, sir! We will do our best to make you comfortable while you stay with us. I beg your pardon, if I have said anything to offend you. The reputation of an establishment like this is a matter of very serious importance. May I hope that you will do us the great favour to say nothing about what has happened upstairs? The two French gentlemen have kindly promised to keep it a secret.'

This apology left Francis no polite alternative but to grant the manager's request. 'There is an end to the Countess's wild scheme,' he thought to himself, as he retired for the night. 'So much the better for the Countess!'

He rose late the next morning. Inquiring for his Parisian friends, he was informed that both the French gentlemen had left for Milan. As he crossed the hall, on his way to the restaurant, he noticed the head porter chalking the numbers of the rooms on some articles of luggage which were waiting to go upstairs. One trunk attracted his attention by the extraordinary number of old travelling labels left on it. The porter was marking it at the moment—and the number was, '13 A.' Francis instantly looked at the card fastened on the lid. It bore the common English name, 'Mrs James'! He at once inquired about the lady. She had arrived early that morning, and she was then in the Reading Room. Looking into the room, he discovered a lady in it alone. Advancing a little nearer, he found himself face to face with the Countess.

She was seated in a dark corner, with her head down and her arms crossed over her bosom. 'Yes,' she said, in a tone of weary impatience, before Francis could speak to her. 'I thought it best not to wait for you—I determined to get here before anybody else could take the room.'

'Have you taken it for long?' Francis asked.

'You told me Miss Lockwood would be here in a week's time. I have taken it for a week.'

'What has Miss Lockwood to do with it?'

'She has everything to do with it—she must sleep in the room. I shall give the room up to her when she comes here.'

Francis began to understand the superstitious purpose that she had in view. 'Are you (an educated woman) really of the same opinion as my sister's maid!' he exclaimed. 'Assuming your absurd superstition to be a serious thing, you are taking the wrong means to prove it true. If I and my brother and sister have seen nothing, how should Agnes Lockwood discover what was not revealed to *us*? She is only distantly related to the Montbarrys—she is only our cousin.'

'She was nearer to the heart of the Montbarry who is dead than any of you,' the Countess answered sternly. 'To the last day of his life, my miserable husband repented his desertion of her. She will see what none of you have seen—she shall have the room.'

Francis listened, utterly at a loss to account for the motives that animated her. 'I don't see what interest *you* have in trying this extraordinary experiment,' he said.

'It is my interest *not* to try it! It is my interest to fly from Venice, and never set eyes on Agnes Lockwood or any of your family again!'

'What prevents you from doing that?'

She started to her feet and looked at him wildly. 'I know no more what prevents me than you do!' she burst out. 'Some will that is stronger than mine drives me on to my destruction, in spite of my own self!' She suddenly sat down again, and waved her hand for him to go. 'Leave me,' she said. 'Leave me to my thoughts.'

Francis left her, firmly persuaded by this time that she was out of her senses. For the rest of the day, he saw nothing of her. The night, so far as he knew, passed quietly. The next morning he breakfasted early, determining to wait in the restaurant for the appearance of the Countess. She came in and ordered her breakfast quietly, looking dull and worn and self-absorbed, as she had looked when he last saw her. He hastened to her table, and asked if anything had happened in the night.

'Nothing,' she answered.

'You have rested as well as usual?'

'Quite as well as usual. Have you had any letters this morning? Have you heard when she is coming?'

'I have had no letters. Are you really going to stay here? Has your experience of last night not altered the opinion which you expressed to me yesterday?'

'Not in the least.'

The momentary gleam of animation which had crossed her face when she questioned him about Agnes, died out of it again when he answered her. She looked, she spoke, she ate her breakfast, with a vacant resignation, like a woman who had done with hopes, done with interests, done with everything but the mechanical movements and instincts of life.

Francis went out, on the customary travellers' pilgrimage to the shrines of Titian and Tintoret.* After some hours of absence, he found a letter waiting for him when he got back to the hotel. It was written by his brother Henry, and it recommended him to return to Milan immediately. The proprietor of a French theatre, recently arrived from Venice, was trying to induce the famous dancer whom Francis had engaged to break faith with him and accept a higher salary.

Having made this startling announcement, Henry proceeded to inform his brother that Lord and Lady Montbarry, with Agnes and the children, would arrive in Venice in three days more. 'They know nothing of our adventures at the hotel,' Henry wrote; 'and they have telegraphed to the manager for the accommodation that they want. There would be something absurdly superstitious in our giving them a warning which would frighten the ladies and children out of the best hotel in Venice. We shall be a strong party this time—too strong a party for ghosts! I shall meet the travellers on their arrival, of course, and try my luck again at what you call the Haunted Hotel. Arthur Barville and his wife have already got as far on their way as Trent;* and two of the lady's relations have arranged to accompany them on the journey to Venice.'

Naturally indignant at the conduct of his Parisian colleague, Francis made his preparations for returning to Milan by the train of that day.

On his way out, he asked the manager if his brother's telegram had been received. The telegram had arrived, and, to the surprise of Francis, the rooms were already reserved. 'I thought you would refuse to let any more of the family into the house,' he said satirically. The manager answered (with the due dash of respect) in the same tone. 'Number 13 A is safe, sir, in the occupation of a stranger. I am the servant of the Company; and I dare not turn money out of the hotel.'

Hearing this, Francis said good-bye—and said nothing more. He was ashamed to acknowledge it to himself, but he felt an irresistible curiosity to know what would happen when Agnes arrived at the hotel. Besides, 'Mrs James' had reposed a confidence in him. He got into his gondola, respecting the confidence of 'Mrs James.'

Towards evening on the third day, Lord Montbarry and his travelling companions arrived, punctual to their appointment.

'Mrs James,' sitting at the window of her room watching for them, saw the new Lord land from the gondola first. He handed his wife to the steps. The three children were next committed to his care. Last of all, Agnes appeared in the little black doorway of the gondola cabin, and, taking Lord Montbarry's hand, passed in her turn to the steps. She wore no veil. As she ascended to the door of the hotel, the Countess (eyeing her through an opera-glass) noticed that she paused to look at the outside of the building, and that her face was very pale.

## CHAPTER XXI

Lord and Lady Montbarry were received by the housekeeper; the manager being absent for a day or two on business connected with the affairs of the hotel.

The rooms reserved for the travellers on the first floor were three in number; consisting of two bedrooms opening into each other, and communicating on the left with a drawing-room. Complete so far, the arrangements proved to be less satisfactory in reference to the third bedroom required for Agnes and for the eldest daughter of Lord Montbarry, who usually slept with her on their travels. The bed-chamber on the right of the drawing-room was already occupied by an English widow lady. Other bed-chambers at the other end of the corridor were also let in every case. There was accordingly no altern-ative but to place at the disposal of Agnes a comfortable room on the second floor. Lady Montbarry vainly complained of this separation of one of the members of her travelling party from the rest. The house-keeper politely hinted that it was impossible for her to ask other travellers to give up their rooms. She could only express her regret, and assure Miss Lockwood that her bed-chamber on the second floor was one of the best rooms in that part of the hotel.

On the retirement of the housekeeper, Lady Montbarry noticed that Agnes had seated herself apart, feeling apparently no interest in the question of the bedrooms. Was she ill? No; she felt a little unnerved by the railway journey, and that was all. Hearing this, Lord Montbarry proposed that she should go out with him, and try the experiment of half an hour's walk in the cool evening air. Agnes gladly accepted the suggestion. They directed their steps towards the square of St Mark, so as to enjoy the breeze blowing over the lagoon. It was the first visit of Agnes to Venice. The fascination of the wonderful city of the waters exerted its full influence over her sensitive nature. The proposed half-hour of the walk had passed away, and was fast expanding to half an hour more, before Lord Montbarry could persuade his companion to remember that dinner was waiting for them. As they returned, passing under the colonnade, neither of them noticed a lady in deep mourning, loitering in the open space of the square. She started as she recognised Agnes walking with the new Lord Montbarry—hesitated for a moment—and then followed them, at a discreet distance, back to the hotel.

Lady Montbarry received Agnes in high spirits—with news of an event which had happened in her absence.

She had not left the hotel more than ten minutes, before a little note in pencil was brought to Lady Montbarry by the housekeeper. The writer proved to be no less a person than the widow lady who occupied the room on the other side of the drawing-room, which her ladyship had vainly hoped to secure for Agnes. Writing under the name of Mrs James, the polite widow explained that she had heard from the housekeeper of the disappointment experienced by Lady Montbarry in the matter of the rooms. Mrs James was quite alone; and as long as her bed-chamber was airy and comfortable, it mattered nothing to her whether she slept on the first or the second floor of the house. She had accordingly much pleasure in proposing to change rooms with Miss Lockwood. Her luggage had already been removed, and Miss Lockwood had only to take possession of the room (Number 13 A), which was now entirely at her disposal.

'I immediately proposed to see Mrs James,' Lady Montbarry continued, 'and to thank her personally for her extreme kindness. But I was informed that she had gone out, without leaving word at what hour she might be expected to return. I have written a little note of thanks, saying that we hope to have the pleasure of personally expressing our sense of Mrs James's courtesy to-morrow. In the mean time, Agnes, I have ordered your boxes to be removed downstairs. Go!—and judge for yourself, my dear, if that good lady has not given up to you the prettiest room in the house!'

With those words, Lady Montbarry left Miss Lockwood to make a hasty toilet for dinner.

The new room at once produced a favourable impression on Agnes. The large window, opening into a balcony, commanded an admirable view of the canal. The decorations on the walls and ceiling were skilfully copied from the exquisitely graceful designs of Raphael in the Vatican. The massive wardrobe possessed compartments of unusual size, in which double the number of dresses that Agnes possessed might have been conveniently hung at full length. In the inner corner of the room, near the head of the bedstead, there was a recess which had been turned into a little dressing-room, and which opened by a second door on the inferior stair-case of the hotel, commonly used by the servants. Noticing these aspects of the room at a glance, Agnes made the necessary change in her dress, as quickly as possible. On her way back to the drawing-room she was addressed by a chambermaid in the corridor who asked for her key. 'I will put your room tidy for the night, Miss,' the woman said, 'and I will then bring the key back to you in the drawing-room.'

While the chambermaid was at her work, a solitary lady, loitering about the corridor of the second storey, was watching her over the bannisters. After a while, the maid appeared, with her pail in her hand, leaving the room by way of the dressing-room and the back stairs. As she passed out of sight, the lady on the second floor (no other, it is needless to add, than the Countess herself) ran swiftly down the stairs, entered the bed-chamber by the principal door, and hid herself in the empty side compartment of the wardrobe. The chambermaid returned, completed her work, locked the door of the dressing-room on the inner side, locked the principal entrance-door on leaving the room, and returned the key to Agnes in the drawing-room.

The travellers were just sitting down to their late dinner, when one of the children noticed that Agnes was not wearing her watch. Had she left it in her bed-chamber in the hurry of changing her dress? She rose from the table at once in search of her watch; Lady Montbarry advising her, as she went out, to see to the security of her bed-chamber, in the event of there being thieves in the house. Agnes found her watch, forgotten on the toilet table, as she had anticipated. Before leaving the room again she acted on Lady Montbarry's advice, and tried the key in the lock of the dressing-room door. It was properly secured. She left the bed-chamber, locking the main door behind her.

Immediately on her departure, the Countess, oppressed by the confined air in the wardrobe, ventured on stepping out of her hiding place into the empty room.

Entering the dressing-room, she listened at the door, until the silence outside informed her that the corridor was empty. Upon this, she unlocked the door, and, passing out, closed it again softly; leaving it to all appearance (when viewed on the inner side) as carefully secured as Agnes had seen it when she tried the key in the lock with her own hand.

While the Montbarrys were still at dinner, Henry Westwick joined them, arriving from Milan.

When he entered the room, and again when he advanced to shake hands with her, Agnes was conscious of a latent feeling which secretly reciprocated Henry's unconcealed pleasure on meeting her again. For a moment only, she returned his look; and in that moment her own observation told her that she had silently encouraged him to hope. She saw it in the sudden glow of happiness which overspread his face; and she confusedly took refuge in the usual conventional inquiries relating to the relatives whom he had left at Milan.

Taking his place at the table, Henry gave a most amusing account of the position of his brother Francis between the mercenary opera-dancer on one side, and the unscrupulous manager of the French theatre on the other. Matters had proceeded to such extremities, that the law had been called on to interfere, and had decided the dispute in favour of Francis. On winning the victory the English manager had at once left Milan, recalled to London by the affairs of his theatre. He was accompanied on the journey back, as he had been accompanied on the journey out, by his sister. Resolved, after passing two nights of terror in the Venetian hotel, never to enter it again, Mrs Norbury asked to be excused from appearing at the family festival, on the ground of ill-health. At her age, travelling fatigued her, and she was glad to take advantage of her brother's escort to return to England.

While the talk at the dinner-table flowed easily onward, the evening-time advanced to night—and it became necessary to think of sending the children to bed.

As Agnes rose to leave the room, accompanied by the eldest girl, she observed with surprise that Henry's manner suddenly changed. He looked serious and pre-occupied; and when his niece wished him good night, he abruptly said to her, 'Marian, I want to know what part of the hotel you sleep in?' Marian, puzzled by the question, answered that she was going to sleep, as usual, with 'Aunt Agnes.' Not satisfied with that reply, Henry next inquired whether the bedroom was near the rooms occupied by the other members of the travelling party. Answering for the child, and wondering what Henry's object could possibly be, Agnes mentioned the polite sacrifice made to her convenience by Mrs James. 'Thanks to that lady's kindness,' she said, 'Marian and I are only on the other side of the drawing-room.' Henry made no remark; he looked incomprehensibly discontented as he opened the door for Agnes and her companion to pass out. After wishing them good night, he waited in the corridor until he saw them enter the fatal corner-room—and then he called abruptly to his brother, 'Come out, Stephen, and let us smoke!'

As soon as the two brothers were at liberty to speak together privately, Henry explained the motive which had led to his strange inquiries about the bedrooms. Francis had informed him of the meeting with the Countess at Venice, and of all that had followed it; and Henry now carefully repeated the narrative to his brother in all its details. 'I am not satisfied,' he added, 'about that woman's purpose in giving up her room. Without alarming the ladies by telling them what I have just told you, can you not warn Agnes to be careful in securing her door?'

Lord Montbarry replied, that the warning had been already given by his wife, and that Agnes might be trusted to take good care of herself and her little bed-fellow. For the rest, he looked upon the story of the Countess and her superstitions as a piece of theatrical exaggeration, amusing enough in itself, but unworthy of a moment's serious attention.

While the gentlemen were absent from the hotel, the room which had been already associated with so many startling circumstances, became the scene of another strange event in which Lady Montbarry's eldest child was concerned.

Little Marian had been got ready for bed as usual, and had (so far) taken hardly any notice of the new room. As she knelt down to say her prayers, she happened to look up at that part of the ceiling above her which was just over the head of the bed. The next instant she alarmed Agnes, by starting to her feet with a cry of terror, and pointing to a small brown spot on one of the white panelled spaces of the carved ceiling. 'It's a spot of blood!' the child exclaimed. 'Take me away! I won't sleep here!'

Seeing plainly that it would be useless to reason with her while she was in the room, Agnes hurriedly wrapped Marian in a dressing-gown, and carried her back to her mother in the drawing-room. Here, the ladies did their best to soothe and reassure the trembling girl. The effort proved to be useless; the impression that had been produced on the young and sensitive mind was not to be removed by persuasion. Marian could give no explanation of the panic of terror that had seized her. She was quite unable to say why the spot on the ceiling looked like the colour of a spot of blood. She only knew that she should die of terror if she saw it again. Under these circumstances, but one alternative was left. It was arranged that the child should pass the night in the room occupied by her two younger sisters and the nurse.

In half an hour more, Marian was peacefully asleep with her arm around her sister's neck. Lady Montbarry went back with Agnes to her room to see the spot on the ceiling which had so strangely frightened the child. It was so small as to be only just perceptible, and it had in all probability been caused by the carelessness of a workman, or by a dripping from water accidentally spilt on the floor of the room above.

'I really cannot understand why Marian should place such a shocking interpretation on such a trifling thing,' Lady Montbarry remarked.

'I suspect the nurse is in some way answerable for what has happened,' Agnes suggested. 'She may quite possibly have been telling Marian some tragic nursery story which has left its mischievous impression behind it. Persons in her position are sadly ignorant of the danger of exciting a child's imagination. You had better caution the nurse to-morrow.'

Lady Montbarry looked round the room with admiration. 'Is it not prettily decorated?' she said. 'I suppose, Agnes, you don't mind sleeping here by yourself?'

Agnes laughed. 'I feel so tired,' she replied, 'that I was thinking of bidding you good-night, instead of going back to the drawing-room.'

Lady Montbarry turned towards the door. 'I see your jewel-case on the table,' she resumed. 'Don't forget to lock the other door there, in the dressing-room.'

'I have already seen to it, and tried the key myself,' said Agnes. 'Can I be of any use to you before I go to bed?'

'No, my dear, thank you; I feel sleepy enough to follow your example. Good night, Agnes—and pleasant dreams on your first night in Venice.'


## CHAPTER XXII

Having closed and secured the door on Lady Montbarry's departure, Agnes put on her dressing-gown, and, turning to her open boxes, began the business of unpacking. In the hurry of making her toilet for dinner, she had taken the first dress that lay uppermost in the trunk, and had thrown her travelling costume on the bed. She now opened the doors of the wardrobe for the first time, and began to hang her dresses on the hooks in the large compartment on one side.

After a few minutes only of this occupation, she grew weary of it, and decided on leaving the trunks as they were, until the next morning. The oppressive south wind, which had blown throughout the day, still prevailed at night. The atmosphere of the room felt close; Agnes threw a shawl over her head and shoulders, and, opening the window, stepped into the balcony to look at the view.

The night was heavy and overcast: nothing could be distinctly seen. The canal beneath the window looked like a black gulf; the opposite houses were barely visible as a row of shadows, dimly relieved against the starless and moonless sky. At long intervals, the warning cry of a belated gondolier was just audible, as he turned the corner of a distant canal, and called to invisible boats which might be approaching him in the darkness. Now and then, the nearer dip of an oar in the water told of the viewless passage of other gondolas bringing guests back to the hotel. Excepting these rare sounds, the mysterious night-silence of Venice was literally the silence of the grave.

Leaning on the parapet of the balcony, Agnes looked vacantly into the black void beneath. Her thoughts reverted to the miserable man who had broken his pledged faith to her, and who had died in that house. Some change seemed to have come over her since her arrival in Venice; some new influence appeared to be at work. For the first time in her experience of herself, compassion and regret were not the only emotions aroused in her by the remembrance of the dead Montbarry. A keen sense of the wrong that she had suffered, never yet felt by that gentle and forgiving nature, was felt by it now. She found herself thinking of the bygone days of her humiliation almost as harshly as Henry Westwick had thought of them—she who had rebuked him the last time he had spoken slightingly of his brother in her presence! A sudden fear and doubt of herself, startled her physically as well as morally. She turned from the shadowy abyss of the dark water as if the mystery and the gloom of it had been answerable for the emotions which had taken her by surprise. Abruptly closing the window, she threw aside her shawl, and lit the candles on the mantelpiece, impelled by a sudden craving for light in the solitude of her room.

The cheering brightness round her, contrasting with the black gloom outside, restored her spirits. She felt herself enjoying the light like a child!

Would it be well (she asked herself) to get ready for bed? No! The sense of drowsy fatigue that she had felt half an hour since was gone. She returned to the dull employment of unpacking her boxes. After a few minutes only, the occupation became irksome to her once more. She sat down by the table, and took up a guide-book. 'Suppose I inform myself,' she thought, 'on the subject of Venice?'

Her attention wandered from the book, before she had turned the first page of it.

The image of Henry Westwick was the presiding image in her memory now. Recalling the minutest incidents and details of the evening, she could think of nothing which presented him under other than a favourable and interesting aspect. She smiled to herself softly, her colour rose by fine gradations, as she felt the full luxury of dwelling on the perfect truth and modesty of his devotion to her. Was the depression of spirits from which she had suffered so persistently on her travels attributable, by any chance, to their long separation from each other—embittered perhaps by her own vain regret when she remembered her harsh reception of him in Paris? Suddenly conscious of this bold question, and of the self-abandonment which it implied, she returned mechanically to her book, distrusting the unrestrained liberty of her own thoughts. What lurking temptations to forbidden tenderness find their hiding-places in a woman's dressing-gown, when she is alone in her room at night! With her heart in the tomb of the dead Montbarry, could Agnes even think of another man, and think of love? How shameful! how unworthy of her! For the second time, she tried to interest herself in the guide-book— and once more she tried in vain. Throwing the book aside, she turned desperately to the one resource that was left, to her luggage—resolved to fatigue herself without mercy, until she was weary enough and sleepy enough to find a safe refuge in bed.

For some little time, she persisted in the monotonous occupation of transferring her clothes from her trunk to the wardrobe. The large clock in the hall, striking mid-night, reminded her that it was getting late. She sat down for a moment in an arm-chair by the bedside, to rest.

The silence in the house now caught her attention, and held it— held it disagreeably. Was everybody in bed and asleep but herself?

Surely it was time for her to follow the general example? With a certain irritable nervous haste, she rose again and undressed herself. 'I have lost two hours of rest,' she thought, frowning at the reflection of herself in the glass, as she arranged her hair for the night. 'I shall be good for nothing to-morrow!'

She lit the night-light, and extinguished the candles—with one exception, which she removed to a little table, placed on the side of the bed opposite to the side occupied by the arm-chair. Having put her travelling-box of matches and the guide-book near the candle, in case she might be sleepless and might want to read, she blew out the light, and laid her head on the pillow.

The curtains of the bed were looped back to let the air pass freely over her. Lying on her left side, with her face turned away from the table, she could see the arm-chair by the dim night-light. It had a chintz covering—representing large bunches of roses scattered over a pale green ground. She tried to weary herself into drowsiness by counting over and over again the bunches of roses that were visible from her point of view. Twice her attention was distracted from the counting, by sounds outside—by the clock chiming the half-hour past twelve; and then again, by the fall of a pair of boots on the upper floor, thrown out to be cleaned, with that barbarous disregard of the comfort of others which is observable in humanity when it inhabits an hotel. In the silence that followed these passing disturbances, Agnes went on counting the roses on the arm-chair, more and more slowly. Before long, she confused herself in the figures—tried to begin counting again—thought she would wait a little first—felt her eyelids drooping, and her head reclining lower and lower on the pillow—sighed faintly—and sank into sleep.

How long that first sleep lasted, she never knew. She could only remember, in the after-time, that she woke instantly.

Every faculty and perception in her passed the boundary line between insensibility and consciousness, so to speak, at a leap. Without knowing why, she sat up suddenly in the bed, listening for she knew not what. Her head was in a whirl; her heart beat furiously, without any assignable cause. But one trivial event had happened during the interval while she had been asleep. The night-light had gone out; and the room, as a matter of course, was in total darkness.

She felt for the match-box, and paused after finding it. A vague sense of confusion was still in her mind. She was in no hurry to light the match. The pause in the darkness was, for the moment, agreeable to her.

In the quieter flow of her thoughts during this interval, she could ask herself the natural question:—What cause had awakened her so suddenly, and had so strangely shaken her nerves? Had it been the influence of a dream? She had not dreamed at all—or, to speak more correctly, she had no waking remembrance of having dreamed. The mystery was beyond her fathoming: the darkness began to oppress her. She struck the match on the box, and lit her candle.

As the welcome light diffused itself over the room, she turned from the table and looked towards the other side of the bed.

In the moment when she turned, the chill of a sudden terror gripped her round the heart, as with the clasp of an icy hand.

She was not alone in her room!

There—in the chair at the bedside—there, suddenly revealed under the flow of light from the candle, was the figure of a woman, reclining. Her head lay back over the chair. Her face, turned up to the ceiling, had the eyes closed, as if she was wrapped in a deep sleep.

The shock of the discovery held Agnes speechless and helpless. Her first conscious action, when she was in some degree mistress of herself again, was to lean over the bed, and to look closer at the woman who had so incomprehensibly stolen into her room in the dead of night. One glance was enough: she started back with a cry of amazement. The person in the chair was no other than the widow of the dead Montbarry—the woman who had warned her that they were to meet again, and that the place might be Venice!

Her courage returned to her, stung into action by the natural sense of indignation which the presence of the Countess provoked.

'Wake up!' she called out. 'How dare you come here? How did you get in? Leave the room—or I will call for help!'

She raised her voice at the last words. It produced no effect. Leaning farther over the bed, she boldly took the Countess by the shoulder and shook her. Not even this effort succeeded in rousing the sleeping woman. She still lay back in the chair, possessed by a torpor like the torpor of death—insensible to sound, insensible to touch. Was she really sleeping? Or had she fainted?

Agnes looked closer at her. She had not fainted. Her breathing was audible, rising and falling in deep heavy gasps. At intervals she ground her teeth savagely. Beads of perspiration stood thickly on her forehead. Her clenched hands rose and fell slowly from time to time on her lap. Was she in the agony of a dream? or was she spiritually conscious of something hidden in the room?

The doubt involved in that last question was unendurable. Agnes determined to rouse the servants who kept watch in the hotel at night.

The bell-handle was fixed to the wall, on the side of the bed by which the table stood.

She raised herself from the crouching position which she had assumed in looking close at the Countess; and, turning towards the other side of the bed, stretched out her hand to the bell. At the same instant, she stopped and looked upward. Her hand fell helplessly at her side. She shuddered, and sank back on the pillow.

What had she seen?

She had seen another intruder in her room.

Midway between her face and the ceiling, there hovered a human head—severed at the neck, like a head struck from the body by the guillotine.

Nothing visible, nothing audible, had given her any intelligible warning of its appearance. Silently and suddenly, the head had taken its place above her. No supernatural change had passed over the room, or was perceptible in it now. The dumbly-tortured figure in the chair; the broad window opposite the foot of the bed, with the black night beyond it; the candle burning on the table—these, and all other objects in the room, remained unaltered. One object more, unutterably horrid, had been added to the rest. That was the only change—no more, no less.

By the yellow candlelight she saw the head distinctly, hovering in mid-air above her. She looked at it steadfastly, spell-bound by the terror that held her.

The flesh of the face was gone. The shrivelled skin was darkened in hue, like the skin of an Egyptian mummy—except at the neck. There it was of a lighter colour; there it showed spots and splashes of the hue of that brown spot on the ceiling, which the child's fanciful terror had distorted into the likeness of a spot of blood. Thin remains of a discoloured moustache and whiskers, hanging over the upper lip, and over the hollows where the cheeks had once been, made the head just recognisable as the head of a man. Over all the features death and time had done their obliterating work. The eyelids were closed. The hair on the skull, discoloured like the hair on the face, had been burnt away in places. The bluish lips, parted in a fixed grin, showed the double row of teeth. By slow degrees, the hovering head (perfectly still when she first saw it) began to descend towards Agnes as she lay beneath. By slow degrees, that strange doubly-blended odour, which the Commissioners had discovered in the vaults of the old palace—which had sickened Francis Westwick in the bed-chamber of the new hotel—spread its fetid exhalations over the room. Downward and downward the hideous apparition made its slow progress, until it stopped close over Agnes—stopped, and turned slowly, so that the face of it confronted the upturned face of the woman in the chair.

There was a pause. Then, a supernatural movement disturbed the rigid repose of the dead face.

The closed eyelids opened slowly. The eyes revealed themselves, bright with the glassy film of death—and fixed their dreadful look on the woman in the chair.

Agnes saw that look; saw the eyelids of the living woman open slowly like the eyelids of the dead; saw her rise, as if in obedience to some silent command—and saw no more.

\* \* \* \* \* \* \*

Her next conscious impression was of the sunlight pouring in at the window; of the friendly presence of Lady Montbarry at the bedside; and of the children's wondering faces peeping in at the door.

## CHAPTER XXIII

'. . . You have some influence over Agnes. Try what you can do, Henry, to make her take a sensible view of the matter. There is really nothing to make a fuss about. My wife's maid knocked at her door early in the morning, with the customary cup of tea. Getting no answer, she went round to the dressing-room—found the door on that side unlocked—and discovered Agnes on the bed in a fainting fit. With my wife's help, they brought her to herself again; and she told the extraordinary story which I have just repeated to you. You must have seen for yourself that she has been over-fatigued, poor thing, by our long railway journeys: her nerves are out of order—and she is just the person to be easily terrified by a dream. She obstinately refuses, however, to accept this rational view. Don't suppose that I have been severe with her! All that a man can do to humour her I have done. I have written to the Countess (in her assumed name) offering to restore the room to her. She writes back, positively declining to return to it. I have accordingly arranged (so as not to have the thing known in the hotel) to occupy the room for one or two nights, and to leave Agnes to recover her spirits under my wife's care. Is there anything more that I can do? Whatever questions Agnes has asked of me I have answered to the best of my ability; she knows all that you told me about Francis and the Countess last night. But try as I may I can't quiet her mind. I have given up the attempt in despair, and left her in the drawing-room. Go, like a good fellow, and try what you can do to compose her.'

In those words, Lord Montbarry stated the case to his brother from the rational point of view. Henry made no remark, he went straight to the drawing-room.

He found Agnes walking rapidly backwards and forwards, flushed and excited. 'If you come here to say what your brother has been saying to me,' she broke out, before he could speak, 'spare yourself the trouble. I don't want common sense—I want a true friend who will believe in me.'

'I am that friend, Agnes,' Henry answered quietly, 'and you know it.'

'You really believe that I am not deluded by a dream?'

'I know that you are not deluded—in one particular, at least.'

'In what particular?'

'In what you have said of the Countess. It is perfectly true—'

Agnes stopped him there. 'Why do I only hear this morning that the Countess and Mrs James are one and the same person?' she asked distrustfully. 'Why was I not told of it last night?'

'You forget that you had accepted the exchange of rooms before I reached Venice,' Henry replied. 'I felt strongly tempted to tell you, even then—but your sleeping arrangements for the night were all made; I should only have inconvenienced and alarmed you. I waited till the morning, after hearing from my brother that you had yourself seen to your security from any intrusion. How that intrusion was accomplished it is impossible to say. I can only declare that the Countess's presence by your bedside last night was no dream of yours. On her own authority I can testify that it was a reality.'

'On her own authority?' Agnes repeated eagerly. 'Have you seen her this morning?'

'I have seen her not ten minutes since.'

'What was she doing?'

'She was busily engaged in writing. I could not even get her to look at me until I thought of mentioning your name.'

'She remembered me, of course?'

'She remembered you with some difficulty. Finding that she wouldn't answer me on any other terms, I questioned her as if I had come direct from you. Then she spoke. She not only admitted that she had the same superstitious motive for placing you in that room which she had acknowledged to Francis—she even owned that she had been by your bedside, watching through the night, "to see what you saw," as she expressed it. Hearing this, I tried to persuade her to tell me how she got into the room. Unluckily, her manuscript on the table caught her eye; she returned to her writing. "The Baron wants money," she said; "I must get on with my play." What she saw or dreamed while she was in your room last night, it is at present impossible to discover. But judging by my brother's account of her, as well as by what I remember of her myself, some recent influence has been at work which has produced a marked change in this wretched woman for the worse. Her mind (since last night, perhaps) is partially deranged.* One proof of it is that she spoke to me of the Baron as if he were still a living man. When Francis saw her, she declared that the Baron was dead, which is the truth. The United States Consul at Milan showed us the announcement of the death in an American newspaper. So far as I can see, such sense as she still possesses seems to be entirely absorbed in one absurd idea—the idea of writing a play for Francis to bring out at his theatre. He admits that he encouraged her to hope she might get money in this way. I think he did wrong. Don't you agree with me?'

Without heeding the question, Agnes rose abruptly from her chair.

'Do me one more kindness, Henry,' she said. 'Take me to the Countess at once.'

Henry hesitated. 'Are you composed enough to see her, after the shock that you have suffered?' he asked.

She trembled, the flush on her face died away, and left it deadly pale. But she held to her resolution. 'You have heard of what I saw last night?' she said faintly.

'Don't speak of it!' Henry interposed. 'Don't uselessly agitate yourself.'

'I must speak! My mind is full of horrid questions about it. I know I can't identify it—and yet I ask myself over and over again, in whose likeness did it appear? Was it in the likeness of Ferrari? or was it—?' she stopped, shuddering. 'The Countess knows, I must see the Countess!' she resumed vehemently. 'Whether my courage fails me or not, I must make the attempt. Take me to her before I have time to feel afraid of it!'

Henry looked at her anxiously. 'If you are really sure of your own resolution,' he said, 'I agree with you—the sooner you see her the better. You remember how strangely she talked of your influence over her, when she forced her way into your room in London?'

'I remember it perfectly. Why do you ask?'

'For this reason. In the present state of her mind, I doubt if she will be much longer capable of realizing her wild idea of you as the avenging angel who is to bring her to a reckoning for her evil deeds. It may be well to try what your influence can do while she is still capable of feeling it.'

He waited to hear what Agnes would say. She took his arm and led him in silence to the door.

They ascended to the second floor, and, after knocking, entered the Countess's room.

She was still busily engaged in writing. When she looked up from the paper, and saw Agnes, a vacant expression of doubt was the only expression in her wild black eyes. After a few moments, the lost remembrances and associations appeared to return slowly to her mind. The pen dropped from her hand. Haggard and trembling, she looked closer at Agnes, and recognised her at last. 'Has the time come already?' she said in low awe-struck tones. 'Give me a little longer respite, I haven't done my writing yet!'

She dropped on her knees, and held out her clasped hands entreatingly. Agnes was far from having recovered, after the shock that she had suffered in the night: her nerves were far from being equal to the strain that was now laid on them. She was so startled by the change in the Countess, that she was at a loss what to say or to do next. Henry was obliged to speak to her. 'Put your questions while you have the chance,' he said, lowering his voice. 'See! the vacant look is coming over her face again.'

Agnes tried to rally her courage. 'You were in my room last night—' she began. Before she could add a word more, the Countess lifted her hands, and wrung them above her head with a low moan of horror. Agnes shrank back, and turned as if to leave the room. Henry stopped her, and whispered to her to try again. She obeyed him after an effort. 'I slept last night in the room that you gave up to me,' she resumed. 'I saw—'

The Countess suddenly rose to her feet. 'No more of that,' she cried. 'Oh, Jesu Maria! do you think I want to be told what you saw? Do you think I don't know what it means for you and for me? Decide for yourself, Miss. Examine your own mind. Are you well assured that the day of reckoning has come at last? Are you ready to follow me back, through the crimes of the past, to the secrets of the dead?'

She turned again to the writing-table, without waiting to be answered. Her eyes flashed; she looked like her old self once more as she spoke. It was only for a moment. The old ardour and impetuosity were nearly worn out. Her head sank; she sighed heavily as she unlocked a desk which stood on the table. Opening a drawer in the desk, she took out a leaf of vellum, covered with faded writing. Some ragged ends of silken thread were still attached to the leaf, as if it had been torn out of a book.

'Can you read Italian?' she asked, handing the leaf to Agnes.

Agnes answered silently by an inclination of her head.

'The leaf,' the Countess proceeded, 'once belonged to a book in the old library of the palace, while this building was still a palace. By whom it was torn out you have no need to know. For what purpose it was torn out you may discover for yourself, if you will. Read it first— at the fifth line from the top of the page.'

Agnes felt the serious necessity of composing herself. 'Give me a chair,' she said to Henry; 'and I will do my best.' He placed himself behind her chair so that he could look over her shoulder and help her to understand the writing on the leaf. Rendered into English, it ran as follows:—

'I have now completed my literary survey of the first floor of the palace. At the desire of my noble and gracious patron, the lord of this glorious edifice, I next ascend to the second floor, and continue my catalogue or description of the pictures, decorations, and other treasures of art therein contained. Let me begin with the corner room at the western extremity of the palace, called the Room of the Caryatides, from the statues which support the mantel-piece. This work is of comparatively recent execution: it dates from the eighteenth century only, and reveals the corrupt taste of the period in every part of it. Still, there is a certain interest which attaches to the mantel-piece: it conceals a cleverly constructed hiding-place, between the floor of the room and the ceiling of the room beneath, which was made during the last evil days of the Inquisition in Venice, and which is reported to have saved an ancestor of my gracious lord pursued by that terrible tribunal. The machinery of this curious place of concealment has been kept in good order by the present lord, as a species of curiosity. He condescended to show me the method of working it. Approaching the two Caryatides, rest your hand on the forehead (midway between the eyebrows) of the figure which is on your left as you stand opposite to the fireplace, then press the head inwards as if you were pushing it against the wall behind. By doing this, you set in motion the hidden machinery in the wall which turns the hearthstone on a pivot, and discloses the hollow place below. There is room enough in it for a man to lie easily at full length. The method of closing the cavity again is equally simple. Place both your hands on the temples of the figure; pull as if you were pulling it towards you—and the hearthstone will revolve into its proper position again.'

'You need read no farther,' said the Countess. 'Be careful to remember what you have read.'

She put back the page of vellum in her writing-desk, locked it, and led the way to the door.

'Come!' she said; 'and see what the mocking Frenchman* called "The beginning of the end."'

Agnes was barely able to rise from her chair; she trembled from head to foot. Henry gave her his arm to support her. 'Fear nothing,' he whispered; 'I shall be with you.'

The Countess proceeded along the westward corridor, and stopped at the door numbered Thirty-eight. This was the room which had been inhabited by Baron Rivar in the old days of the palace: it was situated immediately over the bedchamber in which Agnes had passed the night. For the last two days the room had been empty. The absence of luggage in it, when they opened the door, showed that it had not yet been let.

'You see?' said the Countess, pointing to the carved figure at the fire-place; 'and you know what to do. Have I deserved that you should temper justice with mercy?' she went on in lower tones. 'Give me a few hours more to myself. The Baron wants money—I must get on with my play.'

She smiled vacantly, and imitated the action of writing with her right hand as she pronounced the last words. The effort of concentrating her weakened mind on other and less familiar topics than the constant want of money in the Baron's lifetime, and the vague prospect of gain from the still unfinished play, had evidently exhausted her poor reserves of strength. When her request had been granted, she addressed no expressions of gratitude to Agnes; she only said, 'Feel no fear, miss, of my attempting to escape you. Where you are, there I must be till the end comes.'

Her eyes wandered round the room with a last weary and stupefied look. She returned to her writing with slow and feeble steps, like the steps of an old woman.

## CHAPTER XXIV

Henry and Agnes were left alone in the Room of the Caryatides.

The person who had written the description of the palace—probably a poor author or artist—had correctly pointed out the defects of the mantel-piece. Bad taste, exhibiting itself on the most costly and splendid scale, was visible in every part of the work. It was nevertheless greatly admired by ignorant travellers of all classes; partly on account of its imposing size, and partly on account of the number of variously-coloured marbles which the sculptor had contrived to introduce into his design. Photographs of the mantel-piece were exhibited in the public rooms, and found a ready sale among English and American visitors to the hotel.

Henry led Agnes to the figure on the left, as they stood facing the empty fire-place. 'Shall I try the experiment,' he asked, 'or will you?' She abruptly drew her arm away from him, and turned back to the door. 'I can't even look at it,' she said. 'That merciless marble face frightens me!'

Henry put his hand on the forehead of the figure. 'What is there to alarm you, my dear, in this conventionally classical face?' he asked jestingly. Before he could press the head inwards, Agnes hurriedly opened the door. 'Wait till I am out of the room!' she cried. 'The bare idea of what you may find there horrifies me!' She looked back into the room as she crossed the threshold. 'I won't leave you altogether,' she said, 'I will wait outside.'

She closed the door. Left by himself, Henry lifted his hand once more to the marble forehead of the figure.

For the second time, he was checked on the point of setting the machinery of the hiding-place in motion. On this occasion, the interruption came from an outbreak of friendly voices in the corridor. A woman's voice exclaimed, 'Dearest Agnes, how glad I am to see you again!' A man's voice followed, offering to introduce some friend to 'Miss Lockwood.' A third voice (which Henry recognised as the voice of the manager of the hotel) became audible next, directing the housekeeper to show the ladies and gentlemen the vacant apartments at the other end of the corridor. 'If more accommodation is wanted,' the manager went on, 'I have a charming room to let here.' He opened the door as he spoke, and found himself face to face with Henry Westwick.

'This is indeed an agreeable surprise, sir!' said the manager cheerfully. 'You are admiring our famous chimney-piece, I see. May I ask, Mr Westwick, how you find yourself in the hotel, this time? Have the supernatural influences affected your appetite again?'

'The supernatural influences have spared me, this time,' Henry answered. 'Perhaps you may yet find that they have affected some other member of the family.' He spoke gravely, resenting the familiar tone in which the manager had referred to his previous visit to the hotel. 'Have you just returned?' he asked, by way of changing the topic.

'Just this minute, sir. I had the honour of travelling in the same train with friends of yours who have arrived at the hotel—Mr and Mrs Arthur Barville, and their travelling companions. Miss Lockwood is with them, looking at the rooms. They will be here before long, if they find it convenient to have an extra room at their disposal.'

This announcement decided Henry on exploring the hiding-place, before the interruption occurred. It had crossed his mind, when Agnes left him, that he ought perhaps to have a witness, in the not very probable event of some alarming discovery taking place. The too-familiar manager, suspecting nothing, was there at his disposal. He turned again to the Caryan figure, maliciously resolving to make the manager his witness.

'I am delighted to hear that our friends have arrived at last,' he said. 'Before I shake hands with them, let me ask you a question about this queer work of art here. I see photographs of it downstairs. Are they for sale?'

'Certainly, Mr Westwick!'

'Do you think the chimney-piece is as solid as it looks?' Henry proceeded. 'When you came in, I was just wondering whether this figure here had not accidentally got loosened from the wall behind it.' He laid his hand on the marble forehead, for the third time. 'To my eye, it looks a little out of the perpendicular. I almost fancied I could jog the head just now, when I touched it.' He pressed the head inwards as he said those words.

A sound of jarring iron was instantly audible behind the wall. The solid hearthstone in front of the fire-place turned slowly at the feet of the two men, and disclosed a dark cavity below. At the same moment, the strange and sickening combination of odours, hitherto associated with the vaults of the old palace and with the bed-chamber beneath, now floated up from the open recess, and filled the room.

The manager started back. 'Good God, Mr Westwick!' he exclaimed, 'what does this mean?'

Remembering, not only what his brother Francis had felt in the room beneath, but what the experience of Agnes had been on the previous night, Henry was determined to be on his guard. 'I am as much surprised as you are,' was his only reply.

'Wait for me one moment, sir,' said the manager. 'I must stop the ladies and gentlemen outside from coming in.'

He hurried away—not forgetting to close the door after him. Henry opened the window, and waited there breathing the purer air. Vague apprehensions of the next discovery to come, filled his mind for the first time. He was doubly resolved, now, not to stir a step in the investigation without a witness.

The manager returned with a wax taper in his hand, which he lighted as soon as he entered the room.

'We need fear no interruption now,' he said. 'Be so kind, Mr Westwick, as to hold the light. It is *my* business to find out what this extraordinary discovery means.'

Henry held the taper. Looking into the cavity, by the dim and flickering light, they both detected a dark object at the bottom of it. 'I think I can reach the thing,' the manager remarked, 'if I lie down, and put my hand into the hole.'

He knelt on the floor—and hesitated. 'Might I ask you, sir, to give me my gloves?' he said. 'They are in my hat, on the chair behind you.'

Henry gave him the gloves. 'I don't know what I may be going to take hold of,' the manager explained, smiling rather uneasily as he put on his right glove.

He stretched himself at full length on the floor, and passed his right arm into the cavity. 'I can't say exactly what I have got hold of,' he said. 'But I have got it.'

Half raising himself, he drew his hand out.

The next instant, he started to his feet with a shriek of terror. A human head dropped from his nerveless grasp on the floor, and rolled to Henry's feet. It was the hideous head that Agnes had seen hovering above her, in the vision of the night!

The two men looked at each other, both struck speechless by the same emotion of horror. The manager was the first to control himself. 'See to the door, for God's sake!' he said. 'Some of the people outside may have heard me.'

Henry moved mechanically to the door.

Even when he had his hand on the key, ready to turn it in the lock in case of necessity, he still looked back at the appalling object on the floor. There was no possibility of identifying those decayed and distorted features with any living creature whom he had seen—and, yet, he was conscious of feeling a vague and awful doubt which shook him to the soul. The questions which had tortured the mind of Agnes, were now *his* questions too. *He* asked himself, 'In whose likeness might I have recognised it before the decay set in? The likeness of Ferrari? or the likeness of—?' He paused trembling, as Agnes had paused trembling before him. Agnes! The name, of all women's names the dearest to him, was a terror to him now! What was he to say to her? What might be the consequence if he trusted her with the terrible truth?

No footsteps approached the door; no voices were audible outside. The travellers were still occupied in the rooms at the eastern end of the corridor.

In the brief interval that had passed, the manager had sufficiently recovered himself to be able to think once more of the first and foremost interests of his life—the interests of the hotel. He approached Henry anxiously.

'If this frightful discovery becomes known,' he said, 'the closing of the hotel and the ruin of the Company will be the inevitable results. I feel sure that I can trust your discretion, sir, so far?'

'You can certainly trust me,' Henry answered. 'But surely discretion has its limits,' he added, 'after such a discovery as we have made?'

The manager understood that the duty which they owed to the community, as honest and law-abiding men, was the duty to which Henry now referred. 'I will at once find the means,' he said, 'of conveying the remains privately out of the house, and I will myself place them in the care of the police authorities. Will you leave the room with me? or do you not object to keep watch here, and help me when I return?'

While he was speaking, the voices of the travellers made themselves heard again at the end of the corridor. Henry instantly consented to wait in the room. He shrank from facing the inevitable meeting with Agnes if he showed himself in the corridor at that moment.

The manager hastened his departure, in the hope of escaping notice. He was discovered by his guests before he could reach the head of the stairs. Henry heard the voices plainly as he turned the key. While the terrible drama of discovery was in progress on one side of the door, trivial questions about the amusements of Venice, and facetious discussions on the relative merits of French and Italian cookery, were proceeding on the other. Little by little, the sound of the talking grew fainter. The visitors, having arranged their plans of amusement for the day, were on their way out of the hotel. In a minute or two, there was silence once more.

Henry turned to the window, thinking to relieve his mind by looking at the bright view over the canal. He soon grew wearied of the familiar scene. The morbid fascination which seems to be exercised by all horrible sights, drew him back again to the ghastly object on the floor.

Dream or reality, how had Agnes survived the sight of it? As the question passed through his mind, he noticed for the first time something lying on the floor near the head. Looking closer, he perceived a thin little plate of gold, with three false teeth attached to it, which had apparently dropped out (loosened by the shock) when the manager let the head fall on the floor.

The importance of this discovery, and the necessity of not too readily communicating it to others, instantly struck Henry. Here surely was a chance—if any chance remained—of identifying the shocking relic of humanity which lay before him, the dumb witness of a crime! Acting on this idea, he took possession of the teeth, purposing to use them as a last means of inquiry when other attempts at investigation had been tried and had failed.

He went back again to the window: the solitude of the room began to weigh on his spirits. As he looked out again at the view, there was a soft knock at the door. He hastened to open it—and checked himself in the act. A doubt occurred to him. Was it the manager who had knocked? He called out, 'Who is there?'

The voice of Agnes answered him. 'Have you anything to tell me, Henry?'

He was hardly able to reply. 'Not just now,' he said, confusedly. 'Forgive me if I don't open the door. I will speak to you a little later.'

The sweet voice made itself heard again, pleading with him piteously. 'Don't leave me alone, Henry! I can't go back to the happy people downstairs.'

How could he resist that appeal? He heard her sigh—he heard the rustling of her dress as she moved away in despair. The very thing that he had shrunk from doing but a few minutes since was the thing that he did now! He joined Agnes in the corridor. She turned as she heard him, and pointed, trembling, in the direction of the closed room. 'Is it so terrible as that?' she asked faintly.

He put his arm round her to support her. A thought came to him as he looked at her, waiting in doubt and fear for his reply. 'You shall know what I have discovered,' he said, 'if you will first put on your hat and cloak, and come out with me.'

She was naturally surprised. 'Can you tell me your object in going out?' she asked.

He owned what his object was unreservedly. 'I want, before all things,' he said, 'to satisfy your mind and mine, on the subject of Montbarry's death. I am going to take you to the doctor who attended him in his illness, and to the consul who followed him to the grave.'

Her eyes rested on Henry gratefully. 'Oh, how well you understand me!' she said. The manager joined them at the same moment, on his way up the stairs. Henry gave him the key of the room, and then called to the servants in the hall to have a gondola ready at the steps. 'Are you leaving the hotel?' the manager asked. 'In search of evidence,' Henry whispered, pointing to the key. 'If the authorities want me, I shall be back in an hour.'

## CHAPTER XXV

The day had advanced to evening. Lord Montbarry and the bridal party had gone to the Opera. Agnes alone, pleading the excuse of fatigue, remained at the hotel. Having kept up appearances by accompanying his friends to the theatre, Henry Westwick slipped away after the first act, and joined Agnes in the drawing-room.

'Have you thought of what I said to you earlier in the day?' he asked, taking a chair at her side. 'Do you agree with me that the one dreadful doubt which oppressed us both is at least set at rest?'

Agnes shook her head sadly. 'I wish I could agree with you, Henry—I wish I could honestly say that my mind is at ease.'

The answer would have discouraged most men. Henry's patience (where Agnes was concerned) was equal to any demands on it.

'If you will only look back at the events of the day,' he said, 'you must surely admit that we have not been completely baffled. Remember how Dr Bruno disposed of our doubts:—"After thirty years of medical practice, do you think I am likely to mistake the symptoms of death by bronchitis?" If ever there was an unanswerable question, there it is! Was the consul's testimony doubtful in any part of it? He called at the palace to offer his services, after hearing of Lord Montbarry's death; he arrived at the time when the coffin was in the house; he himself saw the corpse placed in it, and the lid screwed down. The evidence of the priest is equally beyond dispute. He remained in the room with the coffin, reciting the prayers for the dead, until the funeral left the palace. Bear all these statements in mind, Agnes; and how can you deny that the question of Montbarry's death and burial is a question set at rest? We have really but one doubt left: we have still to ask ourselves whether the remains which I discovered are the remains of the lost courier, or not. There is the case, as I understand it. Have I stated it fairly?'

Agnes could not deny that he had stated it fairly.

'Then what prevents you from experiencing the same sense of relief that I feel?' Henry asked.

'What I saw last night prevents me,' Agnes answered. 'When we spoke of this subject, after our inquiries were over, you reproached me with taking what you called the superstitious view. I don't quite admit that—but I do acknowledge that I should find the superstitious view intelligible if I heard it expressed by some other person. Remembering what your brother and I once were to each other in the bygone time, I can understand the apparition making itself visible to Me, to claim the mercy of Christian burial, and the vengeance due to a crime. I can even perceive some faint possibility of truth in the explanation which you described as the mesmeric theory*—that what I saw might be the result of magnetic influence communicated to me, as I lay between the remains of the murdered husband above me and the guilty wife suffering the tortures of remorse at my bedside. But what I do *not* understand is, that I should have passed through that dreadful ordeal; having no previous knowledge of the murdered man in his lifetime, or only knowing him (if you suppose that I saw the apparition of Ferrari) through the interest which I took in his wife. I can't dispute your reasoning, Henry. But I feel in my heart of hearts that you are deceived. Nothing will shake my belief that we are still as far from having discovered the dreadful truth as ever.'

Henry made no further attempt to dispute with her. She had impressed him with a certain reluctant respect for her own opinion, in spite of himself.

'Have you thought of any better way of arriving at the truth?' he asked. 'Who is to help us? No doubt there is the Countess, who has the clue to the mystery in her own hands. But, in the present state of her mind, is her testimony to be trusted—even if she were willing to speak? Judging by my own experience, I should say decidedly not.'

'You don't mean that you have seen her again?' Agnes eagerly interposed.

'Yes. I disturbed her once more over her endless writing; and I insisted on her speaking out plainly.'

'Then you told her what you found when you opened the hiding-place?'

'Of course I did!' Henry replied. 'I said that I held her responsible for the discovery, though I had not mentioned her connection with it to the authorities as yet. She went on with her writing as if I had spoken in an unknown tongue! I was equally obstinate, on my side. I told her plainly that the head had been placed under the care of the police, and that the manager and I had signed our declarations and given our evidence. She paid not the slightest heed to me. By way of tempting her to speak, I added that the whole investigation was to be kept a secret, and that she might depend on my discretion. For the moment I thought I had succeeded. She looked up from her writing with a passing flash of curiosity, and said, "What are they going to do with it?"—meaning, I suppose, the head. I answered that it was to be privately buried, after photographs of it had first been taken. I even went the length of communicating the opinion of the surgeon consulted, that some chemical means of arresting decomposition had been used and had only partially succeeded—and I asked her point-blank if the surgeon was right? The trap was not a bad one—but it completely failed. She said in the coolest manner, "Now you are here, I should like to consult you about my play; I am at a loss for some new incidents." Mind! there was nothing satirical in this. She was really eager to read her wonderful work to me—evidently supposing that I took a special interest in such things, because my brother is the manager of a theatre! I left her, making the first excuse that occurred to me. So far as I am concerned, I can do nothing with her. But it is possible that *your* influence may succeed with her again, as it has succeeded already. Will you make the attempt, to satisfy your own mind? She is still upstairs; and I am quite ready to accompany you.'

Agnes shuddered at the bare suggestion of another interview with the Countess.

'I can't! I daren't!' she exclaimed. 'After what has happened in that horrible room, she is more repellent to me than ever. Don't ask me to do it, Henry! Feel my hand—you have turned me as cold as death only with talking of it!'

She was not exaggerating the terror that possessed her. Henry hastened to change the subject.

'Let us talk of something more interesting,' he said. 'I have a question to ask you about yourself. Am I right in believing that the sooner you get away from Venice the happier you will be?'

'Right?' she repeated excitedly. 'You are more than right! No words can say how I long to be away from this horrible place. But you know how I am situated—you heard what Lord Montbarry said at dinner-time?'

'Suppose he has altered his plans, since dinner-time?' Henry suggested.

Agnes looked surprised. 'I thought he had received letters from England which obliged him to leave Venice to-morrow,' she said.

'Quite true,' Henry admitted. 'He had arranged to start for England to-morrow, and to leave you and Lady Montbarry and the children to enjoy your holiday in Venice, under my care. Circumstances have occurred, however, which have forced him to alter his plans. He must take you all back with him to-morrow because I am not able to assume the charge of you. I am obliged to give up my holiday in Italy, and return to England too.'

Agnes looked at him in some little perplexity: she was not quite sure whether she understood him or not.

'Are you really obliged to go back?' she asked.

Henry smiled as he answered her. 'Keep the secret,' he said, 'or Montbarry will never forgive me!'

She read the rest in his face. 'Oh!' she exclaimed, blushing brightly, 'you have not given up your pleasant holiday in Italy on my account?'

'I shall go back with you to England, Agnes. That will be holiday enough for *me*.'

She took his hand in an irrepressible outburst of gratitude. 'How good you are to me!' she murmured tenderly. 'What should I have done in the troubles that have come to me, without your sympathy? I can't tell you, Henry, how I feel your kindness.'

She tried impulsively to lift his hand to her lips. He gently stopped her. 'Agnes,' he said, 'are you beginning to understand how truly I love you?'

That simple question found its own way to her heart. She owned the whole truth, without saying a word. She looked at him—and then looked away again.

He drew her nearer to him. 'My own darling!' he whispered—and kissed her. Softly and tremulously, the sweet lips lingered, and touched his lips in return. Then her head drooped. She put her arms round his neck, and hid her face on his bosom. They spoke no more.

The charmed silence had lasted but a little while, when it was mercilessly broken by a knock at the door.

Agnes started to her feet. She placed herself at the piano; the instrument being opposite to the door, it was impossible, when she seated herself on the music-stool, for any person entering the room to see her face. Henry called out irritably, 'Come in.'

The door was not opened. The person on the other side of it asked a strange question.

'Is Mr Henry Westwick alone?'

Agnes instantly recognised the voice of the Countess. She hurried to a second door, which communicated with one of the bedrooms. 'Don't let her come near me!' she whispered nervously. 'Good night, Henry! good night!'

If Henry could, by an effort of will, have transported the Countess to the uttermost ends of the earth, he would have made the effort without remorse. As it was, he only repeated, more irritably than ever, 'Come in!'

She entered the room slowly with her everlasting manuscript in her hand. Her step was unsteady; a dark flush appeared on her face, in place of its customary pallor; her eyes were bloodshot and widely dilated. In approaching Henry, she showed a strange incapability of calculating her distances—she struck against the table near which he happened to be sitting. When she spoke, her articulation was confused, and her pronunciation of some of the longer words was hardly intelligible. Most men would have suspected her of being under the influence of some intoxicating liquor. Henry took a truer view—he said, as he placed a chair for her, 'Countess, I am afraid you have been working too hard: you look as if you wanted rest.'

She put her hand to her head. 'My invention has gone,' she said. 'I can't write my fourth act. It's all a blank—all a blank!'

Henry advised her to wait till the next day. 'Go to bed,' he suggested; 'and try to sleep.'

She waved her hand impatiently. 'I must finish the play,' she answered. 'I only want a hint from you. You must know something about plays. Your brother has got a theatre. You must often have heard him talk about fourth and fifth acts—you must have seen rehearsals, and all the rest of it.' She abruptly thrust the manuscript into Henry's hand. 'I can't read it to you,' she said; 'I feel giddy when I look at my own writing. Just run your eye over it, there's a good fellow—and give me a hint.'

Henry glanced at the manuscript. He happened to look at the list of the persons of the drama. As he read the list he started and turned abruptly to the Countess, intending to ask her for some explanation. The words were suspended on his lips. It was but too plainly useless to speak to her. Her head lay back on the rail of the chair. She seemed to be half asleep already. The flush on her face had deepened: she looked like a woman who was in danger of having a fit.

He rang the bell, and directed the man who answered it to send one of the chambermaids upstairs. His voice seemed to partially rouse the Countess; she opened her eyes in a slow drowsy way. 'Have you read it?' she asked.

It was necessary as a mere act of humanity to humour her. 'I will read it willingly,' said Henry, 'if you will go upstairs to bed. You shall hear what I think of it to-morrow morning. Our heads will be clearer, we shall be better able to make the fourth act in the morning.'

The chambermaid came in while he was speaking. 'I am afraid the lady is ill,' Henry whispered. 'Take her up to her room.' The woman looked at the Countess and whispered back, 'Shall we send for a doctor, sir?'

Henry advised taking her upstairs first, and then asking the manager's opinion. There was great difficulty in persuading her to rise, and accept the support of the chambermaid's arm. It was only by reiterated promises to read the play that night, and to make the fourth act in the morning, that Henry prevailed on the Countess to return to her room.

Left to himself, he began to feel a certain languid curiosity in relation to the manuscript. He looked over the pages, reading a line here and a line there. Suddenly he changed colour as he read—and looked up from the manuscript like a man bewildered. 'Good God! what does this mean?' he said to himself.

His eyes turned nervously to the door by which Agnes had left him. She might return to the drawing-room, she might want to see what the Countess had written. He looked back again at the passage which had startled him—considered with himself for a moment—and, snatching up the unfinished play, suddenly and softly left the room.

## CHAPTER XXVI

Entering his own room on the upper floor, Henry placed the manuscript on his table, open at the first leaf. His nerves were unquestionably shaken; his hand trembled as he turned the pages, he started at chance noises on the staircase of the hotel.

The scenario, or outline, of the Countess's play began with no formal prefatory phrases. She presented herself and her work with the easy familiarity of an old friend.

'Allow me, dear Mr Francis Westwick, to introduce to you the persons in my proposed Play. Behold them, arranged symmetrically in a line.

'My Lord. The Baron. The Courier. The Doctor. The Countess.

'I don't trouble myself, you see, to invent fictitious family names. My characters are sufficiently distinguished by their social titles, and by the striking contrast which they present one with another.

'The First Act opens—

'No! Before I open the First Act, I must announce, in justice to myself, that this Play is entirely the work of my own invention. I scorn to borrow from actual events; and, what is more extraordinary still, I have not stolen one of my ideas from the Modern French drama. As the manager of an English theatre, you will naturally refuse to believe this. It doesn't matter. Nothing matters—except the opening of my first act.

'We are at Homburg, in the famous Salon d'Or, at the height of the season. The Countess (exquisitely dressed) is seated at the green table. Strangers of all nations are standing behind the players, venturing their money or only looking on. My Lord is among the strangers. He is struck by the Countess's personal appearance, in which beauties and defects are fantastically mingled in the most attractive manner. He watches the Countess's game, and places his money where he sees her deposit her own little stake. She looks round at him, and says, "Don't trust to my colour; I have been unlucky the whole evening. Place your stake on the other colour, and you may have a chance of winning." My Lord (a true Englishman) blushes, bows, and obeys. The Countess proves to be a prophet. She loses again. My Lord wins twice the sum that he has risked.

'The Countess rises from the table. She has no more money, and she offers my Lord her chair.

'Instead of taking it, he politely places his winnings in her hand, and begs her to accept the loan as a favour to himself. The Countess stakes again, and loses again. My Lord smiles superbly, and presses a second loan on her. From that moment her luck turns. She wins, and wins largely. Her brother, the Baron, trying his fortune in another room, hears of what is going on, and joins my Lord and the Countess.

'Pay attention, if you please, to the Baron. He is delineated as a remarkable and interesting character.

'This noble person has begun life with a single-minded devotion to the science of experimental chemistry, very surprising in a young and handsome man with a brilliant future before him. A profound knowledge of the occult sciences has persuaded the Baron that it is possible to solve the famous problem called the "Philosopher's Stone."* His own pecuniary resources have long since been exhausted by his costly experiments. His sister has next supplied him with the small fortune at her disposal: reserving only the family jewels, placed in the charge of her banker and friend at Frankfort. The Countess's fortune also being swallowed up, the Baron has in a fatal moment sought for new supplies at the gaming table. He proves, at starting on his perilous career, to be a favourite of fortune; wins largely, and, alas! profanes his noble enthusiasm for science by yielding his soul to the all-debasing passion of the gamester.

'At the period of the Play, the Baron's good fortune has deserted him. He sees his way to a crowning experiment in the fatal search after the secret of transmuting the baser metals into gold. But how is he to pay the preliminary expenses? Destiny, like a mocking echo, answers, How?

'Will his sister's winnings (with my Lord's money) prove large enough to help him? Eager for this result, he gives the Countess his advice how to play. From that disastrous moment the infection of his own adverse fortune spreads to his sister. She loses again, and again—loses to the last farthing.

'The amiable and wealthy Lord offers a third loan; but the scrupulous Countess positively refuses to take it. On leaving the table, she presents her brother to my Lord. The gentlemen fall into pleasant talk. My Lord asks leave to pay his respects to the Countess, the next morning, at her hotel. The Baron hospitably invites him to breakfast. My Lord accepts, with a last admiring glance at the Countess which does not escape her brother's observation, and takes his leave for the night.

'Alone with his sister, the Baron speaks out plainly. "Our affairs," he says, "are in a desperate condition, and must find a desperate remedy. Wait for me here, while I make inquiries about my Lord. You have evidently produced a strong impression on him. If we can turn that impression into money, no matter at what sacrifice, the thing must be done."

'The Countess now occupies the stage alone, and indulges in a soliloquy which develops her character.

'It is at once a dangerous and attractive character. Immense capacities for good are implanted in her nature, side by side with equally remarkable capacities for evil. It rests with circumstances to develop either the one or the other. Being a person who produces a sensation wherever she goes, this noble lady is naturally made the subject of all sorts of scandalous reports. To one of these reports (which falsely and abominably points to the Baron as her lover instead of her brother) she now refers with just indignation. She has just expressed her desire to leave Homburg, as the place in which the vile calumny first took its rise, when the Baron returns, overhears her last words, and says to her, "Yes, leave Homburg by all means; provided you leave it in the character of my Lord's betrothed wife!"

'The Countess is startled and shocked. She protests that she does not reciprocate my Lord's admiration for her. She even goes the length of refusing to see him again. The Baron answers, "I must positively have command of money. Take your choice, between marrying my Lord's income, in the interest of my grand discovery—or leave me to sell myself and my title to the first rich woman of low degree who is ready to buy me."

'The Countess listens in surprise and dismay. Is it possible that the Baron is in earnest? He is horribly in earnest. "The woman who will buy me," he says, "is in the next room to us at this moment. She is the wealthy widow of a Jewish usurer. She has the money I want to reach the solution of the great problem. I have only to be that woman's husband, and to make myself master of untold millions of gold. Take five minutes to consider what I have said to you, and tell me on my return which of us is to marry for the money I want, you or I."

'As he turns away, the Countess stops him.

'All the noblest sentiments in her nature are exalted to the highest pitch. "Where is the true woman," she exclaims, "who wants time to consummate the sacrifice of herself, when the man to whom she is devoted demands it? She does not want five minutes—she does not want five seconds—she holds out her hand to him, and she says, Sacrifice me on the altar of your glory! Take as stepping-stones on the way to your triumph, my love, my liberty, and my life!"

'On this grand situation the curtain falls. Judging by my first act, Mr Westwick, tell me truly, and don't be afraid of turning my head:—Am I not capable of writing a good play?'

\*

Henry paused between the First and Second Acts; reflecting, not on the merits of the play, but on the strange resemblance which the incidents so far presented to the incidents that had attended the disastrous marriage of the first Lord Montbarry.

Was it possible that the Countess, in the present condition of her mind, supposed herself to be exercising her invention when she was only exercising her memory?

The question involved considerations too serious to be made the subject of a hasty decision. Reserving his opinion, Henry turned the page, and devoted himself to the reading of the next act. The manuscript proceeded as follows:—

'The Second Act opens at Venice. An interval of four months has elapsed since the date of the scene at the gambling table. The action now takes place in the reception-room of one of the Venetian palaces.

'The Baron is discovered, alone, on the stage. He reverts to the events which have happened since the close of the First Act. The Countess has sacrificed herself; the mercenary marriage has taken place—but not without obstacles, caused by difference of opinion on the question of marriage settlements.

'Private inquiries, instituted in England, have informed the Baron that my Lord's income is derived chiefly from what is called entailed property. In case of accidents, he is surely bound to do something for his bride? Let him, for example, insure his life, for a sum proposed by the Baron, and let him so settle the money that his widow shall have it, if he dies first.

'My Lord hesitates. The Baron wastes no time in useless discussion. "Let us by all means" (he says) "consider the marriage as broken off:" My Lord shifts his ground, and pleads for a smaller sum than the sum proposed. The Baron briefly replies, "I never bargain." My lord is in love; the natural result follows—he gives way.

'So far, the Baron has no cause to complain. But my Lord's turn comes, when the marriage has been celebrated, and when the honeymoon is over. The Baron has joined the married pair at a palace which they have hired in Venice. He is still bent on solving the problem of the "Philosopher's Stone." His laboratory is set up in the vaults beneath the palace—so that smells from chemical experiments may not incommode the Countess, in the higher regions of the house. The one obstacle in the way of his grand discovery is, as usual, the want of money. His position at the present time has become truly critical. He owes debts of honour to gentlemen in his own rank of life, which must positively be paid; and he proposes, in his own friendly manner, to borrow the money of my Lord. My Lord positively refuses, in the rudest terms. The Baron applies to his sister to exercise her conjugal influence. She can only answer that her noble husband (being no longer distractedly in love with her) now appears in his true character, as one of the meanest men living. The sacrifice of the marriage has been made, and has already proved useless.

'Such is the state of affairs at the opening of the Second Act.

'The entrance of the Countess suddenly disturbs the Baron's reflections. She is in a state bordering on frenzy. Incoherent expressions of rage burst from her lips: it is some time before she can sufficiently control herself to speak plainly. She has been doubly insulted—first, by a menial person in her employment; secondly, by her husband. Her maid, an Englishwoman, has declared that she will serve the Countess no longer. She will give up her wages, and return at once to England. Being asked her reason for this strange proceeding, she insolently hints that the Countess's service is no service for an honest woman, since the Baron has entered the house. The Countess does, what any lady in her position would do; she indignantly dismisses the wretch on the spot.

'My Lord, hearing his wife's voice raised in anger, leaves the study in which he is accustomed to shut himself up over his books, and asks what this disturbance means. The Countess informs him of the outrageous language and conduct of her maid. My Lord not only declares his entire approval of the woman's conduct, but expresses his own abominable doubts of his wife's fidelity in language of such horrible brutality that no lady could pollute her lips by repeating it. "If I had been a man," the Countess says, "and if I had had a weapon in my hand, I would have struck him dead at my feet!"

'The Baron, listening silently so far, now speaks. "Permit me to finish the sentence for you," he says. "You would have struck your husband dead at your feet; and by that rash act, you would have deprived yourself of the insurance money settled on the widow—the very money which is wanted to relieve your brother from the unendurable pecuniary position which he now occupies!"

'The Countess gravely reminds the Baron that this is no joking matter. After what my Lord has said to her, she has little doubt that he will communicate his infamous suspicions to his lawyers in England.

If nothing is done to prevent it, she may be divorced and disgraced, and thrown on the world, with no resource but the sale of her jewels to keep her from starving.

'At this moment, the Courier who has been engaged to travel with my Lord from England crosses the stage with a letter to take to the post. The Countess stops him, and asks to look at the address on the letter. She takes it from him for a moment, and shows it to her brother. The handwriting is my Lord's; and the letter is directed to his lawyers in London.

'The Courier proceeds to the post-office. The Baron and the Countess look at each other in silence. No words are needed. They thoroughly understand the position in which they are placed; they clearly see the terrible remedy for it. What is the plain alternative before them? Disgrace and ruin—or, my Lord's death and the insurance money!

'The Baron walks backwards and forwards in great agitation, talking to himself. The Countess hears fragments of what he is saying. He speaks of my Lord's constitution, probably weakened in India—of a cold which my Lord has caught two or three days since—of the remarkable manner in which such slight things as colds sometimes end in serious illness and death.

'He observes that the Countess is listening to him, and asks if she has anything to propose. She is a woman who, with many defects, has the great merit of speaking out. "Is there no such thing as a serious illness," she asks, "corked up in one of those bottles of yours in the vaults downstairs?"

'The Baron answers by gravely shaking his head. What is he afraid of?—a possible examination of the body after death? No: he can set any post-mortem examination at defiance. It is the process of administering the poison that he dreads. A man so distinguished as my Lord cannot be taken seriously ill without medical attendance. Where there is a Doctor, there is always danger of discovery. Then, again, there is the Courier, faithful to my Lord as long as my Lord pays him. Even if the Doctor sees nothing suspicious, the Courier may discover something. The poison, to do its work with the necessary secrecy, must be repeatedly administered in graduated doses. One trifling miscalculation or mistake may rouse suspicion. The insurance offices may hear of it, and may refuse to pay the money. As things are, the Baron will not risk it, and will not allow his sister to risk it in his place.

'My Lord himself is the next character who appears. He has repeatedly rung for the Courier, and the bell has not been answered. "What does this insolence mean?"

'The Countess (speaking with quiet dignity—for why should her infamous husband have the satisfaction of knowing how deeply he has wounded her?) reminds my Lord that the Courier has gone to the post. My Lord asks suspiciously if she has looked at the letter. The Countess informs him coldly that she has no curiosity about his letters. Referring to the cold from which he is suffering, she inquires if he thinks of consulting a medical man. My Lord answers roughly that he is quite old enough to be capable of doctoring himself.

'As he makes this reply, the Courier appears, returning from the post. My Lord gives him orders to go out again and buy some lemons. He proposes to try hot lemonade as a means of inducing perspiration in bed. In that way he has formerly cured colds, and in that way he will cure the cold from which he is suffering now.

'The Courier obeys in silence. Judging by appearances, he goes very reluctantly on this second errand.

'My Lord turns to the Baron (who has thus far taken no part in the conversation) and asks him, in a sneering tone, how much longer he proposes to prolong his stay in Venice. The Baron answers quietly, "Let us speak plainly to one another, my Lord. If you wish me to leave your house, you have only to say the word, and I go." My Lord turns to his wife, and asks if she can support the calamity of her brother's absence—laying a grossly insulting emphasis on the word "brother." The Countess preserves her impenetrable composure; nothing in her betrays the deadly hatred with which she regards the titled ruffian who has insulted her. "You are master in this house, my Lord," is all she says. "Do as you please."

'My Lord looks at his wife; looks at the Baron—and suddenly alters his tone. Does he perceive in the composure of the Countess and her brother something lurking under the surface that threatens him? This is at least certain, he makes a clumsy apology for the language that he has used. (Abject wretch!)

'My Lord's excuses are interrupted by the return of the Courier with the lemons and hot water.

'The Countess observes for the first time that the man looks ill. His hands tremble as he places the tray on the table. My Lord orders his

Courier to follow him, and make the lemonade in the bedroom. The Countess remarks that the Courier seems hardly capable of obeying his orders. Hearing this, the man admits that he is ill. He, too, is suffering from a cold; he has been kept waiting in a draught at the shop where he bought the lemons; he feels alternately hot and cold, and he begs permission to lie down for a little while on his bed.

'Feeling her humanity appealed to, the Countess volunteers to make the lemonade herself. My Lord takes the Courier by the arm, leads him aside, and whispers these words to him: "Watch her, and see that she puts nothing into the lemonade; then bring it to me with your own hands; and, then, go to bed, if you like."

'Without a word more to his wife, or to the Baron, my Lord leaves the room.

'The Countess makes the lemonade, and the Courier takes it to his master.

'Returning, on the way to his own room, he is so weak, and feels, he says, so giddy, that he is obliged to support himself by the backs of the chairs as he passes them. The Baron, always considerate to persons of low degree, offers his arm. "I am afraid, my poor fellow," he says, "that you are really ill." The Courier makes this extraordinary answer: "It's all over with me, Sir: I have caught my death."

'The Countess is naturally startled. "You are not an old man," she says, trying to rouse the Courier's spirits. "At your age, catching cold doesn't surely mean catching your death?" The Courier fixes his eyes despairingly on the Countess.

' "My lungs are weak, my Lady," he says; "I have already had two attacks of bronchitis. The second time, a great physician joined my own doctor in attendance on me. He considered my recovery almost in the light of a miracle. 'Take care of yourself,' he said. 'If you have a third attack of bronchitis, as certainly as two and two make four, you will be a dead man.' I feel the same inward shivering, my Lady, that I felt on those two former occasions—and I tell you again, I have caught my death in Venice."

'Speaking some comforting words, the Baron leads him to his room. The Countess is left alone on the stage.

'She seats herself, and looks towards the door by which the Courier has been led out. "Ah! my poor fellow," she says, "if you could only change constitutions with my Lord, what a happy result would follow for the Baron and for me! If *you* could only get cured of a trumpery cold with a little hot lemonade, and if *he* could only catch his death in your place—!"

'She suddenly pauses—considers for a while—and springs to her feet, with a cry of triumphant surprise: the wonderful, the unparalleled idea has crossed her mind like a flash of lightning. Make the two men change names and places—and the deed is done! Where are the obstacles? Remove my Lord (by fair means or foul) from his room; and keep him secretly prisoner in the palace, to live or die as future necessity may determine. Place the Courier in the vacant bed, and call in the doctor to see him—ill, in my Lord's character, and (if he dies) dying under my Lord's name!'

The manuscript dropped from Henry's hands. A sickening sense of horror overpowered him. The question which had occurred to his mind at the close of the First Act of the Play assumed a new and terrible interest now. As far as the scene of the Countess's soliloquy, the incidents of the Second Act had reflected the events of his late brother's life as faithfully as the incidents of the First Act. Was the monstrous plot, revealed in the lines which he had just read, the offspring of the Countess's morbid imagination? or had she, in this case also, deluded herself with the idea that she was inventing when she was really writing under the influence of her own guilty remembrances of the past? If the latter interpretation were the true one, he had just read the narrative of the contemplated murder of his brother, planned in cold blood by a woman who was at that moment inhabiting the same house with him. While, to make the fatality complete, Agnes herself had innocently provided the conspirators with the one man who was fitted to be the passive agent of their crime.

Even the bare doubt that it might be so was more than he could endure. He left his room; resolved to force the truth out of the Countess, or to denounce her before the authorities as a murderess at large.

Arrived at her door, he was met by a person just leaving the room. The person was the manager. He was hardly recognisable; he looked and spoke like a man in a state of desperation.

'Oh, go in, if you like!' he said to Henry. 'Mark this, sir! I am not a superstitious man; but I do begin to believe that crimes carry their own curse with them. This hotel is under a curse. What happens in the morning? We discover a crime committed in the old days of the palace. The night comes, and brings another dreadful event with it—a death; a sudden and shocking death, in the house. Go in, and see for yourself! I shall resign my situation, Mr Westwick: I can't contend with the fatalities that pursue me here!'

Henry entered the room.

The Countess was stretched on her bed. The doctor on one side, and the chambermaid on the other, were standing looking at her. From time to time, she drew a heavy stertorous breath, like a person oppressed in sleeping. 'Is she likely to die?' Henry asked.

'She is dead,' the doctor answered. 'Dead of the rupture of a blood-vessel on the brain. Those sounds that you hear are purely mechanical—they may go on for hours.'

Henry looked at the chambermaid. She had little to tell. The Countess had refused to go to bed, and had placed herself at her desk to proceed with her writing. Finding it useless to remonstrate with her, the maid had left the room to speak to the manager. In the shortest possible time, the doctor was summoned to the hotel, and found the Countess dead on the floor. There was this to tell—and no more.

Looking at the writing-table as he went out, Henry saw the sheet of paper on which the Countess had traced her last lines of writing. The characters were almost illegible. Henry could just distinguish the words, 'First Act,' and 'Persons of the Drama.' The lost wretch had been thinking of her Play to the last, and had begun it all over again!

## CHAPTER XXVII

Henry returned to his room.

His first impulse was to throw aside the manuscript, and never to look at it again. The one chance of relieving his mind from the dreadful uncertainty that oppressed it, by obtaining positive evidence of the truth, was a chance annihilated by the Countess's death. What good purpose could be served, what relief could he anticipate, if he read more?

He walked up and down the room. After an interval, his thoughts took a new direction; the question of the manuscript presented itself under another point of view. Thus far, his reading had only informed him that the conspiracy had been planned. How did he know that the plan had been put in execution?

The manuscript lay just before him on the floor. He hesitated—then picked it up; and, returning to the table, read on as follows, from the point at which he had left off.

'While the Countess is still absorbed in the bold yet simple combination of circumstances which she has discovered, the Baron returns. He takes a serious view of the case of the Courier; it may be necessary, he thinks, to send for medical advice. No servant is left in the palace, now the English maid has taken her departure. The Baron himself must fetch the doctor, if the doctor is really needed.

' "Let us have medical help, by all means," his sister replies. "But wait and hear something that I have to say to you first." She then electrifies the Baron by communicating her idea to him. What danger of discovery have they to dread? My Lord's life in Venice has been a life of absolute seclusion: nobody but his banker knows him, even by personal appearance. He has presented his letter of credit as a perfect stranger; and he and his banker have never seen each other since that first visit. He has given no parties, and gone to no parties. On the few occasions when he has hired a gondola or taken a walk, he has always been alone. Thanks to the atrocious suspicion which makes him ashamed of being seen with his wife, he has led the very life which makes the proposed enterprise easy of accomplishment.

'The cautious Baron listens—but gives no positive opinion, as yet. "See what you can do with the Courier," he says; "and I will decide when I hear the result. One valuable hint I may give you before you go. Your man is easily tempted by money—if you only offer him enough. The other day, I asked him, in jest, what he would do for a thousand pounds. He answered, 'Anything.' Bear that in mind; and offer your highest bid without bargaining."

'The scene changes to the Courier's room, and shows the poor wretch with a photographic portrait of his wife in his hand, crying. The Countess enters.

'She wisely begins by sympathising with her contemplated accomplice. He is duly grateful; he confides his sorrows to his gracious mistress. Now that he believes himself to be on his death-bed, he feels remorse for his neglectful treatment of his wife. He could resign himself to die; but despair overpowers him when he remembers that he has saved no money, and that he will leave his widow, without resources, to the mercy of the world.

'On this hint, the Countess speaks. "Suppose you were asked to do a perfectly easy thing," she says; "and suppose you were rewarded for doing it by a present of a thousand pounds, as a legacy for your widow?"

'The Courier raises himself on his pillow, and looks at the Countess with an expression of incredulous surprise. She can hardly be cruel enough (he thinks) to joke with a man in his miserable plight. Will she say plainly what this perfectly easy thing is, the doing of which will meet with such a magnificent reward?

'The Countess answers that question by confiding her project to the Courier, without the slightest reserve.

'Some minutes of silence follow when she has done. The Courier is not weak enough yet to speak without stopping to think first. Still keeping his eyes on the Countess, he makes a quaintly insolent remark on what he has just heard. "I have not hitherto been a religious man; but I feel myself on the way to it. Since your ladyship has spoken to me, I believe in the Devil." It is the Countess's interest to see the humorous side of this confession of faith. She takes no offence. She only says, "I will give you half an hour by yourself, to think over my proposal. You are in danger of death. Decide, in your wife's interests, whether you will die worth nothing, or die worth a thousand pounds."

'Left alone, the Courier seriously considers his position—and decides. He rises with difficulty; writes a few lines on a leaf taken from his pocket-book; and, with slow and faltering steps, leaves the room.

'The Countess, returning at the expiration of the half-hour's interval, finds the room empty. While she is wondering, the Courier opens the door. What has he been doing out of his bed? He answers, "I have been protecting my own life, my lady, on the bare chance that I may recover from the bronchitis for the third time. If you or the Baron attempts to hurry me out of this world, or to deprive me of my thousand pounds reward, I shall tell the doctor where he will find a few lines of writing, which describe your ladyship's plot. I may not have strength enough, in the case supposed, to betray you by making a complete confession with my own lips; but I can employ my last breath to speak the half-dozen words which will tell the doctor where he is to look. Those words, it is needless to add, will be addressed to your Ladyship, if I find your engagements towards me faithfully kept."

'With this audacious preface, he proceeds to state the conditions on which he will play his part in the conspiracy, and die (if he does die) worth a thousand pounds.

'Either the Countess or the Baron are to taste the food and drink brought to his bedside, in his presence, and even the medicines which the doctor may prescribe for him. As for the promised sum of money, it is to be produced in one bank-note, folded in a sheet of paper, on which a line is to be written, dictated by the Courier. The two enclosures are then to be sealed up in an envelope, addressed to his wife, and stamped ready for the post. This done, the letter is to be placed under his pillow; the Baron or the Countess being at liberty to satisfy themselves, day by day, at their own time, that the letter remains in its place, with the seal unbroken, as long as the doctor has any hope of his patient's recovery. The last stipulation follows. The Courier has a conscience; and with a view to keeping it easy, insists that he shall be left in ignorance of that part of the plot which relates to the sequestration of my Lord. Not that he cares particularly what becomes of his miserly master—but he does dislike taking other people's responsibilities on his own shoulders.

'These conditions being agreed to, the Countess calls in the Baron, who has been waiting events in the next room.

'He is informed that the Courier has yielded to temptation; but he is still too cautious to make any compromising remarks. Keeping his back turned on the bed, he shows a bottle to the Countess. It is labelled "Chloroform." She understands that my Lord is to be removed from his room in a convenient state of insensibility. In what part of the palace is he to be hidden? As they open the door to go out, the Countess whispers that question to the Baron. The Baron whispers back, "In the vaults!" The curtain falls.'

## CHAPTER XXVIII

So the Second Act ended.

Turning to the Third Act, Henry looked wearily at the pages as he let them slip through his fingers. Both in mind and body, he began to feel the need of repose.

In one important respect, the later portion of the manuscript differed from the pages which he had just been reading. Signs of an overwrought brain showed themselves, here and there, as the outline of the play approached its end. The handwriting grew worse and worse. Some of the longer sentences were left unfinished. In the exchange of dialogue, questions and answers were not always attributed respectively to the right speaker. At certain intervals the writer's failing intelligence seemed to recover itself for a while; only to relapse again, and to lose the thread of the narrative more hopelessly than ever.

After reading one or two of the more coherent passages Henry recoiled from the ever-darkening horror of the story. He closed the manuscript, heartsick and exhausted, and threw himself on his bed to rest. The door opened almost at the same moment. Lord Montbarry entered the room.

'We have just returned from the Opera,' he said; 'and we have heard the news of that miserable woman's death. They say you spoke to her in her last moments; and I want to hear how it happened.'

'You shall hear how it happened,' Henry answered; 'and more than that. You are now the head of the family, Stephen; and I feel bound, in the position which oppresses me, to leave you to decide what ought to be done.'

With those introductory words, he told his brother how the Countess's play had come into his hands. 'Read the first few pages,' he said. 'I am anxious to know whether the same impression is produced on both of us.'

Before Lord Montbarry had got half-way through the First Act, he stopped, and looked at his brother. 'What does she mean by boasting of this as her own invention?' he asked. 'Was she too crazy to remember that these things really happened?'

This was enough for Henry: the same impression had been produced on both of them. 'You will do as you please,' he said. 'But if you will be guided by me, spare yourself the reading of those pages to come, which describe our brother's terrible expiation of his heartless marriage.'

'Have *you* read it all, Henry?'

'Not all. I shrank from reading some of the latter part of it. Neither you nor I saw much of our elder brother after we left school; and, for my part, I felt, and never scrupled to express my feeling, that he behaved infamously to Agnes. But when I read that unconscious confession of the murderous conspiracy to which he fell a victim, I remembered, with something like remorse, that the same mother bore us. I have felt for him to-night, what I am ashamed to think I never felt for him before.'

Lord Montbarry took his brother's hand.

'You are a good fellow, Henry,' he said; 'but are you quite sure that you have not been needlessly distressing yourself? Because some of this crazy creature's writing accidentally tells what we know to be the truth, does it follow that all the rest is to be relied on to the end?'

'There is no possible doubt of it,' Henry replied.

'No possible doubt?' his brother repeated. 'I shall go on with my reading, Henry—and see what justification there may be for that confident conclusion of yours.'

He read on steadily, until he had reached the end of the Second Act. Then he looked up.

'Do you really believe that the mutilated remains which you discovered this morning are the remains of our brother?' he asked. 'And do you believe it on such evidence as this?'

Henry answered silently by a sign in the affirmative.

Lord Montbarry checked himself—evidently on the point of entering an indignant protest.

'You acknowledge that you have not read the later scenes of the piece,' he said. 'Don't be childish, Henry! If you persist in pinning your faith on such stuff as this, the least you can do is to make yourself thoroughly acquainted with it. Will you read the Third Act? No? Then I shall read it to you.'

He turned to the Third Act, and ran over those fragmentary passages which were clearly enough written and expressed to be intelligible to the mind of a stranger.

'Here is a scene in the vaults of the palace,' he began. 'The victim of the conspiracy is sleeping on his miserable bed; and the Baron and the Countess are considering the position in which they stand. The Countess (as well as I can make it out) has raised the money that is wanted by borrowing on the security of her jewels at Frankfort; and the Courier upstairs is still declared by the Doctor to have a chance of recovery. What are the conspirators to do, if the man does recover? The cautious Baron suggests setting the prisoner free. If he ventures to appeal to the law, it is easy to declare that he is subject to insane delusion, and to call his own wife as witness. On the other hand, if the Courier dies, how is the sequestrated and unknown nobleman to be put out of the way? Passively, by letting him starve in his prison? No: the Baron is a man of refined tastes; he dislikes needless cruelty. The active policy remains—say, assassination by the knife of a hired bravo?* The Baron objects to trusting an accomplice; also to spending money on anyone but himself. Shall they drop their prisoner into the canal? The Baron declines to trust water; water will show him on the surface. Shall they set his bed on fire? An excellent idea; but the smoke might be seen. No: the circumstances being now entirely altered, poisoning him presents the easiest way out of it. He has become simply a superfluous person. The cheapest poison will do.—Is it possible, Henry, that you believe this consultation really took place?'

Henry made no reply. The succession of the questions that had just been read to him, exactly followed the succession of the dreams that had terrified Mrs Norbury, on the two nights which she had passed in the hotel. It was useless to point out this coincidence to his brother. He only said, 'Go on.'

Lord Montbarry turned the pages until he came to the next intelligible passage.

'Here,' he proceeded, 'is a double scene on the stage—so far as I can understand the sketch of it. The Doctor is upstairs, innocently writing his certificate of my Lord's decease, by the dead Courier's bedside. Down in the vaults, the Baron stands by the corpse of the poisoned lord, preparing the strong chemical acids which are to reduce it to a heap of ashes—Surely, it is not worth while to trouble ourselves with deciphering such melodramatic horrors as these? Let us get on! let us get on!'

He turned the leaves again; attempting vainly to discover the meaning of the confused scenes that followed. On the last page but one, he found the last intelligible sentences.

'The Third Act seems to be divided,' he said, 'into two Parts or Tableaux. I think I can read the writing at the beginning of the Second Part. The Baron and the Countess open the scene. The Baron's hands are mysteriously concealed by gloves. He has reduced the body to ashes by his own system of cremation, with the exception of the head—'

Henry interrupted his brother there. 'Don't read any more!' he exclaimed.

'Let us do the Countess justice,' Lord Montbarry persisted. 'There are not half a dozen lines more that I can make out! The accidental breaking of his jar of acid has burnt the Baron's hands severely. He is still unable to proceed to the destruction of the head— and the Countess is woman enough (with all her wickedness) to shrink from attempting to take his place—when the first news is received of the coming arrival of the commission of inquiry des- patched by the insurance offices. The Baron feels no alarm. Inquire as the commission may, it is the natural death of the Courier (in my Lord's character) that they are blindly investigating. The head not being destroyed, the obvious alternative is to hide it—and the Baron is equal to the occasion. His studies in the old library have informed him of a safe place of concealment in the palace. The Countess may recoil from handling the acids and watching the process of cremation; but she can surely sprinkle a little disinfecting powder—'

'No more!' Henry reiterated. 'No more!'

'There is no more that can be read, my dear fellow. The last page looks like sheer delirium. She may well have told you that her invention had failed her!'

'Face the truth honestly, Stephen, and say her memory.'

Lord Montbarry rose from the table at which he had been sitting, and looked at his brother with pitying eyes.

'Your nerves are out of order, Henry,' he said. 'And no wonder, after that frightful discovery under the hearth-stone. We won't dis- pute about it; we will wait a day or two until you are quite yourself again. In the meantime, let us understand each other on one point at least. You leave the question of what is to be done with these pages of writing to me, as the head of the family?'

'I do.'

Lord Montbarry quietly took up the manuscript, and threw it into the fire. 'Let this rubbish be of some use,' he said, holding the pages down with the poker. 'The room is getting chilly—the Countess's play will set some of these charred logs flaming again.' He waited a little at the fireplace, and returned to his brother. 'Now, Henry, I have a last word to say, and then I have done. I am ready to admit that you have stumbled, by an unlucky chance, on the proof of a crime committed in the old days of the palace, nobody knows how long ago. With that one concession, I dispute everything else. Rather than agree in the opinion you have formed,

I won't believe anything that has happened. The supernatural influences that some of us felt when we first slept in this hotel—your loss of appetite, our sister's dreadful dreams, the smell that overpowered Francis, and the head that appeared to Agnes—I declare them all to be sheer delusions! I believe in nothing, nothing, nothing!' He opened the door to go out, and looked back into the room. 'Yes,' he resumed, 'there is one thing I believe in. My wife has committed a breach of confidence—I believe Agnes will marry you. Good night, Henry. We leave Venice the first thing to-morrow morning.'

So Lord Montbarry disposed of the mystery of The Haunted Hotel.

## POSTSCRIPT

A last chance of deciding the difference of opinion between the two brothers remained in Henry's possession. He had his own idea of the use to which he might put the false teeth as a means of inquiry when he and his fellow-travellers returned to England.

The only surviving depositary of the domestic history of the family in past years, was Agnes Lockwood's old nurse. Henry took his first opportunity of trying to revive her personal recollections of the deceased Lord Montbarry. But the nurse had never forgiven the great man of the family for his desertion of Agnes; she flatly refused to consult her memory. 'Even the bare sight of my lord, when I last saw him in London,' said the old woman, 'made my finger-nails itch to set their mark on his face. I was sent on an errand by Miss Agnes; and I met him coming out of his dentist's door—and, thank God, that's the last I ever saw of him!'

Thanks to the nurse's quick temper and quaint way of expressing herself, the object of Henry's inquiries was gained already! He ventured on asking if she had noticed the situation of the house. She had noticed, and still remembered the situation—did Master Henry suppose she had lost the use of her senses, because she happened to be nigh on eighty years old? The same day, he took the false teeth to the dentist, and set all further doubt (if doubt had still been possible) at rest for ever. The teeth had been made for the first Lord Montbarry.

Henry never revealed the existence of this last link in the chain of discovery to any living creature, his brother Stephen included. He carried his terrible secret with him to the grave.

There was one other event in the memorable past on which he preserved the same compassionate silence. Little Mrs Ferrari never knew that her husband had been—not, as she supposed, the Countess's victim—but the Countess's accomplice. She still believed that the late Lord Montbarry had sent her the thousand-pound note, and still recoiled from making use of a present which she persisted in declaring had 'the stain of her husband's blood on it.' Agnes, with the widow's entire approval, took the money to the Children's Hospital;* and spent it in adding to the number of the beds.

In the spring of the new year, the marriage took place. At the special request of Agnes, the members of the family were the only persons present at the ceremony. There was no wedding breakfast— and the honeymoon was spent in the retirement of a cottage on the banks of the Thames.

During the last few days of the residence of the newly married couple by the riverside, Lady Montbarry's children were invited to enjoy a day's play in the garden. The eldest girl overheard (and reported to her mother) a little conjugal dialogue which touched on the topic of The Haunted Hotel.

'Henry, I want you to give me a kiss.'

'There it is, my dear.'

'Now I am your wife, may I speak to you about something?'

'What is it?'

'Something that happened the day before we left Venice. You saw the Countess, during the last hours of her life. Won't you tell me whether she made any confession to you?'

'No conscious confession, Agnes—and therefore no confession that I need distress you by repeating.'

'Did she say nothing about what she saw or heard, on that dreadful night in my room?'

'Nothing. We only know that her mind never recovered the terror* of it.'

Agnes was not quite satisfied. The subject troubled her. Even her own brief intercourse with her miserable rival of other days suggested questions that perplexed her. She remembered the Countess's prediction. 'You have to bring me to the day of discovery, and to the punishment that is my doom.' Had the prediction simply failed, like other mortal prophecies?—or had it been fulfilled on the terrible night when she had seen the apparition, and when she had innocently tempted the Countess to watch her in her room?

Let it, however, be recorded, among the other virtues of Mrs Henry Westwick, that she never again attempted to persuade her husband into betraying his secrets. Other men's wives, hearing of this extraordinary conduct (and being trained in the modern school of morals and manners), naturally regarded her with compassionate contempt. They spoke of Agnes, from that time forth, as 'rather an old-fashioned person.'

\*

Is that all?

That is all.

Is there no explanation of the mystery of The Haunted Hotel?

Ask yourself if there is any explanation of the mystery of your own life and death.—Farewell.

# THE GUILTY RIVER

# CONTENTS

# CHAPTER I

## ON THE WAY TO THE RIVER

For reasons of my own, I excused myself from accompanying my stepmother to a dinner-party given in our neighbourhood. In my present humour, I preferred being alone—and, as a means of getting through my idle time, I was quite content to be occupied in catching insects.

Provided with a brush and a mixture of rum and treacle, I went into Fordwitch Wood to set the snare, familiar to hunters of moths, which we call sugaring the trees.

The summer evening was hot and still; the time was between dusk and dark. After ten years of absence in foreign parts, I perceived changes in the outskirts of the wood, which warned me not to enter it too confidently when I might find a difficulty in seeing my way. Remaining among the outermost trees, I painted the trunks with my treacherous mixture—which allured the insects of the night, and stupefied them when they settled on its rank surface. The snare being set, I waited to see the intoxication of the moths.

A time passed, dull and dreary. The mysterious assemblage of trees was blacker than the blackening sky. Of millions of leaves over my head, none pleased my ear, in the airless calm, with their rustling summer song.

The first flying creatures, dimly visible by moments under the gloomy sky, were enemies whom I well knew by experience. Many a fine insect specimen have I lost, when the bats were near me in search of their evening meal.

What had happened before, in other woods, happened now. The first moth that I had snared was a large one, and a specimen well worth securing. As I stretched out my hand to take it, the apparition of a flying shadow passed, swift and noiseless, between me and the tree. In less than an instant the insect was snatched away, when my fingers were within an inch of it. The bat had begun his supper, and the man and the mixture had provided it for him.

Out of five moths caught, I became the victim of clever theft in the case of three. The other two, of no great value as specimens, I was just quick enough to secure. Under other circumstances, my patience as a collector would still have been a match for the dexterity of the bats. But on that evening—a memorable evening when I look back at it now—my spirits were depressed, and I was easily discouraged. My favourite studies of the insect-world seemed to have lost their value in my estimation. In the silence and the darkness I lay down under a tree, and let my mind dwell on myself and on my new life to come.

I am Gerard Roylake, son and only child of the late Gerard Roylake of Trimley Deen.

At twenty-two years of age, my father's death had placed me in possession of his large landed property. On my arrival from Germany, only a few hours since, the servants innocently vexed me. When I drove up to the door, I heard them say to each other: 'Here is the young Squire.' My father used to be called 'the old Squire'. I shrank from being reminded of him—not as other sons in my position might have said, because it renewed my sorrow for his death. There was no sorrow in me to be renewed. It is a shocking confession to make: my heart remained unmoved when I thought of the father whom I had lost.

Our mothers have the most sacred of all claims on our gratitude and our love. They have nourished us with their blood; they have risked their lives in bringing us into the world; they have preserved and guided our helpless infancy with divine patience and love. What claim equally strong and equally tender does the other parent establish on his offspring? What motive does the instinct of his young children find for preferring their father before any other person who may be a familiar object in their daily lives? They love him—naturally and rightly love him—because he lives in their remembrance (if he is a good man) as the first, the best, the dearest of their friends.

My father was a bad man. He was my mother's worst enemy; and he was never my friend.

The little that I know of the world tells me that it is not the common lot in life of women to marry the object of their first love. A sense of duty had compelled my mother to part with the man who had won her heart, in the first days of her maidenhood; and my father had discovered it, after his marriage. His insane jealousy foully wronged the truest wife, the most long-suffering woman that ever lived. I have no patience to write of it. For ten miserable years she suffered her martyrdom; she lived through it, dear angel, sweet suffering soul, for my sake. At her death, my father was able to gratify his hatred of the son whom he had never believed to be his own child. Under pretence of preferring the foreign system of teaching, he sent me to a school in France. My education having been so far completed, I was next transferred to a German University. Never again did I see the place of my birth, never did I get a letter from home, until the family lawyer wrote from Trimley Deen, requesting me to assume possession of my house and lands, under the entail.

I should not even have known that my father had taken a second wife but for some friend (or enemy)—I never discovered the person—who sent me a newspaper containing an announcement of the marriage.

When we saw each other for the first time, my stepmother and I met necessarily as strangers. We were elaborately polite, and we each made a meritorious effort to appear at our ease. On her side, she found herself confronted by a young man, the new master of the house, who looked more like a foreigner than an Englishman—who, when he was congratulated (in view of the approaching season) on the admirable preservation of his partridges and pheasants, betrayed an utter want of interest in the subject; and who showed no sense of shame in acknowledging that his principal amusements were derived from reading books, and collecting insects. How I must have disappointed Mrs Roylake! and how considerately she hid from me the effect that I had produced!

Turning next to my own impressions, I discovered in my newly-found relative, a little light-eyed, light-haired, elegant woman; trim, and bright, and smiling; dressed to perfection, clever to her fingers' ends, skilled in making herself agreeable—and yet, in spite of these undeniable fascinations, perfectly incomprehensible to me. After my experience of foreign society, I was incapable of understanding the extraordinary importance which my stepmother seemed to attach to rank and riches, entirely for their own sakes. When she described my unknown neighbours, from one end of the county to the other, she took it for granted that I must be interested in them on account of their titles and their fortunes. She held me up to my own face, as a kind of idol to myself, without producing any better reason than might be found in my inheritance of an income of sixteen thousand pounds. And when I expressed (in excusing myself for not accompanying her, uninvited, to the dinner-party) a perfectly rational doubt whether I might prove to be a welcome guest, Mrs Roylake held up her delicate little hands in unutterable astonishment. 'My dear Gerard, in *your* position!' She appeared to think that this settled the question. I submitted in silence; the truth is, I was beginning already to despair of my prospects. Kind as my stepmother was, and agreeable as she was, what chance could I see of establishing any true sympathy between us? And, if my neighbours resembled her in their ways of thinking, what hope could I feel of finding new friends in England to replace the friends in Germany whom I had lost? A stranger among my own country people, with the every-day habits and every-day pleasures of my youthful life left behind me—without plans or hopes to interest me in looking at the future—it is surely not wonderful that my spirits had sunk to their lowest ebb, and that I even failed to appreciate with sufficient gratitude the fortunate accident of my birth.

Perhaps the journey to England had fatigued me, or perhaps the controlling influences of the dark and silent night proved irresistible. This only is certain: my solitary meditations under the tree ended in sleep.

I was awakened by a light falling on my face.

The moon had risen. In the outward part of the wood, beyond which I had not advanced, the pure and welcome light penetrated easily through the scattered trees. I got up and looked about me. A path into the wood now showed itself, broader and better kept than any path that I could remember in the days of my boyhood. The moon showed it to me plainly, and my curiosity was aroused.

Following the new track, I found that it led to a little glade which I at once recognised. The place was changed in one respect only. A neglected water-spring had been cleared of brambles and stones, and had been provided with a drinking cup, a rustic seat, and a Latin motto on a marble slab. The spring at once reminded me of a greater body of water—a river, at some little distance farther on, which ran between the trees on one side, and the desolate open country on the other. Ascending from the glade, I found myself in one of the narrow woodland paths, familiar to me in the by-gone time.

Unless my memory was at fault, this was the way which led to an old water-mill on the river-bank. The image of the great turning wheel, which half-frightened half-fascinated me when I was a child, now presented itself to my memory for the first time after an interval of many years. In my present frame of mind, the old scene appealed to me with the irresistible influence of an old friend. I said to myself: 'Shall I walk on, and try if I can find the river and the mill again?' This perfectly trifling question to decide presented to me, nevertheless, fantastic difficulties so absurd that they might have been difficulties encountered in a dream. To my own astonishment, I hesitated—walked back again along the path by which I had advanced—reconsidered my decision, without knowing why—and turning in the opposite direction, set my face towards the river once more. I wonder how my life would have ended, if I had gone the other way?

## CHAPTER II

### THE RIVER INTRODUCES US

I stood alone on the bank of the ugliest stream in England.

The moonlight, pouring its unclouded radiance over open space, failed to throw a beauty not their own on those sluggish waters. Broad and muddy, their stealthy current flowed onward to the sea, without a rock to diversify, without a bubble to break, the sullen surface. On the side from which I was looking at the river, the neglected trees grew so close together that they were undermining their own lives, and poisoning each other. On the opposite bank, a rank growth of gigantic bulrushes hid the ground beyond, except where it rose in hillocks, and showed its surface of desert sand spotted here and there by mean patches of health. A repellent river in itself, a repellent river in its surroundings, a repellent river even in its name. It was called The Loke. Neither popular tradition nor antiquarian research could explain what the name meant, or could tell when the name had been given. 'We call it The Loke; they do say no fish can live in it; and it dirties the clean salt water when it runs into the sea.' Such was the character of the river in the estimation of the people who knew it best. But I was pleased to see The Loke again. The ugly river, like the woodland glade, looked at me with the face of an old friend.

On my right hand side rose the venerable timbers of the water-mill.

The wheel was motionless, at that time of night; and the whole structure looked—as remembered objects will look, when we see them again after a long interval—smaller than I had supposed it to be. Otherwise, I could discover no change in the mill. But the wooden cottage attached to it had felt the devastating march of time. A portion of the decrepit building still stood revealed in its wretched old age; propped, partly by beams which reached from the thatched roof to the ground, and partly by the wall of a new cottage attached, presenting in yellow brick-work a hideous modern contrast to all that was left of its ancient neighbour.

Had the miller whom I remembered, died; and were these changes the work of his successor? I thought of asking the question, and tried the door: it was fastened. The windows were all dark excepting one, which I discovered in the upper storey, at the farther side of the new building. Here, there was a dim light burning. It was impossible to disturb a person, who, for all I knew to the contrary, might be going to bed. I turned back to The Loke, proposing to extend my walk, by a mile or a little more, to a village that I remembered on the bank of the river.

I had not advanced far, when the stillness around me was disturbed by an intermittent sound of splashing in the water. Pausing to listen, I heard next the working of oars in their rowlocks. After another interval a boat appeared, turning a projection in the bank, and rowed by a woman pulling steadily against the stream.

As the boat approached me in the moonlight, this person corrected my first impression, and revealed herself as a young girl. So far as I could perceive she was a stranger to me. Who could the girl be, alone on the river at that time of night? Idly curious I followed the boat, instead of pursuing my way to the village, to see whether she would stop at the mill, or pass it.

She stopped at the mill, secured the boat, and stepped on shore.

Taking a key from her pocket, she was about to open the door of the cottage, when I advanced and spoke to her. As far from recognizing her as ever, I found myself nevertheless thinking of an odd outspoken child, living at the mill in past years, who had been one of my poor mother's favourites at our village school. I ran the risk of offending her, by bluntly expressing the thought which was then in my mind.

'Is it possible that you are Cristel Toller?' I said.

The question seemed to amuse her. 'Why shouldn't I be Cristel Toller?' she asked.

'You were a little girl,' I explained, 'when I saw you last. You are so altered now—and so improved—that I should never have guessed you might be the daughter of Giles Toller of the mill, if I had not seen you opening the cottage door.'

She acknowledged my compliment by a curtsey, which reminded me again of the village school. 'Thank you, young man,' she said smartly; 'I wonder who you are?'

'Try if you can recollect me,' I suggested.

'May I take a long look at you?'

'As long as you like.'

She studied my face, with a mental effort to remember me, which gathered her pretty eyebrows together quaintly in a frown.

'There's something in his eyes,' she remarked, not speaking to me but to herself, 'which doesn't seem to be quite strange. But I don't know his voice, and I don't know his beard.' She considered a little, and addressed herself directly to me once more. 'Now I look at you again, you seem to be a gentleman. Are you one?'

'I hope so.'

'Then you're not making game of me?'

'My dear, I am only trying if you can remember Gerard Roylake.'

While in charge of the boat, the miller's daughter had been rowing with bared arms; beautiful dusky arms, at once delicate and strong. Thus far, she had forgotten to cover them up. The moment I mentioned my name, she started back as if I had frightened her—pulled her sleeves down in a hurry—and hid the objects of my admiration as an act of homage to myself! Her verbal apologies followed.

'You used to be such a sweet-spoken pretty little boy,' she said, 'how should I know you again, with a big voice and all that hair on your face?' It seemed to strike her on a sudden that she had been too familiar. 'Oh, Lord,' I heard her say to herself, 'half the county belongs to him!' She tried another apology, and hit this time on the conventional form. 'I beg your pardon, sir. Welcome back to your own country, sir. I wish you good-night, sir.'

She attempted to escape into the cottage; I followed her to the threshold of the door. 'Surely it's not time to go to bed yet,' I ventured to say.

She was still on her good behaviour to her landlord. 'Not if you object to it, sir,' she answered.

This recognition of my authority was irresistible. Cristel had laid me under an obligation to her good influence for which I felt sincerely grateful—she had made me laugh, for the first time since my return to England.

'We needn't say good-night just yet,' I suggested; 'I want to hear a little more about you. Shall I come in?'

She stepped out of the doorway even more rapidly than she had stepped into it. I might have been mistaken, but I thought Cristel seemed to be actually alarmed by my proposal. We walked up and down the river-bank. On every occasion when we approached the cottage, I detected her in stealing a look at the ugly modern part of it. There could be no mistake this time; I saw doubt, I saw anxiety in her face. What was going on at the mill? I made some domestic inquiries, beginning with her father. Was the miller alive and well?

'Oh yes, sir. Father gets thinner as he gets older—that's all.'

'Did he send you out by yourself, at this late hour, in the boat?'

'They were waiting for a sack of flour down there,' she replied, pointing in the direction of the river-side village. 'Father isn't as quick as he used to be. He's often late over his work now.'

Was there no one to give Giles Toller the help that he must need at his age? 'Do you and your father really live alone in this solitary place?' I said.

A change of expression appeared in her bright brown eyes which roused my curiosity. I also observed that she evaded a direct reply. 'What makes you doubt, sir, if father and I live alone?' she asked.

I pointed to the new cottage. 'That ugly building,' I answered, 'seems to give you more room than you want—unless there is somebody else living at the mill.'

I had no intention of trying to force the reply from her which she had hitherto withheld; but she appeared to put that interpretation on what I had said. 'If you will have it,' she burst out, 'there *is* somebody else living with us.'

'A man who helps your father?'

'No. A man who pays my father's rent.'

I was quite unprepared for such a reply as this: Cristel had surprised me. To begin with, her father was 'well-connected,' as we say in England. His younger brother had made a fortune in commerce, and had vainly offered him the means of retiring from the mill with a sufficient income. Then again, Giles Toller was known to have saved money. His domestic expenses made no heavy demand on his purse; his German wife (whose Christian name was now borne by his daughter) had died long since; his sons were no burden on him; they had never lived at the mill in my remembrance. With all these reasons against his taking a stranger into his house, he had nevertheless, if my interpretation of Cristel's answer was the right one, let his spare rooms to a lodger. 'Mr Toller can't possibly be in want of money,' I said.

'The more money father has, the more he wants. That's the reason,' she added bitterly, 'why he asked for plenty of room when the cottage was built, and why we have got a lodger.'

'Is the lodger a gentleman?'

'I don't know. Is a man a gentleman, if he keeps a servant? Oh, don't trouble to think about it, sir! It isn't worth thinking about.'

This was plain speaking at last. 'You don't seem to like the lodger,' I said.

'I hate him!'

'Why?'

She turned on me with a look of angry amazement—not undeserved, I must own, on my part—which showed her dark beauty in the perfection of its lustre and its power. To my eyes she was at the moment irresistibly charming. I daresay I was blind to the defects in her face. My good German tutor used to lament that there was too much of my boyhood still left in me. Honestly admiring her, I let my favourable opinion express itself a little too plainly. 'What a splendid creature you are!' I burst out. Cristel did her duty to herself and to me; she passed over my little explosion of nonsense without taking the smallest notice of it.

'Master Gerard,' she began—and checked herself. 'Please to excuse me, sir; you have set my head running on old times. What I want to say is: you were not so inquisitive when you were a young gentleman in short jackets. Please behave as you used to behave then, and don't say anything more about our lodger. I hate him because I hate him. There!'

Ignorant as I was of the natures of women, I understood her at last. Cristel's opinion of the lodger was evidently the exact opposite of the lodger's opinion of Cristel. When I add that this discovery did decidedly operate as a relief to my mind, the impression produced on me by the miller's daughter is stated without exaggeration and without reserve.

'Good-night,' she repeated, 'for the last time.' I held out my hand. 'Is it quite right, sir,' she modestly objected, 'for such as me to shake hands with such as you?'

She did it nevertheless; and dropping my hand, cast a farewell look at the mysterious object of her interest—the new cottage. Her variable humour changed on the instant. Apparently in a state of unendurable irritation, she stamped on the ground. 'Just what I didn't want to happen!' she said to herself.

## CHAPTER III

### HE SHOWS HIMSELF

I too, looked at the cottage, and made a discovery that surprised me at one of the upper windows.

If I could be sure that the moon had not deceived me, the most beautiful face that I had ever seen was looking down on us—and it was the face of a man! By the uncertain light I could discern the perfection of form in the features, and the expression of power which made it impossible to mistake the stranger for a woman, although his hair grew long and he was without either moustache or beard. He was watching us intently; he neither moved nor spoke when we looked up at him.

'Evidently the lodger,' I whispered to Cristel. 'What a handsome man!'

She tossed her head contemptuously: my expression of admiration seemed to have irritated her.

'I didn't want him to see you!' she said. 'The lodger persecutes me with his attentions; he's impudent enough to be jealous of me.'

She spoke without even attempting to lower her voice. I endeavoured to warn her. 'He's at the window still,' I said, in tones discreetly lowered; 'he can hear everything you are saying.'

'Not one word of it, Mr Gerard.'

'What do you mean?'

'The man is deaf. Don't look at him again. Don't speak to me again. Go home—pray go home!'

Without further explanation, she abruptly entered the cottage, and shut the door.

As I turned into the path which led through the wood I heard a voice behind me. It said: 'Stop, sir.' I stopped directly, standing in the shadow cast by the outermost line of trees, which I had that moment reached. In the moonlight that I had left behind me, I saw again the man whom I had discovered at the window. His figure, tall and slim; his movements, graceful and easy, were in harmony with his beautiful face. He lifted his long finely-shaped hands, and clasped them with a frantic gesture of entreaty.

'For God's sake,' he said, 'don't be offended with me!'

His voice startled me even more than his words; I had never heard anything like it before. Low, dull, and muffled, it neither rose nor fell; it spoke slowly and deliberately, without laying the slightest emphasis on any one of the words that it uttered. In the astonishment of the moment, I forgot what Cristel had told me. I answered him as I should have answered any other unknown person who had spoken to me.

'What do you want?'

His hands dropped; his head sunk on his breast. 'You are speaking, sir, to a miserable creature who can't hear you. I am deaf.'

I stepped nearer to him, intending to raise my voice in pity for his infirmity. He shuddered, and signed to me to keep back.

'Don't come close to my ear; don't shout.' As he spoke, strong excitement flashed at me in his eyes, without producing the slightest change in his voice. 'I don't deny,' he resumed, 'that I can hear sometimes when people take that way with me. They hurt when they do it. Their voices go through my nerves as a knife might go through my flesh. I live at the mill, sir; I have a great favour to ask. Will you come and speak to me in my room—for five minutes only?'

I hesitated. Any other man in my place, would, I think, have done the same; receiving such an invitation as this from a stranger, whose pitiable infirmity seemed to place him beyond the pale of social intercourse.

He must have guessed what was passing in my mind; he tried me again in words which might have proved persuasive, had they been uttered in the customary variety of tone.

'I can't help being a stranger to you; I can't help being deaf. You're a young man. You look more merciful and more patient than young men in general. Won't you hear what I have to say? Won't you tell me what I want to know?'

How were we to communicate? Did he by any chance suppose that I had learnt the finger alphabet?* I touched my fingers and shook my head, as a means of dissipating his delusion, if it existed.

He instantly understood me.

'Even if you knew the finger alphabet,' he said, 'it would be of no use. I have been too miserable to learn it—my deafness only came on me a little more than a year since. Pardon me if I am obliged to give you trouble—I ask persons who pity me to write their answers when I speak to them. Come to my room, and you will find what you want—a candle to write by.'

Was his will, as compared with mine, the stronger will of the two? And was it helped (insensibly to myself) by his advantages of personal appearance? I can only confess that his apology presented a picture of misery to my mind, which shook my resolution to refuse him. His ready penetration discovered this change in his favour: he at once took advantage of it. 'Five minutes of your time is all I ask for,' he said. 'Won't you indulge a man who sees his fellow-creatures all talking happily round him, and feels dead and buried among them?'

The very exaggeration of his language had its effect on my mind. It revealed to me the horrible isolation among humanity of the deaf, as I had never understood it yet. Discretion is, I am sorry to say, not one of the strong points in my character. I committed one more among the many foolish actions of my life; I signed to the stranger to lead the way back to the mill.

## CHAPTER IV

### HE EXPLAINS HIMSELF

Giles Toller's miserly nature had offered to his lodger shelter from wind and rain, and the furniture absolutely necessary to make a bedroom habitable—and nothing more. There was no carpet on the floor, no paper on the walls, no ceiling to hide the rafters of the roof. The chair that I sat on was the one chair in the room; the man whose guest I had rashly consented to be found a seat on his bed. Upon his table I saw pens and pencils, paper and ink, and a battered brass candlestick with a common tallow candle in it. His changes of clothing were flung on the bed; his money was left on the unpainted wooden chimney-piece; his wretched little morsel of looking-glass (propped up near the money) had been turned with its face to the wall. He perceived that the odd position of this last object had attracted my notice.

'Vanity and I have parted company,' he explained; 'I shrink from myself when I look at myself now. The ugliest man living—if he has got his hearing—is a more agreeable man in society than I am. Does this wretched place disgust you?'

He pushed a pencil and some sheets of writing-paper across the table to me. I wrote my reply: 'The place makes me sorry for you.'

He shook his head. 'Your sympathy is thrown away on me. A man who has lost his social relations with his fellow-creatures doesn't care how he lodges or where he lives. When he has found solitude, he has found all he wants for the rest of his days. Shall we introduce ourselves? It won't be easy for me to set the example.'

I used the pencil again: 'Why not?'

'Because you will expect me to give you my name. I can't do it. I have ceased to bear my family name; and, being out of society, what need have I for an assumed name? As for my Christian name, it's so detestably ugly that I hate the sight and sound of it. Here, they know me as The Lodger. Will you have that? or will you have an appropriate nick-name? I come of a mixed breed; and I'm likely, after what has happened to me, to turn out a worthless fellow. Call me The Cur. Oh, you needn't start! that's as accurate a description of me as any other. What's *your* name?'

I wrote it for him. His face darkened when he found out who I was.

'Young, personally attractive, and a great landowner,' he said. 'I saw you just now talking familiarly with Cristel Toller. I didn't like that at the time; I like it less than ever now.'

My pencil asked him, without ceremony, what he meant.

He was ready with his reply. 'I mean this: you owe something to the good luck which has placed you where you are. Keep your familiarity for ladies in your own rank of life.'

This (to a young man like me) was unendurable insolence. I had hitherto refrained from taking him at his own bitter word in the matter of nick-name. In the irritation of the moment, I now first resolved to adopt his suggestion seriously. The next slip of paper that

I handed to him administered the smartest rebuff that my dull brains could discover on the spur of the moment: 'The Cur is requested to keep his advice till he is asked for it.'

For the first time, something like a smile showed itself faintly on his lips—and represented the only effect which my severity had produced. He still followed his own train of thought, as resolutely and as impertinently as ever.

'I haven't seen you talking to Cristel before to-night. Have you been meeting her in secret?'

In justice to the girl, I felt that I ought to set him right, so far. Taking up the pencil again, I told this strange man that I had just returned to England, after an absence of many years in foreign countries—that I had known Cristel when we were both children— and that I had met her purely by accident, when he had detected us talking outside the cottage. Seeing me pause, after advancing to that point in the writing of my reply, he held out his hand impatiently for the paper. I signed him to wait, and added a last sentence: 'Understand this; I will answer no more questions—I have done with the subject.'

He read what I had written with the closest attention. But his inveterate suspicion of me was not set at rest, even yet.

'Are you likely to come this way again?' he asked.

I pointed to the final lines of my writing, and got up to go.

This assertion of my will against his roused him. He stopped me at the door—not by a motion of his hand but by the mastery of his look. The dim candlelight afforded me no help in determining the colour of his eyes. Dark, large, and finely set in his head, there was a sinister passion in them, at that moment, which held me in spite of myself. Still as monotonous as ever, his voice in some degree expressed the frenzy that was in him, by suddenly rising in its pitch when he spoke to me next.

'Mr Roylake, I love her. Mr Roylake, I am determined to marry her. Any man who comes between me and that cruel girl—ah, she's as hard as one of her father's millstones; it's the misery of my life, it's the joy of my life, to love her—I tell you, young sir, any man who comes between Cristel and me does it at his peril. Remember that.'

I had no wish to give offence—but his threatening me in this manner was so absurd that I gave way to the impression of the moment, and laughed. He stepped up to me, with such an expression of demoniacal rage and hatred in his face that he became absolutely ugly in an instant.

'I amuse you, do I?' he said. 'You don't know the man you're trifling with. You had better know me. You *shall* know me.' He turned away, and walked up and down the wretched little room, deep in thought. 'I don't want this matter between us to end badly,' he said, interrupting his meditations—then returning to them again—and then once more addressing me. 'You're young, you're thoughtless; but you don't look like a bad fellow. I wonder whether I can trust you? Not one man in a thousand would do it. Never mind. I'm the one man in ten thousand who does it. Mr Gerard Roylake, I'm going to trust you.'

With this incoherent expression of a resolution unknown to me, he unlocked a shabby trunk hidden in a corner, and took from it a small portfolio.

'Men of your age,' he resumed, 'seldom look below the surface. Learn that valuable habit, sir—and begin by looking below the surface of Me.' He forced the portfolio into my hand. Once more, his beautiful eyes held me with their irresistible influence; they looked at me with an expression of sad and solemn warning. 'Discover for yourself,' he said, 'what devils my deafness has set loose in me; and let no eyes but yours see that horrid sight. You will find me here to-morrow, and you will decide by that time whether you make an enemy of me or not.'

He threw open the door, and bowed as graciously as if he had been a sovereign dismissing a subject.

Was he mad?

I hesitated to adopt that conclusion. There is no denying it, the deaf man had found his own strange and tortuous way to my interest, in spite of myself. I might even have been in some danger of allowing him to make a friend of me, if I had not been restrained by the fears for Cristel which his language and his manner amply justified, to my mind. Although I was far from foreseeing the catastrophe that really did happen, I felt that I had returned to my own country at a critical time in the life of the miller's daughter. My friendly interference might be of serious importance to Cristel's peace of mind—perhaps even to her personal safety as well.

Eager to discover what the contents of the portfolio might tell me, I hurried back to Trimley Deen. My stepmother had not yet returned from the dinner-party. As one of the results of my ten years' banishment from home, I was obliged to ask the servant to show me the way to my own room, in my own house! The windows looked out on a view of Fordwitch Wood. As I opened the leaves which were to reveal to me the secret soul of the man whom I had so strangely met, the fading moonlight vanished, and the distant trees were lost in the gloom of a starless night.

## CHAPTER V

### HE BETRAYS HIMSELF

The confession was entitled, 'Memoirs of a Miserable Man'. It began abruptly in these words:

I

'I acknowledge, at the outset, that misfortune has had an effect on me which frail humanity is for the most part anxious to conceal. Under the influence of suffering, I have become of enormous importance to myself. In this frame of mind, I naturally enjoy painting my own portrait in words. Let me add that they must be written words because it is a painful effort to me (since I lost my hearing) to speak to anyone continuously, for any length of time.

'I have also to confess that my brains are not so completely under my own command as I could wish.

'For instance, I possess considerable skill (for an amateur) as a painter in water colours. But I can only produce a work of art, when irresistible impulse urges me to express my thoughts in form and colour. The same obstacle to regular exertion stands in my way, if I am using my pen. I can only write when the fit takes me—sometimes at night when I ought to be asleep; sometimes at meals when I ought to be handling my knife and fork; sometimes out of doors when I meet with inquisitive strangers who stare at me. As for paper, the first stray morsel of anything that I can write upon will do, provided I snatch it up in time to catch my ideas as they fly.

'My method being now explained, I proceed to the deliberate act of self-betrayal which I contemplate in producing this picture of myself.

## II

'I divide my life into two Epochs—respectively entitled: Before my Deafness, and After my Deafness. Or, suppose I define the melancholy change in my fortunes more sharply still, by contrasting with each other my days of prosperity and my days of disaster? Of these alternatives, I hardly know which to choose. It doesn't matter; the one thing needful is to go on.

'In any case, then, I have to record that I passed a happy childhood—thanks to my good mother. Her generous nature had known adversity, and had not been deteriorated by undeserved trials. Born of slave-parents, she had not reached her eighteenth year, when she was sold by auction in the Southern States of America. The person who bought her (she never would tell me who he was) freed her by a codicil, added to his will on his deathbed. My father met with her, a few years afterwards, in American society—fell (as I have heard) madly in love with her—and married her in defiance of the wishes of his family. He was quite right: no better wife and mother ever lived. The one vestige of good feeling that I still possess, lives in my empty heart when I dwell at times on the memory of my mother.

'My good fortune followed me when I was sent to school.

'Our head master was more nearly a perfect human being than any other man that I have ever met with. Even the worst-tempered boys among us ended in loving him. Under his encouragement, and especially to please him, I won every prize that industry, intelligence, and good conduct could obtain; and I rose, at an unusually early age, to be the head boy in the first class. When I was old enough to be removed to the University, and when the dreadful day of parting arrived, I fainted under the agony of leaving the teacher—no! the dear friend—whom I devotedly loved. There must surely have been some good in me at that time. What has become of it now?

'The years followed each other—and I was Fortune's spoilt child still.

'Under adverse circumstances, my sociable disposition, my delight in the society of young people of my own age, might have exposed me to serious dangers in my new sphere of action. Happily for me, my father consulted a wise friend, before he sent me to Cambridge. I was entered at one of the smaller colleges; and I fell, at starting, among the right set of men. Good examples were all round me. We formed a little club of steady students; our pleasures were innocent; we were too proud and too poor to get into debt. I look back on my career at Cambridge, as I look back on my career at school, and wonder what has become of my better self.

### III

'During my last year at Cambridge, my father died.

'The profession which he had intended that I should follow was the Bar. I believed myself to be quite unfit for the sort of training imperatively required by the Law; and my mother agreed with me. When I left the University, my own choice of a profession pointed to the medical art, and to that particular branch of it called surgery. After three years of unremitting study at one of the great London hospitals, I started in practice for myself. Once more, my persistent luck was faithful to me at the outset of my new career.

'The winter of that year was remarkable for alternate extremes of frost and thaw. Accidents to passengers in the streets were numerous; and one of them happened close to my own door. A gentleman slipped on the icy pavement, and broke his leg. On sending news of the accident to his house, I found that my chance-patient was a nobleman.

'My lord was so well satisfied with my services that he refused to be attended by any of my elders and betters in the profession. Little did I think at the time, that I had received the last of the favours which Fortune was to bestow on me. I enjoyed the confidence and goodwill of a man possessing boundless social influence; and I was received most kindly by the ladies of his family. In one word, at the time when my professional prospects justified the brightest hopes that I could form, sudden death deprived me of the dearest and truest of all friends—I suffered the one dreadful loss which it is impossible to replace, the loss of my mother. We had parted at night when she was, to all appearance, in the enjoyment of her customary health. The next morning, she was found dead in her bed.

### IV

'Keen observers, who read these lines, will remark that I have said nothing about the male members of my family, and that I have even passed over my father with the briefest possible allusion to his death.

'This curious reticence on my part, is simply attributable to pure ignorance. Until affliction lay heavy on me, my father, my uncle, and my grandfather were hardly better known to me, in their true characters, than if they had been strangers passing in the street. How I contrived to become more intimately acquainted with my ancestors, I am now to reveal.

'In the absence of any instructions to guide me, after my mother's death, I was left to use my own discretion in examining the papers which she had left behind her. Reading her letters carefully, before I decided what to keep and what to destroy, I discovered a packet, protected by an unbroken seal, and bearing an inscription, addressed abruptly to my mother in these words:

"For fear of accidents, my dear, we will mention no names in this place. The sight of my handwriting will remind you of my devotion to your interests in the past, and will satisfy you that I am to be trusted in the service that I now offer to my good sister-friend. In the fewest words, let me tell you that I have heard of the circumstances under which your marriage has taken place. Your origin has unfortunately become known to the members of your husband's family; their pride has been deeply wounded; and the women especially regard you with feelings of malignant hatred. I have good reason for fearing that they may try to excuse their inhuman way of speaking of you, by making public the calamity of your slave-birth. What deplorable influence might be exercised on your husband's mind, by such an exposure as this, I will not stop to inquire. It will be more to the purpose to say that I am able to offer you a sure means of protecting yourself— through information which I have unexpectedly obtained, and the source of which I am obliged to keep secret. If you are ever threatened by your enemies, open the packet which I have now sealed up, and you will command the silence of the bitterest man or woman who longs to injure you. I may add that absolute proof accompanies every assertion which my packet contains. Keep it carefully, as long as you live—and God grant you may never have occasion to break the seal."

'Such was the inscription; copied exactly, word for word.

'I cannot even guess who my mother's devoted friend may have been. Neither can I doubt that she would have destroyed the packet, but for the circumstance of her sudden death.

'After hesitating a little—I hardly know why—I summoned my resolution, and broke the seal. Of the horror with which I read the contents of the packet I shall say nothing. Who ever yet sympathised with the sorrows and sufferings of strangers? Let me merely announce that I knew my ancestors at last, and that I am now able to present them in their true characters, as follows:

## V

'My grandfather was tried on a charge of committing wilful murder—was found guilty on the clearest evidence—and died on the scaffold by the hangman's hands.

'His two sons abandoned the family name, and left the family residence. They were, nevertheless, not unworthy representatives of their atrocious father, as will presently appear.

'My uncle (a captain in the Army) was discovered at the hazard table, playing with loaded dice. Before this abject scoundrel could be turned out of his regiment, he was killed in a duel by one of his brother officers whom he had cheated.

'My father, when he was little more than a lad, deserted a poor girl who had trusted him under a promise of marriage. Friendless and hopeless, she drowned herself and her child. His was the most infamous in the list of the family crimes—and *he* escaped, without answering to a court of law or a court of honour for what he had done.

'Some of us come of one breed, and some of another. There is the breed from which I drew the breath of life. What do you think of me now?

## VI

'I looked back over the past years of my existence, from the time of my earliest recollections to the miserable day when I opened the sealed packet.

'What wholesome influences had preserved me, so far, from moral contamination by the vile blood that ran in my veins? There were two answers to that question which, in some degree, quieted my mind. In the first place, resembling my good mother physically, I might hope to have resembled her morally. In the second place, the happy accidents of my career had preserved me from temptation, at more than one critical period of my life. On the other hand, in the ordinary course of nature, not one half of that life had yet elapsed. What trials might the future have in store for me? and what protection against them would the better part of my nature be powerful enough to afford?

'While I was still troubled by these doubts, the measure of my disasters was filled by an attack of illness which threatened me with death. My medical advisers succeeded in saving my life—and left me to pay the penalty of their triumph by the loss of one of my senses.

'At an early period of my convalescence, I noticed one day, with languid surprise, that the voices of the doctors, when they asked me how I had slept and if I felt better, sounded singularly dull and distant. A few hours later, I observed that they stooped close over me when they had something important to say. On the same evening, my day nurse and my night nurse happened to be in the room together. To my surprise, they had become so wonderfully quiet in their movements, that they opened the door or stirred the fire, without making the slightest noise. I intended to ask them what it meant; I had even begun to put the question, when I was startled by another discovery relating this time to myself. I was certain that I had spoken—and yet, I had not heard myself speak! As well as my weakness would let me, I called to the nurses in my loudest tones. "Has anything happened to my voice?" I asked. The two women consulted together, looking at me with pity in their eyes. One of them took the responsibility on herself. She put her lips close to my ear; the horrid words struck me with a sense of physical pain: "Your illness has left you in a sad state, sir. You are deaf."

## VII

'As soon as I was able to leave my bed, well-meaning people, in and out of the medical profession, combined to torment me with the best intentions.

'One famous aural surgeon after another came to me, and quoted his experience of cases, in which the disease that had struck me down had affected the sense of hearing in other unhappy persons: they had submitted to surgical treatment, generally with cheering results. I submitted in my turn. All that skill could do for me was done, and without effect. My deafness steadily increased; my case was pronounced to be hopeless; the great authorities retired.

'Judicious friends, who had been waiting for their opportunity, undertook the moral management of me next.

'I was advised to cultivate cheerfulness, to go into society, to encourage kind people who tried to make me hear what was going on, to be on my guard against morbid depression, to check myself when the sense of my own horrible isolation drove me away to my room, and, last but by no means least, to beware of letting my vanity disincline me to use an ear-trumpet.

'I did my best, honestly did my best, to profit by the suggestions that were offered to me—not because I believed in the wisdom of my friends, but because I dreaded the effect of self-imposed solitude on my nature. Since the fatal day when I had opened the sealed packet, I was on my guard against the inherited evil lying dormant, for all I knew to the contrary, in my father's son. Impelled by that horrid dread, I suffered my daily martyrdom with a courage that astonishes me when I think of it now.

'What the self-inflicted torture of the deaf is, none but the deaf can understand.

'When benevolent persons did their best to communicate to me what was clever or amusing, while conversation was going on in my presence, I was secretly angry with them for making my infirmity conspicuous, and directing the general attention to me. When other friends saw in my face that I was not grateful to them, and gave up the attempt to help me, I suspected them of talking of me contemptu-ously, and amusing themselves by making my misfortune the subject of coarse jokes.

'Even when I deserved encouragement by honestly trying to atone for my bad behaviour, I committed mistakes (arising out of my helpless position) which prejudiced people against me. Sometimes, I asked questions which appeared to be so trivial, to ladies and gentlemen happy in the possession of a sense of hearing, that they evidently thought me imbecile as well as deaf. Sometimes, seeing the company enjoying an interesting story or a good joke, I ignorantly appealed to the most incompetent person present to tell me what had been said—with this result, that he lost the thread of the story or missed the point of the joke, and blamed my unlucky interference as the cause of it.

'These mortifications, and many more, I suffered patiently until, little by little, my last reserves of endurance felt the cruel strain on them, and failed me. My friends detected a change in my manner which alarmed them. They took me away from London, to try the renovating purity of country air.

'So far as any curative influence over the state of my mind was concerned, the experiment proved to be a failure.

'I had secretly arrived at the conclusion that my deafness was increasing, and that my friends knew it and were concealing it from me. Determined to put my suspicions to the test, I took long solitary walks in the neighbourhood of my country home, and tried to hear the new sounds about me. I was deaf to everything—with the one exception of the music of the birds.

'How long did I hear the little cheering songsters who comforted me?

'I am unable to measure the interval that elapsed: my memory fails me. I only know that the time came, when I could see the skylark in the heavens, but could no longer hear its joyous notes. In a few weeks more the nightingale, and even the loud thrush, became silent birds to my doomed ears. My last effort to resist my own deafness was made at my bedroom window. For some time I still heard, faintly and more faintly, the shrill twittering just above me, under the eaves of the house. When this last poor enjoyment came to an end—when I listened eagerly, desperately, and heard nothing (think of it, *nothing!*)—I gave up the struggle. Persuasions, arguments, entreaties were entirely without effect on me. Reckless what came of it, I retired to the one fit place for me—to the solitude in which I have buried myself ever since.

### VIII

'With some difficulty, I discovered the lonely habitation of which I was in search.

'No language can describe the heavenly composure of mind that came to me, when I first found myself alone; living the death-in-life of deafness, apart from creatures—no longer my fellow-creatures—who could hear: apart also from those privileged victims of hysterical impulse, who wrote me love-letters, and offered to console the "poor beautiful deaf man" by marrying him. Through the distorting medium of such sufferings as I have described, women and men—even young women—were repellent to me alike. Ungratefully impatient of the admiration excited by my personal advantages, savagely irritated by tender looks and flattering compliments, I only consented to take lodgings, on condition that there should be no young women living under the same roof with me. If this confession of morbid feeling looks like vanity, I can only say that appearances lie. I write in sober sadness; determined to present my character, with photographic accuracy, as a true likeness.

'What were my habits in solitude? How did I get through the weary and wakeful hours of the day?

'Living by myself, I became (as I have already acknowledged) important to myself—and, as a necessary consequence, I enjoyed registering my own daily doings. Let passages copied from my journal reveal how I got through the day.

IX

EXTRACTS FROM A DEAF MAN'S DIARY

'Monday.—Six weeks to-day since I first occupied my present retreat.

'My landlord and landlady are two hideous old people. They look as if they disliked me, on the rare occasions when we meet. So much the better; they don't remind me of my deafness by trying to talk, and they keep as much as possible out of my way. This morning, after breakfast, I altered the arrangement of my books—and then I made my fourth attempt, in the last ten days, to read some of my favourite authors. No: my taste has apparently changed since the time when I could hear. I closed one volume after another; caring nothing for what used to be deeply interesting to me.

'Reckless and savage—with a burning head and a cold heart— I went out to look about me.

'After two hours of walking and thinking, I found that I had wandered to our county town. The rain began to fall heavily just as I happened to be passing a bookseller's shop. After some hesitation— for I hate exposing my deafness to strangers—I asked leave to take shelter, and looked at the books.

'Among them was a collection of celebrated Trials. I thought of my grandfather; consulted the index; and, finding his name there, bought the work. The shopman (as I could guess from his actions and looks) proposed sending the parcel to me. I insisted on taking it away. The sky had cleared; and I was eager to read the details of my grandfather's crime.

'Tuesday.—Sat up late last night, reading my new book. My favourite poets, novelists, and historians have failed to interest me.

I devoured the Trials with breathless delight; beginning of course with the murder in which I felt a family interest. Prepared to find my grandfather a ruffian, I confess I was surprised by the discovery that he was also a fool. The officers of justice had no merit in tracing the crime to him; his own stupidity delivered him into their hands. I read the evidence twice over, and put myself in his position, and saw the means plainly by which he might have set discovery at defiance.

'In the Preface to the Trials I found an allusion, in terms of praise, to a work of the same kind, published in the French language. I wrote to London at once, and ordered the book.

'Wednesday.—Is there some mysterious influence, in the silent solitude of my life, that is hardening my nature? Is there something unnatural in the existence of a man who never hears a sound? Is there a moral sense that suffers when a bodily sense is lost?

'These questions have been suggested to me by an incident that happened this morning.

'Looking out of window, I saw a brutal carter, on the road before the house, beating an over-loaded horse. A year since I should have interfered to protect the horse, without a moment's hesitation. If the wretch had been insolent, I should have seized his whip, and applied the heavy handle of it to his own shoulders. In past days, I have been more than once fined by a magistrate (privately in sympathy with my offence) for assaults committed by me in the interests of helpless animals. What did I feel now? Nothing but a selfish sense of uneasiness, at having been accidentally witness of an act which disturbed my composure. I turned away, regretting that I had gone to the window and looked out.

'This was not an agreeable train of thought to follow. What could I do? I was answered by the impulse which commands me to paint.

'I sharpened my pencils, and opened my box of colours, and determined to produce a work of art. To my astonishment, the brutal figure of the carter forced its way into my memory again and again. I felt (without in the least knowing why) as if the one chance of getting rid of this curious incubus, was to put the persistent image of the man on paper. It was done mechanically, and yet done so well, that I was encouraged to add to the picture. I put in next the poor beaten horse (another good likeness!); and then I introduced a life-like portrait of myself, giving the man the sound thrashing that he had deserved.

Strange to say, this representation of what I ought to have done, relieved my mind as if I had actually done it. I looked at the preeminent figure of myself, and felt good, and turned to my Trials, and read them over again, and liked them better than ever.

'Thursday.—The bookseller has found a second-hand copy of the French Trials, and has sent them to me (as he expresses it) "on approval".

'I more than approve—I admire; and I more than admire— I imitate. These criminal stories are told with a dramatic power, which has impelled me to try if I can rival the clever French narrative. I found a promising subject by putting myself in my grandfather's place, and tracing the means by which it had occurred to me that he might have escaped the discovery of his crime.

'I cannot remember having read any novel with a tenth part of the interest that absorbed me, in constructing my imaginary train of circumstances. So completely did the reality of the narrative impress itself on my mind, that I felt as if the murder that I was relating had been a crime committed by myself. It was my own ingenuity that hid the dead body, and removed the traces of blood— and my own self-control that presented me as an innocent person, when the victim was missing, and I was asked (among other respectable people) to say whether I thought he was living or dead.

'A whole week has passed—and has been occupied by my new literary pursuit.

'My inexhaustible imagination invents plots and conspiracies of which I am the happy hero. I set traps which invariably catch my enemies. I place myself in positions which are entirely new to me. Yesterday, for instance, I invented a method of spiriting away a young person, whose disappearance was of considerable importance under the circumstances, and succeeded in completely bewildering her father, her friends, and the police: not a trace of her could they find. If I ever have occasion to do, in reality, what I only suppose myself to do in these exercises of ingenuity, what a dangerous man I may yet prove to be!

'This morning, I rose, planning to amuse myself with a new narrative, when the ideal world in which I am now living, became a world annihilated by collision with the sordid interests of real life.

'In plainer words, I received a written message from my landlord which has annoyed me—and not without good cause. This tiresome person finds himself unexpectedly obliged to give up possession of his house. The circumstances are not worth relating. The result is important—I am compelled to find new lodgings. Where am I to go?

'I left it to chance. That is to say, I looked at the railway time-table, and took a ticket for the first place, of which the name happened to catch my eye. Arrived at my destination, I found myself in a dirty manufacturing town, with an ugly river running through it.

'After a little reflection, I turned my back on the town, and followed the course of the river, in search of shelter and solitude on one or the other of its banks. An hour of walking brought me to an odd-looking cottage, half old and half new, attached to a water-mill. A bill in one of the windows announced that rooms were to be let; and a look round revealed a thick wood on my left hand, and a wilderness of sand and heath on my right. So far as appearances went, here was the very place for me.

'I knocked at the door, and was admitted by a little lean sly-looking old man. He showed me the rooms—one for myself, and one for my servant. Wretched as they were, the loneliness of the situation recommended them to me. I made no objections; and I consented to pay the rent that was asked. The one thing that remained to be done, in the interests of my tranquillity, was to ascertain if any other persons lived in the cottage besides my new landlord. He wrote his answer to the question: "Nobody but my daughter." With serious misgivings, I inquired if his daughter was young. He wrote two fatal figures: "18."

'Here was a discovery which disarranged all my plans, just as I had formed them! The prospect of having a girl in the house, at the age associated with my late disagreeable experience of the sensitive sex, was more than my irritable temper could endure. I saw the old man going to the window to take down the bill. Turning in a rage to stop him, I was suddenly brought to a standstill by the appearance of a person who had just entered the room.

'Was this the formidable obstacle to my tranquillity, which had prevented me from taking the rooms that I had chosen? Yes! I knew the miller's daughter intuitively. Delirium possessed me; my eyes devoured her; my heart beat as if it would burst out of my bosom. The old man approached me; he nodded, and grinned, and pointed to her. Did he claim his parental interest in her? Did he mean that she belonged to him? No! she belonged to me. She might be his daughter. She was My Fate.

'I don't know what it was in the girl that took me by storm. Nothing in her look or her manner expressed the slightest interest in me. That famous "beauty" of mine which had worked such ravages in the hearts of other young women, seemed not even to attract her notice. When her father put his hand to his ear, and told her (as I guessed) that I was deaf, there was no pity in her splendid brown eyes; they expressed a momentary curiosity, and nothing more. Possibly she had a hard heart? or perhaps she took a dislike to me, at first sight? It made no difference to my mind, either way. Was she the most beautiful creature I had ever seen? Not even that excuse was to be made for me. I have met with women of her dark complexion who were, beyond dispute, her superiors in beauty, and have looked at them with indifference. Add to this, that I am one of the men whom women offend if they are not perfectly well-dressed. The miller's daughter was badly dressed; her magnificent figure was profaned by the wretchedly-made gown that she wore. I forgave the profanation. In spite of the protest of my own better taste, I resigned myself to her gown. Is it possible adequately to describe such infatuation as this? Quite possible! I have only to acknowledge that I took the rooms at the cottage—and there is the state of my mind, exposed without mercy!

'How will it end?'

## CHAPTER VI

### THE RETURN OF THE PORTFOLIO

With that serious question the last of the leaves entrusted to me by the Lodger at the Mill came to an end.

I betray no confidence in presenting this copy of his confession. Time has passed since I first read it, and changes have occurred in the interval, which leave me free to exercise my own discretion, and to let the autobiography speak for itself.

If I am asked what impression of the writer those extraordinary pages produced on me, I feel at a loss how to reply.

Not one impression, but many impressions, troubled and confused my mind. Certain passages in the confession inclined me to believe that the writer was mad. But I altered my opinion at the next leaf, and set him down as a man with a bitter humour, disposed to make merry over his own bad qualities. At one time, his tone in writing of his early life, and his allusions to his mother, won my sympathy and respect. At another time, the picture of himself in his later years, and the defiant manner in which he presented it, almost made me regret that he had not died of the illness which had struck him deaf. In this state of uncertainty I may claim the merit of having arrived, so far as my own future conduct was concerned, at one positive conclusion. As strangers he and I had first met. As strangers I was determined we should remain.

Having made up my mind, so far, the next thing to do (with the clock on the mantel-piece striking midnight) was to go to bed.

I slept badly. The events that had happened, since my arrival in England, had excited me I suppose. Now and then, in the wakeful hours of the night, I thought of Cristel with some anxiety. Taking the Lodger's exaggerated language for what it was really worth, the poor girl (as I was still inclined to fear) might have serious reason to regret that he had ever entered her father's cottage.

At the breakfast table, my stepmother and I met again.

Mrs Roylake—in an exquisite morning dress; with her smile in perfect order—informed me that she was dying with curiosity. She had heard, from the servants, that I had not returned to the house until past ten o'clock on the previous night; and she was absolutely bewildered by the discovery. What could her dear Gerard have been doing, out in the dark by himself, for all that time?

'For some part of the time,' I answered, 'I was catching moths in Fordwitch Wood.'

'What an extraordinary occupation for a young man! Well? And what did you do after that?'

'I walked on through the wood, and renewed my old associations with the river and the mill.'

Mrs Roylake's fascinating smile disappeared when I mentioned the mill. She suddenly became a cold lady—I might even say a stiff lady.

'I can't congratulate you on the first visit you have paid in our neighbourhood,' she said. 'Of course that bold girl contrived to attract your notice?'

I replied that I had met with the 'bold girl' purely by accident, on her side as well as on mine; and then I started a new topic. 'Was it a pleasant dinner-party last night?' I asked—as if the subject really interested me. I had not been quite four and twenty hours in England yet, and I was becoming a humbug already.

My stepmother was her charming self again the moment my question had passed my lips. Society—provided it was not society at the mill—was always attractive as a topic of conversation. 'Your absence was the only drawback,' she answered. 'I have asked the two ladies (my lord has an engagement) to dine here to-day, without ceremony. They are most anxious to meet you. My dear Gerard! you look surprised. Surely you know who the ladies are?'

I was obliged to acknowledge my ignorance.

Mrs Roylake was shocked. 'At any rate,' she resumed, 'you have heard of their father, Lord Uppercliff?'

I made another shameful confession. Either I had forgotten Lord Uppercliff, during my long absence abroad, or I had never heard of him.

Mrs Roylake was disgusted. 'And this is a foreign education!' she exclaimed. 'Thank Heaven, you have returned to your own country! We will drive out after luncheon, and pay a round of visits.' When this prospect was placed before me, I remembered having read in books of sensitive persons receiving impressions which made their blood run cold; I now found myself one of those persons, for the first time in my life. 'In the meanwhile,' Mrs Roylake continued, 'I must tell you—excuse me for laughing; it seems so very absurd that you should not know who Lord Uppercliff's daughters are—I must tell you that Lady Rachel is the eldest. She is married to the Honourable Captain Millbay, of the Navy, now away in his ship. A person of extraordinary strength of mind (I don't mean the Captain; I mean Lady Rachel); I admire her intellect, but her political and social opinions I must always view with regret. Her younger sister, Lady Lena—not married, Gerard; remember that!—is simply the most charming girl in England. If you don't fall in love with her, you will be the only young man in the county who has resisted Lady Lena. Poor Sir George—she refused him last week; you really *must* have heard of Sir George; our member of parliament; conservative of course; quite broken-hearted about Lady Lena; gone away to America to shoot bears. You seem to be restless. What are you fidgeting about? Ah, I know! You want to smoke after breakfast. Well, I won't be in your way. Go out on the terrace; your poor father always took his cigar on the terrace. They say smoking leads to meditation; I leave you to meditate on Lady Lena. Don't forget—luncheon at one o'clock, and the carriage at two.'

She smiled, and kissed her hand, and fluttered out of the room. Charming; perfectly charming. And yet I was ungrateful enough to wish myself back in Germany again.

I lit my cigar, but not on the terrace. Leaving the house, I took the way once more that led to Fordwitch Wood. What would Mrs Roylake have said, if she had discovered that I was going back to the mill? There was no other alternative. The portfolio was a trust confided to me; the sooner I returned it to the writer of the confession—the sooner I told him plainly the conclusion at which I had arrived—the more at ease my mind would be.

The sluggish river looked muddier than ever, the new cottage looked uglier than ever, exposed to the searching ordeal of sunlight. I knocked at the door on the ancient side of the building.

Cristel's father—shall I confess I had hoped that it might be Cristel herself?—let me in. In by-gone days, I dimly remembered him as old and small and withered. Advancing years had wasted him away, in the interval, until his white miller's clothes hung about him in empty folds. His fleshless face would have looked like the face of a mummy, but for the restless brightness of his little watchful black eyes. He stared at me in momentary perplexity, and, suddenly recovering himself, asked me to walk in.

'Are you the young master, sir? Ah, yes, yes; I thought so. My girl Cristy said she saw the young master last night. Thank you kindly, sir; I'm pretty well, considering how I've fallen away in my flesh. I have got a fine appetite, but somehow or other, my meals don't show on me. You will excuse my receiving you in the kitchen, sir; it's the best room we have. Did Cristy tell you how badly we are off here for repairs? You being our landlord, we look to you to help us. We are falling to pieces, as it were, on this old side of the house. There's first the drains——'

He proceeded to reckon up the repairs, counting with his fleshless thumb on his skinny fingers, when he was interrupted by a curious succession of sounds which began with whining, and ended with scratching at the cottage door.

In a minute after, the door was opened from without. A brown dog, of the companionable retriever breed, ran in and fawned upon old Toller. Cristel followed (from the kitchen garden), with a basket of vegetables on her arm. Unlike the river and the cottage, she gained by being revealed in the brilliant sunlight. I now saw, in their full beauty, the lustre of her brown eyes, the warm rosiness of her dark complexion, the delightful vivacity of expression which was the crowning charm of her face. She paused confusedly in the doorway, and tried to resist me when I insisted on relieving her of the basket.

'Mr Gerard,' she protested, 'you are treating me as if I was a young lady. What would they say at the great house, if they knew you had done that?'

My answer would no doubt have assumed the form of a foolish compliment, if her father had not spared her that infliction. He returned to the all-important question, the question of repairs.

'You see, sir, it's no use speaking to the bailiff. Saving your presence, he's a miser with his master's money. He says, "All right," and he does nothing. There's first, as I told you just now, the truly dreadful state of the drains——'

I tried to stop him by promising to speak to the bailiff myself. On hearing this good news, Mr Toller's gratitude became ungovernable: he was more eager than ever, and more eloquent than ever, in returning to the repairs.

'And then, sir, there's the oven. They do call bread the staff of life. It's a burnt staff at one time, and a clammy staff at another, in our domestic experience. Satisfy yourself, sir; do please cross the kitchen and look with your own eyes at the state, the scandalous state, of the oven.'

His daughter interfered, and stopped him at the critical moment when he was actually offering his arm to conduct me in state across the kitchen. Cristel had just put her pretty brown hand over his mouth, and said, 'Oh, father, do pray be quiet!' when we were all three disturbed by another interruption.

A second door communicating, as I concluded from its position, with the new cottage, was suddenly opened. In the instant before the person behind it appeared, the dog looked that way—started up, frightened—and took refuge under the table. At the next moment, the deaf Lodger walked into the room. It was he beyond all doubt who had frightened the dog, forewarned by instinct of his appearance.

What I had read of his writing disposed me, now that I saw the man by daylight, to find something devilish in the expression of his face. No! strong as it was, my prejudice failed to make any discoveries that presented him at a disadvantage. His personal attractions triumphed in the clear searching light. I now perceived that his eyes were of that deeply dark blue, which is commonly and falsely described as resembling the colour of the violet. To my thinking, they were so entirely beautiful that they had no right to be in a man's face. I might have felt the same objection to the pale delicacy of his complexion, to the soft profusion of his reddish-brown hair, to his finely shaped sensitive lips, but for two marked peculiarities in him which would have shown me to be wrong—that is to say: the expression of power about his head, and the signs of masculine resolution presented by his mouth and chin.

On entering the room, the first person, and the only person, who attracted his attention was Cristel.

He bowed, smiled, possessed himself abruptly of her hand, and kissed it. She tried to withdraw it from his grasp, and met with an obstinate resistance. His gallantry addressed her in sweet words; and his voice destroyed their charm by the dreary monotony of the tone in which he spoke. 'On this lovely day, Cristel, Nature pleads for me. Your heart feels the sunshine and softens towards the poor deaf man who worships you. Ah, my dear, it's useless to say No. My affliction is my happiness, when you say cruel things to me. I live in my fool's paradise; I don't hear you.' He tried to draw her nearer to him. 'Come, my angel; let me kiss you.'

She made a second attempt to release herself; and this time, she wrenched her hand out of his grasp with a strength for which he was not prepared.

That fiercest anger which turns the face pale, was the anger that had possession of Cristel as she took refuge with her father. 'You asked me to bear with that man,' she said, 'because he paid you a good rent. I tell you this, father; my patience is coming to an end. Either he must go, or I must go. Make up your mind to choose between your money and me.'

Old Toller astonished me. He seemed to have caught the infection of his daughter's anger. Placed between Cristel and his money, he

really acted as if he preferred Cristel. He hobbled up to his lodger,
and shook his infirm fists, and screamed at the highest pitch of his old
cracked voice: 'Let her be, or I won't have you here no longer! You
deaf adder,* let her be!'

The sensitive nerves of the deaf man shrank as those shrill tones
pierced them. 'If you want to speak to me, write it!' he said, with rage
and suffering in every line of his face. He tore from his pocket his little
book, filled with blank leaves, and threw it at Toller's head. 'Write,'
he repeated. 'If you murder me with your screeching again, look out
for your skinny throat—I'll throttle you.'

Cristel picked up the book. She was gratefully sensible of her
father's interference. 'He shall know what you said to him,' she
promised the old man. 'I'll write it myself.'

She took the pencil from its sheath in the leather binding of the
book. Controlling himself, the lover whom she hated advanced
towards her with a persuasive smile.

'Have you forgiven me?' he asked. 'Have you been speaking kindly
of me? I think I see it in your face. There are some deaf people who
can tell what is said by looking at the speaker's lips. I am too stupid, or
too impatient, or too wicked to be able to do that. Write it for me,
dear, and make me happy for the day.'

Cristel was not attending to him, she was speaking to me. 'I hope,
sir, you don't think that father and I are to blame for what has
happened this morning,' she said. He looked where she was looking—and discovered, for the first time, that I was in the room.

He had alluded to his wickedness a moment since. When his face
turned my way, I thought it bore witness to his knowledge of his own
character.

'Why didn't you come to my side of the house?' he said to me.
'What am I to understand, sir, by seeing you here?'

Cristel dropped his book on the table, and hurried to me in breathless surprise. 'He speaks as if he knew you!' she cried. 'What does it
mean?'

'Only that I met him last night,' I explained, 'after leaving you.'

'Did you know him before that?'

'No. He was a perfect stranger to me.'

He picked up his book from the table, and took his pencil out of
Cristel's hand, while we were speaking. 'I want my answer,' he said,
handing me the book and the pencil. I gave him his answer.

'You find me here, because I don't wish to return to your side of the house.'

'Is that the impression,' he asked, 'produced by what I allowed you to read?'

I replied by a sign in the affirmative. He inquired next if I had brought his portfolio with me. I put it at once into his hand.

In some way unknown to me, I had apparently roused his suspicions. He opened the portfolio, and counted the loose leaves of writing in it carefully. While he was absorbed in this occupation, old Toller's eccentricity assumed a new form. His little restless black eyes followed the movements of his lodger's fingers, as they turned over leaf after leaf of the manuscript, with such eager curiosity and interest that I looked at him in surprise. Finding that he had attracted my notice, he showed no signs of embarrassment—he seized the opportunity of asking for information.

'Did my gentleman trust you, sir, with all that writing?' he began.

'Yes.'

'Did he want you to read it?'

'He did.'

'What's it all about, sir?'

Confronted by this cool inquiry, I informed Mr Toller that the demands of curiosity had their limits, and that he had reached them. On this ground, I declined to answer any more questions. Mr Toller went on with his questions immediately.

'Do you notice, sir, that he seems to set a deal of store by his writings? Perhaps you can say what the value of them may be?'

I shook my head. 'It won't do, Mr Toller!'

He tried again—I declare it positively, he tried again. 'You'll excuse me, sir? I've never seen his portfolio before. Am I right if I think you know where he keeps it?'

'Spare your breath, Mr Toller. Once more, it won't do!'

Cristel joined us, amazed at his pertinacity. 'Why are you so anxious, father, to know about that portfolio?' she asked.

Her father seemed to have reasons of his own for following my example, and declining to answer questions. More polite, however, than I had been, he left his resolution to be inferred. His daughter was answered by a few general remarks, setting forth the advantage to the landlord of having a lodger who had lost one of his senses.

'You see there's something convenient, my dear, in the circumstance of that nice-looking gentleman over there being deaf. We can talk about him before his face, just as comfortably as if it was behind his back. Isn't that so, Mr Gerard? Don't you see it yourself, Cristy? For instance, I say it without fear in his presence: 'tis the act of a fool to be fumbling over writings, when there's nothing in them that's not well known to himself already—unless indeed they are worth money, which I don't doubt is no secret to *you*, Mr Gerard? Eh? I beg your pardon, sir, did you speak? No? I beg your pardon again. Yes, yes, Cristy, I'm noticing him; he's done with his writings. Suppose I offer to put them away for him? You can see in his face he finds the tale of them correct. He's coming this way. What's he going to do next?'

He was going to establish a claim on my gratitude, by relieving me of Giles Toller.

'I have something to say to Mr Roylake,' he announced, with a haughty look at his landlord. 'Mind! I don't forget your screaming at me just now, and I intend to know what you meant by it. That will do. Get out of the way.'

The old fellow received his dismissal with a low bow, and left the kitchen with a look at the Lodger which revealed (unless I was entirely mistaken) a sly sense of triumph. What did it mean?

The deaf man addressed me with a cold and distant manner. 'We must understand each other,' he said. 'Will you follow me to my side of the cottage?' I shook my head. 'Very well,' he resumed; 'we will have it out, here. When I trusted you with my confession last night, I left you to decide (after reading it) whether you would make an enemy of me or not. You remember that?' I nodded my head. 'Then I now ask you, Mr Roylake: Which are we—enemies or friends?'

I took the pencil, and wrote my reply:

'Neither enemies nor friends. We are strangers from this time forth.'

Some internal struggle produced a change in his face—visible for one moment, hidden from me in a moment more. 'I think you will regret the decision at which you have arrived.' He said that, and saluted me with his grandly gracious bow. As he turned away, he perceived Cristel at the other end of the room, and eagerly joined her.

'The only happy moments I have are my moments passed in your presence,' he said. 'I shall trouble you no more for to-day. Give me a little comfort to take back with me to my solitude. I didn't notice that there were other persons present when I asked leave to kiss you. May I hope that you forgive me?'

He held out his hand; it was not taken. He waited a little, in the vain hope that she would relent: she turned away from him.

A spasm of pain distorted his handsome face. He opened the door that led to his side of the cottage—paused—and looked back at Cristel. She took no notice of him. As he moved again to the door and left us, the hysterical passion in him forced its way outward—he burst into tears.

The dog sprang up from his refuge under the table, and shook himself joyfully. Cristel breathed again freely, and joined me at my end of the room. Shall I make another acknowledgment of weakness? I began to fear that we might all of us (even including the dog!) have been a little hard on the poor deaf wretch who had gone away in such bitter distress. I communicated this view of the matter to Cristel. She failed to see it as I did.

The dog laid his head on her lap, asking to be caressed. She patted him while she answered me.

'I agree with this old friend, Mr Gerard. We were both of us frightened, on the very first day, when the person you are pitying came to lodge with us. I have got to hate him, since that time—perhaps to despise him. But the dog has never changed; he feels and knows there is something dreadful in that man. One of these days, poor Ponto may turn out to be right.—May I ask you something, sir?'

'Of course!'

'You won't think I am presuming on your kindness?'

'You ought to know me better than that, Cristel!'

'The truth is, sir, I have been a little startled by what I saw in our Lodger's face, when he asked if you were his enemy or his friend. I know he is thought to be handsome—but, Mr Gerard, those beautiful eyes of his sometimes tell tales; and I have seen his pretty complexion change to a colour that turned him into an ugly man. Will you tell me what you wrote when you answered him?'

I repeated what I had written, word for word. It failed to satisfy her.

'He is very vain,' she said, 'and you may have wounded his vanity by treating him like a stranger, after he had given you his writings to read, and invited you to his room. But I thought I saw something much worse than mortification in his face. Shall I be taking a liberty, if I ask how it was you got acquainted with him last night?'

She was evidently in earnest. I saw that I must answer her without reserve; and I was a little afraid of being myself open to a suspicion of vanity, if I mentioned the distrust which I had innocently excited in the mind of my new acquaintance. In this state of embarrassment I took a young man's way out of the difficulty, and spoke lightly of a serious thing.

'I became acquainted with your deaf Lodger, Cristel, under ridiculous circumstances. He saw us talking last night, and did me the honour to be jealous of me.'

I had expected to see her blush. To my surprise she turned pale, and vehemently remonstrated.

'Don't laugh, sir! There's nothing to be amused at in what you have just told me. You didn't go into his room last night? Oh, what made you do that!'

I described his successful appeal to my compassion—not very willingly, for it made me look (as I thought) like a weak person. Little by little, she extracted from me the rest: how he objected to find a young man, especially in my social position, talking to Cristel; how he insisted on my respecting his claims, and engaging not to see her again; how, when I refused to do this, he gave me his confession to read, so that I might find out what a formidable man I was setting at defiance; how I had not been in the least alarmed, and had treated him (as Cristel had just heard) on the footing of a perfect stranger.

'There's the whole story,' I concluded. 'Like a scene in a play, isn't it?'

She protested once more against the light tone that I persisted in assuming.

'I tell you again, sir, this is no laughing matter. You have roused his jealousy. You had better have roused the fury of a wild beast. Knowing what you know of him, why did you stay here, when he came in? And, oh, why did I humiliate him in your presence? Leave us, Mr Gerard—pray, pray leave us, and don't come near this place again till father has got rid of him.'

Did she think I was to be so easily frightened as that? My sense of my own importance was up in arms at the bare suspicion of it!

'My dear child,' I said grandly, 'do you really suppose I am afraid of that poor wretch? Am I to give up the pleasure of seeing you, because a mad fellow is simple enough to think you will marry him? Absurd, Cristel—absurd!'

The poor girl wrung her hands in despair.

'Oh, sir, don't distress me by talking in that way! Do please remember who you are, and who I am. If I was the miserable means of your coming to any harm—I can't bear even to speak of it! Pray don't think me bold; I don't know how to express myself. You ought never to have come here; you ought to go; you *must* go!'

Driven by strong impulse, she ran to the place in which I had left my hat, and brought it to me, and opened the door with a look of entreaty which it was impossible to resist. It would have been an act of downright cruelty to persist in opposing her. 'I wouldn't distress you, Cristel, for the whole world,' I said—and left her to conclude that I had felt the influence of her entreaties in the right way. She tried to thank me; the tears rose in her eyes—she signed to me to leave her, poor soul, as if she felt ashamed of herself. I was shocked; I was grieved; I was more than ever secretly resolved to go back to her. When we said good-bye—I have been told that I did wrong; I meant no harm—I kissed her.

Having traversed the short distance between the cottage and the wood, I remembered that I had left my walking-stick behind me, and returned to get it.

Cristel was leaving the kitchen; I saw her at the door which communicated with the Lodger's side of the cottage. Her back was turned towards me; astonishment held me silent. She opened the door, passed through it, and closed it behind her.

Going to that man, after she had repelled his advances, in my presence! Going to the enemy against whom she had warned me, after I had first been persuaded to leave her! Angry thoughts these—and surely thoughts unworthy of me? If it had been the case of another man, I should have said he was jealous. Jealous of the miller's daughter—in my position? Absurd! contemptible! But I was still in such a vile temper that I determined to let Cristel know she had been discovered. Taking one of my visiting cards, I wrote on it: 'I came back for my stick, and saw you go to him.' After I had pinned this spiteful little message to the door, so that she might see it when she returned, I suffered a disappointment. I was not half so well satisfied with myself as I had anticipated.

# CHAPTER VII

## THE BEST SOCIETY

Leaving the cottage for the second time, I was met at the door by a fat man of solemn appearance dressed in black, who respectfully touched his hat. My angry humour acknowledged the harmless stranger's salute by a rude inquiry: 'What the devil do you want?' Instead of resenting this uncivil language, he indirectly reproved me by becoming more respectful than ever.

'My mistress desires me to tell you, sir, that luncheon is waiting.'

I was in the presence of a thoroughbred English servant—and I had failed to discover it until he spoke of his mistress! I had also, by keeping luncheon waiting, treated an English institution with contempt. And, worse even than this, as a misfortune which personally affected me, my stepmother evidently knew that I had paid another visit to the mill.

I hurried along the woodland path, followed by the fat domestic in black. Not used apparently to force his legs into rapid motion, he articulated with the greatest difficulty in answering my next question: 'How did you know where to find me?'

'Mrs Roylake ordered inquiries to be made, sir. The head gardener—' There his small reserves of breath failed him.

'The head gardener saw me?'

'Yes, sir.'

'When?'

'Hours ago, sir—when you went into Toller's cottage.'

I troubled my fat friend with no more questions.

Returning to the house, and making polite apologies, I discovered one more among Mrs Roylake's many accomplishments. She possessed two smiles—a sugary smile (with which I was already acquainted), and an acid smile which she apparently reserved for special occasions. It made its appearance when I led her to the luncheon table.

'Don't let me detain you,' my stepmother began.

'Won't you give me some luncheon?' I inquired.

'Dear me! hav'n't you lunched already?'

'Where should I lunch, my dear lady?' I thought this would induce the sugary smile to show itself. I was wrong.

'Where?' Mrs Roylake repeated. 'With your friends at the mill, of course. Very inhospitable not to offer you lunch. When are we to have flour cheaper?'

I began to get sulky. All I said was: 'I don't know.'

'Curious!' Mrs Roylake observed. 'You not only don't get luncheon among your friends: you don't even get information. To know a miller, and not to know the price of flour, is ignorance presented in one of its most pitiable aspects. And how is Miss Toller looking? Perfectly charming?'

I was angry by this time. 'You have exactly described her,' I said.

Mrs Roylake began to get angry, on her side.

'Surely a little coarse and vulgar?' she suggested, reverting to poor Cristel.

'Would you like to judge for yourself?' I asked. 'I shall be happy, Mrs Roylake, to take you to the mill.'

My stepmother's knowledge of the world implied considerable acquaintance—how obtained I do not pretend to know—with the characters of men. Discovering that she was in danger of overstepping the limits of my patience, she drew back with a skill which performed the retrograde movement without permitting it to betray itself.

'We have carried our little joke, my dear Gerard, far enough,' she said. 'I fancy your residence in Germany has rather blunted your native English sense of humour. You don't suppose, I hope and trust, that I am so insensible to our relative positions as to think of interfering in your choice of friends or associates. If you are not aware of it already, let me remind you that this house is now yours; not mine. I live here—gladly live here, my dear boy—by your indulgence; fortified (I am sure) by your regard for your excellent father's wishes as expressed in his will—'

I stopped her there. She had got the better of me with a dexterity which I see now, but which I was not clever enough to appreciate at the time. In a burst of generosity, I entreated her to consider Trimley Deen as her house, and never to mention such a shocking subject as my authority again.

After this, need I say that the most amiable of women took me out in her carriage, and introduced me to some of the best society in England?

If I could only remember all the new friends to whom I made my bow, as well as the conversation in which we indulged, I might write a few pages here, interesting in a high degree to persons with well-balanced minds. Unhappily, so far as my own impressions were concerned, the best society proved to be always the same society. Every house that we entered was in the same beautiful order; every mistress of the house was dressed in the best taste; every master of the house had the same sensible remarks to make on conservative prospects at the coming election; every young gentleman wanted to know how my game preserves had been looked after in my absence; every young lady said: 'How nice it must have been, Mr Roylake, to find yourself again at Trimley Deen.' Has anybody ever suffered as I suffered, during that round of visits, under the desire to yawn and the effort to suppress it? Is there any sympathetic soul who can understand me, when I say that I would have given a hundred pounds for a gag, and for the privilege of using it to stop my stepmother's pleasant chat in the carriage, following on our friends' pleasant chat in the drawing-room? Finally, when we got home, and when Mrs Roylake kindly promised me another round of visits, and more charming people in the neighbourhood to see, will any good Christian forgive me, if I own that I took advantage of being alone to damn the neighbourhood, and to feel relieved by it?

Now that I was no longer obliged to listen to polite strangers, my thoughts reverted to Cristel, and to the suspicions that she had roused in me.

Recovering its influence, in the interval that had passed, my better nature sharply reproached me. I had presumed to blame Cristel, with nothing to justify me but my own perverted view of her motives. How did I know that she had not opened that door, and gone to that side of the cottage, with a perfectly harmless object in view? I was really anxious, if I could find the right way to do it, to make amends for an act of injustice of which I felt ashamed. If I am asked why I was as eager to set myself right with a miller's daughter, as if she had been a young lady in the higher ranks of life, I can only reply that no such view of our relative positions as this ever occurred to me. A strange state of mind, no doubt. What was the right explanation of it?

The right explanation presented itself at a later time, when troubles had quickened my intellect, and when I could estimate the powerful influence of circumstances at its true value.

I had returned to England, to fill a prominent place in my own little world, without relations whom I loved, without friends whose society I could enjoy. Hopeful, ardent, eager for the enjoyment of life, I had brought with me to my own country the social habits and the free range of thought of a foreign University; and, as a matter of course, I failed to feel any sympathy with the society—new to me—in which my lot had been cast. Beset by these disadvantages, I had met with a girl, possessed of remarkable personal attractions, and associated with my earliest remembrances of my own happy life and of my mother's kindness—a girl, at once simple and spirited; unspoilt by the world and the world's ways, and placed in a position of peril due to the power of her own beauty, which added to the interest that she naturally inspired. Estimating these circumstances at their true value, did a state of mind which rendered me insensible to the distinctions that separate the classes in England, stand in any need of explanation? As I thought—and think still—it explained itself.

My stepmother and I parted on the garden terrace, which ran along the pleasant southern side of the house.

The habits that I had contracted, among my student friends in Germany, made tobacco and beer necessary accompaniments to the process of thinking. I had nearly exhausted my cigar, my jug, and my thoughts, when I saw two men approaching me from the end of the terrace.

As they came nearer, I recognised in one of the men my fat domestic in black. He stopped the person who was accompanying him, and came on to me by himself.

'Will you see that man, sir, waiting behind me?'

'Who is he?'

'I don't know, sir. He says he has got a letter to give you, and he must put it in your own hands. I think myself he's a beggar. He's excessively insolent—he insists on seeing you. Shall I tell him to go?'

The servant evidently expected me to say Yes. He was disappointed; my curiosity was roused; I said I would see the insolent stranger.

As he approached me, the man certainly did not look like a beggar.
Poor he might be, judging by his dress. The upper part of him was
clothed in an old shooting jacket of velveteen; his legs presented a pair
of trousers, once black, now turning brown with age. Both garments
were too long for him, and both were kept scrupulously clean. He was
a short man, thickly and strongly made. Impenetrable composure
appeared on his ugly face. His eyes were sunk deep in his head; his
nose had evidently been broken and not successfully mended; his
grey hair, when he took off his hat on addressing me, was cut short,
and showed his low forehead and his bull neck. An Englishman of the
last generation would, as I have since been informed, have set him
down as a retired prize-fighter. Thanks to my ignorance of the
pugilistic glories of my native country, I was totally at a loss what to
make of him.

'Have I the honour of speaking to Mr Roylake?' he asked.

His quiet steady manner prepossessed me in his favour; it showed
no servile reverence for the accident of birth, on the one hand, and
no insolent assertion of independence, on the other. When I had
told him that my name was Roylake, he searched one of the large
pockets of his shooting jacket, produced a letter, and silently offered
it to me.

Before I took the letter—seeing that he was a stranger, and that he
mentioned no name known to me—I thought it desirable to make
some inquiry.

'Is it a letter of your own writing?' I asked.

'No, sir.'

'Who sends you with it?'

He was apparently a man of few words. 'My master,' was the
guarded answer that this odd servant returned.

I became as inquisitive as old Toller himself.

'Who is your master?' I went on.

The reply staggered me. Speaking as quietly and respectfully as
ever, he said: 'I can't tell you, sir.'

'Do you mean that you are forbidden to tell me?'

'No, sir.'

'Then what do you mean?'

'I mean that I don't know my master's name.'

I instantly took the letter from him, and looked at the address. For
once in a way, I had jumped at a conclusion and I had proved to be

right. The handwriting on the letter, and the handwriting of the confession which I had read overnight, were one and the same.

'Are you to wait for an answer?' I asked, as I opened the envelope.

'I am to wait, sir, if you tell me to do so.'

The letter was a long one. After running my eye over the first sentences, I surprised myself by acting discreetly. 'You needn't wait,' I said; 'I will send a reply.' The man of few words raised his shabby hat, turned about in silence, and left me.

## CHAPTER VIII

### THE DEAF LODGER

The letter was superscribed: 'Private and Confidential.' It was written in these words:

'Sir,—You will do me grievous wrong if you suppose that I am trying to force myself on your acquaintance. My object in writing is to prevent you (if I can) from misinterpreting my language and my conduct, on the only two occasions when we happen to have met.

'I am conscious that you must have thought me rude and ungrateful—perhaps even a little mad—when I returned your kindness last night, in honouring me with a visit, by using language which has justified you in treating me as a stranger.

'Fortunately for myself, I gave you my autobiography to read. After what you now know of me, I may hope that your sense of justice will make some allowance for a man, tried (I had almost written, cursed) by such suffering as mine.

'There are other deaf persons, as I have heard, who set me a good example.

'They feel the consolations of religion. Their sweet tempers find relief even under the loss of the most precious of all the senses. They mix with society; submitting to their dreadful isolation, and preserving unimpaired sympathy with their happier fellow-creatures who can hear. I am not one of those persons. With sorrow I say it—I never have submitted, I never can submit, to my hard fate.

'Let me not omit to ask your indulgence for my behaviour, when we met at the cottage this morning.

'What unfavourable impression I may have produced on you, I dare not inquire. So little capable am I of concealing the vile feelings which sometimes get the better of me, that Miss Cristel (observe that I mention her with respect) appears to have felt positive alarm, on your account, when she looked at me.

'I may tell you, in confidence, that this charming person came to my side of the cottage, as soon as you had taken your departure, to intercede with me in your favour. "If your wicked mind is planning to do evil to Mr Roylake," she wrote in my book, "either you will promise me to give it up, or I will never allow me to see me again; I will even leave home secretly, to be out of your way." In that strong language she expressed—how shall I refer to it?—shall I say the sisterly interest that she felt in your welfare?'

I laid down the letter for a moment. If I had not already reproached myself for having misjudged Cristel—and if I had not, in that way, done her some little justice in my own better thoughts—I should never have recovered my self-respect after reading the deaf man's letter. The good girl! The dear good girl! Yes: that was how I thought of her, under the windows of my stepmother's boudoir—while Mrs Roylake, for all I knew to the contrary, might be looking down at me, and when Lady Lena, the noble and beautiful, was coming to dinner!

The letter concluded as follows:

'To return to myself. I gave Miss Cristel the promise on which she had insisted; and then, naturally enough, I inquired into her motive for interfering in your favour.

'She frankly admitted that she was interested in you. First: in grateful remembrance of old times, when you and your mother had been always good to her. Secondly: because she had found you as kind and as friendly as ever, now that you were a man and had become the greatest landowner in the county. There was the explanation I had asked for, at my service. And, on that, she left me.

'Did I believe her when I was meditating on our interview, alone in my room? Or did I suspect you of having robbed me of the only consolation that makes my life endurable?

'No such unworthy suspicion as this was admitted to my mind. With all my heart, I believe her. And with perfect sincerity, I trust You.

'If your knowledge of me has failed to convince you that there is any such thing as a better side to my nature, you will no doubt conclude that this letter is a trick of mine to throw you off your guard; and you will continue to distrust me as obstinately as ever. In that case, I will merely remind you that my letter is private and confidential, and I will not ask you to send me a reply.

'I remain, Sir, yours as you may receive me,

'THE DEAF LODGER.'

I wonder what another man, in my position, would have done when he had read this letter? Would he have seen in it nothing to justify some respect and some kindly feeling towards the writer? Could he have reconciled it to his conscience to leave the afflicted man who had trusted him without a word of reply?

For my part (do not forget what a young man I was in those days), I made up my mind to reply in the friendliest manner—that is to say, in person.

After consulting my watch, I satisfied myself that I could go to the mill, and get back again, before the hour fixed for our late dinner—supper we should have called it in Germany. For the second time that day, and without any hesitation, I took the road that led to Fordwitch Wood.

Crossing the glade, I encountered a stout young woman, filling a can with water from the spring. She curtseyed on seeing me. I asked if she belonged to the village.

The reply informed me that I had taken another of my servants for a stranger. The stout nymph of the spring was my kitchen-maid; and she was fetching the water which we drank at the house; 'and there's no water, sir, like *yours* for all the country round.' Furnished with these stores of information, I went my way, and the kitchen-maid went hers. She spoke, of course, of having seen her new master, on returning to the servants' hall. In this manner, as I afterwards heard, the discovery of me at the spring, and my departure by the path that led to the mill, reached Mrs Roylake's ears—the medium of information being the lady's own maid. So far, Fordwitch Wood seemed to be a place to avoid, in the interests of my domestic tranquillity.

Arriving at the cottage, I found the Lodger standing by the open window at which I had first seen him.

But, on this occasion, his personal appearance had undergone a singular process of transformation. The lower part of his face, from his nostrils to his chin, was hidden by a white handkerchief tied round it. He had removed the stopper from a strangely shaped bottle, and was absorbed in watching some interesting condition in a dusky liquid that it contained. To attract his attention by speaking was of course out of the question; I could only wait until he happened to look my way.

My patience was not severely tried: he soon replaced the stopper in the bottle, and, looking up from it, saw me. With his free hand, he quickly removed the handkerchief, and spoke.

'Let me ask you to wait in the boat-house,' he said; 'I will come to you directly.' He pointed round the corner of the new cottage; indicating of course the side of it that was farthest from the old building.

Following his directions, I first passed the door that he used in leaving or returning to his room, and then gained the bank of the river. On my right hand rose the mill building, with its big water-wheel—and, above it, a little higher up the stream, I recognised the boat-house; built out in the water on piles, and approached by a wooden pier.

No structure of this elaborate and expensive sort would have been set up by my father, for the miller's convenience. The boat-house had been built, many years since, by a rich retired tradesman with a mania for aquatic pursuits. Our ugly river had not answered his expectations, and our neighbourhood had abstained from returning his visits. When he left us, with his wherries and canoes and outriggers, the miller took possession of the abandoned boat-house. 'It's the sort of fixture that don't pay nohow,' old Toller remarked. 'Suppose you remove it—there's a waste of money. Suppose you knock it to pieces—is it worth a rich gentleman's while to sell a cartload of firewood?' Neither of these alternatives having been adopted, and nobody wanting an empty boat-house, the clumsy mill boat, hitherto tied to a stake, and exposed to the worst that the weather could do to injure it, was now snugly sheltered under a roof; with empty lockers (once occupied by aquatic luxuries) gaping on either side of it.

I was looking out on the river, and thinking of all that had happened since my first meeting with Cristel by moonlight, when the voice of the deaf man made itself discordantly heard, behind me.

'Let me apologise for receiving you here,' he said; 'and let me trouble you with one more of my confessions. Like other unfortunate deaf people, I suffer from nervous irritability. Sometimes, we restlessly change our places of abode. And sometimes, as in my case, we take refuge in variety of occupation. You remember the ideal narratives of crime which I was so fond of writing at one time?'

I gave the affirmative answer, in the usual way.

'Well,' he went on, 'my literary inventions have ceased to interest me. I have latterly resumed the chemical studies, associated with that happy time in my life when I was entering on the medical profession. Unluckily for you, I have been trying an experiment to-day, which makes such an abominable smell in my room that I dare not ask you to enter it. The fumes are not only disagreeable, but in some degree dangerous. You saw me at the window, perhaps, with my nose and mouth protected before I opened the bottle?'

I repeated the affirmative sign. He produced his little book of blank leaves, and opened it ready for use.

'May I hope,' he said, 'that your visit is intended as a favourable reply to my letter?'

I took the pencil, and answered him in these terms:

'Your letter has satisfied me that I was mistaken in treating you like a stranger. I have come here to express my regret at having failed to do you justice. Pray be assured that I believe in your better nature, and that I accept your letter in the spirit in which you have written it.'

He read my reply, and suddenly looked at me.

Never had I seen his beautiful eyes so brightly soft, so irresistibly tender, as they appeared now. He held out his hand to me. It is one of my small merits to be (in the popular phrase) as good as my word. I took his hand; well knowing that the action committed me to accepting his friendship.

In relating the events which form this narrative, I look back at the chain, as I add to it link by link—sometimes with surprise, sometimes with interest, and sometimes with the discovery that I have omitted a circumstance which it is necessary to replace. But I search my memory in vain, while I dwell on the lines that I have just written, for a recollection of some attendant event which might have warned me of the peril towards which I was advancing blindfold. My remembrance presents us as standing together with clasped hands; but nothing in the slightest degree ominous is associated with the picture. There was no sinister chill communicated from his hand to mine; no shocking accident happened close by us in the river; not even a passing cloud obscured the sunlight, shining in its gayest glory over our heads.

After having shaken hands, neither he nor I had apparently anything more to say. A little embarrassed, I turned to the boat-house window, and looked out. Trifling as the action was, my companion noticed it.

'Do you like that muddy river?' he asked.

I took the pencil again: 'Old associations make even the ugly Loke interesting to me.'

He sighed as he read those words. 'I wish, Mr Roylake, I could say the same. Your interesting river frightens me.'

It was needless to ask for the pencil again. My puzzled face begged for an explanation.

'When you were in my room,' he said, 'you may have noticed a second window which looks out on The Loke. I have got into a bad habit of sitting by that window on moonlight nights. I watch the flow of the stream, and it seems to associate itself with the flow of my thoughts. Nothing remarkable, so far—while I am awake. But, later, when I get to sleep, dreams come to me. All of them, sir, without exception connect Cristel with the river. Look at the stealthy current that makes no sound. In my last night's sleep, it made itself heard; it was flowing in my ears with a water-music of its own. No longer my deaf ears; I heard, in my dream, as well as you can hear. Yes; the same water-music, singing over and over again the same horrid song: "Fool, fool, no Cristel for you; bid her good-bye, bid her good-bye." I saw her floating away from me on those hideous waters. The cruel current held me back when I tried to follow her. I struggled and screamed and shivered and cried. I woke up with a start that shook me to pieces, and cursed your interesting river. Don't write to me about it again. Don't look at it again. Why did you bring up the subject? I beg your pardon; I had no right to say that. Let me be polite; let me be hospitable. I beg to invite you to come and see me, when my room is purified from its pestilent smell. I can only offer you a cup of tea. Oh, that river, that river, what devil set me talking about it? I'm not mad, Mr Roylake; only wretched. When may I expect you? Choose your own evening next week.'

Who could help pitying him? Compared with my sound sweet dreamless sleep, what dreadful nights were his!

I accepted his invitation as a matter of course. When we had completed our arrangements, it was time for me to think of returning to Trimley Deen. Moving towards the door, I accidentally directed his attention to the pier by which the boat-house was approached.

His face instantly reminded me of Cristel's description of him, when he was strongly and evilly moved. I too saw 'his beautiful eyes tell tales, and his pretty complexion change to a colour which turned him into an ugly man.' He seized my arm, and pointed to the pier, at the end of it which joined the river-bank. 'Pray accept my excuses; I can't answer for my temper if that wretch comes near me.' With this apology he hurried away; and sly Giles Toller, having patiently waited until the coast was clear, accosted me with his best bow, and said: 'Beautiful weather, isn't it, sir?'

I had no remarks to make on the weather; but I was interested in discovering what had happened at the cottage.

'You have mortally offended the gentleman who has just left me,' I said. 'What have you done?'

Mr Toller had purposes of his own to serve, and kept those purposes (as usual) exclusively in view: *he* presented deaf ears to me now!

'I don't think I ever remember such wonderful weather, sir, in my time; and I'm an old fellow, as I needn't tell you. Being at the mill just now, I saw you in the boat-house, and came to pay my respects. Would you be so good as to look at this slip of paper, Mr Gerard? If you will kindly ask what it is, you will in a manner help me.'

I knew but too well what it was. 'The repairs again!' I said resignedly. 'Hand it over, you obstinate old man.'

Mr Toller was so tickled by my discovery, and by the cheering prospect consequent on seeing his list of repairs safe in my pocket, that he laughed until I really thought he would shake his lean little body to pieces. By way of bringing his merriment to an end, I assumed a look of severity, and insisted on knowing how he had offended the Lodger. My venerable tenant, trembling for his repairs, drifted into a question of personal experience, and seemed to antici-pate that it might improve my temper.

'When you have a woman about the house, Mr Gerard, you may have noticed that she's an everlasting expense to you—especially when she's a young one. Isn't that so?'

I inquired if he applied this remark to his daughter.

'That's it, sir; I'm talking of Cristy. When her back's up, there isn't her equal in England for strong language. My gentleman has misbe-haved himself in some way (since you were with us this morning, sir); how, I don't quite understand. All I can tell you is, I've given him notice to quit. A clear loss of money to me every week, and Cristy's responsible for it. Yes, sir! I've been worked up to it by my girl. If Cristy's mother had asked me to get rid of a paying lodger, I should have told her to go to——we won't say where, sir; you'll know where when you're married yourself. The upshot of it is that I have offended my gentleman, for the sake of my girl: which last is a luxury I can't afford, unless I let the rooms again. If you hear of a tenant, say what a good landlord I am, and what sweet pretty rooms I've got to let.'

I led the way to the bank of the river, before Mr Toller could make any more requests.

We passed the side of the old cottage. The door was open; and I saw Cristel employed in the kitchen.

My watch told me that I had still two or three minutes to spare; and my guilty remembrance of the message that I had pinned to the door suggested an immediate expression of regret. I approached Cristel with a petition for pardon on my lips. She looked distrustfully at the door of communication with the new cottage, as if she expected to see it opened from the other side.

'Not now!' she said—and went on sadly with her household work.

'May I see you to-morrow?' I asked.

'It had better not be here, sir,' was the only reply she made.

I offered to meet her at any other place which she might appoint. Cristel persisted in leaving it to me; she spoke absently, as if she was thinking all the time of something else. I could propose no better place, at the moment, than the spring in Fordwitch Wood. She consented to meet me there, on the next day, if seven o'clock in the morning would not be too early for me. My German habits had accustomed me to early rising. She heard me tell her this—and looked again at the Lodger's door—and abruptly wished me good evening.

Her polite father was shocked at this unceremonious method of dismissing the great man, who had only to say the word and stop the repairs. 'Where are your manners, Cristy?' he asked indignantly. Before he could say another word, I was out of the cottage.

As I passed the spring on my way home, I thought of my two appointments. On that evening, my meeting with the daughter of the lord. On the next morning, my meeting with the daughter of the miller. Lady Lena at dinner; Cristel before breakfast. If Mrs Roylake found out *that* social contrast, what would she say? I was a merry young fool; I burst out laughing.

# CHAPTER IX

## MRS ROYLAKE'S GAME: FIRST MOVE

The dinner at Trimley Deen has left in my memory little that I can distinctly recall. Only a faintly-marked vision of Lady Lena rewards me for doing my best to remember her. A tall slim graceful person, dressed in white with a simplicity which is the perfection of art, presents to my admiration gentle blue eyes, a pale complexion delicately touched with colour, a well-carried head crowned by lovely light brown hair. So far, time helps the reviving past to come to life again—and permits nothing more. I cannot say that I now remember the voice once so musical in my ears, or that I am able to repeat the easy unaffected talk which once interested me, or that I see again (in my thoughts) the perfect charm of manner which delighted everybody, not forgetting myself. My unworthy self, I might say; for I was the only young man, honoured by an introduction to Lady Lena, who stopped at admiration, and never made use of opportunity to approach love.

On the other hand, I distinctly recollect what my stepmother and I said to each other when our guests had wished us good-night.

If I am asked to account for this, I can only reply that the conspiracy to lead me into proposing marriage to Lady Lena first showed itself on the occasion to which I have referred. In her eagerness to reach her ends, Mrs Roylake failed to handle the fine weapons of deception as cleverly as usual. Even I, with my small experience of worldly women, discovered the object that she had in view.

I had retired to the seclusion of the smoking-room, and was already encircled by the clouds which float on the heaven of tobacco, when I heard a rustling of silk outside, and saw the smile of Mrs Roylake beginning to captivate me through the open door.

'If you throw away your cigar,' cried this amiable person, 'you will drive me out of the room. Dear Gerard, I like your smoke.'

My fat man in black, coming in at the moment to bring me some soda water, looked at his mistress with an expression of amazement and horror, which told me that he now saw Mrs Roylake in the smoking-room for the first time. I involved myself in new clouds. If I suffocated my stepmother, her own polite equivocation would justify the act. She settled herself opposite to me in an armchair.

The agonies that she must have suffered, in preventing her face from expressing emotions of disgust, I dare not attempt to imagine, even at this distance of time.

'Now, Gerard, let us talk about the two ladies. What do you think of my friend, Lady Rachel?'

'I don't like your friend, Lady Rachel.'

'You astonish me. Why?'

'I think she's a false woman.'

'Heavens, what a thing to say of a lady—and that lady my friend! Her politics may very reasonably have surprised you. But surely her vigorous intellect ought to have challenged your admiration; you can't deny that?'

I was not clever enough to be able to deny it. But I was bold enough to say that Lady Rachel seemed to me to be a woman who talked for the sake of producing effect. She expressed opinions, as I ventured to declare, which (in her position) I did not believe she could honestly entertain.

Mrs Roylake entered a vigorous protest. She assured me that I was completely mistaken. 'Lady Rachel,' she said, 'is the most perfectly candid person in the whole circle of my acquaintance.'

With the best intentions on my part, this was more than I could patiently endure.

'Isn't she the daughter of a nobleman?' I asked. 'Doesn't she owe her rank and her splendour, and the respect that people show to her, to the fortunate circumstance of her birth? And yet she talks as if she was a red republican. You yourself heard her say that she was a thorough Radical, and hoped she might live to see the House of Lords abolished. Oh, I heard her! And what is more, I listened so attentively to such sentiments as these, from a lady with a title, that I can repeat, word for word, what she said next. "We hav'n't deserved our own titles; we hav'n't earned our own incomes; and we legislate for the country, without having been trusted by the country. In short, we are a set of impostors, and the time is coming when we shall be found out." Do you believe she really meant that? All as false as false can be—that's what I say of it.'

There I stopped, privately admiring my own eloquence.

Quite a mistake on my part; my eloquence had done just what Mrs Roylake wished me to do. She wanted an opportunity of dropping Lady Rachel, and taking up Lady Lena, with a producible reason which forbade the imputation of a personal motive on her part. I had furnished her with the reason. Thus far, I cannot deny it, my step-mother was equal to herself.

'Really, Gerard, you are so violent in your opinions that I am sorry I spoke of Lady Rachel. Shall I find you equally prejudiced, and equally severe, if I change the subject to dear Lady Lena? Oh, don't say you think She is false, too!'

Here Mrs Roylake made her first mistake. She over-acted her part; and, when it was too late, she arrived, I suspect, at that conclusion herself.

'If you hav'n't seen that I sincerely admire Lady Lena,' I said, as smartly as I could, 'the sooner you disfigure yourself with a pair of spectacles, my dear lady, the better. She is very pretty, perfectly unaffected, and, if I may presume to judge, delightfully well-bred and well-dressed.'

My stepmother's face actually brightened with pleasure. Reflecting on it now, I am strongly disposed to think that she had not allowed her feelings to express themselves so unreservedly, since the time when she was a girl. After all, Mrs Roylake was paying her step-son a compliment in trying to entrap him into a splendid marriage. It was my duty to think kindly of my ambitious relative. I did my duty.

'You really like my sweet Lena?' she said. 'I am so glad. What were you talking about, with her? She made you exert all your powers of conversation, and she seemed to be deeply interested.'

More over-acting! Another mistake! And I could see through it! With no English subject which we could discuss in common, Lady Lena's ready tact alluded to my past life. Mrs Roylake had told her that I was educated at a German University. She had heard vaguely of students with long hair, who wore Hessian boots,* and fought duels; and she appealed to my experience to tell her something more. I did my best to interest her, with very indifferent success, and was un-deservedly rewarded by a patient attention, which presented the unselfish refinements of courtesy under their most perfect form.

But let me do my step-mother justice. She contrived to bend me to her will, before she left the smoking-room—I am sure I don't know how.

'You have entertained the charming daughters at dinner,' she reminded me; 'and the least you can do, after that, is to pay your respects to their noble father. In your position, my dear boy, you cannot neglect our English customs without producing the worst possible impression.'

In two words, I found myself pledged, under pretence of visiting my lord, to improve my acquaintance with Lady Lena on the next day.

'And pray be careful,' Mrs Roylake proceeded, still braving the atmosphere of the smoking-room, 'not to look surprised if you find Lord Uppercliff's house presenting rather a poor appearance just now.'

I was dying for another cigar, and I entirely misunderstood the words of warning which had just been addressed to me. I tried to bring our interview to a close by making a generous proposal.

'Does he want money?' I asked. 'I'll lend him some with the greatest pleasure.'

Mrs Roylake's horror expressed itself in a little thin wiry scream.

'Oh, Gerard, what people you must have lived among! What shocking ignorance of my lord's enormous fortune! He and his family have only just returned to their country seat, after a long absence— parliament you know, and foreign baths, and so on—and their English establishment is not yet complete. I don't know what mistake you may not make next. Do listen to what I want to say to you.'

Listening, I must acknowledge, with an absent mind, my attention was suddenly seized by Mrs Roylake—without the slightest conscious effort towards that end, on the part of the lady herself.

The first words that startled me, in her flow of speech, were these:

'And I must not forget to tell you of poor Lord Uppercliff's misfortune. He had a fall, some time since, and broke his leg. As I think, he was so unwise as to let a plausible young surgeon set the broken bone. Anyway, the end of it is that my lord slightly limps when he walks; and pray remember that he hates to see it noticed. Lady Rachel doesn't agree with me in attributing her father's lameness to his surgeon's want of experience. Between ourselves, the man seems to have interested her. Very handsome, very clever, very agreeable, and the manners of a gentleman. When his medical services came to an end, he was quite an acquisition at their parties in London—with one drawback: he mysteriously disappeared, and has never been heard of since. Ask Lady Lena about it. She will give you all the details, without her elder sister's bias in favour of the handsome young man. What a pretty compliment you are paying me! You really look as if I had interested you.'

Knowing what I knew, I was unquestionably interested.

Although the recent return of Lord Uppercliff and his daughter to their country home had, as yet, allowed no opportunity of a meeting, out of doors, between the deaf Lodger and the friends whom he had lost sight of—no doubt at the time of his serious illness—still, the inevitable discovery might happen on any day. What result would follow? And what would be the effect on Lady Rachel, when she met with the fascinating young surgeon, and discovered the terrible change in him?

## CHAPTER X

### WARNED!

We were alone in the glade, by the side of the spring. At that early hour there were no interruptions to dread; but Cristel was ill at ease. She seemed to be eager to get back to the cottage as soon as possible.

'Father tells me,' she began abruptly, 'he saw you at the boat-house. And it seemed to him, that you were behaving yourself like a friend to that terrible man.'

I reminded her of my having expressed the fear that we had been needlessly hard on him; and, I added that he had written a letter which confirmed me in that opinion. She looked, not only disappointed, but even alarmed.

'I had hoped,' she said sadly, 'that father was mistaken.'

'So little mistaken,' I assured her, 'that I am going to drink tea with the man who seems to frighten you. I hope he will ask you to meet me.'

She recoiled from the bare idea of an invitation.

'Will you hear what I want to tell you?' she said earnestly. 'You may alter your opinion if you know what I have been foolish enough to do, when you saw me go to the other side of the cottage.'

'Dear Cristel, I know what I owe to your kind interest in me on that occasion!' Before I could say a word of apology for having wronged her by my suspicions, she insisted on an explanation of what I had just said.

'Did he mention it in his letter?' she asked.

I owned that I had obtained my information in this way. And I declared that he had expressed his admiration of her, and his belief in her, in terms which made it a subject of regret to me not to be able to show what he had written.

Cristel forgot her fear of our being interrupted. Her dismay expressed itself in a cry that rang through the wood.

'You even believe in his letter?' she exclaimed. 'Mr Gerard! His writing in that way to You about Me is a proof that he lies; and I'll make you see it. If you were anybody else but yourself, I would leave you to your fate. Yes, your fate,' she passionately repeated. 'Oh, forgive me, sir! I'm behaving disrespectfully; I beg your pardon. No, no; let me go on. When I spoke to him in your best interests (as I did most truly believe) I never suspected what mischief I had done, till I looked in his face. Then, I saw how he hated you, and how vilely he was thinking in secret of me—'

Pure delusion! How could I allow it to go on? I interrupted her.

'My dear, you have quite mistaken him. As I have already said, he sincerely respects you—and he owns that he misjudged me when he and I first met.'

'What! Is *that* in his letter too? It's worse even than I feared. Again, and again, and again, I say it'—she stamped on the ground in the fervour of her conviction—'he hates you with the hatred that never forgives and never forgets. You think him a good man. Do you suppose I would have begged and prayed of my father to send him away, without having reasons that justified me? Mr Gerard, you force me to tell you what my unlucky visit did put into his head. Yes, he does believe—believes firmly—that you have forgotten what is due to your rank; that I have been wicked enough to forget it too; and that you are going to take me away from him. Say what he may, and write what he may, he is deceiving you for his own wicked ends. If you go to drink tea with him, God only knows what cause you may have to regret it. Forgive me for being so violent, sir; I have done now. You have made me very wretched, but you are too good and kind to mean it. Good-bye.'

I took her hand, I pressed it tenderly; I was touched, deeply touched.

No! let me write honestly. Her eyes betrayed her, her voice betrayed her, while she said her parting words. What I saw, what

I heard, was no longer within the limits of doubt. The sweet girl's interest in my welfare was not the merely friendly interest which she herself believed it to be. And I said just now that I was 'touched'. Cant! Lies! I loved her more dearly than I had ever loved her yet. There is the truth—stripped of poor prudery, and the mean fear of being called Vain!

What I might have said to her, if the opportunity had offered itself, may be easily imagined. Before I could open my lips, a man appeared on the path which led from the mill to the spring—the man whom Cristel had secretly suspected of a design to follow her.

I felt her hand trembling in my hand, and gave it a little encouraging squeeze. 'Let us judge him,' I suggested, 'by what he says and does, on finding us together.'

Without an attempt at concealment on his part, he advanced towards us briskly, smiling and waving his hand.

'What, Mr Roylake, you have already found out the virtues of your wonderful spring, and you are drinking the water before breakfast! I have often done it myself when I was not too lazy to get up. And this charming girl,' he went on, turning to Cristel, 'has she been trying the virtues of the spring by your advice? She won't listen to me, or I should have recommended it long since. See me set the example.'

He took a silver mug from his pocket, and descended the few steps that led to the spring. Allowing for the dreadful deaf monotony in his voice, no man could have been more innocently joyous and agreeable. While he was taking his morning draught, I appealed to Cristel's better sense.

'Is this the hypocrite, who is deceiving me for his own wicked ends?' I asked. 'Does he look like the jealous monster who is plotting my destruction, and who will succeed if I am fool enough to accept his invitation?'

Poor dear, she was as obstinate as ever! 'Think over what I have said to you—think, for your own sake,' was her only reply.

'And a little for *your* sake?' I ventured to add.

She ran away from me, taking the path which would lead her home again. The deaf man and I were left together. He looked after her until she was out of sight. Then he produced his book of blank leaves. But, instead of handing it to me as usual, he began to write in it himself.

'I have something to say to you,' he explained.

It was only possible, while the book was in his possession, to remind him that I could hear, and that he could speak, by using the language of signs. I touched my lips, and pointed to him; I touched my ear, and pointed to myself.

'Yes,' he said, understanding me with his customary quickness; 'but I want you to remember as well as to hear. When I have filled this leaf, I shall beg you to keep it about you, and to refer to it from time to time.'

He wrote on steadily, until he had filled both sides of the slip of paper.

'Quite a little letter,' he said. 'Pray read it.'

This is what I read:

'You must have seen for yourself that I was incapable of insulting you and Miss Cristel by an outbreak of jealousy, when I found you together just now. Only remember that we all have our weaknesses, and that it is my hard lot to be in a state of contest with the inherited evil which is the calamity of my life. With your encouragement, I may resist temptation in the future, and keep the better part of me in authority over my thoughts and actions. But, be on your guard, and advise Miss Cristel to be on her guard, against false appearances. As we all know, they lie like truth. Consider me. Pity me. I ask no more.'

Straightforward and manly and modest—I appeal to any unprejudiced mind whether I should not have committed a mean action, if I had placed an evil construction on this?

'Am I understood?' he asked.

I signed to him to give me his book, and relieved him of anxiety in these words:

'If I had failed to understand you, I should have felt ashamed of myself. May I show what you have written to Cristel?'

He smiled, more sweetly and pleasantly than I had seen him smile yet.

'If you wish it,' he answered. 'I leave it entirely to you. Thank you—and good morning.'

Having advanced a few steps on his way to the cottage, he paused, and reminded me of the tea-drinking: 'Don't forget to-morrow evening, at seven o'clock.'

# CHAPTER XI

## WARNED AGAIN!

The breakfast hour had not yet arrived when I got home. I went into the garden to refresh my eyes—a little weary of the solemn uniformity of colour in Fordwitch Wood—by looking at the flowers.

Reaching the terrace, in the first place, I heard below me a man's voice, speaking in tones of angry authority, and using language which expressed an intention of turning somebody out of the garden. I at once descended the steps which led to the flower-beds. The man in authority proved to be one of my gardeners; and the man threatened with instant expulsion was the oddly-dressed servant of the friend whom I had just left.

The poor fellow's ugly face presented a picture of shame and contrition, the moment I showed myself. He piteously entreated me to look over it, and to forgive him.

'Wait a little,' I said. 'Let me see if I have anything to forgive.' I turned to the gardener. 'What is your complaint of this man?'

'He's a trespasser on your grounds, sir. And, his impudence, to say the least of it, is such as I never met with before.'

'What harm has he done?'

'Harm, sir?'

'Yes—harm. Has he been picking the flowers?'

The gardener looked round him, longing to refer me to the necessary evidence, and failing to discover it anywhere. The wretched trespasser took heart of grace, and said a word in his own defence.

'Nobody ever knew me to misbehave myself in a gentleman's garden,' he said; 'I own, sir, to having taken a peep at the flowers, over the wall.'

'And they tempted you to look a little closer at them?'

'That's the truth, sir.'

'So you are fond of flowers?'

'Yes, sir. I once failed in business as a nurseryman—but I don't blame the flowers.'

The delightful simplicity of this was lost on the gardener. I heard the brute mutter to himself: 'Gammon!'* For once I asserted my authority over my servant.

'Understand this,' I said to him: 'I don't confine the enjoyment of my garden to myself and my friends. Any well-behaved persons are welcome to come here and look at the flowers. Remember that. Now you may go.'

Having issued these instructions, I next addressed myself to my friend in the shabby shooting jacket; telling him to roam wherever he liked, and to stay as long as he pleased. Instead of thanking me and using his liberty, he hesitated, and looked thoroughly ill at ease.

'What's the matter now?' I asked.

'I'm afraid you don't know, sir, who it is you are so kind to. I've been something else in my time, besides a nurseryman.'

'What have you been?'

'A prize-fighter.'

If he expected me to exhibit indignation or contempt, he was disappointed. My ignorance treated him as civilly as ever.

'What is a prize-fighter?' I inquired.

The unfortunate pugilist looked at me in speechless bewilderment. I told him that I had been brought up among foreigners, and that I had never even seen an English newspaper for the last ten years. This explanation seemed to encourage the man of few words: it set him talking freely at last. He delivered a treatise on the art of prize-fighting, and he did something else which I found more amusing— he told me his name. To my small sense of humour his name, so to speak, completed this delightfully odd man: it was Gloody. As to the list of his misfortunes, the endless length of it became so unendurably droll, that we both indulged in unfeeling fits of laughter over the sorrows of Gloody. The first lucky accident of the poor fellow's life had been, literally, the discovery of him by his present master.

This event interested me. I said I should like to hear how it had happened.

Gloody modestly described himself as 'one of the starving lot, sir, that looks out for small errands. I got my first dinner for three days, by carrying a gentleman's portmanteau for him. And he, if you please, was afterwards my master. He lived alone. Bless you, he was as deaf then as he is now. He says to me, "If you bawl in my ears, I'll knock you down." I thought to myself, you wouldn't say that, master, if you knew how I was employed twenty years ago. He took me into his service, sir, because I was ugly. "I'm so handsome myself," he says, "I want a contrast of something ugly about me." You may have noticed that he's a bitter one—and bitterly enough he sometimes behaved to me. But there's a good side to him. He gives me his old clothes, and sometimes he speaks almost as kindly to me as you do. But for him, I believe I should have perished of starvation—'

He suddenly checked himself. Whether he was afraid of wearying me, or whether some painful recollection had occurred to him, it was of course impossible to say.

The ugly face, to which he owed his first poor little morsel of prosperity, became overclouded by care and doubt. Bursting into expressions of gratitude which I had certainly not deserved—expressions, so evidently sincere, that they bore witness to constant ill-usage suffered in the course of his hard life—he left me with a headlong haste of movement, driven away as I fancied by an unquiet mind.

I watched him retreating along the path, and saw him stop abruptly, still with his back to me. His deep strong voice travelled farther than he supposed. I heard him say to himself: 'What an infernal rascal I am!' He waited a little, and turned my way again. Slowly and reluctantly, he came back to me. As he approached I saw the man, who had lived by the public exhibition of his courage, looking at me with fear plainly visible in the change of his colour, and the expression of his face.

'Anything wrong?' I inquired.

'Nothing wrong, sir. Might I be so bold as to ask —'

We waited a little; I gave him time to collect his thoughts. Perhaps the silence confused him. Anyhow, I was obliged to help him to get on.

'What do you wish to ask of me?' I said.

'I wished to speak, sir—'

He stopped again.

'About what?' I asked.

'About to-morrow evening.'

'Well?'

He burst out with it, at last. 'Are you coming to drink tea with my master?'

'Of course, I am coming! Mr Gloody, do you know that you rather surprise me?'

'I hope no offence, sir.'

'Nonsense! It seems odd, my good fellow, that your master shouldn't have told you I was coming to drink tea with him. Isn't it your business to get the things ready?'

He shifted from one foot to another, and looked as if he wished himself out of my way. At a later time of my life, I have observed that these are signs by which an honest man is apt to confess that he has told, or is going to tell, a lie. As it was, I only noticed that he answered confusedly.

'I can't quite say, Mr Roylake, that my master didn't mention the thing to me.'

'But you failed to understand him—is that it?'

'Well, sir, if I want to ask him anything I have to write it. I'm slow at writing, and bad at writing, and he isn't always patient. However, as you reminded me just now, I have got to get the things ready. To cut it short, perhaps I might say that I didn't quite expect the tea-party would come off.'

'Why shouldn't it come off?'

'Well, sir, you might have some other engagement.'

Was this a hint? or only an excuse? In either case it was high time, if he still refused to speak out, that I should set him the example.

'You have given me some curious information,' I said, 'on the subject of fighting with the fists; and you have made me understand the difference between "fair hitting" and "foul hitting". Are you hitting fair now? Very likely I am mistaken—but you seem to me to be trying to prevent my accepting your master's invitation.'

He pulled off his hat in a hurry.

'I beg your pardon, sir; I won't detain you any longer. If you will allow me, I'll take my leave.'

'Don't go, Mr Gloody, without telling me whether I am right or wrong. Is there really some objection to my coming to tea to-morrow?'

'Quite a mistake, sir,' he said, still in a hurry. 'I've led you wrong without meaning it—being an ignorant man, and not knowing how to express myself. Don't think me ungrateful, Mr Roylake! After your kindness to me, I'd go through fire and water for you—I would!'

His sunken eyes moistened, his big voice faltered. I let him leave me, in mercy to the strong feeling which I had innocently roused. But I shook hands with him first. Yielding to one of my headlong impulses? Yes. And doing a very indiscreet thing? Wait a little—and we shall see.

## CHAPTER XII
### WARNED FOR THE LAST TIME!

My loyalty towards the afflicted man, whose friendly advances I had
seen good reason to return, was in no sense shaken. His undeserved
misfortunes, his manly appeal to me at the spring, his hopeless attachment to the beautiful girl whose aversion towards him I had unhappily
encouraged, all pleaded with me in his favour. I had accepted his
invitation; and I had no other engagement to claim me: it would have
been an act of meanness amounting to a confession of fear, if I had sent
an excuse. Still, while Cristel's entreaties and Cristel's influence
had failed to shake me, Gloody's strange language and Gloody's
incomprehensible conduct had troubled my mind. I felt vaguely
uneasy; irritated by my own depression of spirits. If I had been a
philosopher, I should have recognised the symptoms of a very
common attack of a very widely-spread moral malady. The meanest
of all human infirmities is also the most universal; and the name of it is
Self-esteem.

It is perhaps only right to add that my patience had been tried by
the progress of domestic events, which affected Lady Lena and
myself—viewed as victims.

Calling, with my stepmother, at Lord Uppercliff's house later in
the day, I perceived that Lady Rachel and Mrs Roylake found (or
made) an opportunity of talking together confidentially in a corner;
and, once or twice, I caught them looking at Lady Lena and at me.
Even Lord Uppercliff (perhaps not yet taken into their confidence)
noticed the proceedings of the two ladies, and seemed to be at a loss to
understand them.

When Mrs Roylake and I were together again, on our way home,
I was prepared to hear the praise of Lady Lena, followed by a delicate
examination into the state of my heart. Neither of these anticipations
was realized. Once more, my clever stepmother had puzzled me.

Mrs Roylake talked as fluently as ever; exhausting one commonplace subject after another, without the slightest allusion to my lord's
daughter, to my matrimonial prospects, or to my visits at the mill.
I was secretly annoyed, feeling that my stepmother's singular indifference to domestic interests of paramount importance, at other
times, must have some object in view, entirely beyond the reach of

my penetration. If I had dared to commit such an act of rudeness, I should have jumped out of the carriage, and have told Mrs Roylake that I meant to walk home.

The day was Sunday. I loitered about the garden, listening to the distant church-bell ringing for the afternoon service. Without any cause that I knew of to account for it, I was so restless that nothing I could do attracted me or quieted me.

Returning to the house, I tried to occupy myself with my collection of insects, sadly neglected of late. Useless! My own moths failed to interest me.

I went back to the garden. Passing the open window of one of the lower rooms which looked out on the terrace, I saw Mrs Roylake reading a book in sad-coloured binding. She was yawning over it fearfully, when she discovered that I was looking at her. Equal to any emergency, this remarkable woman instantly handed to me a second and similar volume. 'The most precious sermons, Gerard, that have been written in our time.' I looked at the book; I opened the book; I recovered my presence of mind, and handed it back. If a female humbug was on one side of the window, a male humbug was on the other. 'Please keep it for me till the evening,' I said; 'I am going for a walk.'

Which way did I turn my steps?

Men will wonder what possessed me—women will think it a proceeding that did me credit—I took the familiar road which led to the gloomy wood and the guilty river. The longing in me to see Cristel again, was more than I could resist. Not because I was in love with her; only because I had left her in distress.

Beyond the spring, and within a short distance of the river, I saw a lady advancing towards me on the path which led from the mill.

Brisk, smiling, tripping along like a young girl, behold the mock-republican, known in our neighbourhood as Lady Rachel! She held out both hands to me. But for her petticoats, I should have thought I had met with a jolly young man.

'I have been wandering in your glorious wood, Mr Roylake. Anything to escape the respectable classes on Sunday, patronising piety on the way to afternoon church. I must positively make a sketch of the cottage by the mill—I mean, of course, the picturesque side of it. That fine girl of Toller's was standing at the door. She is really handsomer than ever. Are you going to see her, you wicked man?

Which do you admire—that gipsy complexion, or Lena's lovely skin? Both, I have no doubt, at your age. Good-bye.'

When we had left each other, I thought of the absent Captain in the Navy who was Lady Rachel's husband. He was a perfect stranger— but I put myself in his place, and felt that I too should have gone to sea.

Old Toller was alone in his kitchen, evidently annoyed and angry.

'We are all at sixes and sevens, Mr Gerard. I've had another row with that deaf-devil—my new name for him, and I think it's rather clever. He swears, sir, that he won't go at the end of his week's notice. Says, if I think I'm likely to get rid of him before he has married Cristy, I'm mistaken. Threatens, if any man attempts to take her away, he'll shoot her, and shoot the man, and shoot himself. Aha! old as I am, if he believes he's going to have it all his own way, he's mistaken. I'll be even with him. You mark my words: I'll be even with him.'

That old Toller—the most exasperating of men, judged by a quick temper—had irritated my friend into speaking rashly was plain enough. Nevertheless, I felt some anxiety (jealous anxiety, I am afraid) about Cristel. After looking round the kitchen again, I asked where she was.

'Sitting forlorn in her bedroom, crying,' her father told me. 'I went out for a walk by the river, and I sat down, and (being Sunday) I fell asleep. When I woke, and got home again just now, that was how I found her. I don't like to hear my girl crying; she's as good as gold and better. No, sir; our deaf-devil is not to blame for this. He has given Cristy no reason to complain of him. She says so herself—and she never told a lie yet.'

'But, Mr Toller,' I objected, 'something must have happened to distress her. Has she not told you what it is?'

'Not she! Obstinate about it. Leaves me to guess. It's clear to my mind, Mr Gerard, that somebody has got at her in my absence, and said something to upset her. You will ask me who the person is. I can't say I have found that out yet.'

'But you mean to try?'

'Yes; I mean to try.'

He answered me with little of the energy which generally distinguished him. Perhaps he was fatigued, or perhaps he had something else to think of. I offered a suggestion.

'When we are in want of help,' I said, 'we sometimes find it, nearer than we had ventured to expect—at our own doors.'

The ancient miller rose at that hint like a fish at a fly.

'Gloody!' he cried.

'Find him at once, Mr Toller.'

He hobbled to the door—and looked round at me. 'I've got burdens on my mind,' he explained, 'or I should have thought of it too.' Having done justice to his own abilities, he bustled out. In less than a minute, he was back again in a state of breathless triumph. 'Gloody has seen the person,' he announced; 'and (what do you think, sir?) it's a woman!'

I beckoned to Gloody, waiting modestly at the door, to come in, and tell me what he had discovered.

'I saw her outside, sir—rapping at the door here, with her parasol.' That was the servant's report.

Her parasol? Not being acquainted with the development of dress among female servants in England, I asked if she was a lady. There seemed to be no doubt of it in the man's mind. She was also, as Gloody supposed, a person whom he had never seen before.

'How is it you are not sure of that?' I said.

'Well, sir, she was waiting to be let in; and I was behind her, coming out of the wood.'

'Who let her in?'

'Miss Cristel.' His face brightened with an expression of interest when he mentioned the miller's daughter. He went on with his story without wanting questions to help him. 'Miss Cristel looked like a person surprised at seeing a stranger—what *I* should call a free and easy stranger. She walked in, sir, as if the place belonged to her.'

I am not suspicious by nature, as I hope and believe. But I began to be reminded of Lady Rachel already.

'Did you notice the lady's dress?' I asked.

A woman who had seen her would have been able to describe every morsel of her dress from head to foot. The man had only observed her hat; and all he could say was that he thought it 'a smartish one'.

'Any particular colour?' I went on.

'Not that I know of. Dark green, I think.'

'Any ornament in it?'

'Yes! A purple feather.'

The hat I had seen on the head of that hateful woman was now sufficiently described—for a man. Sly old Toller, leaving Gloody unnoticed, and keeping his eye on me, saw the signs of conviction in my face, and said with his customary audacity: 'Who is she?'

I followed, at my humble distance, the example of Sir Walter Scott, when inquisitive people asked him if he was the author of the Waverley Novels.* In plain English, I denied all knowledge of the stranger wearing the green hat. But, I was naturally desirous of discovering next what Lady Rachel had said; and I asked to speak with Cristel. Her far-seeing father might or might not have perceived a chance of listening to our conversation. He led me to the door of his daughter's room; and stood close by, when I knocked softly, and begged that she would come out.

The tone of the poor girl's voice—answering, 'Forgive me, sir; I can't do it'—convicted the she-socialist (as I thought) of merciless conduct of some sort. Assuming this conclusion to be the right one, I determined, then and there, that Lady Rachel should not pass the doors of Trimley Deen again. If her bosom-friend resented that wise act of severity by leaving the house, I should submit with resignation, and should remember the circumstance with pleasure.

'I am afraid you are ill, Cristel?' was all I could find to say, under the double disadvantage of speaking through a door, and having a father listening at my side.

'Oh no, Mr Gerard, not ill. A little low in my mind, that's all. I don't mean to be rude, sir—pray be kinder to me than ever! pray let me be!'

I said I would return on the next day; and left the room with a sore heart.

Old Toller highly approved of my conduct. He rubbed his fleshless hands, and whispered: 'You'll get it out of Cristy to-morrow, and I'll help you.'

I found Gloody waiting for me outside the cottage. He was anxious about Miss Cristel; his only excuse, he told me, being the fear that she might be ill. Having set him at ease, in that particular, I said: 'You seem to be interested in Miss Cristel.'

His answer raised him a step higher in my estimation.

'How can I help it, sir?'

An odd man, with a personal appearance that might excite a prejudice against him, in some minds. I failed to see it myself in that light. It struck me, as I walked home, that Cristel might have made many a worse friend than the retired prize-fighter.

A change in my manner was of course remarked by Mrs Roylake's ready observation. I told her that I had been annoyed, and offered no other explanation. Wonderful to relate, she showed no curiosity and no surprise. More wonderful still, at every fair opportunity that offered, she kept out of my way.

My next day's engagement being for seven o'clock in the evening, I put Mrs Roylake's self-control to a new test. With prefatory excuses, I informed her that I should not be able to dine at home as usual. Impossible as it was that she could have been prepared to hear this, her presence of mind was equal to the occasion. I left the house, followed by my stepmother's best wishes for a pleasant evening.

Hoping to speak with Cristel alone, I had arranged to reach the cottage before seven o'clock.

On the river-margin of the wood, I was confronted by a wild gleam of beauty in the familiar view, for which previous experience had not prepared me. Am I wrong in believing that all scenery, no matter how magnificent or how homely it may be, derives a splendour not its own from favouring conditions of light and shade? Our gloomy trees and our repellent river presented an aspect superbly transfigured, under the shadows of the towering clouds, the fantastic wreaths of the mist, and the lurid reddening of the sun as it stooped to its setting. Lovely interfusions of sobered colour rested, faded, returned again, on the upper leaves of the foliage as they lightly moved. The mist, rolling capriciously over the waters, revealed the grandly deliberate course of the flowing current, while it dimmed the turbid earthy yellow that discoloured and degraded the stream under the full glare of day. While my eyes followed the successive transformations of the view, as the hour advanced, tender and solemn influences breathed their balm over my mind. Days, happy days that were past, revived. Again, I walked hand in hand with my mother, among the scenes that were round me, and learnt from her to be grateful for the beauty of the earth, with a heart that felt it. We were tracing our way along our favourite woodland path; and we found a companion of tender years, hiding from us. She showed herself, blushing, hesitating, offering a nosegay of wild flowers. My mother whispered to me—I thanked the little mill-girl, and gave her a kiss. Did I feel the child's breath, in my day-dream, still fluttering on my cheek? Was I conscious of her touch? I started, trembled, returned reluctantly to my present self. A visible hand touched my arm. As I turned suddenly, a living breath played on my face. The child had faded into a vanishing shade: the perfected woman who had grown from her had stolen on me unawares, and was asking me to pardon her. 'Mr Gerard, you were lost in your thoughts; I spoke, and you never heard me.'

I looked at her in silence.

Was this the dear Cristel so well known to me? Or was it a mockery of her that had taken her place?

'I hope I have not offended you?' she said.

'You have surprised me,' I answered. 'Something must have happened, since I saw you last. What is it?'

'Nothing.'

I advanced a step, and drew her closer to me. A dark flush discoloured her face. An overpowering brilliancy flashed from her eyes; there was an hysterical defiance in her manner. 'Are you excited? are you angry? are you trying to startle me by acting a part?' I urged those questions on her, one after another; and I was loudly and confidently answered.

'I dare say I am excited, Mr Gerard, by the honour that has been done me. You are going to keep your engagement, of course? Well, your friend, your favourite friend, has invited me to meet you. No! that's not quite true. I invited myself—the deaf gentleman submitted.'

'Why did you invite yourself?'

'Because a tea-party is not complete without a woman.'

Her manner was as strangely altered as her looks. That she was beside herself for the moment, I clearly saw. That she had answered me unreservedly, it was impossible to believe. I began to feel angry, when I ought to have made allowances for her.

'Is this Lady Rachel's doing?' I said.

'What do you know of Lady Rachel, sir?'

'I know that she has visited you, and spoken to you.'

'Do you know what she has said?'

'I can guess.'

'Mr Gerard, don't abuse that good and kind lady. She deserves your gratitude as well as mine.'

Her manner had become quieter; her face was more composed; her expression almost recovered its natural charm while she spoke of Lady Rachel. I was stupefied.

'Try, sir, to forget it and forgive it,' she resumed gently, 'if I have misbehaved myself. I don't rightly know what I am saying or doing.'

I pointed to the new side of the cottage, behind us.

'Is the cause there?' I asked.

'No! no indeed! I have not seen him; I have not heard from him. His servant often brings me messages. Not one message to-day.'

'Have you seen Gloody to-day?'

'Oh, yes! There's one thing, if I may make so bold, I should like to know. Mr Gloody is as good to me as good can be; we see each other continually, living in the same place. But you are different; and he tells me himself he has only seen you twice. What have you done, Mr Gerard, to make him like you so well, in that short time?'

I told her that he had been found in my garden, looking at the flowers. 'As he had done no harm,' I said, 'I wouldn't allow the servant to turn him out; and I walked round the flower-beds with him. Little enough to deserve such gratitude as the poor fellow expressed—and felt, I don't doubt it.'

I had intended to say no more than this. But the remembrance of Gloody's mysterious prevarication, and of the uneasiness which I had undoubtedly felt when I thought of it afterwards, led me (I cannot pretend to say how) into associating Cristel's agitation with something which this man might have said to her. I was on the point of putting the question, when she held up her hand, and said, 'Hush!'

The wind was blowing towards us from the river-side village, to which I have already alluded. I am not sure whether I have mentioned that the name of the place was Kylam. It was situated behind a promontory of the river-bank, clothed thickly with trees, and was not visible from the mill. In the present direction of the wind, we could hear the striking of the church clock. Cristel counted the strokes.

'Seven,' she said. 'Are you determined to keep your engagement?'

She had repeated—in an unsteady voice, and with a sudden change in her colour to paleness—the strange question put to me by Gloody. In his case I had failed to trace the motive. I tried to discover it now.

'Tell me why I ought to break my engagement,' I said.

'Remember what I told you at the spring,' she answered. 'You are deceived by a false friend who lies to you and hates you.'

The man she was speaking of turned the corner of the new cottage. He waved his hand gaily, and approached us along the road.

'Go!' she said. 'Your guardian angel has forgotten you. It's too late now.'

Instead of letting me precede her, as I had anticipated, she ran on before me—made a sign to the deaf man, as she passed him, not to stop her—and disappeared through the open door of her father's side of the cottage.

I was left to decide for myself. What should I have done, if I had been twenty years older?

Say that my moral courage would have risen superior to the poorest of all fears, the fear of appearing to be afraid, and that I should have made my excuses to my host of the evening—how would my moral courage have answered him, if he had asked for an explanation? Useless to speculate on it! Had I possessed the wisdom of middle life, his book of leaves would not have told him, in my own handwriting, that I believed in his better nature, and accepted his friendly letter in the spirit in which he had written it.

Explain it who can—I knew that I was going to drink tea with him, and yet I was unwilling to advance a few steps, and meet him on the road!

'I find a new bond of union between us,' he said, as he joined me. 'We both feel *that*.' He pointed to the grandly darkening view. 'The two men who could have painted the mystery of those growing shadows and fading lights, lie in the graves of Rembrandt and Turner. Shall we go to tea?'

On our way to his room we stopped at the miller's door.

'Will *you* inquire,' he said, 'if Miss Cristel is ready?'

I went in. Old Toller was in the kitchen, smoking his pipe without appearing to enjoy it.

'What's come to my girl?' he asked, the moment he saw me. 'Yesterday she was in her room, crying. To-day she's in her room, praying.'

The warnings which I had neglected rose in judgment against me. I was silent; I was awed. Before I recovered myself, Cristel entered the kitchen. Her father whispered, 'Look at her!'

Of the excitement which had disturbed—I had almost said, profaned—her beautiful face, not a vestige remained. Pale, composed, resolute, she said, 'I am ready,' and led the way out.

The man whom she hated offered his arm. She took it!

# CHAPTER XIII

## THE CLARET JUG

I perceived but one change in the Lodger's miserable room, since I had seen it last.

A second table was set against one of the walls. Our boiling water for the tea was kept there, in a silver kettle heated by a spirit-lamp. I next observed a delicate little china vase which held the tea, and a finely-designed glass claret jug, with a silver cover. Other men, possessing that beautiful object, would have thought it worthy of the purest Bordeaux wine which the arts of modern adulteration permit us to drink. This man had filled the claret jug with water.

'All my valuable property, ostentatiously exposed to view,' he said, in his bitterly facetious manner. 'My landlord's property matches it on the big table.'

The big table presented a coarse earthenware teapot; cups and saucers with pieces chipped out of them; a cracked milk jug; a tumbler which served as a sugar basin; and an old vegetable dish, honoured by holding delicate French sweet-meats for the first time since it had left the shop.

My deaf friend, in boisterously good spirits, pointed backwards and forwards between the precious and the worthless objects on the two tables, as if he saw a prospect that delighted him.

'I don't believe the man lives,' he said, 'who enjoys Contrast as I do.—What do you want now?'

This question was addressed to Gloody, who had just entered the room. He touched the earthenware teapot. His master answered: 'Let it alone.'

'I make the tea at other times,' the man persisted, looking at me.

'What does he say? Write it down for me, Mr Roylake. I beg you will write it down.'

There was anger in his eyes as he made that request. I took his book, and wrote the words—harmless words, surely? He read them, and turned savagely to his unfortunate servant.

'In the days when you were a ruffian in the prize-ring, did the other men's fists beat all the brains out of your head? Do you think you can make tea that is fit for Mr Roylake to drink?'

He pointed to an open door, communicating with another bed-room. Gloody's eyes rested steadily on Cristel: she failed to notice him, being occupied at the moment in replacing the pin of a brooch which had slipped out of her dress. The man withdrew into the second bedroom, and softly closed the door.

Our host recovered his good humour. He took a wooden stool, and seated himself by Cristel.

'Borrowed furniture,' he said, 'as well as borrowed tea-things. What a debt of obligation I owe to your excellent father. How quiet you are, dear girl. Do you regret having followed the impulse which made you kindly offer to drink tea with us?' He suddenly turned to me. 'Another proof, Mr Roylake, of the sisterly interest that she feels in you; she can't hear of your coming to my room, without wanting to be with you. Ah, you possess the mysterious attractions which fascin-ate the sex. One of these days, *some* woman will love you as never man was loved yet.' He addressed himself again to Cristel. 'Still out of spirits? I dare say you are tired of waiting for your tea. No? You have had tea already? It's Gloody's fault; he ought to have told me that seven o'clock was too late for you. The poor devil deserved that you should take no notice of him when he looked at you just now. Are you one of the few women who dislike an ugly man? Women in general, I can tell you, prefer ugly men. A handsome man matches them on their own ground, and they don't like that. "We are so fond of our ugly husbands; they set us off to such advantage." Oh, I don't report what they say; I speak the language in which they think.—Mr Roylake, does it strike you that the Cur is a sad cynic? By-the-by, do you call me "the Cur" (as I suggested) when you speak of me to other people—to Miss Cristel, for instance? My charming young friends, you both look shocked; you both shake your heads. Perhaps I am in one of my tolerant humours to-day; I see nothing disgraceful in being a Cur. He is a dog who represents different breeds. Very well, the English are a people who represent different breeds: Saxons, Normans, Danes. The consequence, in one case, is a great nation. The consequence, in the other case, is the cleverest member of the whole dog family—as you may find out for yourself if you will only teach him. Ha—how I am running on. My guests try to slip in a word or two, and can't find their opportunity. Enjoyment, Miss Cristel. Excitement, Mr Roylake. For more than a year past, I have not luxuriated in the pleasures of society. I feel the social glow; I love the human family; I never, never, never was such a good man as I am now. Let vile slang express my emotions: isn't it jolly?'

Cristel and I stopped him, at the same moment. We instinctively lifted our hands to our ears.

In his delirium of high spirits, he had burst through the invariable monotony of his articulation. Without the slightest gradation of sound, his voice broke suddenly into a screech, prolonged in its own discord until it became perfectly unendurable to hear. The effect that he had produced upon us was not lost on him. His head sank on his breast; horrid shudderings shook him without mercy; he said to himself, not to us:

'I had forgotten I was deaf.'

There was a whole world of misery in those simple words. Cristel kept her place, unmoved. I rose, and put my hand kindly on his shoulder. It was the best way I could devise of assuring him of my sympathy.

He looked up at me, in silence.

His book of leaves was on the table; he did once more, what he had already done at the spring. Instead of using the book as usual, he wrote in it himself, and then handed it to me.

'Let me spare your nerves a repetition of my deaf discord. Sight, smell, touch, taste—I would give them all to be able to hear. In reminding me of that vain aspiration, my infirmity revenges itself: my deafness is not accustomed to be forgotten. Well! I can be silently useful; I can make the tea.'

He rose, and, taking the teapot with him, went to the table that had been placed against the wall. In that position, his back was turned towards us.

At the same time, I felt his book gently taken out of my hand. Cristel had been reading, while I read, over my shoulder. She wrote on the next blank leaf: 'Shall I make the tea?'

'Now,' she said to me, 'notice what happens.'

Following him, she touched his arm, and presented her request. He shook his head in token of refusal. She came back to her place by me.

'You expected that?' I said.

'Yes.'

'Why did you ask me to notice his refusal?'

'Because I may want to remind you that he wouldn't let me make the tea.'

'Mysteries, my dear?'

'Yes: mysteries.'

'Not to be mentioned more particularly?'

'I will mention one of them more particularly. After the tea has been made, you may possibly feel me touch your knee under the table.'

I was fool enough to smile at this, and wise enough afterwards to see in her face that I had made a mistake.

'What is your touch intended to mean?' I asked.

'It means, "Wait," she said.'

My sense of humour was, by this time, completely held in check. That some surprise was in store for me, and that Cristel was resolved not to take me into her confidence, were conclusions at which I naturally arrived. I felt, and surely not without good cause, a little annoyed. The Lodger came back to us with the tea made. As he put the teapot on the table, he apologised to Cristel.

'Don't think me rude, in refusing your kind offer. If there is one thing I know I can do better than anybody else, that thing is making tea. Do you take sugar and milk, Mr Roylake?'

I made the affirmative sign. He poured out the tea. When he had filled two cups, the supply was exhausted. Cristel and I noticed this. He saw it, and at once gratified our curiosity.

'It is a rule,' he said, 'with masters in the art of making tea, that one infusion ought never to be used twice. If we want any more, we will make more; and if you feel inclined to join us, Miss Cristel, we will fill the third cup.'

What was there in this (I wondered) to make her turn pale? And why, after what he had just said, did I see her eyes willingly rest on him, for the first time in my experience? Entirely at a loss to understand her, I resignedly stirred my tea. On the point of tasting it next, I felt her hand on my knee, under the table.

Bewildered as I was, I obeyed my instructions, and went on stirring my tea. Our host smiled.

'Your sugar takes a long time to melt,' he said—and drank his tea. As he emptied the cup, the touch was taken off me. I followed his example.

In spite of his boasting, the tea was the worst I ever tasted. I should have thrown it out of the window, if they had offered us such nasty stuff at Trimley Deen. When I set down my cup, he asked facetiously if I wished him to brew any more. My negative answer was a master-piece of strong expression, in the language of signs.

Instead of sending for Gloody to clear the table, he moved away the objects near him, so as to leave an empty space at his disposal.

'I ought perhaps to have hesitated, before I asked you to spend the evening with me,' he said, speaking with a gentleness and amiability of manner, strongly in contrast with his behaviour up to this time. 'It is my misfortune, as you both well know, to be a check on conversation. I dare say you have asked yourselves: How is he going to amuse us, after tea? If you will allow me, I propose to amuse you by exhibiting the dexterity of my fingers and thumbs. Before I was deaf, I should have preferred the piano for this purpose. As it is, an inferior accomplishment must serve my turn.'

He opened a cupboard in the wall, close by the second table, and returned with a pack of cards.

Cristel imitated the action of dealing cards for a game. 'No,' he said, 'that is not the amusement which I have in view. Allow me to present myself in a new character. I am no longer the Lodger, and no longer the Cur. My new name is more honourable still—I am the Conjurer.'

He shuffled the pack by pouring it backwards and forwards from one hand to the other, in a cascade of cards. The wonderful ease with which he did it prepared me for something worth seeing. Cristel's admiration of his dexterity expressed itself by a prolonged clapping of hands, and a strange uneasy laugh. As his excitement subsided, her agitation broke out. I saw the flush again on her face, and the fiery brightness in her eyes. Once, when his attention was engaged, she stole a look at the door by which Gloody had left the room. Did this indicate another of the mysteries which, by her own confession, she had in preparation for me? My late experience had not inclined me favourably towards mysteries. I devoted my whole attention to the Conjurer.

Whether he chose the easiest examples of skill in sleight of hand is more than I know. I can only say that I never was more completely mystified by any professor of legerdemain on the public platform. After the performance of each trick, he asked leave to 'time himself' by looking at his watch; being anxious to discover if he had lost his customary quickness of execution through recent neglect of the necessary practice.

Of Cristel's conduct, while he was amusing us, I can only say that it justified Mrs Roylake's spiteful description of her as a bold girl. The more cleverly the tricks were performed, the more they seemed to annoy and provoke her.

'I hate being puzzled!' she said, addressing herself of course to me. 'Yes, yes; his fingers are quicker than my eyes—I have heard that explanation before. When he has done one of his tricks, I want to know how he does it. Conjurers are people who ask riddles, and, when one can't guess them, refuse to say what the answer is. It's as bad as calling me a fool, to suppose that I like being deceived. Ah,' she cried, with a shocking insolence of look and manner, 'if our friend could only hear what I am saying!'

He had paused while she was speaking, observing her attentively. 'Your face doesn't encourage me,' he said, with a patience and courtesy of manner which it was impossible not to admire. 'I am coming gradually to my greatest triumph; and I think I can surprise and please you.'

He timed his last trick, and returned to the table placed against the wall.

'Excuse me for a moment,' he resumed; 'I am suffering as usual, after drinking tea. I so delight in it that the temptation to-night was more than I could resist. Tea disagrees with my weak stomach. It always produces thirst.'

'What nonsense he talks!' Cristel exclaimed. 'All mere fancy! He reminds me of the old song called 'The Nervous Man.'* Do you know it, Mr Roylake?'

In spite of my efforts to prevent her, she burst out with the first verse of a stupid comic song. Spared by his deafness from this infliction of vulgarity, our host filled a tumbler from the water in the claret jug, and drank it.

As he set the tumbler down, we were startled by an accident in the next room. The floor was suddenly shaken by the sound of a heavy fall. The fall was followed by a groan which instantly brought me to my feet.

Although his infirmity made him unconscious of the groan, my friend felt the vibration of the floor, and saw me start up from my chair. He looked even more alarmed than I was, judging by the ghastly change that I saw in his colour; and he reached the door of the second room as soon as I did. It is needless to say that I allowed him to enter first.

On the point of following him, I felt myself roughly pulled back. When I turned round, and saw Cristel, I did really and truly believe that she was mad. The furious impatience in her eyes, the frenzied strength of her grasp on my arm, would have led most other men to form the same conclusion.

'Come!' she cried. 'No! not a word. There isn't a moment to lose.'

She dragged me across the room to the table on which the claret jug stood. She filled the tumbler from it, as *he* had filled the tumbler. The material of which the jug had been made was so solid (crystal, not glass as I had supposed) that the filling of the two tumblers emptied it. Cristel held the water out to me, gasping for breath, trembling as if she saw some frightful reptile before her instead of myself.

'Drink it,' she said, 'if you value your life!'

I should of course have found it perfectly easy to obey her, strange as her language was, if I had been in full possession of myself. Between distress and alarm, my mind (I suppose) had lost its balance. With or without a cause, I hesitated.

She crossed the room, and threw open the window which looked out on the river.

'You shan't die alone,' she said. 'If you don't drink it, I'll throw myself out!'

I drank from the tumbler to the last drop.

It was not water.

It had a taste which I can compare to no drink, and to no medicine, known to me. I thought of the other strange taste peculiar to the tea. At last, the tremendous truth forced itself on my mind. The man in whom my boyish generosity had so faithfully believed had attempted my life.

Cristel took the tumbler from me. My poor angel clasped her free arm round my neck, and pressed her lips, in an ecstasy of joy, on my cheek. The next instant, she seized the claret jug, and dashed it into pieces on the floor. 'Get the jug from his washhand-stand,' she said. When I gave it to her, she poured some of the water upon the broken fragments of crystal scattered on the floor. I had put the jug back in its place, and was returning to Cristel, when the poisoner showed himself, entering from the servant's room.

'Don't be alarmed,' he said. 'Gloody's name ought to be Glutton. An attack of giddiness, thoroughly well deserved. I have relieved him. You remember, Mr Roylake, that I was once a surgeon —'

The broken claret jug caught his eye.

We have all read of men who were petrified by terror. Of the few persons who have really witnessed that spectacle, I am one. The utter stillness of him was really terrible to see. Cristel wrote in his book an excuse, no doubt prepared beforehand: 'That fall in the next room frightened me, and I felt faint. I went to get some water from the jug you drank out of, and it slipped from my hand.'

She placed those words under his eyes—she might just as well have shown them to the dog. A dead man, erect on his feet—so he looked to our eyes. So he still looked, when I took Cristel's arm, and led her out of that dreadful presence.

'Take me into the air!' she whispered.

A burst of tears relieved her, after the unutterable suspense that she had so bravely endured. When she was in some degree composed again, we walked gently up and down for a minute or two in the cool night air. 'Don't speak to me,' she said, as we stopped before her father's door. 'I am not fit for it yet; I know what you feel.' I pressed her to my heart, and let the embrace speak for me. She yielded to it, faintly sighing. 'To-morrow?' I whispered. She bent her head, and left me.

Walking home through the wood, I became aware, little by little, that my thoughts were not under the customary control. Over and over again, I tried to review the events of that terrible evening, and failed. Fragments of other memories presented themselves—and then deserted me. Nonsense, absolute nonsense, found its way into my mind next, and rose in idiotic words to my lips. I grew too lazy even to talk to myself. I strayed from the path. The mossy earth began to rise and sink under my feet, like the waters in a ground-swell at sea. I stood still, in a state of idiot-wonder. The ground suddenly rose right up to my face. I remember no more.

My first conscious exercise of my senses, when I revived, came to me by way of my ears. Leaden weights seemed to close my eyes, to fetter my movements, to silence my tongue, to paralyse my touch. But I heard a wailing voice, speaking close to me, so close that it might have been my own voice: I distinguished the words; I knew the tones.

'Oh, my master, my lord, who am I that I should live—and you die! and you die!'

Was it her warm young breath that quickened me with its vigorous life? I only know that the revival of my sense of touch did certainly spring from the contact of her lips, pressed to mine in the reckless abandonment of grief without hope. Her cry of joy, when my first sigh told her that I was still a living creature, ran through me like an electric shock. I opened my eyes; I held out my hand; I tried to help her when she raised my head, and set me against the tree under which I had been stretched helpless. With an effort I could call her by her name. Even that exhausted me. My mind was so weak that I should have believed her, if she had declared herself to be a spirit seen in a dream, keeping watch over me in the wood.

Wiser than I was, she snatched up my hat, ran on before me, and was lost in the darkness.

An interval, an unendurable interval, passed. She returned, having filled my hat from the spring. But for the exquisite coolness of the water falling on my face, trickling down my throat, I should have lost my senses again. In a few minutes more, I could take that dear hand, and hold it to me as if I was holding to my life. We could only see each other obscurely, and in that very circumstance (as we confessed to each other afterwards) we found the needful composure before we could speak.

'Cristel! what does it mean?'

'Poison,' she answered. 'And *he* has suffered too.'

To my astonishment, there was no anger in her tone: she spoke of him as quietly as if she had been alluding to an innocent man.

'Do you mean that he has been at death's door, like me?'

'Yes, thank God—or I should never have found you here. Poor old Gloody came to us, in search of help. "My master's in a swoon, and I can't bring him to." Directly I heard that, I remembered that you had drunk what he had drunk. What had happened to him, must have happened to you. Don't ask me how long it was before I found you, and what I felt when I did find you. I do so want to enjoy my happiness! Only let me see you safely home, and I ask no more.'

She helped me to rise, with the encouraging words which she might have used to a child. She put my arm in hers, and led me carefully along through the wood, as if I had been an old man.

Cristel had saved my life—but she would hear of no allusion to it. She knew how the poisoner had plotted to get rid of me—but nothing that I could say induced her to tell me how she had made the discovery. In view of Trimley Deen, my guardian angel dropped my arm.

'Go on,' she said, 'and let me see the servant let you in, before I run home.'

If she had not been once more wiser than I was, I should have taken her with me to the house; I should have positively refused to let her go back by herself. Nothing that I could say or do had the slightest effect on her resolution. Does the man live who could have taken leave of her calmly, in my place? She tore herself away from me, with a sigh of bitterness that was dreadful to hear.

'Oh, my darling,' I said, 'do I distress you?'

'Horribly,' she answered; 'but you are not to blame.'

Those were her farewell words. I called after her. I tried to follow her. She was lost to me in the darkness.

## CHAPTER XIV

### GLOODY SETTLES THE ACCOUNT

A night of fever; a night, when I did slumber for a few minutes, of horrid dreams—this was what I might have expected, and this is what really happened. The fresh morning air, flowing through my open window, cooled and composed me; the mercy of sleep found me. When I woke, and looked at my watch, I was a new man. The hour was noon.

I rang my bell. The servant announced that a man was waiting to see me. 'The same man, sir, who was found in the garden, looking at your flowers.' I at once gave directions to have him shown up into my bedroom. The delay of dressing was more than I had patience to encounter. Unless I was completely mistaken, here was the very person whom I wanted to enlighten me.

Gloody showed himself at the door, with a face ominously wretched, as well as ugly. I instantly thought of Cristel.

'If you bring me bad news,' I said, 'don't keep me waiting for it.'

'It's nothing that need trouble You, sir. I'm dismissed from my master's service—that's all.'

It was plainly not 'all'. Relieved even by that guarded reply, I pointed to a chair by the bedside.

'Do you believe that I mean well by you?' I asked.

'I do, sir, with all my heart.'

'Then sit down, Gloody, and make a clean breast of it.'

He lifted his enormous fist, by way of emphasising his answer.

'I was within a hair's breadth, sir, of striking him. If I hadn't kept my temper, I might have killed him.'

'What did he do?'

'Flew into a furious rage. I don't complain of that; I daresay I deserved it. Please to excuse my getting up again. I can't look you in the face, and tell you of it.' He walked away to the window. 'Even a poor devil, like me, does sometimes feel it when he is insulted. Mr Roylake, he kicked me. Say no more about it, sir! I would never have mentioned it, if I hadn't had something else to tell you; only I don't know how.' In this difficulty, he came back to my bedside. 'Look here, sir! What I say is—that kick has wiped out the debt of thanks I owe him. Yes. I say the account between us two is settled now, on both sides. In two words, sir, if you mean to charge him before the magistrates with attempting your life, I'll take my Bible oath he did attempt it, and you may call me as your witness. There! Now it's out.'

What his master had no doubt inferred, was what I saw plainly too. Cristel had saved my life, and had been directed how to do it by the poor fellow who had suffered in my cause.

'We will wait a little before we talk of setting the law in force,' I said. 'In the meantime, Gloody, I want you to tell me what you would tell the magistrate if I called you as a witness.'

He considered a little. 'The magistrate would put questions to me—wouldn't he, sir? Very good. You put questions to me, and I'll answer them to the best of my ability.'

The investigation that followed was far too long and too wearisome to be related here. If I give the substance of it, I shall have done enough.

Sometimes when he was awake, and supposed that he was alone—sometimes when he was asleep and dreaming—the Cur had betrayed himself. (It was a paltry vengeance, I own, to gratify a malicious pleasure—as I did now—in thinking of him and speaking of him by the degrading name which his morbid humility had suggested. But are the demands of a man's dignity always paid in the ready money of prompt submission?) Anyway, it appeared that Gloody had heard enough, in the sleeping moments and the solitary moments of his master, to give him some idea of the jealous hatred with which the Cur regarded me. He had done his best to warn me, without actually betraying the man who had rescued him from starvation or the workhouse—and he had failed.

But his resolution to do me good service, in return for my kindness to him, far from being shaken, was confirmed by circumstances.

When his master returned to the chemical studies which have been already mentioned, Gloody was employed as assistant, to the extent of his limited capacity for making himself useful. He had no reason to suppose that I was the object of any of the experiments, until the day before the tea-party. Then, he saw the dog enticed into the new cottage, and apparently killed by the administration of poison of some sort. After an interval, a dose of another kind was poured down the poor creature's throat, and he began to revive. A lapse of a quarter of an hour followed; the last dose was repeated; and the dog soon sprang to his feet again, as lively as ever. Gloody was thereupon told to set the animal free; and was informed at the same time that he would be instantly dismissed, if he mentioned to any living creature what he had just seen.

By what process he arrived at the suspicion that my safety might be threatened, by the experiment on the dog, he was entirely unable to explain.

'It was borne in on my mind, sir; and that's all I can tell you,' he said. 'I didn't dare speak to you about it; you wouldn't have believed me. Or, if you did believe me, you might have sent for the police. The one way of putting a stop to murdering mischief (if murdering mischief it might be) was to trust Miss Cristel. That she was fond of you—I don't mean any offence, sir—I pretty well guessed. That she was true as steel, and not easily frightened, I didn't need to guess; I knew it.'

Gloody had done his best to prepare Cristel for the terrible confidence which he had determined to repose in her, and had not succeeded. What the poor girl must have suffered, I could but too readily understand, on recalling the startling changes in her look and manner when we met at the river-margin of the wood. She was pledged to secrecy, under penalty of ruining the man who was trying to save me; and to her presence of mind was trusted the whole responsibility of preserving my life. What a situation for a girl of eighteen!

'We made it out between us, sir, in two ways,' Gloody proceeded. 'First and foremost, she was to invite herself to tea. And, being at the table, she was to watch my master. Whatever she saw him drink, she was to insist on your drinking it too. You heard me ask leave to make the tea?'

'Yes.'

'Well, that was one of the signals agreed on between us. When he sent me away, we were certain of what he had it in his mind to do.'

'And when you looked at Miss Cristel, and she was too busy with her brooch to notice you, was that another signal?'

'It was, sir. When she handled her silver ornament, she told me that I might depend on her to forget nothing, and to be afraid of nothing.'

I remembered the quiet firmness in her face, after the prayer that she had said in her own room. Her steady resolution no longer surprised me.

'Did you wonder, sir, what possessed her,' Gloody went on, 'when she burst out singing? That was a signal to me. We wanted him out of our way, while you were made to drink what he had drunk out of the jug.'

'How did you know that he would not drink the whole contents of the jug?'

'You forget, sir, that I had seen the dog revived by two doses, given with a space of time between them.'

I ought to have remembered this, after what he had already told me. My intelligence brightened a little as I went on.

'And your accident in the next room was planned, of course?' I said. 'Do you think he saw through it? I should say, No; judging by his looks. He turned pale when he felt the floor shaken by your fall. For once in a way, he was honest—honestly frightened.'

'I noticed the same thing, sir, when he picked me up, off the floor. A man who can change his complexion, at will, is a man we hav'n't heard of yet, Mr Roylake.'

I had been dressing for some time past; longing to see Cristel, it is needless to say.

'Is there anything more,' I asked, 'that I ought to know?'

'Only one thing, Mr Roylake, that I can think of,' Gloody replied. 'I'm afraid it's Miss Cristel's turn next.'

'What do you mean?'

'While the deaf man lodges at the cottage, he means mischief, and his eye is on Miss Cristel. Early this morning, sir, I happened to be at the boat-house. Somebody (I leave you to guess who it is) has stolen the oars.'

I was dressed by this time, and so eager to get to the cottage, that I had already opened my door. What I had just heard brought me back into the room. As a matter of course, we both suspected the same person of stealing the oars. Had we any proof to justify us?

Gloody at once acknowledged that we had no proof. 'I happened to look at the boat,' he said, 'and I missed the oars. Oh, yes; I searched the boat-house. No oars! no oars!'

'And nothing more that you have forgotten, and ought to tell me?'

'Nothing, sir.'

I left Gloody to wait my return; being careful to place him under the protection of the upper servants—who would see that he was treated with respect by the household generally.

## CHAPTER XV

### THE MILLER'S HOSPITALITY

On the way to Toller's cottage, my fears for Cristel weighed heavily on my mind.

That the man who had tried to poison me was capable of committing any other outrage, provided he saw a prospect of escaping with impunity, no sane person could hesitate to conclude. But the cause of my alarm was not to be traced to this conviction. It was a doubt that made me tremble.

After what I had myself seen, and what Gloody had told me, could I hope to match my penetration, or the penetration of any person about me whom I could trust, against the fathomless cunning, the Satanic wickedness, of the villain who was still an inmate with Cristel, under her father's roof?

I have spoken of his fathomless cunning, and his Satanic wickedness. The manner in which the crime had been prepared and carried out would justify stronger expressions still. Such was the deliberate opinion of the lawyer whom I privately consulted, under circumstances still to be related.

'Let us arrive at a just appreciation of the dangerous scoundrel whom we have to deal with,' this gentleman said. 'His preliminary experiment with the dog; his resolution to make suspicion an impossibility, by drinking from the same tea which he had made ready for you; his skilled preparation of an antidote, the colour of which might court appearances by imitating water—are there many poisoners clever enough to provide themselves beforehand with such a defence as this? How are you to set the circumstances in their true light, on your side? You may say that you threw out the calculations, on which he had relied for securing his own safety, by drinking his second dose of the antidote while he was out of the room; and you can appeal to the fainting-fits from which you and he suffered on the same evening, as a proof that the action of the poison was partially successful; in your case and in his, because you and he were insufficiently protected by half doses only of the antidote. A bench of Jesuits* would understand these refinements. A bench of British magistrates would look at each other, and say: Where is the medical evidence? No, Mr Roylake, we must wait. You can't even turn him out of the cottage before he has had the customary notice to quit. The one thing to take care of—in case some other suspicions of ours turn out to be well founded—is that our man shall not give us the slip. One of my clerks, and one of your gamekeepers shall keep watch on his lodgings, turn and turn about, till his time is up. Go where he may after that, he shall not escape us.'

I may now take up the chain of events again.

On reaching Toller's cottage, I was distressed (but hardly surprised) to hear that Cristel, exhausted after a wakeful night, still kept her bed, in the hope of getting some sleep. I was so anxious to know if she was at rest, that her father went upstairs to look at her.

I followed him—and saw Ponto watching on the mat outside her door. Did this indicate a wise distrust of the Cur? 'A guardian I can trust, sir,' the old man whispered, 'while I'm at the mill.'

He looked into Cristel's room, and permitted me to look over his shoulder. My poor darling was peacefully asleep. Judging by the miller's manner, which was as cool and composed as usual, I gathered that Cristel had wisely kept him in ignorance of what had happened on the previous evening.

The inquiry which I had next in my mind was forestalled by old Toller.

'Our deaf-devil, Mr Gerard, has done a thing this morning which puzzles me,' he began; 'and I should like to hear what you think of it. For the first time since we have had him here, he has opened his door to a visitor. And—what a surprise for you!—it's the other devil with the hat and feather who got at my Cristy, and made her cry.'

That this meeting would be only too likely to happen, in due course of time, I had never doubted. That it had happened, now, confirmed me in my resolution to keep guard over Cristel at the cottage, till the Cur left it.

I asked, of course, how those two enemies of mine had first seen each other.

'She was just going to knock at our door, Mr Gerard, when she happened to look up. There he was, airing himself at his window as usual. Do you think she was too much staggered at the sight of him to speak? At any rate, he got the start of her. "Wait till I come down," says he—and there he was, almost as soon as he said it. They went into his place together; and for best part of an hour they were in each other's company. Every man has his failings; I don't deny that I'm a little inquisitive by nature. Between ourselves, I got under the open window and listened. At a great disadvantage, I needn't tell you; for she was obliged to write what she had to say. But *he* talked. I was too late for the cream of it; I only heard him wish her good-bye. "If your ladyship telegraphs this morning," says he, "when will the man come to me?" Now what do you say to that?'

'More than I have time to say now, Mr Toller. Can you find me a messenger to take a note to Trimley Deen?'

'We have no messengers in this lonesome place, sir.'

'Very well. Then I must take my own message. You will see me again, as soon as I can get back.'

Mr Toller's ready curiosity was roused in a moment.

'Perhaps, you wish to have a look at the repairs?' he suggested in his most insinuating manner.

'I wish to see what her ladyship's telegram brings forth,' I said; 'and I mean to be here when "the man" arrives.'

My venerable tenant was delighted. 'Turn him inside out, sir, and get at his secrets. I'll help you.'

Returning to Trimley Deen, I ordered the pony-chaise to be got ready, and a small portmanteau to be packed—speaking in the hall. The sound of my voice brought Mrs Roylake out of the morning-room. She was followed by Lady Rachel. If I could only have heard their private conference, I should have seen the dangerous side of the Cur's character under a new aspect.

'Gerard!' cried my stepmother, 'what did I hear just now? You can't be going back to Germany!'

'Certainly not,' I answered.

'Going to stay with some friends perhaps?' Lady Rachel suggested. 'I wonder whether I know them?'

It was spitefully done—but, in respect of tone and manner, done to perfection.

The pony-chaise drew up at the door. This was another of the rare occasions in my life on which I acted discreetly. It was necessary for me to say something. I said, 'Good morning.'

Nothing had happened at the cottage, during the interval of my absence. Clever as he was, old Toller had never suspected that I should return to him (with luggage!) in the character of a self-invited guest. His jaw dropped, and his wicked little eyes appealed to the sky. Merciful Providence! what have I done to deserve this? There, as I read him, was the thought in the miller's mind, expressed in my best English.

'Have you got a spare bed in the house?' I asked.

Mr Toller forgot the respect due to the person who could stop the repairs at a moment's notice. He answered in the tone of a man who had been grossly insulted: 'No!'

But for the anxieties that oppressed me, I should have only perceived the humorous side of old Toller's outbreak of temper. He had chosen his time badly, and he got a serious reply.

'Understand this,' I said: 'either you receive me civilly—or you make up your mind to find a flour-mill on some other property than mine.'

This had its effect. The miller's servility more than equalled his insolence. With profuse apologies, he offered me his own bedroom. I preferred a large old-fashioned armchair which stood in a corner of the kitchen. Listening in a state of profound bewilderment—longing to put inquisitive questions, and afraid to do so—Toller silently appealed to my compassion. I had nothing to conceal; I mentioned my motive. Without intending it, I had wounded him in one of his most tender places; the place occupied by his good opinion of himself. He said with sulky submission:

'Much obliged, Mr Gerard. My girl is safe under *my* protection. Leave it to me, sir—leave it to me.'

I had just reminded old Toller of his age, and of the infirmities which age brings with it, when his daughter—pale and languid, with signs of recent tears in her eyes—entered the kitchen. When I approached her, she trembled and drew back; apparently designing to leave the room. Her father stopped her. 'Mr Gerard has something to tell you,' he said. 'I'm off to the mill.' He took up his hat, and left us.

Submitting sadly, she let me take her in my arms, and try to cheer her. But when I alluded to what I owed to her admirable devotion and courage, she entreated me to be silent. 'Don't bring it all back!' she cried, shuddering at the remembrances which I had awakened. 'Father said you had something to tell me. What is it?'

I repeated (in language more gentle and more considerate) what I had already said to her father. She took my hand, and kissed it gratefully. 'You have your mother's face, and your mother's heart,' she said; 'you are always good, you are never selfish. But it mustn't be. How can I let you suffer the discomfort of staying here? Indeed, I am in no danger; you are alarming yourself without a cause.'

'How can you be sure of that?' I asked.

She looked reluctantly at the door of communication.

'Must I speak of him?'

'Only to tell me,' I pleaded, 'whether you have seen him since last night.'

She had both seen him and heard from him, on reaching home. 'He opened that door,' she told me, 'and threw on the floor one of the leaves out of his book. After doing that, he relieved me from the sight of him.'

'Show me the leaf, Cristel.'

'Father has got it. I thought he was asleep in the armchair. He snatched it out of my hand. It isn't worth reading.'

She turned pale, nevertheless, when she replied in those terms. I could see that I was disturbing her, when I asked if she remembered what the Cur had written. But our position was far too serious to be trifled with. 'I suppose he threatened you?' I said, trying to lead her on. 'What did he say?'

'He said, if any attempt was made to remove me out of his reach, after what had happened that evening, my father would find him on the watch day and night, and would regret it to the end of his life. The wretch thinks me cruel enough to have told my father of the horrors we went through! You know that he has dismissed his poor old servant? Was I wrong in advising Gloody to go to you?'

'You were quite right. He is at my house—and I should like to keep him at Trimley Deen; but I am afraid he and the other servants might not get on well together?'

'Will you let him come here?'

She spoke earnestly; reminding me that I had thought it wrong to leave her father, at his age, without someone to help him.

'If an accident separated me from him,' she went on, 'he would be left alone in this wretched place.'

'What accident are you thinking of?' I asked. 'Is there something going on, Cristel, that I don't know of?'

Had I startled her? or had I offended her?

'Can we tell what may or may not happen to us, in the time to come?' she asked abruptly. 'I don't like to think of my father being left without a creature to take care of him. Gloody is so good and so true; and they always get on well together. If you have nothing better in view for him—?'

'My dear, I have nothing half so good in view; and Gloody, I am sure, will think so too.' I privately resolved to insure a favourable reception for the poor fellow, by making him the miller's partner. Bank notes in Toller's pocket! What a place reserved for Gloody in Toller's estimation!

But I confess that Cristel's allusion to a possible accident rather oppressed my mind, situated as we were at that time. What we talked of next has slipped from my memory. I only recollect that she made an excuse to go back to her room, and that nothing I could say or do availed to restore her customary cheerfulness.

As the twilight was beginning to fade, we heard the sound of a carriage. The new man had arrived in a fly from the station. Before bedtime, he made his appearance in the kitchen, to receive the domestic instructions of which a stranger stood in need. A quiet man and a civil man: even my prejudiced examination could discover nothing in him that looked suspicious. I saw a well-trained servant— and I saw nothing more.

Old Toller made a last attempt to persuade me that it was not worth a gentleman's while to accept his hospitality, and found me immovable. I was equally obstinate when Cristel asked leave to make up a bed for me in the counting-house at the mill.

With the purpose that I had in view, if I accepted her proposal I might as well have been at Trimley Deen.

Left alone, I placed the armchair and another chair for my feet, across the door of communication. That done, I examined a little door behind the stairs (used I believe for domestic purposes) which opened on a narrow pathway, running along the river-side of the house. It was properly locked. I have only to add that nothing happened during the night.

The next day showed no alteration for the better, in Cristel. She made an excuse when I proposed to take her out with me for a walk. Her father's business kept him away from the cottage, and thus gave me many opportunities of speaking to her in private. I was so uneasy, or so reckless—I hardly know which—that I no longer left it to be merely inferred that I had resolved to propose marriage to her.

'My sweet girl, you are so wretched, and so unlike yourself, in this place, that I entreat you to leave it. Come with me to London, and let me make you safe and happy as my wife.'

'Oh, Mr Roylake!'

'Why do you call me, "Mr Roylake"? Have I done anything to offend you? There seems to be some estrangement between us. Do you believe that I love you?'

'I wish I could doubt it!' she answered.

'Why?'

'You know why.'

'Cristel! Have I made some dreadful mistake? The truth! I want the truth! Do you love me?'

A low cry of misery burst from her. Was she mastered by love, or by despair? She threw herself on my breast. I kissed her. She murmured, 'Oh don't tempt me! Don't tempt me!' Again and again, I kissed her. 'Ah,' I broke out, in the ecstasy of my sense of relief, 'I know that you love me, now!'

'Yes,' she said, simply and sadly, 'I do love you.'

My selfish passion asked for more even than this.

'Prove it by being my wife,' I answered.

She put me back from her, firmly and gently.

'I will prove it, Gerard, by not letting you disgrace yourself.'

With those horrible words—put into her mouth, beyond all doubt by the woman who had interfered between us—she left me. The long hours of the day passed: I saw her no more.

People who are unable to imagine what I suffered, are not the people to whom I now address myself. After all the years that have passed—after age and contact with the world have hardened me—it is still a trial to my self-control to look back to that day. Events I can remember with composure. To events, therefore, let me return.

No communication of any sort reached us from the Cur. Towards evening, I saw him pacing up and down on the road before the cottage, and speaking to his new servant. The man (listening attentively) had the master's book of leaves in his hand, and wrote in it from time to time as replies were wanted from him. He was probably receiving instructions. The Cur's discretion was a bad sign. I should have felt more at ease, if he had tried to annoy Cristel, or to insult me.

Towards bedtime, old Toller's sense of hospitality exhibited marked improvement. He was honoured and happy to have me under his poor roof—a roof, by the way, which was also in need of repairs—but he protested against my encountering the needless hardship of sleeping in a chair, when a bed could be set up for me in the counting-house. 'Not what you're used to, Mr Gerard. Empty barrels, and samples of flour, and account-books smelling strong of leather, instead of velvet curtains and painted ceilings; but better than a chair, sir—better than a chair!'

I was as obstinate as ever. With thanks, I insisted on the chair.

Feverish, anxious, oppressed in my breathing—with nerves unstrung, as a doctor would have put it—I disturbed the order of the household towards twelve o'clock by interfering with old Toller in the act of locking up the house-door.

'Let me get a breath of fresh air,' I said to him, 'or there will be no sleep for me to-night.'

He opened the door with a resignation to circumstances, so exemplary that it claimed some return. I promised to be back in a quarter of an hour. Old Toller stifled a yawn. 'I call that truly considerate,' he said—and stifled another yawn. Dear old man!

Stepping into the road, I first examined the Cur's part of the cottage. Not a sound was audible inside; not a creature was visible outside. The usual dim light was burning behind the window that looked out on the road. Nothing, absolutely nothing, that was suspicious could I either hear or see.

I walked on, by what we called the upper bank of the river; leading from the village of Kylam. The night was cloudy and close. Now the moonlight reached the earth at intervals; now again it was veiled in darkness. The trees, at this part of the wood, so encroached on the bank of the stream as considerably to narrow and darken the path. Seeing a possibility of walking into the river if I went on much farther, I turned back again in the more open direction of Kylam, and kept on briskly (as I reckon) for about five minutes more.

I had just stopped to look at my watch, when I saw something dark floating towards me, urged by the slow current of the river. As it came nearer, I thought I recognised the mill-boat.

It was one of the dark intervals when the moon was overcast. I was sufficiently interested to follow the boat, on the chance that a return of the moonlight might show me who could possibly be in it. After no very long interval, the yellow light for which I was waiting poured through the lifting clouds.

The mill-boat, beyond all doubt—and nobody in it! The empty inside of the boat was perfectly visible to me. Even if I had felt inclined to do so, it would have been useless to jump into the water and swim to the boat. There were no oars in it, and therefore no means of taking it back to the mill. The one thing I could do was to run to old Toller and tell him that his boat was adrift.

On my way to the cottage, I thought I heard a sound like the shutting of a door. I was probably mistaken. In expectation of my return, the door was secured by the latch only; and the miller, looking out of his bedroom window, said: 'Don't forget to lock it, sir; the key's inside.'

I followed my instructions, and ascended the stairs. Surprised to hear me in that part of the house, he came out on the landing in his nightgown.

'What is it?' he asked.

'Nothing very serious,' I said. 'The boat's adrift. I suppose it will run on shore somewhere.'

'It will do that, Mr Gerard; everybody along the river knows the boat.' He held up his lean trembling hand. 'Old fingers don't always tie fast knots.'

He went back into his bed. It was opposite the window; and the window, being at the side of the old cottage, looked out on the great open space above the river. When the moonlight appeared, it shone straight into his eyes. I offered to pull down the blind.

'Thank you kindly, sir; please to let it be. I wake often in the night, and I like to see the heavens when I open my eyes.'

Something touched me behind: it was the dog. Like his noble and beautiful race, Ponto knew his friends. He licked my hand, and then he walked out through the bedroom door. Instead of taking his usual place, on the mat before Cristel's room, he smelt for a moment under the door—whined softly—and walked up and down the landing.

'What's the matter with the dog?' I asked.

'Restless to-night,' said old Toller. 'Dogs *are* restless sometimes. Lie down!' he called through the doorway.

The dog obeyed, but only for a moment. He whined at the door again—and then, once more, he walked up and down the landing.

I went to the bedside. The old man was just going to sleep. I shook him by the shoulder.

'There's something wrong,' I said. 'Come out and look at Ponto.'

He grumbled—but he came out. 'Better get the whip,' he said.

'Before you do that,' I answered, 'knock at your daughter's door.'

'And wake her?' he asked in amazement.

I knocked at the door myself. There was no reply. I knocked again, with the same result.

'Open the door,' I said, 'or I will do it myself.'

He obeyed me. The room was empty; and the bed had not been slept in.

Standing helpless on the threshold of the door, I looked into the empty room; hearing nothing but my heart thumping heavily, seeing nothing but the bed with the clothes on it undisturbed.

The sudden growling of the dog shook me back (if I may say so) into the possession of myself. He was looking through the balusters that guarded the landing. The head of a man appeared, slowly ascending the stairs. Acting mechanically, I held the dog back. Thinking mechanically, I waited for the man. The face of the new servant showed itself. The dog frightened him: he spoke in tones that trembled, standing still on the stairs.

'My master has sent me, sir—'

A voice below interrupted him. 'Come back,' I heard the Cur say; 'I'll do it myself. Toller! where is Toller?'

The enraged dog, barking furiously, struggled to get away from me. I dragged him—the good honest creature who was incapable of concealments and treacheries!—into his master's room. In the moment before I closed the door again, I saw Toller down on his knees with his arms laid helplessly on the window-sill, staring up at the sky as if he had gone mad. There was no time for questions; I drove poor Ponto back into the room, and shut the door.

On the landing, I found myself face to face with the Cur.

'*You!*' he said.

I lifted my hand. The servant ran between us. 'For God's sake, control yourself, sir! We mean no harm. It's only to tell Mr Toller that his boat is missing.'

'Mr Toller knows it already,' I said. 'No honest man would touch your master if he could help it. I warn him to go; and I make him understand me by a sign.' I pointed down the stairs, and turned my head to look at him.

He was no longer before me. His face, hideously distorted by rage and terror, showed itself at the door of Cristel's empty room. He rushed out on me; his voice rose to the detestable screech which I had heard once already.

'Where have you hidden her? Give her back to me—or you die.' He drew a pistol out of the breast-pocket of his coat. I seized the weapon by the barrel, and snatched it away from him. As the charge exploded harmlessly between us, I struck him on the head with the butt-end of the pistol. He dropped on the landing.

The door of Toller's room opened behind me. He stood speechless; the report of the pistol had terrified him. In the instant when I looked at the old man, I saw, through the window of his room, a rocket soar into the sky, from behind the promontory between us and Kylam.

Some cry of surprise must, I suppose, have escaped me. Toller suddenly looked round towards the window, just as the last fiery particles of the rocket were floating slowly downwards against the black clouds.

I had barely time enough to see this, before a trembling hand was laid on my shoulder, from behind. The servant, white with terror, pointed to his master.

'Have you killed him?' the man said.

The same question must have been in the mind of the dog. He was quiet now. Doubtfully, reluctantly, he was smelling at the prostrate human creature. I knelt down, and put my hand on the wretch's heart. Ponto, finding us both on a level together, gave me the dog's kiss; I returned the caress with my free hand. The servant saw me, with my attention divided in this way between the animal and the man.

'Damn it, sir,' he burst out indignantly, 'isn't a Christian of more importance than a dog?'

A Christian!—but I was in no humour to waste words. 'Are you strong enough to carry him to his own side of the house?' I asked.

'I won't touch him, if he's dead!'

'He is *not* dead. Take him away!'

All this time my mind was pre-occupied by the extraordinary appearance of the rocket, rising from the neighbourhood of a lonely little village between midnight and one in the morning. How I connected that mysterious signal with a possibility of tracing Cristel, it is useless to inquire. That was the thought in me, when I led my lost darling's father back to his room. Without stopping to explain myself, I reminded him that the cottage was quiet again, and told him to wait my return.

In the kitchen, I overtook the servant and his burden. The door of communication (by which they had entered) was still open.

'Lock that door,' I said.

'Lock it yourself,' he answered; 'I'll have nothing to do with this business.' He passed through the doorway, and along the passage, and ascended his master's stairs.

It struck me directly that the man had suggested a sure way of protecting Toller, during my absence. The miller's own door was already secured; I took the key, so as to be able to let myself in again—then passed through the door of communication—fastened it—and put the key in my pocket. The third door, by which the Cur entered his lodgings, was of course at my disposal. I had just closed it, when I discovered that I had a companion. Ponto had followed me.

I felt at once that the dog's superior powers of divination might be of use, on such an errand as mine was. We set out together for Kylam.

Wildly hurried—without any fixed idea in my mind—I ran to Kylam, for the greater part of the way. It was now very dark. On a sandy creek, below the village, I came in contact with something solid enough to hurt me for the moment. It was the stranded boat.

A smoker generally has matches about him. Helped by my little short-lived lights, I examined the interior of the boat. There was absolutely nothing in it but a strip of old tarpaulin—used, as

I guessed, to protect the boat, or something that it carried, in rainy weather.

The village population had long since been in bed. Silence and darkness mercilessly defied me to discover anything. For a while I waited, encouraging the dog to circle round me and exercise his sense of smell. Any suspicious person or object he would have certainly discovered. Nothing—not even the fallen stick of the rocket—rewarded our patience. Determined to leave nothing untried, I groped, rather than found, my way to the village ale house, and succeeded at last in rousing the landlord. He hailed me from the window (naturally enough) in no friendly voice. I called out my name. Within my own little limits, it was the name of a celebrated person. The landlord opened his door directly; eager to answer my questions if he could do it. Nothing in the least out of the common way had happened at Kylam. No strangers had been seen in, or near, the place. The stranded boat had not been discovered; and the crashing flight of the rocket into the air had failed to disturb the soundly-sleeping villagers.

On my melancholy way back, fatigue of body—and, far worse, fatigue of mind—forced me to take a few minutes' rest.

The dimly-flowing river was at my feet; the river on which I had seen Cristel again, for the first time since we were children. Thus far, the dreadful loss of her had been a calamity, held away from me in some degree by events which had imperatively taken possession of my mind. In the darkness and the stillness, the misery of having lost her was free to crush me. My head dropped on the neck of the dog, nestling close at my side. 'Oh, Ponto!' I said to him, 'she's gone!' Nobody could see me; nobody could despise me—I burst out crying.

## CHAPTER XVI

### BRIBERY AND CORRUPTION

Twice, I looked into Toller's room during the remainder of the night, and found him sleeping. When the sun rose, I could endure the delay no longer. I woke him.

'What is it?' he asked peevishly.

'You must be the last person who saw Cristel,' I answered. 'I want to know all that you can tell me.'

His anger completely mastered him; he burst out with a furious reply.

'It's you two—you my landlord, and him my lodger—who have driven Cristy away from her home. She said she would go, and she *has* gone. Get out of my place, sir! You ought to be ashamed to look at me.'

It was useless to reason with him, and it was of vital importance to lose no time in instituting a search. After the reception I had met with, I took care to restore the key of the door leading into the new cottage, before I left him. It was his key; and the poor distracted old man might charge me with taking away his property next.

As I set forth on my way home, I found the new man-servant on the look-out.

His first words showed that he was acting under orders. He asked if I had found the young lady; and he next informed me that his master had revived some hours since, and 'bore no malice'. This outrageous assertion suddenly fired me with suspicion. I believed that the Cur had been acting a part when he threatened me with his pistol, and that he was answerable for the disappearance of Cristel. My first impulse now was to get the help of a lawyer.

The men at my stables were just stirring when I got home. In ten minutes more, I was driving to our town.

The substance of the professional opinion which I received has been already stated in these pages.

One among my answers to the many questions which my legal adviser put to me led him to a conclusion that made my heart ache. He was of opinion that my brief absence, while I was taking that fatal 'breath of air' on the banks of the river, had offered to Cristel her opportunity of getting away without discovery. 'Her old father,' the lawyer said, 'was no doubt in his bed, and you yourself found nobody watching, in the neighbourhood of the cottage.'

'Employ me in some way!' I burst out. 'I can't endure my life, if I'm not helping to trace Cristel.'

He was most kind. 'I understand,' he said. 'Try what you can get those two ladies to tell you—and you may help us materially.'

Mrs Roylake was nearest to me. I appealed to her womanly sympathies, and was answered by tears. I made another attempt; I said

I was willing to believe that she meant well, and that I should be sorry to offend her. She got up, and indignantly left the room.

I went to Lady Rachel next.

She was at home, but the servant returned to me with an excuse: her ladyship was particularly engaged. I sent a message upstairs, asking when I might hope to be received. The servant was charged with the delivery of another excuse: her ladyship would write. After waiting at home for hours I was foolish enough to write, on my side; and (how could I help it?) to express myself strongly. The she-socialist's reply is easy to remember: 'Dear Mr Roylake, when you have recovered your temper, you will hear from me again.'

Even my stepmother gained by comparison with this.

To rest, and do nothing, was to exercise a control over myself of which I was perfectly incapable. I went back to the cottage. Having no hopeful prospect in any other quarter, I persisted in believing that Toller must have seen something or heard something that might either help me, or suggest an idea to my legal adviser.

On entering the kitchen, I found the door of communication wide open, and the new servant established in the large armchair.

'I'm waiting for my master, sir.'

He had got over his fright, and had recovered his temper. The respectful side of him was turned to me again.

'Your master is with Mr Toller?'

'Yes, sir.'

What I felt, amply justified the lawyer in having exacted a promise from me to keep carefully out of the Cur's presence. 'You might knock him on the head again, Mr Roylake, and might hit a little too hard next time.'

But I had an idea of my own. I said, as if speaking to myself: 'I would give a five pound note to know what is going on upstairs.'

'I shall be glad to earn it, sir,' the fellow said. 'If I make a clean breast of what I know already, and if I tell you to-morrow what I can find out—will it be worth the money?'

I began to feel degraded in my own estimation. But I nodded to him, for all that.

'I am the innocent cause, sir, of what happened last night,' he coolly resumed. 'We kept a look-out on the road and saw you, though you didn't see us. But my master never suspected you (for reasons which he kept to himself) of making use of the boat. I reminded him

that one of us had better have an eye on the slip of pathway, between
the cottage and the river. This led to his sending me to the boat-
house—and you know what happened afterwards. My master, as
I suppose, is pumping Mr Toller. That's all, sir, for to-night.
When may I have the honour of expecting you to-morrow morning?'

I appointed an hour, and left the place.

As I entered the wood again, I found a man on the watch. He
touched his hat, and said: 'I'm the clerk, sir. Your gamekeeper is
wanted for his own duties to-night; he will relieve me in the morning.'

I went home with my mind in a ferment of doubt. If I could believe
the servant, the Cur was as innocent of the abduction of Cristel as
I was. But could I trust the servant?

The events of the next morning altered the whole complexion of
affairs fatally for the worse.

Arriving at the cottage, I found a man prostrate on the road, dead
drunk—and the Cur's servant looking at him.

'May I ask something?' the man said. 'Have you been having my
master watched?'

'Yes.'

'Bad news, in that case, sir. Your man there is a drunken vagabond;
and my master has gone to London by the first train.'

When I had recovered the shock, I denied, for the sake of my own
credit, that the brute on the road could be a servant of mine.

'Why not, sir?'

'Do you think I should have been kept in ignorance of it, if my
gamekeeper had been a drunkard? His fellow servants would have
warned me.'

The man smiled. 'I'm afraid, sir, you don't know much about
servants. It's a point of honour among us never to tell tales of each
other to our masters.'

I began to wish that I had never left Germany. The one course to
take now was to tell the lawyer what had happened. I turned away to
get back, and drive at once to the town. The servant remembered,
what I had forgotten—the five pound note.

'Wait and hear my report, sir,' he suggested.

The report informed me: First, that Mr Toller was at the mill, and
had been there for some time past. Secondly: that the Cur had been
alone, for a while, on Mr Toller's side of the cottage, in Mr Toller's
absence—for what purpose his servant had not discovered. Thirdly:

that the Cur had returned to his room in a hurry, and had packed a few things in his travelling-bag. Fourthly: that he had ordered the servant to follow, with his luggage, in a fly which he would send from the railway station, and to wait at the London terminus for further orders. Fifthly, and lastly: that it was impossible to say whether the drunkenness of the gamekeeper was due to his own habits, or to temptation privately offered by the very person whose movements he had been appointed to watch.

I paid the money. The man pocketed it, and paid me a compliment in return: 'I wish I was your servant, sir.'

## CHAPTER XVII

### UTTER FAILURE

My lawyer took a serious view of the disaster that had overtaken us. He would trust nobody but his head clerk to act in my interests, after the servant had been followed to the London terminus, and when it became a question of matching ourselves against the deadly cunning of the man who had escaped us.

Provided with money, and with a letter to the police authorities in London, the head clerk went to the station. I accompanied him to point out the servant (without being allowed to show myself), and then returned to wait for telegraphic information at the lawyer's office.

This was the first report transmitted by the telegram:

The Cur had been found waiting for his servant at the terminus; and the two had been easily followed to the railway hotel close by. The clerk had sent his letter of introduction to the police—had consulted with picked men who joined him at the hotel—had given the necessary instructions—and would return to us by the last train in the evening.

In two days, the second telegram arrived.

Our man had been traced to the Thames Yacht Club in Albemarle Street—had consulted a yachting list in the hall—and had then travelled to the Isle of Wight. There, he had made inquiries at the Squadron Yacht Club, and the Victoria Yacht Club—and had returned to London, and the railway hotel.

The third telegram announced the utter destruction of all our hopes. As far as Marseilles, the Cur had been followed successfully, and in that city the detective officers had lost sight of him.

My legal adviser insisted on having the men sent to him to explain themselves. Nothing came of it but one more repetition of an old discovery. When the detective police force encounters intelligence instead of stupidity, in seven cases out of ten the detective police force is beaten.

There were still two persons at our disposal. Lady Rachel might help us, as I believed, if she chose to do it. As for old Toller, I suggested (on reflection) that the lawyer should examine him. The lawyer declined to waste any more of my money. I called again on Lady Rachel. This time, I was let in. I found the noble lady smoking a cigarette and reading a French novel.

'This is going to be a disagreeable interview,' she said. 'Let us get it over, Mr Roylake, as soon as possible. Tell me what you want—and speak as freely as if you were in the company of a man.'

I obeyed her to the letter; and I got these replies:

'Yes; I did have a talk, in your best interests, with Miss Toller. She is as sensible as she is charming, and as good as she is sensible. We entirely agreed that the sacrifice must be on her side; and that it was due to her own self-respect to prevent a gentleman of your rank from ruining himself by marrying a miller's daughter.'

The next reply was equally free from the smallest atom of sympathy on Lady Rachel's part.

'You are quite right—your deaf man was at his window when I went by. We recognised each other and had a long talk. If I remember correctly, he said you knew of his reasons for concealing his name. I gave my promise (being a matter of perfect indifference to me) to conceal it too. One thing led to another, and I discovered that you were his hated rival in the affections of Miss Toller. I proved worthy of his confidence in me. That is to say, I told him that Mrs Roylake and I would be only too glad, as representing your interests, if he succeeded in winning the young lady. I asked if he had any plans. He said one of his plans had failed. What it was, and how it had failed, he did not mention. I asked if he could devise nothing else. He said, "Yes, if I was not a poor man." In my place, you would have offered, as I did, to find the money if the plan was approved of. He produced some manuscript story of an abduction of a lady, which he had

written to amuse himself. The point of it was that the lover successfully carried away the lady, by means of a boat, while the furious
father's attention was absorbed in watching the high road. It seemed
to me to be a new idea. "If you think you can carry it out," I said,
"send your estimate of expenses to me and Mrs Roylake, and we will
subscribe." We received the estimate. But the plan has failed, and the
man is off. I am quite certain myself that Miss Toller has done what
she promised to do. Wherever she may be now, she has sacrificed
herself for your sake. When you have got over it, you will marry my
sister. I wish you good morning.'

Between Lady Rachel's hard insolence, and Mrs Roylake's sentimental hypocrisy, I was in such a state of irritation that I left Trimley
Deen the next morning, to find forgetfulness, as I rashly supposed, in
the gay world of London.

I had been trying my experiment for something like three weeks,
and was beginning to get heartily weary of it, when I received a letter
from the lawyer.

'Dear Sir,—Your odd tenant, old Mr Toller, has died suddenly of rupture
of a blood-vessel on the brain, as the doctor thinks. There is to be an
inquest, as I need hardly tell you. What do you say to having the report of
the proceedings largely copied in the newspapers? If it catches his daughter's eye, important results may follow.'

To speculate in this way on the impulse which might take its rise in
my poor girl's grief—to surprise her, as it were, at her father's
grave—revolted me. I directed the lawyer to take no steps whatever
in the matter, and to pay the poor old fellow's funeral expenses, on my
account. He had died intestate. The law took care of his money until
his daughter appeared; and the mill, being my property, I gave to
Toller's surviving partner—our good Gloody.

And what did I do next? I went away travelling; one of the
wretchedest men who ever carried his misery with him to foreign
countries. Go where I might on the continent of Europe, the dreadful
idea pursued me that Cristel might be dead.

# CHAPTER XVIII

### THE MISTRESS OF TRIMLEY DEEN

Three weary months had passed, when a new idea was put into my head by an Englishman whom I met at Trieste. He advised turning my back on Europe, and trying the effect of scenes of life that would be new to me. I hired a vessel, and sailed out of the civilised world. When I next stood on *terra firma*,* my feet were on the lovely beach of one of the Pacific Islands.

What I suffered I have not told yet, and do not design to tell. The bitterness of those days hid itself from view at the time—and shall keep its concealment still. Even if I could dwell on my sorrows with the eloquence of a practised writer, some obstinate inner reluctance would persist in holding me dumb.

More than a year had passed before I returned to Trimley Deen, and alarmed my stepmother by 'looking like a foreign sailor.'

The irregular nature of my later travels had made it impossible to forward the few letters that had arrived for me. They were neatly laid out on the library table.

The second letter that I took up bore the postmark of Genoa. I opened it, and discovered that the —

No! I cannot write of him by that mean name; and his own name is still unknown to me. Let me call him—and, oh, don't think that I am deceived again!—let me call him the Penitent.

The letter had been addressed to me from his deathbed, and had been written under dictation. It contained an extraordinary enclosure—a small torn fragment of paper with writing on it.

'Read the poor morsel that I send to you first' (the letter began). 'My time on earth is short; you will save me explanations which may be too much for my strength.'

On one side of the fragment, I found these words:

'. . . cruise to the Mediterranean for my wife's health. If Cristel isn't afraid of passing some months at sea . . .'

On the other side, there was a fragment of conclusion:

'. . . thoroughly understand. All ready. Write word what night, and what . . . loving brother, Stephen Toller.'

I instantly remembered the miller's rich brother; thinking of him for the first time since he had been in my mind for a moment, on the night of my meeting with Cristel. On the fourteenth page* of this narrative Toller's brother will be found briefly alluded to in a few lines.

I returned eagerly to the letter. Thus it was continued:

'That bit of torn paper I found under the bed, while I was secretly searching Mr Toller's room. I had previously suspected You. From my own examination of his face, when he refused to humour my deafness by writing what I asked him to tell me, I suspected Mr Toller next. You will see in the fragment, what I saw—that Toller the brother had a yacht, and was going to the Mediterranean; and that Toller the miller had written, asking him to favour Cristel's escape. The rest, Cristel herself can tell you.

'I know you had me followed. At Marseilles, I got tired of it, and gave your men the slip. At every port in the Mediterranean I inquired for the yacht, and heard nothing of her. They must have changed their minds on board, and gone somewhere else. I refer you to Cristel again.

'Arrived at Genoa, on my way back to England, I met with a skilled Italian surgeon. He declared that he could restore my hearing—but he warned me that I was in a weak state of health, and he refused to answer for the result of the operation. Without hesitating for a moment, I told him to operate. I would have given fifty lives for one exquisite week of perfect hearing. I have had three weeks of perfect hearing. Otherwise, I have had a life of enjoyment before I die.

'It is useless to ask your pardon. My conduct was too infamous for that. Will you remember the family taint, developed by a deaf man's isolation among his fellow-creatures? But I had some days when my mother's sweet nature tried to make itself felt in me, and did not wholly fail. I am going to my mother now: her spirit has been with me ever since my hearing was restored; her spirit said to me last night: "Atone, my son! Give the man whom you have wronged, the woman whom he loves." I had found out the uncle's address in England (which I now enclose) at one of the Yacht Clubs. I had intended to go to the house, and welcome her on her return. You must go instead of me; you will see that lovely face when I am in my grave. Good-bye, Roylake. The cold hand that touches us all, sooner or later, is very near to me. Be merciful to the next scoundrel you meet, for the sake of The Cur.'

I say there *was* good in that suffering man; and I thank God I was not quite wrong about him after all.

Arriving at Mr Stephen Toller's country seat, by the earliest train that would take me there, I found a last trial of endurance in store for me. Cristel was away with her uncle, visiting some friends.

Cristel's aunt received me with kindness which I can never forget. 'We have noticed lately that Cristel was in depressed spirits; no uncommon thing,' Mrs Stephen Toller continued, looking at me with a gentle smile, 'since a parting which I know you must have felt deeply too. No, Mr Roylake, she is not engaged to be married— and she will never be married, unless you forgive her. Ah, you forgive her because you love her! She thought of writing to tell you her motives, when she visited her father's grave on our return to England. But I was unable to obtain your address. Perhaps, I may speak for her now?'

I knew how Lady Rachel's interference had appealed to Cristel's sense of duty and sense of self-respect; I had heard from her own lips that she distrusted herself, if she allowed me to press her. But she had successfully concealed from me the terror with which she regarded her rejected lover, and the influence over her which her father had exercised. Always mindful of his own interests, the miller knew that he would be the person blamed if he allowed his daughter to marry me. 'They will say I did it, with an eye to my son-in-law's money; and gentlefolks may ruin a man who lives by selling flour.' That was how he expressed himself in a letter to his brother.

The whole of the correspondence was shown to me by Mrs Stephen Toller.

After alluding to his wealthy brother's desire that he should retire from business, the miller continued as follows:

'What you are ready to do for me, I want you to do for Cristy. She is in danger, in more ways than one, and I am obliged to get her away from my house as if I was a smuggler, and my girl contraband goods. I am a bad hand at writing, so I leave Cristy to tell you the particulars. Will you receive her, brother Stephen? and take care of her? and do it as soon as possible?'

Mr Stephen Toller's cordial reply mentioned that his vessel was ready to sail, and would pass the mouth of The Loke on her southward voyage. His brother caught at the idea thus suggested.

I have alluded to Giles Toller's sly look to his lodger, when I returned the manuscript of the confession. The old man's unscrupulous curiosity had already applied a second key to the cupboard in the lodger's room. There he had found the 'criminal stories' mentioned in the journal—including the story of abduction referred to by Lady Rachel. This gave him the very idea which his lodger had already relied on for carrying Cristel away by the river (under the influence, of course, of a soporific drug), while her father was keeping watch on the road. The secreting of the oars with this purpose in view, had failed as a measure of security. The miller's knowledge of the stream, and his daughter's ready courage, had suggested the idea of letting the boat drift, with Cristel hidden in it. Two of the yacht's crew, hidden among the trees, watched the progress of the boat until it rounded the promontory, and struck the shore. There, the yacht's boat was waiting. The rocket was fired to re-assure her father; and Cristel was rowed to the mouth of the river, and safely received on board the yacht. Thus (with his good brother's help) the miller had made the River his Guilty accomplice in the abduction of his own child!

When I had read the correspondence, we spoke again of Cristel.

'To save time,' Mrs Stephen Toller said, 'I will write to my husband to-day, by a mounted messenger. He shall only tell Cristel that you have come back to England, and you shall arrange to meet her in our grounds when she returns. I am a childless woman, Mr Roylake—and I love her as I should have loved a daughter of my own. Where improvement (in external matters only) has seemed to be possible, it has been my delight to improve her. Your stepmother and Lady Rachel will acknowledge, even from their point of view, that there is a mistress who is worthy of her position at Trimley Deen.'

When Cristel returned the next day, she found that her uncle had deserted her, and suddenly discovered a man in the shrubbery. What that man said and did, and what the result of it was, may be inferred if I relate a remarkable event. Mrs Roylake has retired from the domestic superintendence of Trimley Deen.

# APPENDIX
## COLLINS'S PREFACES

Preface to *Miss or Mrs? And Other Stories in Outline*, published by
Richard Bentley and Son in 1873

In their original form of publication, the stories contained in this
volume were restricted within limits which alike precluded elaborate
development of character and subtle handling of events. They are
emphatically what I have called them in the title-page — Stories in
Outline. As such, they take their modest place in the Gallery of
Fiction. They have their attraction for the writer, as special studies
in his Art; and their attraction for the reader, as narratives which
endeavour to interest him without making large demands on his
attention and his time.

The first story in the present series originally appeared in the
Christmas Number of the *Graphic* Illustrated Newspaper, for 1871.
'Miss or Mrs?' was fortunate enough to find its way at once to the
favour of an unusually large circle of readers. In England and the
English Colonies, in the United States, and on the Continent of
Europe, I have to thank the public kindness, on this occasion, for
the same hearty welcome.

The two shorter stories which follow were contributed to the
Christmas Numbers of *All the Year Round*, for 1859 and 1861. Trifles
as they are, they were both favourites with the kindest reader my
works have ever had — my dear lost friend, Charles Dickens.

W.C.

*December 1872, London*

\*

Preface to the 1879 Chatto & Windus edition of '*The Haunted
Hotel: A Mystery of Modern Venice*' to which is added '*My Lady's
Money*'

The public favour, at home and abroad, has shown such marked
approval of 'The Haunted Hotel,' during its periodical appearance,

that I may trust the work to speak for itself in the form under which it now appeals to other circles of readers.

The second story was originally published in the Christmas Number of the *Illustrated London News* for 1877. Imperative necessity, connected with the question of space, left the friendly and considerate authorities at the Office no other alternative than to print 'My Lady's Money' in a type which presented serious obstacles (spectacles notwithstanding) to readers who had arrived at a mature time of life. I have now the honour of directing the attention of these ladies and gentlemen to the marked consideration for their convenience exhibited by the printers of the story in its present form. Adding one word more, in relation to the purely literary side of the question, I would venture to hope that the studies of character in this little work will be found faithfully drawn from Nature — and that all friends of dogs will discover something which is true also of their dogs in the pen-and-ink portrait of 'Tommie.'

W.C.

*October 1878, London*

# EXPLANATORY NOTES

## MISS OR MRS?

3 *dedication*: Baron Christian Bernhard von Tauchnitz (1816–95) founded in 1837 in Leipzig a publishing house that in 1841 began to issue a series of English-language titles eventually known as the 'Collection of British and American Authors'. These small volumes, often in paper wrappers, though strictly speaking intended for sale only on the Continent, came to be sold worldwide over a period of more than a hundred years; by 1943, no fewer than 5,370 titles had appeared, and it has been estimated that sales totalled some forty million. The firm issued reprints of a number of Collins's novels, beginning with *After Dark* (1856).

7 *Levant*: former term for the region of the eastern Mediterranean now occupied by Lebanon, Syria and Israel.

8 *perpendicular*: the reference to 'architecture' suggests that Collins intends a facetious allusion, somewhat in the manner of Dickens, to the style of medieval English Gothic architecture known as Perpendicular.

10 *nankeen*: hard-wearing cotton fabric.

13 *pilot-boat*: boat used by pilots cruising off-shore while awaiting the arrival of incoming vessels.

*nautical miles*: a nautical mile is 6,080 feet and hence slightly longer than a land mile ('common mile').

*Dr Johnson*: while the sentiment has a distinct Johnsonian flavour, enquiries (kindly assisted by Mr Jack Lynch, University of Pennsylvania) have failed to identify a precise source for this remark, though a letter to Dr Charles Burney dated 1 November 1784 and quoted by Boswell expresses the same idea at greater length. Probably Collins is half-remembering something he has read or heard rather than alluding to a specific text.

28 *davits*: according to *OED*, one of the meanings of the term is 'a pair of cranes on the side or stern of a ship, fitted with tackle for suspending or lowering a boat'.

29 *Smyrna*: ancient city and important trading centre (now Izmir) on the west coast of Turkey.

32 *...solvent man*: an ironic adaptation of Pope's famous line, 'An honest man's the noblest work of God' (*Essay on Man*, iv. 248).

*Fallen Angel*: Satan, also known as Lucifer and popularly referred to as the Devil.

40 *Banns*: the alternative to marriage by special licence was the calling of banns in the parish or parishes in which the couple resided: 'First the banns ... must be published in the Church, three several Sundays, during

the time of Morning Service, or of Evening Service . . .' (Book of Common Prayer).

41  *Old Bailey*: Central Criminal Court of the City of London.

43  *Lady Winwood . . . but for You!*': the final paragraph of this chapter does not appear in the serial but was added to the first volume edition.

*beadle*: 'An inferior parish officer appointed to keep order in church, punish petty offenders, give notices of vestry meetings, etc.' (*OED*).

44  '. . . *hold his peace*': the 'Form of Solemnization of Matrimony' in the Book of Common Prayer requires the officiating clergyman, before uniting the couple, to declare to those present that 'if any man can shew any just cause, why they may not lawfully be joined together, let him now speak, or else hereafter for ever hold his peace'.

46  *chemisette*: underbodice of lace or other material, worn to cover the area left uncovered by a low-cut dress.

56  *table*: the serial version has 'window'. Collins must have realized belatedly that Turlington has moved from the window to the table, as indicated a few lines earlier ('Turlington struck his hand excitedly on the table').

*Gazette*: the *London Gazette*, a government publication that contained, among other announcements, lists of bankruptcies.

66  *the horrors*: popular expression defined in Eric Partridge's *Dictionary of Slang and Unconventional English* as 'the first stage of *delirium tremens*' (the Latin phrase signifying a psychotic condition associated with chronic alcoholism and often involving hallucinations). Partridge dates the expression 'from ca. 1859'.

## THE HAUNTED HOTEL

87  *dedication*: Sebastian Schlesinger was a Boston businessman with whom Collins struck up a friendship during his visits to that city in the course of his American reading-tour in 1873–4. According to Catherine Peters, Collins 'spent all his spare time at Schlesinger's house' and described his host in a letter as 'the brightest, nicest kindest little fellow I have met with for many a long day . . . he also makes the best cocktail in America' (*The King of Inventors: A Life of Wilkie Collins*, 362).

89  *London season*: the period in the year, from May to July, when the Court and fashionable society gathered in the capital.

95  *evil genius*: 'genius' is used here in the sense of 'spirit'. Collins later used the phrase 'the evil genius' as the title of a novel (1886).

99  *Dalmatian*: Dalmatia is a region of Croatia bordering on the Adriatic.

*Rip-van-Winkle*: in Washington Irving's famous story, published in *The Sketch-Book* (1820), the hero sleeps for twenty years and finds the world bewilderingly changed on waking.

100  *Homburg*: town in Prussia formerly popular as a spa.

*'Peerage'*: published list of noble and titled families.

101 *rent-charge*: 'rent forming a charge upon lands, etc., granted or reserved by deed to one who is not the owner . . .' (*OED*).

119 *'My Lady's Money'*: Collins's story appeared in volume form together with *The Haunted Hotel* (see Note on the Text).

133 *Thomas*: according to St John's Gospel (20: 25), St Thomas demanded physical evidence of Christ's identity when he appeared to his apostles after the Resurrection; hence the proverbial expression 'a doubting Thomas'.

142 *'. . . speak of him too.'*: at this point, in revising his text for the first edition in volume form, Collins cut a passage of about 150 words that had appeared in the serial version, as follows:

> To Henry's astonishment, Agnes stopped her. 'Wait a moment, Lady Montbarry. I have something to ask on my side.'
>
> Lady Montbarry paused on the instant — silently submissive as if she had heard a word of command. Henry drew Agnes away to the other end of the room, and remonstrated with her.
>
> 'You do wrong to call that person back,' he said: — 'No,' Agnes whispered, 'I have had time to remember.' — 'To remember what?' — 'To remember Ferrari's wife: Lady Montbarry may have heard something of the lost man.' —'Lady Montbarry may have heard, but she won't tell.' — 'It may be so, Henry, but, for Emily's sake, I must try.' — Henry yielded. 'Your kindness is inexhaustible,' he said, with his admiration of her kindling in his eyes. 'Always thinking of others; never of yourself!'
>
> Meanwhile, Lady Montbarry waited, with a resignation that could endure any delay. Agnes returned to her, leaving Henry by himself. 'Pardon me for keeping you waiting,' she said in her gentle courteous way. 'You have spoken of Ferrari. I wish to speak of him too.'
>
> Lady Montbarry bent her head in silence. Her hand . . .

Collins presumably noticed that Agnes's having left Henry by himself does not tally with what follows, for some lines below comes the sentence, 'Henry could keep silence no longer.', showing that he is within hearing.

151 *Funds*: securities issued by the Government and therefore regarded as a safe investment.

158 *Palladian*: style of architecture based on classical models and introduced by the Italian architect Andrea Palladio (1518–80).

168 *Americans*: this passage seems to represent a graceful compliment to the friendships Collins had formed in America a few years earlier (see also the note above on the dedication).

170 *table-d'hôte*: used here in the earlier meaning of a meal served in a hotel at a fixed time and price and sometimes eaten at a common table.

182 *maraschino*: liqueur made from cherries.

182 *Queen Caroline*: the wife of the Prince of Wales, subsequently Prince Regent and George IV. She lived on the Continent between 1813 and 1820 after being rejected by her husband.

183 *'I shall have a sketch or outline of my play ready . . .'*: In the serial version this reads: '"I shall go to England, and I shall write a sketch or outline of my play . . ."'. Collins must on reflection have decided that the Countess's notion of going to England is not in keeping with her fatal obsession with Venice.

185 *'Corsican Brothers'*: play adapted from the French by the prolific dramatist Dion Boucicault and successfully produced in 1852.

190 *Titian and Tintoret*: Anglicized forms of the names of Tiziano Vecelli (d. 1576) and Jacopo Tintoretto (1518–94), two of the leading painters of the Venetian school. During his boyhood visit to Venice in 1836 Collins and his family had lived in lodgings opposite Titian's house, and according to Catherine Peters he 'especially admired Tintoretto' (p. 139).

191 *Trent*: Trento, an Italian town north of Lake Garda and close to what is now the Austrian border.

205 *'Her mind . . . partially deranged'*: the serial version has 'Her mind is, in certain respects, unquestionably deranged'.

208 *the mocking Frenchman*: when he heard of the defeat of Napoleon at Borodino (1812), the French statesman Talleyrand is said to have remarked 'Voilà le commencement de la fin' (This is the beginning of the end). The anecdote is recounted by Sainte-Beuve in his *M. de Talleyrand* (1870).

216 *mesmeric theory*: mesmerism, named after the Austrian physician Friedrich Mesmer (1734–1815), was a forerunner of hypnotism. Also known as animal magnetism, it also became associated with what later came to be known as telepathic communication. Collins would have been aware of Dickens' strong interest in the subject: see Fred Kaplan, *Dickens and Mesmerism* (Princeton, 1975).

222 *Philosopher's stone*: legendary substance sought by the alchemists in the belief that it would transmute base metals into gold.

236 *bravo*: hired assassin.

239 *Children's Hospital*: the Hospital for Sick Children in Great Ormond Street, London, founded in 1852. Dickens had helped with fund-raising and had given it publicity in *Our Mutual Friend* (1865).

*recovered the terror*: 'recovered' for 'recovered from' is, according to *OED*, a common nineteenth-century usage.

# THE GUILTY RIVER

256 *finger alphabet*: an alphabet for the deaf, the letters of which are represented by positions and motions of the hand and fingers.

278 *deaf adder*: echoing Psalm 58: 4: 'Their poison is like the poison of a serpent; they are like the deaf adder that stoppeth her ear.'

299 *Hessian boots*: tasseled high boots, first worn by the troops of Hesse in Germany and fashionable in the nineteenth century.

305 *'Gammon!'*: slang term for 'nonsense'.

313 *Waverley Novels*: a series of more than two dozen historical novels by Sir Walter Scott (1771–1832). The first of them, *Waverley* (1814), gave its name to the series. The novels were published anonymously as 'by the author of *Waverley*'.

323 *'The Nervous Man'*: comic song of 1834, music by Jonathan Blewitt, words by I. Francis. The first verse runs:

> I really am a nervous Man, and don't know what to do;
> I tremble so where'er I go, at plays or in my pew.
> I'm always sad, I'm never glad, for do the best I can,
> I shiver, shake, all o'er me quake, I'm such a nervous Man.
> I'm such a nervous, such a nervous, such a nervous Man.

332 *Jesuits*: the name given to members of the Society of Jesus, founded by Ignatius Loyola in 1533. 'Owing to the casuistical principles maintained by many of its leaders, the name Jesuit acquired an opprobrious signification, and a *Jesuit* or *Jesuitical person* means (secondarily) a deceiver, a prevaricator, etc.' (*Brewer's Dictionary of Phrase and Fable*). Here the reference is to casuistry in a derogatory sense—that is, false but clever use of arguments dealing with a legal case.

350 *terra firma*: solid earth, dry land (Latin).

351 *'On the fourteenth page of this narrative'*: p. 252 of the present edition.